LAUREN GREENE

Fight for Us

Palm Cove Book 3

Autumn
Ink
Press

For anyone who's felt broken beyond repair - You're strong and you're not alone

Content Warning

Dear Readers,

Fight For Us can be read as a standalone, but I'd recommend reading *Fight For It* and *Fight For Her* first to get a full picture of our Krav family. Please be aware that *Fight For Us* contains consensual sexual activity and explicit language as well as some sensitive topics including mention of sexual assault (non-graphic), medical trauma (non-graphic, mention of amputation, surgeries, and hospital stays), PTSD, child custody, bullying, victim blaming, use of ableist slur, and death of loved ones.

Your mental health is important.

Hugs,

Lauren

Chapter 1

Olivia

THE SOUND OF FISTS striking padded vinyl put me into a meditative state.

Punch, grunt, shuffle. Punch, grunt, shuffle.

I could see why Mia loved Krav Maga.

Pushing myself to the brink of exhaustion quieted my mind. Baking did too, although it was easier to imagine my unknown abusers face on a blocking pad than on a cake. Each punch made me feel more empowered. Knowing I could put up a good fight stifled my anxious intrusive thoughts.

Punch.

Just try and touch me now.

Crouch. Punch lower. Hit him where it hurts.

I'm no one's victim.

Sidestep. Punch high.

Never again.

"Why do you look like you could commit murder?" Kendahl asked, lowering the practice pad. I heaved a breath into my chest and wiped a bead of sweat from my brow. Kendahl gave me a second before handing me the pad so she could take her turn practicing high and low punches.

"I do not." A distant memory from years ago flashed through my mind. The one that always tended to show up when my emotions ran high. His saccharine voice as he handed me a drink. *"Let's go somewhere to talk."* I didn't need a mirror to know I was scrunching up my face in a scowl.

"There it is again." Kendahl's blond messy bun flopped as she got into position. "Please tell me that look isn't for me."

I forced my focus on the present, locking that memory away in its neat little compartment in my head.

"It's not. Come on, punch lady. We only have ten minutes of class left and I need another round." As exhausted as I was, pent up stress still had my chest tight and jaw clenched. Work earlier in the day was a mess. I spent an extra hour cleaning up after hurricane Wes.

"On second thought." She grabbed the pad again. "You go ahead. I can picture Coby's face on the pad tomorrow night."

I stood in place. "Shit, you're right. I'm sorry. I'm being selfish. You go."

"Something wrong, ladies?" Shawn came up beside us, wearing his black assistant teacher T-shirt. "Need help on your form?"

I glanced at my sister's boyfriend, thinking for the millionth time since I met him that the guy resembled Thor. "We're good. Just trying to decide who gets to let off more steam tonight."

"Ah. Got you." He nodded and ran a hand through his sandy hair. "I'll let you get to it." He set off to help another pair looking mildly afraid.

"I think we scared him." Kendahl grinned. "I'd be scared of us, too. Look at my mean punching skills." She punched with dramatic flair while I held in a laugh.

Class ended with both of us breathless and coated in sweat. I watched Alex run into the gym from his spot in the waiting area and get his usual fist bumps from the other students before heading over to the practice dummies and throwing some punches of his own.

"How's the new place? Unpacked yet?" Kendahl asked while we collected our stuff from the cubbies. I mentally groaned. "There's that face again. Bad question?"

"No, it's fine. I love the new place. It's a dream to be beachside, even if I'm discovering a new hatred of sand." How and why does it get into every single crevice? Kendahl chuckled as I went on, "We're somewhat unpacked. I should give myself more credit since it's only been a few weeks since we moved across the country. Between learning the ropes at work, coming here a few nights a week, and entertaining Alex, I haven't had much time to make the place feel like home yet."

"It's been a lot of changes lately. Give yourself some credit. Not many people would move to Florida in August." She patted my arm before pulling her hand away, laughing. "Wow, you worked up a sweat."

"You saw me. Of course I did." I peeked over at Alex and found Shawn had joined him and was showing him the proper way to punch the lifelike dummy. Shawn's face lit with a grin as he watched Alex go at it.

"Anyway," Kendahl continued, "How about I come over this weekend and help you unpack? And before you argue, no, I do not have anything else going on. I could use some girl time too. You know, conversation where we're not choking each other."

I broke my gaze away from Alex and Shawn, focusing back on my friend. She had her gloves tucked under her arm while she attempted to fix her bun. I reached out and took them to help her out. I wanted to argue that I'd be fine. That I didn't need the help. My dumb pride and all. But who was I kidding? It's been weeks and I was still fishing underwear out of suitcases.

"With all my empty space, we could get some practice in while we unpack," I suggested. She was not amused. "Okay, okay. No choking during girls night."

Just then, Mia came into the gym and spotted us with a wide grin. Her gaze found Shawn immediately after, like she had a radar that pulled her to him.

"I'd hug you guys but wow, you're sweaty. I take it class went well?" she asked, coming to our side.

"Yup. Seems we both had some stress to relieve tonight," Kendahl said.

"What did I miss?" Mia pulled her gloves out of her bag before storing it in an empty cubby. Her level two class was starting in five minutes.

"Just me attempting to force help on your sister here."

"Good luck with that," Mia said. "I've been trying for over a week." Guilt gnawed at my gut. Pushing people out hadn't gotten me far in New York. It almost caused me to lose my relationship with my sister all together. And if I was being honest, I was lonely. And exhausted. Oh, and did I mention stressed?

"I'm sorry. I'm just getting used to all the changes. But yes, let me check my work schedule and I'll let you know. I'd love the help." Mia pulled me into a hug. "I thought you didn't want to get all sweaty and gross," I said against her shoulder.

"Eh, what's a little sweat between siblings?" Her body vibrated with a laugh and I clung on for another long second before pulling back.

Mark and Dina, the married couple who owned and taught at the gym, took up their position at the front of the room. "Alright level two, time to warm up."

"That's our cue to go," Kendahl said, ruffling Mia's messy bun. I called for Alex and waved goodbye to Shawn before following Kendahl out to the parking lot.

Humidity smacked me in the face. I looked up at the gray sky, thick with clouds. A storm was brewing and I hoped like hell I didn't get stuck driving in it.

"I'll text you once I know my schedule." I unlocked the doors and Alex climbed into the back seat. "And Ken, thank you."

"Anytime, bestie. I'm glad you're here. We both are."

"Mom, are you going to be talking forever again? I'm hungry." And just when I was feeling warm and fuzzy, poof, the stress fairy tapped me with her magic wand of doom.

"Mom duty calls," I said to Kendahl. "Talk soon."

As soon as I shut my car door, fat drops of rain splattered my windshield. I knew it. Maybe I was becoming a true Florida resident after all.

I cooked a box of mac and cheese and some frozen veggies for our dinner. It was the second day in a row of mac and cheese and Alex's eye roll wasn't helping the situation. As pathetic as it was, I never learned to cook. Never needed to since we always had an in-home chef when we lived with my parents. I guess I could have learned, but I never had the interest. Baking on the other hand, I gravitated toward. Still did when my feelings got too big and I needed to clear my head.

I've tried to pinpoint what it was about baking that helped. Maybe it was the precision of measuring ingredients. Could be the step by step process, requiring my total focus. Whatever it was, I was grateful for it. Alex shared my love for it too. Most of the time at least.

With Alex fed and settled, I took a minute to check my phone. When I went to Krav, I always kept it stored and on silent. That was my me time. Unless someone was gravely injured, I was taking it. I brushed sand off our hand me down couch, because of course sand made its way there—the evil substance—and sat tucking my feet underneath me. I had three voicemails from Wes. Somehow that didn't surprise me.

"Hey do you know where the deposit envelope is? I can't find it in my office." I groaned. That man couldn't find an asteroid if it landed on his head. "Nevermind. It was under the inventory sheet." I hit delete and clicked next. He needed to get an iPhone and text. I was almost embarrassed for him. "That was the wrong envelope. Sorry, Tiger. Call me when you get this."

I clicked his name and hit call. Knowing Wes, he was probably still searching for it even though he sent these messages over two hours ago.

"Hey, Tiger." His gravelly voice traveled through the phone and settled somewhere deep in my center.

"You know I hate when you call me that," I lied.

"Nah, you love it. It's the perfect name for you since you're always getting ready to pounce."

"Maybe because you're so good at riling me up," I said, re-membering how I held my tongue yesterday. In my defense, I had a grumpy customer sassing me because Wes got my order tickets mixed in with Kelly's. He knew I was still learning on the fly. Kelly was no real help and Wes... He was a hot mess.

"Who me?" He feigned innocence. "I only do my job. Can't help it if you aren't used to restaurant life yet."

"Right. Restaurant life." Because that's what caused my blood pressure to rise. Not my disorganized tornado of a boss. "So, the deposit envelope?"

"I checked my desk and it's not there. I wanted to hit the bank before five o'clock but that didn't happen." The sounds of shuffling papers in the background made its way through the line. I chewed my lip, trying to put myself into Wes's enormous shoes.

"What else was going on when you were getting ready to leave with the deposit?"

The shuffling sounds stopped. Oh good, he was focusing. "Nothing really. Derek had just come in to relieve me. I went into the office to grab my stuff and..." He hesitated.

"And?" I asked, waiting for his *aha* moment.

"I think my phone rang." I heard the creak of his chair and a small hiss that told me he'd pushed to a stand.

"Who called?"

"The rep from Sysco. She was letting me know they were out of the chicken strips I ordered."

Our voices connected like two ends of a string as we said in unison, "The walk-in."

I waited a few seconds, while Wes made his way into the industrial sized freezer. "Find it yet?"

"Yup, got it. Right there next to our last bag of said chicken strips."

I leaned my head against the couch sending a silent prayer to the universe for strength. "There ya go. Problem solved."

"What would I do without you, Tiger?" The rumble of his voice caused my face to heat. I ignored the familiar feeling.

"You survived without me for years. You'd make it." Although he might lose his head in the process.

"I thought I was doing okay. But now that I have you, I realized how much of a shit show the place was."

I smiled at the compliment, feeling the heat spread to my ears. It didn't feel warranted though. *Not really.* Yeah, I added some much needed organization and cleanliness to the place, but I was a crap waitress. My scant collection of tips showed as much.

"Nah, it's not me. Kelly's the one who keeps the place going. It should be renamed Kelly's, instead of Sunshine."

He responded with a growly *hmph.* A sound that I've come to learn was so very Wes.

"Anyway, if that's all, I should get going. Working the breakfast shift tomorrow." My eyelids grew heavy but I still needed a quick shower before getting into bed.

"Get some rest." I pushed off the couch, my shoulders aching from exertion. "And Tiger?"

"Yeah?"

"Thanks."

In a matter of seconds I let myself forget about his mess from earlier and his order ticket mix up. One thanks and he had a clean slate. It wouldn't last long. Tomorrow he'd do something or another to get under my skin, but for tonight, I'd take the reprieve.

"Anytime," I said. And I meant it.

Chapter 2

Olivia

Two Months Earlier

THE FIRST TIME I met Wesley Reed, I ripped him a new one. That's right. I chewed him out, hauled him over the coals, gave him a tongue lashing.

But who could blame me? It was a parent's job to keep their children safe. And he needed a little reminder of that fact.

"Alex, time to pack up. Dinner will be ready any minute." I stood, brushing sand off the back of my thighs. I didn't want to track it inside and make more work for the already overloaded housekeeper. She was sweet enough to stay and work for our family while we were guests at the estate.

"One more, Mom. Please. Look at that wave coming." He pointed at the monster of a wave heading toward the shore and clutched his boogie board like his life depended on it. I inhaled the salty sea air and counted to three before nodding.

"One more. That's it." My mother would scold me out for having the audacity to show up five minutes late to dinner. A dinner she did nothing to prepare for, might I add.

Alex held the board against his lanky frame and ran straight into the breaking wave, flopping down a second too late. My fault for making him wait during my calming breath, I guessed. I couldn't help it. This little private beach had no lifeguard and my ten year old thought he was invincible. Anxious thoughts were bound to chime in.

The evening sun sank toward the horizon, casting out a net of bright orange hues. While Alex went in for a second wave, I took a moment to ground myself. Despite the stress of Alex in the ocean, I'd never been more at peace than when I was at the beach. The sounds, the smells... I could press mute on the static in my head, if only for a few moments. After the first week in Florida, I'd already decided that I wanted to live there. Needed to. But making it happen would be a challenge.

"Let's go ask my mom." Alex's voice jolted me from my thoughts. He ran toward me with a little girl who looked to be about his age. I turned, searching the area for an adult. Surely she didn't appear out of thin air all alone?

"Who's your friend?" I asked Alex while offering a smile to the girl. Up close I could see her cheeks pink with sunburn and a bobby pin hanging on by the smallest piece of hair near her ear. She wore cutoff jean shorts, stained with what looked like paint, and a *Minecraft* T-shirt. Her feet were bare and dirty. I didn't see a pair of shoes nearby.

"I'm Lilly." She dug her toes into the sand and set her attention back on Alex. "Wanna play tag?"

Alex looked at me with questioning eyes, both of us sharing the same thoughts. Where the heck had this child come from and where did she belong? I couldn't leave her here. No way.

I placed my hand on Alex's shoulder to stop him from bolting off. If he was challenged to tag, there wasn't much I could do to keep him rooted in place.

"Lilly, where's your parents?"

"My mom's at work. Or maybe at Jeff's house. She goes there a lot."

Okay. Stay calm. I could figure this out. I stooped down to meet her at eye level, noticing specks of moss green in her big brown eyes. This kid was a prime target for a kidnapper. When I found her mother, I'd give her a piece of my mind. How dare she let her kid wander alone. I took a lungful of ocean air before my head spun.

"So you're here all alone? How'd you get here?" Her gaze drifted over my shoulder but she kept her mouth zipped. "I want to help you. I can't leave you here alone. I—"

"Lillian Elena Reed."

I stood and let my gaze follow the deep, booming voice. The man stalking toward us matched the voice, that was for sure. One word. Huge. The guy would tower over me. My pulse sped up as I unconsciously stepped in front of the children.

"Who's that?" Alex asked.

"I don't know—"

"My dad."

Lilly and I both spoke at the same time and I registered what she said. *Oh.* This was her father. I caught myself gawking at him as he walked. Was I imagining things or did time slow?

A breeze blew pieces of his hair and the sun picked that exact moment to glow against his perfectly tanned face. Handsome face at that. He had facial hair that looked to be a few weeks worth of growth, but neatly trimmed along a cut jawline. Thick brown brows framed smoldering eyes. Long brown hair brightened with golden sun-kissed highlights. Each step he took reminded me of a reality show opening sequence.

My eyes drifted south when I noticed that his gait was a bit different, but then I tried to place his outfit. Black loose pants and a white button-up jacket. He stepped closer and it hit me. A chef's coat.

I steeled myself. *Do not look at his tattooed forearms.* Stupid rolled up sleeves. *You're pissed at this man.* He left his young daughter to run around on a beach alone. *You will scold him.* But oh my. His face. Why did his face have to look like *that?*

"Lilly, for the love of God. You scared the shit out of me." He blew out a breath and ran a hand through the pieces of hair that had escaped his bun. I stopped breathing when he looked right into my eyes. Or at least I think I did. My autonomic nervous system definitely misfired. "Thank you for taking care of my girl."

Those eyes, exactly the same as Lilly's, studied my face. I blinked a few times. Wait. He was talking to me.

"You're—uh—you're welcome." The corner of his lips tilted up. No. This was not how I wanted this to go. I glanced down at Alex, who was watching the exchange with a raised brow. "Actually. You're *not* welcome."

"Excuse me?" He crossed his massive arms and tilted his head. I forced myself to avoid staring at the intricate black swirls along his flexed forearm muscles.

"Did I stutter? How could you let your daughter wander the beach alone? What if I was some kind of criminal? This world is full of sickos, you know. And no shoes either. What if she cut her foot? Imagine if I hadn't found her. She could be halfway to the interstate right now, barefoot and alone."

My chest heaved as blood rushed to the tips of my ears. Ripping this guy a new one made me feel alive. I'd started this tirade and I wasn't done. I gathered air into my lungs and went on while he continued to stare at me.

"Furthermore, this beach has no lifeguard. Do you even know how dangerous riptides are? Thousands of people get swept away every year. It doesn't matter if you're a strong swimmer. One of those babies catches you and you're a goner." With a hand on my hip and a finger pointed at his chest I stepped closer, close enough that one more inch would have us touching. I jabbed his chest, my anger rising to a peak. "How would it feel to be responsible for something terrible happening to someone you love? Something you could never ever fix."

The air whooshed out of me as those last words slipped out. His nostrils flared as he wrapped his hand around my wrist and guided it back to my side. Crap. I didn't exactly mean to take it *that* far. I bit my lower lip and chanced a peek into his hurt eyes. Well, now I felt like a jerk.

He blinked and a haze lifted as his expression morphed back to neutral. "You done?" His deep voice and the adrenaline rush I'd just put myself through had my body burst into full-scale shivers.

"Mom? Do we have to go?" I took a few steps back and felt my pulse return to a normal rhythm.

"Yeah. Can we play now?" Lilly asked, her gaze bouncing between her father and me. I was already late for dinner and would have to face my mother's wrath. Yet, I couldn't find my voice to respond.

"Young lady," he said, bracing his hands on his knees and crouching down slowly. "We are going to have a discussion later. You know better than to run off like that on Grandpa."

"Sorry, Dad. Grandpa fell asleep in his chair and I was so bored." She had the preteen angsty whine down to a T, complete with a full eye roll.

"I don't care how bored you were. This lady is right. Something bad could have happened to you. You're my responsibility this weekend."

I clocked his words. So he's divorced. Or separated. Not that I cared or anything.

"But Mom lets me walk to the store alone all the time. And sometimes even to the pool." He huffed, standing back up with a grunt. A muscle ticked in his jaw. Maybe I should help hammer his point home.

"Lilly, everyone parents differently. When you're with your dad, it's best to follow his rules okay?"

"Okay," she echoed.

The golden sun grazed the water's surface as the waves and sand turned shades of gray.

"Alex, we should get going. I need to get some dinner in you."

"Oh man. I wanted to play tag though." He zipped his lips once I gave him my *I mean business* look. I bent to collect all of our scattered belongings. My hands trembled from the dispersed adrenaline and the knowledge that my ass was pointed directly at this guy didn't help. I was exhausted. Releasing my thoughts drained the last dregs of my energy for the day. Maybe I was hungry too. Hanger was a real thing for Alex and me.

"Hey, um, can I buy you two some pizza? As a thank you." His voice was soft and kind. It took me by surprise.

Teetering on my heels to collect sand toys, I almost fell at his offer. My usual "a man is interested in me" alarm bells were missing. That was a first. But I knew my answer. I didn't even know his name. No way were we having dinner with him.

"Pizza? Sweet!" Alex said. "Mom, can we? I'm tired of all Grandma's healthy dinners. Why does anyone need that many vegetables at one time?"

Lilly piped up. "How many?"

"Like three. And there's always salad. Like every single day."

Lilly's dad chuckled, watching our kids exchange before bringing his gaze back to me. His brow raised and he shrugged.

"Thanks, but we've got to get going." I stood and brushed my palms against my sandy shorts before giving Lilly a pat on the shoulder. "It was nice to meet you Lilly. Maybe we'll see you again at the beach. If," I glanced up toward her father's towering figure, "you ask your dad first."

"Nice to meet you too," she said, sounding far more grown up than she looked.

"I'm Olivia, by the way. And this is Alex." I offered a tentative smile, unsure why I was sharing our names with these complete strangers. He was a huge, tattooed guy with arms that could crush a boulder. I should be at least mildly put off, even though the way he spoke to his daughter was endearing. And maybe he wasn't as negligent as I'd originally thought. In any case, I could unpack all of that later.

"Wes Reed," he said, sticking out his tattoo-covered hand to Alex, who gave him an enthusiastic shake. My father would be proud since he'd been working on handshake etiquette with Alex lately. Then he extended his hand to me. He studied my face with his dark eyes as I wrapped my palm in his. "Nice to meet you, Olivia."

I was most definitely *not* feeling an electric buzz where our skin met. And I was so *not* blushing from his amused grin and extended eye contact. Not at all.

"Okay." I cleared my suddenly dry throat and withdrew my hand. "See you around. Let's go, Alex."

Wes winked at me. *Winked.* Who does that? I let out a frazzled laugh and wave combo before I turned on my heel, beckoning Alex to follow.

Alex dragged his sand coated boogie board by the string and took his sweet time walking paces behind me. Whether he didn't want to leave the beach or was still sulking about pizza deprivation, I didn't know. But I wanted to get behind closed doors as soon as possible so I could replay every interaction from the last ten minutes through my mind again and again.

Maybe Wes watched us head home. I didn't want to turn around and check. But the little voice in my head told me he did.

For the next three Saturdays, Lilly joined us at the beach. Each time, she promised me that her grandpa knew where she was, pointing across the street to their bungalow home. I felt even worse about going off on Wes once I realized they lived so close. I couldn't help that my brain automatically went to her walking five miles with no shoes.

She and Alex would play tag, build intricate sand castles, and he'd boogie board while she preferred to venture no farther than the shoreline. I was thankful for that since I already had my hands full trying to keep myself from panicking at Alex's affinity for going too far into the water. I was curious about Lilly, but never wanted to pry into her life. It's not like I could overhear much about anything of importance when Alex and her only talked about video games and whose sandcastle was bigger.

Each Saturday, Wes would show up right around sunset, arms folded while he thanked me for keeping an eye on his daughter right before he scolded her for bothering us. And each Saturday he'd ask us if he could buy us pizza as a thank you. I'd graciously refuse, pack up, and we'd go on our way.

Until my mind shifted.

Maybe it was seeing my sister gloriously happy for the first time in forever. Or maybe it was that I had this whole comforting familiarity thing going with Wes. But on the fourth Saturday he asked us, I said yes.

"Okay, okay. We'll accept your offering of pizza." With one hand holding my beach bag and the other on my hip, I added, "But we are pineapple lovers, and I will accept no criticism."

He laughed, warm and rich. I found myself smiling. *Really* smiling.

"I'll keep my opinions to myself. I wouldn't want you to yell at me." He reached out, taking the beach bag from my hand and slinging it over his shoulder. "Again." My face heated at the memory of our first encounter. "You like beer, Olivia? Because I know I can use one."

"I do."

As I followed him and his daughter to their home, I checked my internal cues, surprised to find none of them firing. No tight chest. No racing heart. No overwhelming need to flee.

Only contentment and a feeling entirely new to me when it came to men: curiosity.

Chapter 3

Wes

"HANDS," I CALLED, SLIDING the hot plate stacked with pancakes and sausages onto the window and turning to plate up the next ticket. We were slammed for a Wednesday morning. According to Kelly, some meeting at the town hall let out, bringing in a group of twenty. I shouldn't complain, we needed the customers. But damn, I wished I had better help in the kitchen.

"Sharp," Thea called as she passed behind me. I glanced her way, to see her heading back to her station with a sack of potatoes in one hand and a knife in the other. At least I had one hardworking person on the line. Caleb was hanging around by the walk-in most definitely fucking around on his phone.

Breathe, Wes. You were a dumb kid once too. Fucking phones though. It was like they couldn't go a minute without checking them.

I cleared my throat raising my voice so I reached him over the sizzle of the griddle. "I hope whoever you're texting is more important than your job, kid." I kept my tone playful so I didn't lose my shit. It wasn't worth it.

Caleb snapped his head up. "Sorry, boss man."

"It's all good. Put that thing away though."

He slipped his phone into his pocket without another word. Anyone who worked with me knew how I felt about the damn things. I'm surprised he had the balls to bring one into my kitchen.

Halfway through the morning rush I felt that unmistakable buzz at the back of my neck. I didn't have to hear her voice to know she'd arrived for her shift. She bustled around the serving station, pouring herself a cup of coffee. I wiped my palms on a towel and stepped away from the counter. Caleb could carry his weight for five minutes.

"Morning, Tiger. Rough one?" She grimaced, patted her pocket, and pulled out her vibrating phone. I ground my teeth.

"Sorry, it's just my sister getting back to me. I'll text her later."

"You can use my office if you need to call her back." Caleb overheard me and scoffed.

"No, it's fine." She took a deep sip of coffee and smacked her lips together. Her pouty pink lips. Not that I noticed them every day. "Well, I better get out there. I hope it's okay that I brought Alex again today? Mia had a meeting this morning and I still haven't found a sitter. He has his iPad and promised he'll be good."

"Yeah, no problem. I'll make him his favorite." She reached out and gave my hand a squeeze. An appreciative squeeze, nothing more. But I couldn't help reveling in the way her soft palm felt against my skin.

"Thank you. I hate to be a bother. Only one more week until school starts thankfully. Then it'll be a whole new type of morning chaos." A humorless laugh escaped her lips.

"While I'm thinking of it, Kelly asked if you could take the next big table? She needs a break. Ankles swollen like a sausage." I formed my hands together in a circle for emphasis.

"Nice visual." She finished off the remainder of her coffee, leaving the empty mug there for her next cup. "Of course, whatever I can do to help."

I had a read on Olivia in the short time I'd known her. She liked to feel needed, even if she gave me shit for my messes. I've seen her secretly smiling while organizing my desk. I wasn't short on ways to make her feel needed. She *was* needed, very much so, even if I didn't deserve her help.

"Hey, Chef," Thea called. "I've got these diced potatoes ready to go." I tipped my chin in Thea's direction.

Turning back to Olivia, I said, "Give me ten minutes for Alex's breakfast."

"Will do." She turned on her heel and made her way onto the floor, swaying her perfect ass in her tight black pants.

As usual, my old man was seated at the counter nursing his cup of coffee and listening in on any and all gossip that came his way. His brow raised as he spied me ogling Olivia. He's badgered me at least ten times this week, asking when I'm going to quit being a dumbass and lock that woman down. Like it was so easy.

"Morning, Olivia," he said, turning her way. "Looking good today."

"Morning, Walt. Need a refill yet?" She stopped beside him and rested a hand on his shoulder.

"Nah, can't have too much or I'll get the jitters. Alex doing okay over there?"

"He's alright. He'd much rather be playing at the beach but your son is making him pancakes, so that makes up for it." My father spotted me listening and hit me with a smile. That was my cue to get back to work.

"I'll go sit with him. Tell him stories about my time in the Army. He liked that last time he was here." I rolled my eyes. Sorry kid. If I could rescue you, I would.

Oliva handled my old man like a champ, though. "Nothing violent this time, Walter. Remember he's only ten." My father nodded, shooing her off like she was being ridiculous and took his coffee cup over to Alex's booth.

"Hey, Tiger," I called, catching Olivia's attention before she went to her first table.

"Yeah?"

"Make sure he doesn't tell him about the time they went to the brothel. That's a favorite of his." The look of abject horror on her face had me biting back a laugh.

"You're kidding right?"

"Wish I was. You can even ask my mom. It was before they got together and his most overused story. He likes to claim all the ladies had to have him. Either way, it can get pretty R-rated, so keep an ear out."

"Well now I need to hear the story." She laughed. "Maybe just the PG version though."

She set off in the direction of their table and I had to forcefully pull myself back to the line. I knocked over Thea's freshly diced potatoes in my distracted state—my first mess of the day. Thea, being the kind and gracious person she was, held back her expletives and helped me clean up.

"Uh, Thea," I said. "Tell everyone on the floor to eighty-six the potato hash will you?"

"If it means I don't have to dice ten pounds of potatoes again, gladly."

We made it through the rest of breakfast unscathed. A couple more four-tops came through, keeping me busy on the line. As for Olivia, she seemed to get into a groove after her rough start to the day. I was about ready to take a break and get some paperwork done when Kelly stuck her head into the back.

"Boss, you should probably come out here."

I quirked a brow and huffed. Another disgruntled customer she didn't want to handle, most likely. Wiping my hands on a towel, I pushed through the back door and past the server's station. Lilly was standing next to Alex's booth, chatting with him and my father. My eyes snagged on the two suitcases next to her feet and the overstuffed backpack hanging off her shoulders. I went to them, needing to know what the hell was going on.

"Lilly? What are you doing here sweetheart?"

A hush settled over the place as the couple of diners turned to listen to my conversation. Bunch of busy bodies. Lilly's gaze met mine, then she turned and pointed toward the entrance where my ex-wife, Savannah, stood tapping on her phone.

"Mom brought me. She said she has to go on a trip and I can't come. That I gotta stay with you for a while."

Every muscle in my body pulled taut as I looked between my daughter and my least favorite person. I slid Lilly's backpack off her shoulders and dropped it down with the rest of her stuff. "Why don't you sit with Alex and I'll go talk to your mom?"

Olivia came from the restrooms and I caught her eye. Her gaze bounced between Lilly and me, then to the bags. She hurried over. "Hey Lilly, can I get you a drink sweetie?"

I mouthed thanks to her and took a centering breath. I needed it before communicating with Sav.

Her hair was dyed a golden blonde color, which was new, but she still smelled of apple body spray and Marlboro Lights from a few feet away. Not much has changed there. I made it my business to avoid the woman as much as I could during drop off and pick up on the weekends. My parents usually stepped in. Being in Sav's presence only pissed me off and I didn't need that shit, not when I was finally living without the massive chip on my shoulder since she left me in my time of need.

She looked up from her phone when I'd nearly reached her. Her gaze traveled the length of my body, lingering a second too long on my covered prosthesis. She scrunched up her nose and winced—her pity look. I was all too familiar with it.

"Let's go outside." I pointed to the door and waited for her to step out first. Moisture saturated the air like viscous syrup and sweat immediately gathered on the back of my neck. She reached into her purse and pulled out a cigarette and lighter, glancing over her shoulder toward the parking lot. "What are you doing here, Sav?"

"Hello to you, too. I see you're doing better since I last saw you." She lit her cigarette and inhaled the noxious fumes. "Lilly tells me you're working out again. I didn't think that would be possible—" She looked down at my legs again. "—with your disability."

"I know you're not here to make small talk and frankly I don't want to waste a minute of my time talking to you." I stood up to my full height and crossed my arms over my chest. "Why are you here? Is everything okay with Lilly?"

She blew a stream of smoke toward my face and smiled. "Our daughter is fine. If you checked your email more than once a year you'd know why I'm here." I clenched my fists at my side, glaring at her. "Jeff and I are going to Europe for a few months. I got a modeling contract overseas and as much as I'd love to take Lilly with me, I can't. You know I've sacrificed so much to take care of her all these years and no shade to you, but you haven't been the most hands-on father."

"Not because I didn't want to," I said.

"I know, I know. Your leg and your friend and your tragic life. I get it. But I can't let this opportunity go. It's time for you to step up."

Anger, sharp and hot, burned through me. "Nice of you to talk about Dylan that way." I shifted to take pressure off my throbbing hip. "You can't just up and leave. Lilly's not a fucking pet, she's a child. She needs you." It took everything in me not to raise my voice for the entire town to hear.

"You up and left us all the time. Even when you *were* here, you weren't ever *here*, Wesley. You're the poster boy for emotionally unavailable." I scoffed while she took a long drag on her cigarette. "All her important paperwork is in her backpack and she starts school next week."

I was stunned silent. She was serious?

"You're really leaving her here? Without so much as a goodbye?" I asked, dumbfounded.

"I've said my goodbyes. She knew this was coming all week. Lilly wants me to be happy. She's mature enough to understand. Plus, it'll only be a few months. Six, tops." She sucked another drag on her cigarette before stomping it into the cement with her flip-flop. "I've gotta go, Jeff is waiting for me in the car. I know you're unhappy, but look at this as an opportunity for you to get closer to your daughter. You both need that."

She walked toward an idling white Camaro, where a dude obscured by tinted windows sat waiting. This couldn't be happening. I loved Lilly with all my being but I wasn't cut out to parent full-time. I could barely handle her one day a week with my work schedule. The slam of the car door broke me out of my haze.

"Sav, get back here!" I yelled and took off toward the car. Jeff backed it out with a squeal and peeled out of the parking lot before I could get anywhere near it. "Shit!"

I forced air into my chest and counted down from five. Going back inside filled with anger wouldn't help anything. I'd call Sav and work this out. Lilly was my daughter and I loved her, but I couldn't do this alone. I was barely holding on as it was trying to keep the restaurant going. I hadn't made it to the gym this month because of my workload. Taking a break from Sunshine wasn't an option. It's been in my family for too long to let it go to shit.

I wiped sweat from my brow and made my way back inside. Every customer kept their eyes trained on me as I walked toward Lilly's booth, like I was about to lash out. I wanted to. Smashing a few plates in the back would feel fucking amazing right about now. This was just like Sav. She walked out on me with nothing more than a shoulder shrug and a half-hearted apology. Why wouldn't I believe she was capable of abandoning our kid?

Lilly was watching a video with Alex on his device. Maybe a few minutes to blow off some steam would be okay? Then I could come back and have a rational conversation with my family.

A warm palm on my shoulder stopped me in my tracks. I flinched a bit at the unexpected contact before realizing who was touching me. "Is everything okay?" Concern dripped from Olivia's voice as thick as the humidity outside. With one look into her eyes, some of the tightness in my chest loosened. She was my employee. I didn't need to dump my personal life onto her. But shit, if I didn't talk this through right now a part of me that I didn't want Lilly to see would sneak its way out.

"Not really." I blinked, looking around with clearer eyes. People had gone back to eating and chatting like normal. Everyone except my father, who sat back in the vinyl booth watching me like a hawk. "Dad, can you keep an eye on the kids?"

He waved me off. "Go ahead. We'll be right here."

"Let's go to my office."

Chapter 4

Wes

Two Months Earlier

I COULDN'T BELIEVE SHE finally took me up on my offer. It was the least I could do after weeks of her keeping an eye on Lilly while my father had his afternoon nap. That kid would be the death of me.

I couldn't say I wasn't clenching my ass cheeks that second Saturday when I got home from the restaurant and found Lilly missing again. But to my surprise, Olivia didn't yell at me. Maybe there was a tinge of annoyance in her stance when I showed up. Her arms were crossed against her chest and her head was tilted as I gave Lilly another talking to. But that fire in her eyes stayed banked. Which was too bad, considering Olivia yelling at me was the first time I felt much of anything in years.

Olivia walked by my side, likely slowing her pace for me. My body ached but I tried not to show it. I could whine after I put Lilly to bed. For now, I had to suck it up.

She was so fucking gorgeous, I didn't know what to say to her. When was the last time I had a conversation with an attractive woman?

"Do you enjoy living on the beach?"

I breathed a sigh of relief. Thank God she started the conversation. "Yeah. It's peaceful."

"You're lucky. I'd love to step out my door every morning to that view." She turned her head to gaze back at the crashing waves.

"Do you live inland?"

"We're only here for the summer. My parents are friends with the Richardsons down the street. They're letting us stay in their home while they're vacationing in Europe."

My stomach sank. I'd known a woman like her appearing out of thin air across the street from my house was too good to be true.

She continued. "But I think I'm ready for a change. I've fallen in love with the beach during my time here."

I led them across the driveway of my parent's modest home. Compared to the mansions in the area, ours was a shack. But my parents had saved up every penny and when the restaurant was in its prime, they bought the two-bedroom for a steal.

"My mom always wanted to live on the water. That's why they bought this house about ten years ago. I still remember the day my father surprised her with the keys." I felt my lips tip up.

"That's so sweet." Her voice had a wistful quality. Musical even. "Is she home too? I know you mentioned your dad watching Lilly."

"Not yet. She volunteers most Saturdays with her church. Feeds homeless folks, helps collect donations, stuff like that."

"She sounds like an absolute saint. Nothing like my mother."

"A saint?" I chuckled. "Trust me, she has some unholy moments." Namely anything that comes out of her mouth about my ex-wife. I kept that thought to myself. "She used to bring Lilly with her until an incident at the shelter involving a man, a trench coat, and a police report. I'll let you fill in the blanks."

"That's utterly disturbing."

"My thoughts exactly. Thankfully Lilly didn't see anything, but to be safe, she stays here with my dad while I'm at work."

I held the door open for them to go inside. The kids pushed through first and Lilly said, "Come on, I brought my Switch from my mom's house. Let's play games."

"What do you have?" Alex asked as they jogged down the hallway.

"Nothing violent," Olivia yelled at their retreating frames.

"Don't worry, I think it's *Mario Bros.*," I said. Olivia passed through the doorway, brushing my chest with her shoulder. The top of her head reached below my chin. I could smell her hair. Faint hints of lavender and mint—what I'd imagine the feeling of calm smelled like.

"Come on in, make yourself at home." I gestured toward the wooden kitchen table, scattered with paper and markers from Lilly. "Sorry about the mess."

"Please, I'm a mom to a ten year old boy. This is nothing." She tidied the table, piling the paper and sliding the markers back in their box. She held up a picture Lilly must have drawn earlier of a cartoon looking cat. "She's really good. I can't believe this was done with magic markers."

I opened the fridge and grabbed two beers, popping the tops off with my magnetic bottle opener stuck to the fridge. "Yeah, she definitely doesn't get that talent from me. Here you go."

She took the beer with a thanks and drank a long sip. I watched the way her lips molded around the open bottle and the way her delicate fist wrapped around the base. Her throat bobbed as the sip slid down it and I had to force myself to turn my head and gulp down a sip of my own. I was staring like a creep. And hell, my pants were tighter than they'd been five minutes ago.

"That hits the spot," she said. "It has no business being this humid outside."

"Welcome to Florida—humidity, bugs, and gators. Oh, and tourists. Lots of those." I pulled out the chair opposite her and slowly sank down, biting back a groan.

"Can't wait to be a resident." She laughed. "Honestly where I'm from isn't much better. Upstate New York has awful humidity, killer mosquitos, and way too many hikers. I don't understand the appeal."

"Not a nature person?"

I found myself sitting forward waiting on bated breath for her every word. She broke her gaze away from the soggy beer label and pinned it on me.

"Nope. Not unless you'd call the beach nature. Sand I can do, but dirt?" She visibly shuddered while bringing the bottle back to her lips.

"How's that working out for you, being a mom to a boy? Does your husband do the outdoorsy stuff with him?" *Slick, Wes. Real slick.* She choked on a sip of beer. "Shit, you okay?"

"Yup," she said in between coughs. "Went down wrong." When she'd composed herself she answered, "No husband. I'm painfully single."

Was I mistaken, or did a blush spread across her freckled cheeks? Either way, a burst of warmth hit my chest like a bullet. What the hell was this feeling?

"Painfully single, huh?"

"Yup. And not looking to change that anytime soon." She raised a brow and studied my face.

"Noted." I smirked, adding, "I'll have to tell the line of single guys that followed us over here to hit the road."

Her eyes flicked to the door and back again. "Smooth."

"I thought so." I chuckled and pulled at my beer.

"So... about that pizza you promised?" she asked.

"Right. The menu is somewhere in the kitchen. I'll grab it."

"Should I check on the kids?"

"Sure. They're around the corner. Lilly gets my bedroom when she's here and I take the couch."

She nodded and I realized I'd just invited this woman into my bedroom. Not in a creepy way, our kids were in there. But still, it felt weirdly intimate. She left her beer on the table and turned the corner, heading toward the sounds of video game music.

I dug through the junk drawer for the menu to NY Slice. This woman was from New York. No way was I ordering Domino's like I normally would. As I cursed under my breath, I heard the unmistakable footsteps of my father clomping through the front door.

"For Christ's sake, Wesley. You could have called me and told me you were home. You find Lilly?"

"Fortunately, yes. She wasn't abducted on your watch." I found the menu jammed in the back of the drawer and yanked it out. "What the hell, Dad? You fell asleep again and she went roaming the neighborhood."

He groaned, dropped his keys into the bowl on the kitchen island, and pulled out a beer for himself. "It was only for a few minutes. I was watching reruns of *Everybody Loves Raymond* and I must've dozed. Last I saw she was coloring at the table, complaining that she was bored. I was gonna take her for ice cream later."

He looked genuinely distraught. My father was many things, but an attentive parent was not one of them. I had my mother for that, when she wasn't too busy bestowing her support on strangers.

"It's fine. I gotta find a sitter for her, I guess. Or bring her to the restaurant. Can't have her running off every weekend. I'd take off if I could, but Saturdays have been nuts."

"I can watch her. No need to spend money on a sitter," he grumbled.

I huffed and unfolded the menu. "I'm gonna order some pizzas for dinner."

"Pizza again?" I narrowed my brows at him. The last thing I wanted to do after cooking most of the day was cook at home. "Sounds good to me," he chirped.

Olivia came around the corner and I swear my father almost fell over. It took him a second to compose himself before he glanced at me for an explanation.

"This is Olivia. Her and her son Alex found Lilly roaming the beach." I didn't mention that it's been weeks since we'd officially met. He'd hound me about waiting so long to bring her over for dinner. My father's eyes widened. He may be in his sixties, but I knew he was still checking Olivia out. I anchored a hand on his shoulder and gave a gentle squeeze. "Olivia, this is my father, Walter Reed."

She stuck out a hand and my father accepted it, shaking hers vigorously. "Call me Walt."

"Ah, Walt, the dozing babysitter." Olivia was quick-witted and I loved it. My face broke into a grin.

"It won't happen again." He tucked his head. "And don't tell my wife. She'd never let me hear the end of it."

I interrupted whatever pity party rabbit hole my father was about to spiral down. "I found the menu. You mentioned pineapple. Anything else you guys like?"

"Pineapple?" My father asked in a tone that implied I was about to feed him rat poison. I glared at him again and he cleared his throat. "Sounds good."

"Pineapple pizza is great. Thank you." She met my gaze with a half smile and my heart stuttered.

"I'll call it in." I reached into my pocket and took out my phone, flipping it open to dial the number.

"You have a flip phone?" Olivia asked, amused. I'd gotten this remark before and it never bothered me.

"Yup. Sure do."

"Wow. I haven't seen one of those since middle school."

"Even I have an iPhone," my father said. "Wes here is anti-technology. Or at least *now* he is."

"Okay, Dad. Why don't you go turn on a show? I'll let you know when the pizza gets here." My old man would spill national secrets to Russia if he had the opportunity. If I hadn't distracted him he'd tell Olivia my entire life story.

"Alright, no need to get testy. I know when I'm not wanted." Finally, grabbing his beer, he went to his favorite spot on the couch and flipped on what looked like *Law and Order* while Olivia held in a laugh.

"Kids alright?" I asked.

"Yeah, they're having an epic showdown of *Mario Kart*. I'm glad Alex has someone to play with."

"Me too. For Lilly I mean." I gestured to my phone. "I'll call the order in and then would you want to sit outside? It shouldn't be as humid now that the sun's set. We get a nice breeze from the beach."

"Sure." She had the prettiest smile I'd ever seen in my thirty years.

I called in the order, adding in a meat lovers for Dad and me, and a plain for Lilly, as well as some cans of Sprite. It would be here in about forty-five minutes. Which meant I had to make conversation with this stunning woman, distraction free, the entire time. I should have been happy, but I was terrified.

I showed her out to the porch after checking in on the kids again and we settled down in the pair of worn wooden rockers. My joints ached from a busy day at the restaurant but sitting in companionable silence with Olivia made it easier to not focus on the pain.

"What do you do for fun? You know, besides yelling at people." My lip twitched as I took in a ghost of a smile on her face in the dim light.

"Fun? Let's see." She tapped her chin. "Does playing Legos with Alex count? Because I can build a hefty set in record time."

"No shit? Sounds thrilling." I sipped my nearly empty beer, wishing I'd gotten a second one before sitting down.

"Oh, it is. It's all fun and games until you step on a Lego shark and nearly lose a limb."

I smirked, thinking how someone uttering that phrase a few years ago would have sent me into a shitty mood. I bent at the waist and lifted my pant leg to reveal my prosthetic leg. "Courtesy of a Lego shark. There's no nearly about it. I stepped on that thing and did lose a limb."

The tiniest hint of shock played out on her face before she brought a palm to her forehead. "Oh my God. I'm so sorry. Wow, that was a real insert foot in mouth moment."

"I don't know if I should. See, the shark only left one foot and I'm not sure it can reach my mouth." I chuckled watching her horrified expression.

"Shit, I did it again." A combination of a groan and a squeal came from underneath her palm.

"Olivia, I'm kidding. You gave me the perfect in."

She peeked one eye out from between spread fingers, reading my playful expression. "I'm going to go bury my head in the sand now. Tell Alex if he needs me, to find a shovel."

"Come on, Tiger. No need to hide. It's all good." She shook her head from side to side, still hidden behind her palm. Her dark painted nails gave off a luster from the single light of the porch. "That had to be the single best way I've ever told someone yet."

She dragged her hand down her face, inch by inch. When her fingers slid against her full bottom lip I had to avert my eyes. It was too easy to let my mind run wild. With a sigh and another sip of her beer, she finally responded, "Do you want to talk about it?" She gestured toward my leg. I garnered from our few encounters that she was polite, but I didn't expect her to ask about it. I'd usually get an uncomfortable apology before whoever it was suddenly remembered they needed to be somewhere else.

"Nah. Not tonight at least."

She nodded, not prying for more. "I can't help but notice the chef uniform. Where do you work?"

"This?" I pointed to my coat. "This is my costume for the strip club. The ladies love it. I get more tips than the fireman and the construction worker."

"Wow... Well, more power to you." She laughed and I was reminded again how much I enjoyed the sound. "I guess I'm missing out on the real fun in town. Too busy holed up in my room with Star Wars Legos."

"Get your singles ready. Oh, and insider tip, don't order the food there, no matter how tempting it sounds. Baby oil is known to make its way into the kitchen." I didn't know where this side of me was coming from, but hell, it felt good. Like a tiny sliver of myself was waking up from a years long nap.

"I'll keep that in mind."

"To answer your question... yes, I'm a chef. Not classically trained or anything. I did a program in high school and got a culinary certificate."

"Culinary certificate. So fancy."

"Yup. That's me. Fancy as can be. We own a restaurant in town. It's been in my mother's family for a few generations."

"That's awesome. You must be so proud to be a part of that."

"Yeah, you could say that." Proud isn't exactly the term I'd use. More like obligated. I guess I shouldn't complain. It pays the bills and gives me a reason to get out of bed. That, and when Lilly is here on Saturdays and I fumble my way through single fatherhood one night a week. "When are you thinking of moving here?"

"As soon as I can figure out a plan. My life is sort of complicated." I caught her gazing out at the waves. "Moving over a thousand miles away isn't a decision I'd make lightly. But it's time for a change."

We made more small talk. I asked about their hometown and Olivia answered in short one or two word responses. When she wasn't teasing me, she sat back and quietly listened to the sounds of the shore and buzzing insects.

Our peace didn't last long though. My father pushed through the front door, muttering under his breath. "Kelly called me."

"What now?" I huffed. I left the restaurant less than an hour ago and everything was fine.

"That new waitress quit. Walked right out in the middle of her shift." My father didn't handle much with the business. Not anymore. Kelly must have called him since I left my phone inside. I scrubbed a hand over my jaw. "Shit. I'll have to go back."

I couldn't leave the rest of the dinner rush to Kelly and my bare bones kitchen crew. Derek was already struggling to get orders out on time and needed the servers to be on his ass.

"I can help," Olivia offered. Her dark eyes widened as if she too was surprised by the words that came out of her mouth. My father and I both looked at her like she'd just offered us a million bucks.

"Do you have experience?" my father asked.

She squeaked out a noise that sounded like a balloon releasing air while tilting her hand side to side in the so-so gesture. "But how hard can it be?"

I chuckled and kept my tongue tied. It wasn't a difficult job, but it was fast paced. "You're hired, Tiger. Dad, you got the kids?"

"Oh, you meant right now?" she asked.

"Yup. Pizza will have to wait. Let's go."

Chapter 5

Olivia

I KNEW THE LOOK in Wes's eyes. He was about to lose it. Whatever his ex said must have triggered him because in the few months I'd known this man, I'd never seen him look so furious before. Pissed at some of his kitchen staff for fumbling an order or annoyed at his parents, many times. But he'd always kept that slight tilt in his lips and gleam in his eye.

After making sure Walt would be okay with the kids for a few minutes, I followed Wes into his office. He paced the length of his desk, head down, clenching and unclenching his fists at his side. I closed the door behind me and leaned against it. What could I say or do to help him? I tried to put myself in Mia's shoes. She was always good at helping people through a crisis. She'd probably coo over him and offer hugs. I loved that about her. But that wasn't me or my way.

"Wesley," I said his name in a clear, firm tone. "Stop pacing and look at me." He froze and looked up. I took a tentative step closer and decided to throw caution to the wind and say exactly what I was thinking. "I don't know what happened outside or what was said. I don't know anything about this situation." The way he pinned me with his intense gaze should have rattled me. Instead it emboldened me to go on. "But I know the look in your eyes. You're about two seconds from losing your shit." He released a breath and leaned against his desk. "And I know you well enough to know you'd never want Lilly to witness that. Or your customers. But most importantly, Lilly. So talk to me if you want to. I'm here. Or if you want to throw something, I'll help clean up the mess. Just whatever happened outside, don't keep it in. That shit will be a ticking time bomb."

I waited on a response while my pulse pounded in my ears. I had no right to talk to him this way. Hopefully he wouldn't fire me. I thought of Lilly sitting out in that booth and stood firm. I was being tough on him for her. Just like the first time we met when I'd given him a piece of my mind.

The seconds ticked by and Wes's shoulders sunk. His lips settled into a hard line, but the rest of his features seemed to sag. "You're right."

"I usually am." I managed a grin, hoping to lighten the mood. He focused his gaze on the ceiling and shook his head. "Want to talk about it?"

"Is throwing things still an option?"

I grabbed a stack of Post-it notes from his desk and passed them over. "Have at it."

The corner of his mouth creeped up. "Don't think these will give me the release I'm looking for."

My cheeks flushed. *Don't go there, Olivia.* That is most definitely not the type of release he implied.

"Sorry, your office is fresh out of glassware." I came to his side and knocked my thigh against his. There was so much about this man that was a mystery to me, yet I felt like I knew him. Like we were kindred spirits. Not in most of the outward ways we went about our lives, but deep down, where it counted. "So, your ex seems like a peach."

He made a sound like he was trying to clear sand from his throat. "If that peach grew from hell and was rotten and infested with parasites."

"Damn. Tell me how you really feel." That got an actual laugh out of him, and dry as it was, I'd take it.

"Savannah, my ex. She dropped Lilly off so she can fulfill a modeling contract overseas."

I let his words sink in, but even when they did, I still couldn't believe what I'd heard.

"She left? Like poof, she's gone and not coming back?"

"Not for a few months." He pressed his tongue into his cheek. "I gotta call her, see if there's another way. It's not that I don't want Lilly..." He trailed off.

"Calling her sounds like a good plan. Lilly must be upset to be away from her mom for that long." My heart was breaking for that little girl. "Wait. Does Lilly know what's going on?"

"Apparently she does and knew this was coming. It's all news to me though, in case that wasn't obvious."

I fixed my ponytail to give my hands something to do. From what little I'd heard about Lilly's mom, I didn't think much of the woman, but her dropping Lilly off without warning took the cake. Wes moved to sit behind his desk and without thinking I took hold of his hand. I didn't expect him to wrap his fingers around mine the way he did. They were warm and calloused and strong.

"I'm sorry. If there's anything I can do to help, please let me know." I squeezed gently, trying to convey that I meant it. I was used to being a single parent, but I'd also had help my entire life. It wasn't until moving that I'd been slapped in the face with the reality of not just parenting on my own but also learning the hard way what it took to function as an adult in this world. I was lucky enough to have Mia and Kendahl and the support of the Krav family behind me. Knowing I had them here, even as a small anchor, was a comfort I never appreciated until I moved. I didn't know who Wes had in his life other than his parents, but the look on his face told me he needed to know he had me in his corner.

He nodded and I pulled my hand away. "I should get back on the floor to check on Alex and handle my tables. I'll let you make your calls." I gestured toward the door with my thumb, and turned to leave.

"Thanks, Tiger." His words were barely a whisper, but I heard them. I hoped he knew I'd meant what I said. With a quick glance over my shoulder, I saw him shuffling papers around, likely looking for his cellphone. I shook my head at the endearing disaster that seemed to surround him, wondering how the hell this man was going to take care of a kid like Lilly.

After my shift, Alex and I went to the beach for a quick swim before the late afternoon thunderstorm rolled in. Clouds hung low and the air was heavy. Splashing cool water over my sweaty brow was just what I needed.

I was reluctant to leave Lilly at the restaurant, but Wes insisted they were fine and that his father would bring her home shortly. I didn't argue. The man had a rough enough day and I'd already said my piece about being there for them. I couldn't help but think about them the entire time I watched Alex play, though. Being away from my son would break my heart—not hearing his laugh or seeing his eyes light up when he discovered something new. Even hearing him yell at his video games in frustration held a place in my heart, because it was him.

I had an explicit set of words for my parents and how they'd conducted their lives all these years but at least they were there. They stuck with me when I was at my lowest and they never stopped supporting me and Alex when I'd needed them. They weren't the warmest people, and they sure as hell weren't what I'd call good parents, but I had to give them credit where it was due.

I hoped Wes could figure his shit out enough tonight so Lilly would know he wanted her there. I knew he did, deep down. He was just terrible at showing it. As for his ex, who was I to judge? I didn't know anything about her or their past. Just because I couldn't be away from my son for an extended period of time didn't mean all parents felt that way.

After rinsing our sandy selves off, I microwaved our last bag of frozen veggies and warmed up some of Alex's nuggets. Learning to cook needed to be higher up on my to-do list. Funny thing was, I worked in a restaurant and my only real friend back home was our chef. You'd think I would have picked up a few tips.

My phone rang just as I finished cleaning the kitchen and was about to start unpacking a few boxes in my tiny closet. I groaned seeing my mother's contact photo flash across the screen of my phone. Better to get this out of the way, I thought, hitting accept.

"Hello, Mother." I hit the speakerphone button so at least I could have free hands to unpack while I listened to her drone on.

"Can you believe what your father did today?"

I didn't even get a greeting. Not that I was super surprised at that. This was how most of our calls started since I'd moved.

"Am I supposed to know what he did or are you going to tell me?" I tried to keep my tone pleasant. I really did. But it was a long day and I felt my eye starting to twitch.

She huffed. "I don't need that tone from you. Not today of all days."

"Sorry, Mother. Please go on. I am so eager to hear what slight my father dealt upon you today."

"He froze all the joint credit cards." Clearly my sarcasm went right over her head. "I have never been so embarrassed in my life. I was out to lunch with Geneva from The Met. You remember her from the last gala I organized. We were discussing details for my upcoming charity event. Oh Olivia, it's going to be sublime. The theme is vintage couture."

I let out a few well placed *oh wows* and *uh huhs*, focusing instead on organizing my small collection of purses on the top shelf.

"Can you imagine anything more humiliating than having your credit card decline at the Four Seasons? My blood pressure is skyrocketing at the mere memory of it."

"That must have been awful. What did you do?"

"I knew it was your father's doing. He's been livid that I've been staying in the city while he's home upstate. I called him immediately and demanded he fix the problem."

This story was more interesting than I'd thought it would be.

"And did he?"

"Of course. Your father hates a scene more than anyone I know. Thank goodness we have an appointment with the mediator next week. I can't live like this."

I bit back a laugh. If anything, separating from my father has upped my mother's drama factor by ten. This personality must have been tucked away behind years of politician's wife plastered on smiles and repressed sexuality. Oh, and lots of vodka tonics.

"I'm sure you'll get it figured out." I hoped it didn't continue to be the mess it's been since word got out that my mother had cheated on my father with a senator. My parents had been in the public eye my entire life. My father went from high profile attorney, to judge, to attorney general. Neil and Pamela Murphy always put on a great show. If they were good at one thing, it was just that, acting.

"I can't tell you how relieved I am that you're finally on your own. Imagine if I still had you and Alex to care for?" She let out a humorless laugh. "What a mess that would be."

Don't let her get to you. She was right even if my clenched jaw begged to differ. I was almost thirty years old, it was about time I left the nest. It didn't feel great to hear my mother practically having a party over it though.

"Yup," I said.

"Oh don't be that way. You know what I mean. It's just chaotic over here, is all. And our finances are a mess, mostly frozen and untouchable. I even had to let go of Samuel."

I racked my brain but came up empty. "Samuel?"

"My chef here in the city. My lawyer told me to tighten my spending for the time being. Anyway, I won't keep you, you must be busy with Alex. Tell him hello from me."

"I will."

She said a quick goodbye and ended the call while I leaned against my closet door rubbing my tight shoulders. Every time my body hurt from a long day at the restaurant or Wes annoyed me by misplacing something, I thought about the toxicity of my parents lives in New York and was suddenly grateful to have gotten out at the right time. Whatever happened with them had nothing to do with me. I repeated that mantra for the rest of the night. *Their choices, their problems.* Even if it stung to hear how glad she was to be rid of us.

By the time I let my thoughts settle, I'd unpacked two boxes and organized my purses and shoes. With such a small space, I needed to be intentional about what I kept and where I put everything. This bungalow was a far cry from the opulence of our New York home, but that's what I loved about it. Creaky wooden floors with sand embedded in each crack, faded nautical wallpaper in the bedrooms and salt crusted windows that took finessing to open. The place reminded me of a boat at sea. I'd fill this little home with as much love as I could. Alex would know he was always wanted and welcome no matter his age or what happened in life.

At bedtime, I gave him an extra hug, which was met with a groan. His brown eyes searched mine as he played with the leg of his precious stuffed duck, Quackers. In that moment he looked like my little boy again and not the preteen he was turning into. "Will Lilly be okay?"

I ruffled his curls and tidied the stack of comic books on his side table. "Yeah, she'll be okay, honey. Why do you ask?"

"She looked sad today. I think she was trying not to be but I could tell."

My chest ached but I kept my tone neutral. "She has some big changes going on in her life. Kind of like us." I smiled. "The best thing we can do is be her friend."

"I guess I can do that." His mouth tipped in a mischievous grin.

"You guess?"

"She's cool, even if she always hits me with red shells in *Mario Kart*. But I have a plan to win."

I laughed, watching his eyes sparkle with ideas. "I'm sure you do, buddy. Okay, time for bed. We need to get you back on a good schedule for school next week."

"Not school," he groaned. "I don't want to go."

"I know, I know. But I have a feeling you'll like your new school. Want to drive by it tomorrow to check it out?" He thought it over for a second before I added, "We can get ice cream afterwards."

"Okay."

When in doubt, I bribed with ice cream. I said another good-night and turned his light off, grabbing his phone to charge in the kitchen.

As I laid in my own bed, tossing and turning, I considered texting my sister or Kendahl to get my thoughts out there about the day and the exhaustion of it all. The darkened screen on my phone reflected light from my reading lamp, beckoning me to pick it up and type something, even if how I was feeling couldn't easily be articulated.

I huffed and flipped onto my stomach. I didn't want to bother them. They had their own problems to deal with. No one forced me to move here and take on this new life. That choice was all mine to own. I wished I knew how hard it would be. Still, I didn't think I'd have stayed in New York, even knowing I'd be counting every last dollar to buy groceries.

I closed my eyes, focusing on the soft sounds of rolling waves that squeezed through the cracks in the old windows. I pictured Wes in my mind's eye and said a little prayer to the universe that he was doing alright.

Chapter 6

Wes

AFTER THE MORNING RUSH, I was finally able to take a load off in my office. Sweat coated my skin as I cranked the air lower, shrugged out of my chef's coat, and reclined in my chair. It was humid as hell outside and Sunshine seemed to soak the moisture up like a sponge.

I rolled up my pant leg and took my prosthesis off to give my leg some air. Days like this one, where I sweat through my liners, could be dangerous if I didn't keep dry.

Leaning my head back, I groaned and rubbed my tired eyes. It had been a rough few weeks getting accustomed to having Lilly full time. I knew one thing for sure. I had to move out of my parent's place as soon as possible. Sleeping on the couch, with its coiled springs poking me in the back, was fucking me up and making it hard to get through the work day. We all needed our own space. My mom's been up all night reading and shuffling around the kitchen, while my dad snores loud enough to blow the roof off. It's a wonder I haven't fallen asleep standing and face-planted into the fryer by now.

Someone knocked softly on my office door. "Yeah?"

Olivia opened it a crack. Seeing her gorgeous face peeking through helped my mood shift immediately. "Question for you. Can I come in?"

"Always." She pushed the door open. I noticed her rosy cheeks before anything else.

"Oh my God, it's so nice and cool in here." She walked underneath the vent in the ceiling and tilted her face up. "It's almost as nice as the walk-in."

"That's my goal," I said with a smile. My gaze trailed lower, noticing her tight nipples visible through her white shirt. I cleared my throat. "Did you have a question for me?"

"Oh, sorry. I got caught up in my love affair with the air conditioning unit. Do you think your mom could keep an eye on Alex for me tonight? My sister is bugging me to go to a girls night dinner and I'm sure he'd rather play with Lilly than be stuck sitting with my sister's boyfriend." She perched on the edge of my desk and fiddled with my pen holder, flipping the pens so they were all facing down.

"No need to ask my mom. I can watch him." Lilly always seemed happier when she got to hang out with Alex.

"You don't have to work late?"

"Nope, I'm heading home around the same time as you today." I stretched my arms over my head, feeling the pull of my tight muscles. "I told Lilly we'd play some games after school. She'll be psyched to have Alex join in."

Olivia's gaze followed the path of my arms and lingered on my hands. I brought them back to my desk and she seemed to come back to life. "As long as you're sure..."

"Tiger," I grumbled. "I said I'm sure. Alex is a cool kid and honestly, having him over helps me with Lilly. So what's happening for girls night?" I lowered my tone and raised a brow.

"Knowing Mia, it's probably something quiet like a movie and dinner. But if our friend Kendahl is planning, I'm in for a wild night." She hugged her arms to her chest and I spotted goosebumps pebbled along her skin. "Okay, I take back my previous air conditioning comment. It's icy in here."

"I'd give you my coat, but I doubt you'd want it. It's probably still damp with sweat."

"I'll be fine. I should head out and grab some lunch before the next rush." She stood and took a step toward the door.

"You're going out to buy food? You can eat anything you want. Just ask one of the guys or Thea to make you something." Has she been spending money on eating out the whole time she's worked here? I felt like a dumbass.

"I don't want to bother them. Everyone's tired from the rush. I'll be quick, just grabbing a smoothie from the spot down the street."

A smoothie as a meal? That wasn't enough food, especially for someone who's been working as hard as she has all day.

"Give me a minute. I'm making you lunch." She started to protest like I knew she would, but I put my hand out. "I won't take no for an answer. Meet me in the kitchen in a minute."

She bit her bottom lip, clearly holding back a protest. When I didn't drop eye contact with her, she huffed. "Fine, but you don't have to make a fuss."

A grin tugged at my cheeks. It wasn't often that my Tiger gave in, but when it happened I felt like tiny bubbles were bursting in my chest.

Quickly, before she snuck out to get her smoothie anyway, I pulled a clean liner out of my desk drawer and put my prosthesis back on. Hell, it felt amazing to be on two feet every single time, but I'd be lying if I said it wasn't painful sometimes, especially when I was swollen.

Giving myself a minute to adjust, I tugged a sweatband over my head, positioning it to hold my hair back, and put my coat back on, buttoning most of the buttons.

Olivia waited for me in the kitchen, making herself busy wiping down the counter. Thea was in her own world prepping salads and Caleb must have been taking an extra long smoke break.

"What would you like to eat?"

"Hmm…" She bit her bottom lip and peeked around the kitchen. "I don't know. Honestly, I don't care as long as it's edible."

I took a few steps toward her and that tingle in my veins started. The feeling showed up anytime she was in arms length. "Well, give me some ideas. When you're home, what do you cook?"

She laughed and I wanted to capture the sound to replay later. "Anything that comes in a box with instructions."

"You're kidding?" My culinary-loving heart shattered.

"Sadly, no. I can't cook." With her face angled down, she added, "Growing up we always had a chef cook all our meals. I wouldn't even know where to start."

I moved so my body crowded hers. Her breath hitched as I reached behind her for an empty mixing bowl. "I'm going to teach you how to make a meal. Come on, let's see what we have prepped."

"Oh, okay." Her voice wobbled and hitched again as I took her hand and led her to the walk-in. I couldn't feel the cold air—not with her hand in mine, soft and warm.

I reluctantly let go of her to grab some eggs, washed veggies, and cheddar. She quietly watched me gather everything, like she was studying my moves.

I set the items on the counter. "The first thing every cook should learn is how to prepare eggs. According to all my culinary school teachers, if you can't cook eggs, you have no business in a kitchen." I softened my voice when I saw her shoulders fall. "Don't worry. This is easy, I promise."

"Easy for you," she said. "I burn everything I touch."

"Not going to happen today. I'll help you every step of the way. You okay with peppers and onions?"

"Sure." She studied my movements, soaking in everything as I arranged the ingredients.

"Perfect. First, we're going to dice these veggies." I grabbed one of my knives and arranged the pre-cut strips onto the cutting board in front of us. "Come closer, Tiger. I won't bite."

With a cute glare, she stepped right beside me. "Watch how I cut these. You'll want them to be this size so they cook evenly." I handed her the knife and stepped aside so she could try.

"Like this?" She diced a few but they were not even close to being even.

Moving behind her, I reached around her side and grasped the knife handle over her hand, guiding her movement. "Slowly. Just like that." She sucked in a breath but kept chopping until all the strips of peppers were diced. "Now the onion." With her hand under mine, I steered her movements. Pressed against her back, I could smell her hair—so fucking sweet. I had to remind myself to concentrate, but it was increasingly tough while I was this close to her.

"How am I doing?" The usual edge to her tone was gone, replaced with a reserved hush.

"You're doing so well," I murmured close to her ear. "You're a natural."

At that point she could have continued on her own but I wasn't ready to put space between us. Not when it felt so fucking good to have a reason to touch her.

She let out a low laugh. "I wouldn't call myself a natural, but at least I haven't lost a finger yet."

"I'd never let that happen," I said. "As long as I'm here with you, you're perfectly safe."

We'd finished chopping the onion and I realized my hand was still grasping hers. I ran my thumb along the ridges of her knuckles before stepping aside to grab the eggs.

"I think I can do the egg part," she said. "Same as with baking, right?"

Did I want to agree with her? Then I wouldn't have a reason to help her closely again. "It's similar, but I have a secret for fluffy eggs."

With a hand on her hip, she asked, "Is that so?"

"I'd never lie to you, especially not about my culinary talents." I smirked and stepped behind her again. "Let's crack these eggs, and I'll show you how I whisk them."

My skin buzzed when our hands touched again. How long has it been since a woman affected me this way? With Olivia, it was more than simple attraction. I wanted to know everything about her, what made her happy, what worried her. To see her smile or hear her laugh physically affected me, and if I was being honest that scared me. *Come on Wes, you're teaching her how to cook eggs. It's not like you're marrying the woman.*

That thought didn't freak me out like it should have.

She picked up the whisk and dipped it into the bowl. "Let's add some room temperature water. That's great, Tiger. Keep going."

With my palm wrapped around hers and my other hand holding the bowl, I had her boxed in. Was I imagining it, or did she push back against me slightly? Fuck, if she did, there's no way she didn't feel how hard she was making me.

We picked up the pace, whisking until the eggs were nice and frothy. "How's this?" she asked, sounding breathless.

"Keep going, up and down. Just like that." Christ, my voice just shook. I leaned in closer. One more small step and I'd be flush against her. The air between us was heavy and I swore her hand shook beneath mine.

"Hey, Chef, did you have something specific in mind for the soup? You think anyone's gonna order soup in this heat anyway?" Thea called as she turned the corner. I bounced back and dropped my hands to my side. "Oh, sorry. I didn't realize you were busy." She smirked but didn't turn away.

"No, it's fine," I stammered, trying to get control of myself. "You're right, let's cut soup from the specials. It's too damn hot."

"Got it," Thea said before rounding the corner again.

I brought my attention back to Olivia, who was still whisking slowly. "Sorry. I think we're ready to fire it up."

When she faced me, I noticed her flushed cheeks and moist bottom lip, plump from being bitten. I had to stop looking at her lips or I'd never be able to finish this simple omelet.

"I think I'll just watch that part," she said.

I nodded with a grin and brought our thoroughly whisked eggs and other ingredients over to the burners, pulling down a pan. She watched with rapt attention while I finished cooking the omelet and plated it beautifully.

"That looks amazing. I doubt I'll be able to recreate it, but maybe I can try one day."

"I know you can. You did so well." She beamed while I handed her a fork. "Eat up. No one likes cold eggs."

While she ate, I cleaned up the station and took some inconspicuous deep breaths to calm my racing heart. Did she feel what I felt? I couldn't tell from the look on her face, but fuck, I'd be lying if I said I wasn't hoping she felt the same spark too.

Chapter 7

Olivia

Two months into the school year and Alex was no better at waking up on time than on the first day. I've seen slugs move faster and that's not even a joke. There was a slug outside Sunshine the other day and it hauled ass compared to my son. Where was this energy level at bedtime?

I sipped my first cup of coffee and shoved toast into my mouth while stuffing Alex's homework folder into his backpack. Too bad I didn't have time to attempt to cook eggs. "Alex, five minutes until we have to leave. Do you have your shoes on?"

He came trudging out of his room wearing a crumpled *Mario Bros.* T-shirt and shorts that definitely didn't match. I noticed his scowl and decided I'd pick my battles.

"Here, have some toast." I grabbed a piece I'd slathered with peanut butter and extended the offering to him like I was trying not to startle a wild animal.

"I'm not hungry," he grumbled, but took it from my hand anyway. "Can I have coffee, too?"

Instead of shooting his request down immediately, I thought for a second. A few ounces wouldn't hurt him. And maybe it would give the illusion of drinking magical wake up juice. I was too late to argue.

"Here, you can finish mine." He took my offering with a slight grin. I glanced at his feet as I grabbed my work sneakers. "Hey, I don't think wearing flip-flops is a good idea at school. You should change."

"Everyone wears these. It's fine. I don't even have P.E. today."

I looked at my watch again and decided once again that this battle wasn't worth it. "Alright. Grab your bag. You'll have to finish eating in the car." I turned off the coffee maker and the kitchen lights and followed Alex outside.

"Are we picking up Lilly again today?" he asked between sips of coffee.

"Not today. Her grandma is driving her." Thank God since we would have had to leave twenty minutes ago if that were the case. If Alex moved at the speed of a slimy invertebrate in the morning, Lilly moved half the speed. She was the sloth from *Zootopia* personified. Watching her drag herself out the door was like watching a video in slow motion. "How's Lilly doing in school?"

Luck was on our side when Alex and Lilly ended up in the same class at school. Although from what Alex has told me, Lilly was having a tough time adjusting to the move. I thought about the spunky girl I met on the beach with her paint splattered shorts and tangled hair. She still had such a baby face but spoke like she was much older than her ten years.

"I'm not sure. She hasn't really talked about it much. But there's these mean girls that are always laughing when she walks by their desks." I white-knuckled my steering wheel. Kids could be such assholes.

"Well, I'm glad she has you as her friend. Keep on being there for her, okay, bud." I peeked at Alex in my rearview mirror just in time to see a slight eye roll.

"I know, I know."

It was my turn to roll my eyes back at him. I desperately needed more coffee.

"I thought that table would never leave," Kelly groaned, dumping a few dirty plates into the bus box at our server station. She wiped her brow with a napkin and neatly folded it into her pants pocket.

"Which one?" I asked. I was busy enough with my own tables in the morning breakfast rush that I hadn't paid mind to what she was doing. Other than when we crossed paths picking up orders or refilling drinks. Kelly filled a glass with cold water from the machine, sipping and leaving a ring of bright red lipstick on the rim.

"Table nine. Loud couple. You didn't hear them arguing?"

I finished cashing out my ticket and glanced over toward the table in question. "Nope, I guess I was in my own head."

"Guess so. You know who didn't miss a word, though?" I smiled when my gaze found Walter at the counter, his body turned toward the other diners. "That man collects gossip worse than my granny's church group."

"Can't blame him. He needs something to do all day," I said. "And I know he just loves irritating Wes."

Kelly chuckled and finished off her glass. "It's like a circle of irritation in this place. Walt gets under Wesley's skin and Wesley gets under yours."

I titled my head. Her analogy was spot on. "And what about me? Who do I irritate?"

She pinned me with a look and raised her thinly plucked brow. "I think you already know the answer to that question."

We both laughed. "Love you too, Kel." I hip bumped her on my way out to the floor. In my time here, I'd messed up more than I could count, mixing our orders, standing in her way, taking the wrong tables. But I'd slowly grown on her like I was the little sister she never wanted. She was in her forties with a grown son and a grandbaby on the way. As much as our personalities clashed, I valued her knowledge.

"Oh, by the way, dimple guy is here again. He's sitting in your section." Kelly peeked around the corner to scope out our new regular. I don't know anything about him, except that he always sits in the same booth by the window and alternates between our turkey club and our chef's salad. "I think he's looking for you," she singsonged.

"Doubtful," I retorted. Although, he was glancing around the place. I pulled my order pad out, ready to go when I felt the unmistakable presence of Wes behind me.

"Ladies." He nodded at us and filled a glass with Coke. Wayward strands of light brown hair escaped his hair tie. I itched to put them back in their place. "Did you both get a break yet?"

"I'm about to run to the pharmacy before the lunch crowd," Kelly said. "Looks like there's only the one table and I think he's waiting for the newbie."

I huffed and narrowed my eyes at Kelly. "Whatever it is you're thinking, I'm sure you're dead wrong."

"What does she mean?" Wes asked. He craned his neck to get a peek at the guest and crossed his arms. Of course my gaze traveled directly to Wes's flexed forearms down to his wrist where intricate swirls merged into the shape of a lotus flower on his hand. I pulled my gaze away from him before he noticed me staring. "That guy bothering you?"

"No, it's fine. Kelly means nothing. I swear you're both as bad as Walter." I grabbed a place setting and left them staring after me. I could have sworn I heard Wes grumble, "What did I say?"

Dimple guy put his phone down as I reached his table and greeted me with a smile. A perfect smile, might I add. It matched nicely with the rest of his attractive features. But still, he was nothing more than another random customer.

"What can I do for you?" I asked.

He chuckled, the sound warm and inviting. I had no idea why he was laughing but to hide that, I let out an awkward laugh of my own. "What's your name, beautiful?"

"Olivia." I shuffled my feet and fiddled with my pen. Manners dictated that I ask him his name now, but I didn't need that information, no matter how dazzling his smile may have been.

"Damon." He stuck his hand out and gave me a look I could only describe as a smolder. I placed my hand in his, still holding my pen, and he squeezed gently. "Nice to officially meet you."

"Yeah—uh—same." I took a step back, feeling uncomfortable after his touch. It was only a handshake. There was nothing suspicious about it, or him. But a lump formed in my throat nonetheless. "Do—" I swallowed. "Do you know what you'd like today?"

His face lit up and I took notice of his eyes, golden brown and gleaming. "I do know what I'd like, Olivia."

"To eat," I clarified and stood straighter. People who repeated someone's name a lot gave me uncomfortable feelings. I'd heard somewhere it was a psychological sales tactic. Whatever he was trying to sell, I wasn't interested. My phone vibrated in my pocket and I fought the urge to reach for it.

"I'll have the turkey club." My phone continued vibrating, distracting me from fully hearing his next words.

"Sorry, turkey club. What else did you say?"

His dimples popped as he grinned. "I said instead of fries on the side, I'd love your number."

My cheeks flamed but I didn't have time to respond as Kelly appeared behind me and tapped my shoulder.

She pulled me aside.

"Phone call for you. It's Alex's school." My pulse skyrocketed before I internally talked myself down. Maybe he had a stomach ache or a slight fever. "Go on, I've got him," Kelly whispered, patting my shoulder.

"Thanks, be right back." I didn't have time to unpack my feelings about my number being subbed as a side. As I walked toward the nearest phone, I noticed Wes watching my every move. His eyes bounced from me to Dimples and as I got closer I could clearly see the scowl lining his lips.

I grabbed the phone next to the server station and hit the hold button. "Hello, this is Olivia Murphy speaking."

"Mrs. Murphy, this is Mr. Berkus, the nurse at Sunset Elementary. Alex is going to be fine, please don't be alarmed."

"What's wrong? Did something happen?" I could barely recognize the sound of my voice. My hands trembled so much that I had to wedge the phone into the crook of my neck so I didn't drop it.

"He's on his way over to the hospital. He had a fall on the playground and I believe he broke his leg."

"Oh my God. He must be terrified." I grabbed the wall for support. My breaths came in shallow pants. I needed to go. My baby was hurting and I wasn't there. "Is he alone?"

"Mrs. Nolan is with him—his teacher." The nurse rattled off the information for the closest hospital while I tried to jot it down on my order pad. My hands were shaking so badly I could hardly grip my pen. I felt a palm on my shoulder, warm and large. When I looked up I was face to face with Wes, his brows scrunched. He reached for the phone while I forced a breath into my chest.

"This is Alex's father," he said into the receiver. "My wife is shaken up. Can you repeat that information please?"

His stoic expression remained unchanged, while he jotted down the information I was unable to. God, I was such a mess. My son needed me and I couldn't even write an address down on a piece of paper. What kind of mother was I?

"Thank you. We're leaving now." He ended the call and turned to me. His calloused fingers cupped my chin, lifting it so I met his gaze. "Tiger, go get your things."

I nodded, choking down another breath. "I can cover someone else's shift tomorrow. I don't want to inconvenience anyone. Kelly was supposed to leave and I don't know when and oh shit, table nine, the turkey club. And I don't even know where I'm going. I—"

"Get your things. I'm driving." His deep voice cut through my rambling.

"But, the kitchen?"

"Tiger," he practically growled, wrapping his hands around my waist and turning me in the direction of his office. "Get your things and meet me outside."

"Okay."

I forced myself not to think about Alex in pain while I collected my purse at rapid speed. That would only make me spiral into a panic I didn't know if I could come out of. I needed to be there for my son. He only had me after all.

Out in the parking lot Wes stood at the passenger side of his car waiting on me. When he saw me coming he held the door open and ushered me in, reaching across to buckle my seatbelt. I breathed in his comforting scent—a mix of herbs and garlic from the kitchen and sea air. My pulse slowed.

While he walked around to the driver's side I let myself think about the way it felt when he said, *"Alex's father and my wife."* Something about those words coming from his lips didn't feel as wrong as they should. I'd contemplate that another time.

Chapter 8

Wes

FUCKING HOSPITALS. I HATED everything about them. The stark walls that they try to liven up with shitty artwork. The smell of antiseptic permeating the air. It crawls up your nostrils the moment you step foot inside the doors. Worst of all the way every doctor or nurse walked around like seeing suffering didn't affect them. Like witnessing horrors and medical trauma was just any other Wednesday. It was unnatural and unnerving to say the least.

The woman doing intake sat behind her desk with a fake smile plastered on her lips. She passed us a clipboard while Olivia fished out her ID. Her hands still shook so hard, anyone could see. I wished I could take care of this shit for her. The only thing she needed to worry about was getting to Alex, not filling out bullshit paperwork.

"Sir, are you immediate family?" the woman asked, eyes bouncing between Olivia and me. "Yes." I answered without hesitation, taking out my wallet to give her my ID. Her smile widened and she took it, continuing to check us in.

I glanced at Olivia, searching for an objection, but she didn't lift her gaze from the paperwork. No way in hell was I leaving her here alone. I didn't care if I had to lie, cheat or steal, I'd stay with her. Even if my skin crawled with each passing second inside this building.

Guest badges secured, a nurse led us through the dim winding halls of the emergency room toward the sound of a keening wail. Olivia grabbed my hand, gripping it tightly.

"It'll be okay," I said. Nausea took hold of my insides. "That's not him." I fucking hoped.

Hours later, I sat in a shitty, hard chair in the hospital waiting area tuning out the TV blaring a news channel in the corner. Olivia paced the length of the room while her sister, Mia, sat beside me chewing her lip. "How much longer do you think?" Mia asked, looking at me with wide brown eyes identical to Alex's.

"I wish I could tell you." I didn't miss the way she glanced at my prosthesis, like she could see it through the fabric of my clothes. There was no pity in her expression, more curiosity, the same as most. I didn't blame her for asking me. Anyone would think I was some sort of leg injury expert. Fact was, I was drugged up to the nines for the majority of my hospital stays. Time existed in a vacuumed haze.

As for Alex, turns out he suffered a complex leg fracture with the injury close to his growth plate. After weighing their options, the doctors recommended surgery to position his bones and secure with plates and screws. Olivia kept a brave face at Alex's bedside, her hand in his as the poor little guy drifted in and out of sleep from the pain meds he was given.

The second we made it out into the hallway, she collapsed against my chest, sobbing silently. I did what I could to console her, whispering in her ear that it was okay. That Alex was in good hands. All the while, bile threatened to make its way up my throat. When Mia got here, my chest caved in relief. I rushed to the small bathroom off the waiting area and emptied the contents of my stomach.

I wiped my clammy hands on my pants for what felt like the hundredth time in the hour we'd been waiting. Thinking about the little guy laying on an operating table had me sweating bricks. Mia's quiet tapping on her cell phone screen drew my attention.

"Just letting my parents know what's going on," she said. "Olivia will probably be pissed, but that's their grandson and despite them being dicks, they still love Alex."

I nodded, tucking this piece of information away for later. "I should probably call mine. Let them know where I am." Mia tilted her head to the side. "They pick up my daughter from school for me. I'm usually coming home from work around now."

"Oh gotcha," she said. "I thought for a second there that you had to report your comings and goings to mommy." She released her lip from her teeth and smirked. Tiger's sister had a smart mouth too... noted.

I pushed to stand and walked toward Olivia, who'd stopped pacing to check her phone. As I got closer she looked up with bloodshot eyes and a splotchy red face. My heart cracked in two. I lowered my voice, talking in a near whisper. "I'm going to go call my mom and check on Lilly. I'll be right back. You need anything?"

"Oh God, you've been here with me for so long. You should go. Mia's here now and really there's nothing you can do. Lilly needs you home. I—"

For the second time that day, I tipped her chin up, forcing her to look me in the eye. I didn't know why her trying to dismiss me irked me the way it did. Didn't fucking know why I had to be here with them even though the hospital was the last place on earth I'd want to spend my time. But I knew damn well that I wasn't leaving. "I'll be outside for five minutes, tops. I'm not going anywhere, okay?"

A lone tear leaked from the corner of her eye and I watched it trail down her cheek, itching to smooth it off. She sniffed and nodded as I stepped away, reluctant to leave her side.

I followed the labyrinth to the exit and stepped out for some air. The late afternoon sun crept low behind a wall of clouds giving us some reprieve from the heat. I dialed my mom and sighed in relief as she answered the phone. Being here put me on edge, I needed to know that everyone I loved was safe.

"If you're on your way can you grab a poster board? Lilly has a project to work on. Oh, and we need bread. Your father fed the rest to the darn ducks."

"Mom," I interrupted. "I'm at the hospital."

"What? Are you okay? What happened?" Shit, I didn't mean to make her frantic.

"I'm fine. I'm with Olivia. Alex got hurt at school and he's in surgery now." Faint sounds of her shuffling around in the background quieted.

"Oh, my. Come to think of it, Lilly mentioned Alex getting hurt at school but she didn't say it was serious. What can I do to help? Should I organize a meal train? Do they need help from the church?"

"No, Mom, they're fine. As good as can be expected with the situation. It's his leg, a bad break."

"Oh." She paused, and I knew what she was thinking. His leg—I must be losing my shit. But apart from hating the hospital I was surprisingly fine. "How are *you* doing?"

"You know how I feel about hospitals." I pushed a piece of hair behind my ear. "But I'm fine too. You're okay putting Lilly to bed? I don't know how long I'll be here."

"Of course. Please let me know how I can help." I swallowed a lump in my throat. If there was one thing my mother knew well, it was how to be a caretaker. "Hold on, Lilly wants to talk to you."

I smiled despite the situation as my mother passed her phone over. "Dad, is Alex okay?"

"Yeah, he'll be okay, sweet girl. I don't want you to worry."

"Okay." She sounded so young over the phone, her voice so squeaky. "I feel bad."

"I know. But the doctors are fixing him up and he'll be good as new soon." A moment went by while I waited for her to respond. "You there, Lil?"

"Is he going to lose his leg too, like you did?"

Her little voice broke me. I leaned back against the rough exterior wall, my body feeling the stress of the day like a weight. Did I do this to my little girl? Passed along my trauma because I couldn't suck it up and have a proper conversation about my limb loss with her?

"No, sweetheart. He'll be in a cast but he won't lose his leg. When you're ready, we can sit down and talk about what happened to Daddy and why I had to lose mine, okay?"

I could almost hear her nodding. "Dad?"

"Yeah?"

"Tell Alex thank you for me."

"Okay," I said, confused. "Thank you for what?"

The line went quiet and just when I thought she'd hung up she said, "I can't say. But he'll know."

Once Alex was out of recovery and moved into a room, I said my goodbyes, giving the groggy kiddo a pat on the head. Mia was grabbing some dinner for them, then staying until visitors had to leave, so at least they wouldn't be alone. I knew too well what it felt like to be alone in a hospital and I wouldn't wish that on anyone.

"Thank you for today." Olivia's tired eyes met mine and she offered a weak smile. "I appreciate you staying to make sure Alex was okay."

I stayed for you just as much as for him, was what I wanted to say, but I held back.

"Of course. I'll call you in the morning. Try and get some rest."

"Shoot, my shift for tomorrow. I can call Kelly, see if she'll cover." She started to pull her phone out of her purse.

"Tiger, don't worry about it. You're needed here. I think we can manage without you for as long as you need."

"If you're sure?"

"Damn right I'm sure. Matter of fact if you try to come in I'll march you back home."

"Try not to burn the place down without me." She cracked a small grin that I felt deep in my chest.

"Had to call the fire department twice last year and the place still stands."

Alex shifted in bed and Olivia jumped to his side. With a low goodbye I slid out into the hallway, releasing a breath. Exhaustion and another feeling settled into my bones. Something that had my body physically resist walking away from that room. But I pushed forward, the exhaustion winning. "Alex will be okay," I repeated for the hundredth time.

Once I folded into the seat of my car I put my head in my hands, counted down from ten, and then made the drive home, thinking of the pain in Olivia's dark eyes the entire time.

Chapter 9

Olivia

"I need to take this call. Be right back." I adjusted Alex's blanket and stepped into the living area. My phone flashed this local number twice already since I woke up and I didn't think they'd stop calling anytime soon. I took a breath and answered.

"Is this the parent of Alexander Murphy?"

My mind flashed back to his school calling a few days ago and the panicked haze that followed.

"Yes, this is Olivia Murphy."

"Ms. Murphy, this is Sharon from billing at Palm Cove Hospital. It seems there was a mistake and your insurance information wasn't collected for your son's stay. I can take that information now."

I knew this was coming but I didn't think it would be so soon. I paced the length of my couch. "We're currently uninsured. I recently moved and started a new job and the transition has been slow." I stopped rambling. Fact was Sharon didn't care about my life. She had a job to do and that job was collecting insurance information.

"I see." Judgement laced her tone. "I'll forward you some information for our payment plans. Is the email on file correct?"

"Yes. Thank you."

"Fill it out as soon as possible, Ms. Murphy. You'll be hearing from billing in the upcoming weeks." Her voice softened as she added, "Best of luck to you."

I hit end as someone knocked at my door. Since Alex's surgery, Mia and Kendahl have come by every day with food and toys. It's only been a few days and my fridge was full. I wasn't used to this much kindness.

"One second." I tossed my phone on the couch and padded over, pulling the stiff door frame open to find Kendahl standing on the other side holding a stuffed toy. She walked in and plopped her things on my small round kitchen table.

"You okay?" she asked, appraising me with a keen eye. It was like she and Mia were taking turns being on Olivia watch, just waiting for me to break down. I didn't blame them. My track record for handling stressful situations wasn't the best.

"Yeah. I'm fine. Just tired." The lie slipped through my lips easily. If Kendahl found out I'd likely be in thousands upon thousands of dollars of debt because I was a shit mother who didn't even think of health insurance for her kid when I stopped leeching off my parents she'd tell Mia. And Mia would tell my mother, who would get on me even more. They were clear when I decided to move that I was on my own, which meant no more financial help. And that was *before* their assets were frozen.

Kendahl pushed her sunglasses onto her head and scrutinized me. "I call bullshit. But I won't press."

"What'd you bring?" I changed the subject. She grabbed the stuffed toy from the table and held it in front of her. It looked familiar.

"It's some *Minecraft* thing. I don't know, I found it in the game section of Target and knew I'd heard him mention that game like a hundred times."

"He'll love it." I smiled. "Alex, Auntie Kendahl is here." I raised my voice a bit over the sound of his YouTube video.

"I'll go say hi," she said. "Oh, and Mi is coming by in a bit. She was grabbing us lunch." I thought about the trays of food sitting in my fridge and sighed. It made me uncomfortable that everyone was doting on us this way. I knew it was how they showed their love, but it felt more like them not trusting that I could handle things.

"I have to fill out some paperwork and make some calls real quick. You've got him?"

"Of course. Why don't you go take a walk and get some sun. I know you've been cooped up for days, missing Krav among other things. I've got the little man, don't worry." She patted my shoulder with a sympathetic grin.

"I guess my emails can wait." Some fresh air and sun did sound good.

Ken carried her present into Alex's room and I spotted a bag of Skittles tucked under her arm too. I shook my head. He was going to be so spoiled by the time he was back on his feet. Grabbing my flip-flops and throwing my hair into a quick bun, I took another look around the room before saying an internal *screw it*. Everything else could wait.

I opened my door and came face to face with a startled Wes. A curse slipped out of his mouth and I jumped back a step.

"Damn, you scared me, Tiger." His chest heaved while Lilly barked a laugh beside him.

"Wes, what are you doing here? Hey, Lilly."

"Hi. Can I go see Alex?" she asked tentatively.

"Sure, he's in his room. My friend Kendahl is in there with him." We watched her march straight back to Alex's room like she owned the place.

I took a second to look Wes over. For an unknown reason, my stomach fluttered. Maybe it was seeing him in a fitted black T-shirt that hugged his corded arms and thick chest. It was rare that I saw him in anything but his chef's coat. His tattoos were on full display. Swirls of gray and black that looked like waves crashing interweaved with a name I couldn't make out. I spotted skulls and flowers, too.

"How's it going?" he asked. I realized we were still standing there awkwardly while I ogled him. I brought my gaze back to his smirking face.

"It's fine," I lied for the second time that day. "I was actually about to go for a walk."

Wes cleared his throat and lifted the tray he was holding. I'd only just noticed it in his hands. "I won't keep you. I came to drop this off. It's my homemade mac and cheese."

"Thanks, that's so nice of you. Let's put it in the fridge." I left the door open for Wes to come inside.

"How's Alex doing?" He peeked around my small place, taking in the few personal touches I'd added recently. A framed photo of Alex and me on an end table, a vase filled with shells we've been collecting. Nothing much, but it was better than the mostly empty rooms. His large frame filled the space almost comically.

"He's hanging in there. He can head back to school next week with crutches." I stacked the foil tray of food on top of the other three trays. "Although every time we talk about school he shuts down. I'm still not one hundred percent sure how he broke his leg, and he won't tell me much."

Shutting the fridge, I turned to face him, noticing his expression was pinched. Kendahl walked into the room, sizing Wes up. "I thought I heard a deep voice out here. Wesley, right?"

"That's me." He shook Kendahl's hand.

She bounced her gaze between us as she stepped toward the door. "I—uh—left something in the car. Be right back."

"I should go, too. Don't want to bother you guys," Wes said.

"You're not. I haven't gotten to say how much I appreciate the time off. I bet Kelly wants to pull her hair out by now."

"She's getting by." He chuckled.

"And you? Any disasters since I've been gone?" I fiddled with my water bottle to keep my hands busy.

"Ah you know, just the occasional lost ticket or knocked over plate. Nothing I can't handle." He flashed me a grin that had the butterflies in my stomach zipping around wildly. Where was this coming from? They needed a serious chill pill.

His cell phone started ringing from his pocket and he cursed under his breath. I knew how much he hated the things. He pulled it out and scowled. "Sorry. I've gotta take this."

I waved him off and made myself busy at the sink while he stepped outside. So much for my walk on the beach. I would have invited him to join me but I was still unsure about his limitations. I'd seen him walk on the beach for short spurts when he'd pick up Lilly from me those first few weeks but that was different from walking along the softer sand on the shore. Knowing Wes, he'd be happy to answer my questions once I figured out how to ask them without being awkward.

Kendahl came back inside with Mia in tow. Mia held a paper bag stuffed to the brim. I spotted a bag of her favorite cheddar sour cream chips peeking out the top.

"Sissy, I brought sandwiches." She set the bag on the table and came to envelop me in a hug. I squeezed her back feeling my chest lighten. "Is Wes okay? He was staring out at the beach with a look that could kill. I said hi and he didn't respond."

She started to unpack the food and Kendahl added, "Yeah the vibe was different than five minutes ago when the two of you were making googly eyes at each other."

I huffed. "We were not making googly eyes. We were just catching up."

Mia passed me a wrapped sandwich and I took it, suddenly starving. "That snack of a man definitely likes you, sister. I can tell."

"Oh my God, can we please not do this? He's my boss and our kids are friends. That's all." I unwrapped my sandwich at the kitchen counter and practically drooled from the smell of the fresh ciabatta roll.

"Right," Kendahl said, drawing out the word. "I'll go give Alex his food while you sit here in denial."

Thank the universe Wes chose that moment to come back inside. They were right, he looked upset.

"You hungry?" Mia asked. "I have an extra Italian combo here with your name on it."

"Nah, I've gotta get going. Thank you though." Maybe it was just me but he sounded as tired as I felt. His shoulders sagged as he took a few steps toward the bedrooms to call for Lilly. She dragged her feet on the weathered floors before Wes narrowed his brows in her direction.

"I'll see you in a few days," he said to me. "If you need anything give me a call. Lilly, say bye."

"Can Alex go to the beach again soon?" she asked.

"I'm not sure, sweetie. His cast isn't supposed to get wet. But you can come over to play after school next week, okay?"

"Alex is coming back to school?" Her eyes widened.

"Yup. He'll be back on Monday." I softened my voice. "He's going to need a helper to carry his backpack. Would you like the job?" She nodded, still looking mildly horrified. "Thanks, Lil."

We said goodbye and I focused my attention back on my sandwich. Mia chewed slowly before smiling at me.

"What now?" I grumbled.

"Oh, nothing. I'm just picturing my sister as a girl mom. You're so cute with Lilly." Her tone softened as she added, "Reminds me of how you were with me when we were young." She averted her gaze and she shoved another chip into her mouth.

"It's fine, you can say it."

"I don't know what you mean," she lied.

"How I was *before* the party. I won't break down, Mi."

She winced. "I'm sorry. I'm not used to being so open with you, I guess. But I meant it. You'd be great with Lilly."

"She's a good kid who's going through a lot of changes. It's hard not to sympathize. Plus she's gotta deal with tornado Wes as a father. That man seriously needs to learn how to dress a girl and do her hair."

"Maybe he needs a little help from a certain sexy waitress." Mia wiggled her brows and I tossed a chip at her. As much as she drove me crazy, I loved being close to my sister again. I missed this.

"What did I miss?" Kendahl asked, grabbing her sandwich from the bag and looking between us.

"Nothing," I said. "Alex okay?"

"Yeah, he's eating. But I did hear an interesting bit of conversation as Lilly was leaving." She settled into a chair and unwrapped her lunch.

"Oh?" I asked. I'd usually tuned out their conversations since they mostly consisted of video game talk, memes, or YouTube videos they'd watched. Oh, and Lilly occasionally bugging Alex to draw with her.

"She said she'd protect him."

"That's weird," I said. "Maybe they were talking about a game."

Kendahl shrugged. "Maybe. Kids are interesting little creatures. Glad I only have to be the cool aunt who brings candy."

"Yeah I caught that bag of Skittles you smuggled in."

Mia added, "I feel like I'll be ready to be a mom one day soon. Maybe in a few years. I don't know." She looked wistfully out the window.

"Well you're certainly not lacking in the trying department. You and Shawn go at it like animals." Kendahl laughed and Mia smacked her arm playfully.

"You're not wrong, though. That man is something."

"Don't rub it in," Kendahl huffed. "Although, I'm glad one of us is experiencing orgasms that aren't self-induced."

Heat crept across my cheeks. "Change of subject please. I really don't need to hear about my little sister's orgasms."

They busted into laughter. Kendahl grabbed my arm and said matter of factly. "Point taken. But give it a few months and you'll be joining us in our TMI dirty talk sessions. We just have to ease you in."

"That's what she said," Mia yelled.

I shook my head, letting out an uncomfortable laugh. "It's not like I'm a prude." Kendahl raised a brow my way. "I'm not! I may have lived with the king and queen of uptight land for years, but that doesn't mean I haven't had any fun."

"You're so not getting out of sharing now," Mia said.

I narrowed my eyes at her. "You're my sister... no way."

Kendahl sipped her drink and shrugged. "Like I said, we'll ease you in. By the end of the year you'll be sharing all the dirty details. I'd put money on it."

"Assuming I actually meet someone I'd want to date," I said. They gave each other conspiratorial looks and I huffed. "Oh look, it's time for Alex's meds."

I hopped up and made myself busy at the counter but I didn't miss their shared whispers.

Chapter 10

Wes

I FLIPPED THE BURGERS on the grill, pressing Lilly's down so it would end up like the hockey puck she requested. How was she my kid? That well done meat shit was all her mother's doing. I guess it was to be expected since Sav came from the fiery pits of hell. I smirked to myself, picturing Sav with horns and a red face.

I hadn't heard a word from her in the three months since she dropped Lilly off. Life was chaotic but if she wasn't going to reach out, I didn't need to either. I was struggling to keep up with work and Lilly but not bad enough that I'd go begging her to come back. Fuck that. Lilly didn't ask about her much either, at least not anymore. If Sav was contacting Lilly on her phone, I wasn't aware, but my instincts told me it wasn't often.

Sav's fucking mother has been up my ass nonstop though. I never liked her parents when we were together and they made it clear they couldn't stand me. Their little girl deserved so much better. I didn't blame Sav for limiting her relationship with them when Lilly was born. It made me wonder why Regina was contacting me now. Had Sav asked her to keep dibs on me?

My mom pulled the sliding glass door open and joined me on the patio. "Burgers almost done?"

"Yeah, except Lilly's. You know how she likes hers burned to a crisp." I shook my head.

"Okay, I pulled some potato salad out of the fridge. You should take your burger to-go so you're not late." She took out her phone to check the time. "Meeting starts in fifteen minutes."

"Shit."

Her eyes narrowed at me for cussing. "Excuse me?"

I cleared my throat. "Sorry. You sure you don't want to go instead? You've been the one doing homework with her."

She held the plate out to me so I could start taking the burgers off the grill. "You need to go. You're her parent, not me. It's important to see how she's doing in school."

"You're right." I wiped my hands on the leg of my shorts.

"Plus, you won't be alone. Olivia should be here any second." The smirk on my mother's lips was nothing less than villainous. "I offered to watch Alex for her."

On cue, Lilly dashed to the front door while Alex walked slowly beside her. He'd gotten his cast removed recently and was in physical therapy but he had to take it slow. Mom patted my shoulder and walked the burgers inside, greeting Olivia and Alex.

After turning off the grill, I fixed my hair, hoping I didn't look as grubby as I felt after a day of work and being in the heat. Not that I was worried about my looks for any particular reason.

"Ready to go? I'll drive," Olivia said. As I turned, I got a glimpse of her and lost my footing, tripping inside. She noticed my misstep and rushed over to me. Luckily, the doorframe kept me upright. "You okay?"

No, I was not okay. Olivia looked like my personal wet dream and I was so not prepared for that. She wore a deep purple cropped shirt, exposing her entire taut middle, and black work-out leggings that hugged the curve of her hips. Her wavy hair was thrown up in a messy bun and her face was flushed pink.

I always noticed how beautiful she was. Anyone would. But I'd tried so hard not to sexualize her. She was my employee and more than that, my friend. And I was a fucking train wreck. But now I couldn't tear my eyes away from her body. I was in so much trouble.

"Yeah. Lost my footing." I cleared my throat and forced myself to look anywhere but at Olivia's bare skin. Yeah that wasn't going to happen. Especially not since she took that moment to step in front of me, reach up and pull something out of my hair. I looked down at her glowing face. Could she hear my heart pounding? See my uneven breaths?

"You had a leaf." She held it in front of me and our eyes met for a fleeting second.

"Thanks." I ran a hand over the top of my head. "Ready?"

"Bye kids, be good," My father said, coming into the kitchen at the smell of grilled meat. I desperately needed to get my own place again.

On our way to Olivia's car, my phone buzzed. I knew who it was and didn't want to talk to her. Maybe if I kept ignoring her, she'd take the hint. Lilly was my daughter and Sav's mother could fuck right off.

"Ready to go sit in chairs five sizes too small, Goldilocks?" Olivia asked, turning on the car. A deep voice spoke through her car's speakers. Not spoke, growled. And then there was a moan. "Oh my God!" Her hand shot out to yank the volume dial all the way down.

"Was that porn, Tiger?" I chuckled and lifted a brow, ignoring the uncomfortable tightness in my shorts.

She groaned and swiped on her phone screen. "No, it's not porn."

"Really?" I teased. "So that wasn't suggestive moaning then?"

"Oh my God. Can you not?" Her already flushed cheeks flamed to the tips of her ears. "Just forget this ever happened."

"You may be a tiger but I'm an elephant." I leaned in. "I never forget."

My eyes were glued to her face as she bit her lower lip. She turned her head and I could see the change in her expression.

The fire in her eyes. She glanced down at my lap and smirked. "Doesn't look like an elephant to me."

I choked on a laugh as she backed up and hopped on the main road toward our kids school.

I clenched my jaw as we walked through the claustrophobic halls of the elementary school. The place smelled like a mix of Pine-Sol and day-old pizza. Olivia shrugged on the hoodie she'd grabbed from her backseat. Thank fuck because I couldn't stop thinking about how badly I wanted to splay my palm around her waist the entire car ride, especially after that audiobook mishap. Not the most opportune time for my mind to be hovering in the gutter.

School employees waved at us, offering smiles and polite *how are yous*. I nodded, following Olivia who seemed to know where we were headed.

"Here's their classroom. I had to walk Alex in a few times after the surgery." We peeked through the window of the closed door to see the teacher deep in conversation with a set of parents. "I guess we'll have to wait here," she said.

I took in the walls lined with holiday artwork and writing assignments. It had been so long since I'd stepped foot inside a school. Guilt gnawed at my gut. Lilly was ten and this was my first time at one of these parent teacher conferences. I really was a shit father.

"Hey, I think this is Lilly's." Olivia pointed at a hanging paper on the wall a few steps from me. She read it over and cleared her throat.

"What is it?"

"Take a look," she said in a quiet voice.

It was an essay. The title at the top read, *All About Me*. I scanned the sprawling penmanship.

> *I'm supposed to write an essay about myself but why bother? I'm not important or cool. No one would want to read it and I'll probably get an F anyways. But here it goes. All about me. I'm Lilly and I'm 10. I live with my dad and my grand-parents. I really want a cat but my dad says no. He says no a lot. I think he's just sad all the time. I like to draw and play video games but I'm not very good. All in all, that's pretty much it.*

I ground my teeth until my jaw hurt. "Well, that stings."

"I can't believe she hung that out here."

I hadn't thought of that but now that Olivia brought it up, I was pissed. Confused too, but mainly pissed. "What am I supposed to do with that?" I asked, pointing at the paper.

"We can ask her to take it down."

"I meant, with what she wrote." I stared up at the popcorn ceiling. "I knew she'd been acting off."

"Alex has, too." Her sigh mirrored how I was feeling. "They've gone through a lot of changes. Plus they're at this weird age, right between being a kid and a teen. It's not easy."

I knew everything she said made sense but I couldn't help but think it was my shitty parenting that was messing everything up. The classroom door opened and the teacher's voice drifted out the door. "I can see whoever's next."

I looked at Olivia. "You can go."

"No it's fine. Go ahead," she said, gesturing toward the door.

I glanced into the empty classroom then back to Olivia. "Together?"

She hesitated a moment before nodding. "Okay."

"Thanks for coming in, I'm Mrs. Nolan." She extended her hand to me and smiled at Olivia. "Hello again, Olivia. Have a seat."

Olivia wasn't kidding about the Goldilocks chairs. I looked down and my immediate thought was that I'd break that thing. Then I thought about the low squat I'd have to do to get in the thing and how much my body didn't love those. My back and hips already ached from a long day. Olivia noticed my hesitation and said, "I think we'll stand, thanks."

"Okie dokie," the teacher said. "I knew Alex and Lilly were close, but I didn't realize they were siblings."

"Oh. They're not." Olivia gestured between us. She let out a breathless laugh. "We just work together. Right, Wes? We're not dating."

"Yup, definitely not together romantically." She continued to laugh nervously, knocking my ego down a flight of stairs.

"I'm sorry for assuming," Mrs. Nolan said. She flipped through a stack of folders on the desk, pulling out two red ones. "Shall we begin?"

"What are we going to do?" Olivia asked, pouring syrup onto her stack of pancakes.

We stopped at a diner after the meeting, equal parts hungry and distressed. Both of us needing to go over what we'd learned from their teacher.

"You're the seasoned parent here," I said as I squirted ketchup onto my burger. "What do you do when your kid is failing fifth grade?"

"I don't know." She stared intently at a neon beer sign on the wall. "Alex never had trouble in school. He's always gotten good grades. Been a math wiz. This is all my fault. I shouldn't have moved him when he was doing so well."

"It's not your fault. Obviously breaking his leg set him back. Maybe he just needs to catch up. Lilly on the other hand, I have no idea what kind of student she was. She barely talks to me anymore and my mom is the one who does homework with her." I dipped a fry in ketchup and held it in front of me. "If this is anyone's fault, it's mine."

She unzipped her hoodie and shoved it next to her. My eyes bugged out all over again. "It's hot in here." *Yes, it was.* "We're missing the point. Blaming ourselves isn't going to help anything. Obviously we need to talk with our kids. Find out what's going on in their heads."

I chewed my fry slowly. "You're right. I've been spending too much time at Sunshine. So have you." I pointed a fry at her for emphasis. "They come first."

"Right," she said, snagging the fry out of my grasp. My gaze followed it right to her lips and lingered there. "Earth to Wes. Did you hear me?"

"What? I spaced out for a second."

"I noticed. Let's talk to them tonight and report back tomorrow at work."

"Report back? I didn't realize I was under your command," I teased.

"You are and you've just been given an important and deadly mission. Getting your tween daughter to open up to you." She patted my forearm and smiled sweetly. "Good luck soldier."

I'd need it.

I paid the check and Olivia dropped me off at home. The mood between us grew somber as we both knew the heavy conversations that we had coming. After helping Alex to the car, I waved them off, feeling that same pull I always felt when Olivia left my side.

I faced the beach, taking a few gulps of sea air to clear my head. I could do this. Whatever Lilly needed, I'd take care of. A tutor, a therapist, both. Hell, she wanted a damn cat, I'd take her to the shelter tomorrow.

As I turned to head inside my phone buzzed. "Dammit."

I yanked it open and said a gruff hello.

"You finally decided to answer me," Regina's nasally voice rang through the phone. "I thought your mother raised you to respect your elders?"

"She did, but ex in-laws who think they're God's gift to earth don't count." She scoffed in response. "What do you want, Regina?"

"I just had a lovely conversation with a Mrs. Nolan about my granddaughter. Seems she's not doing so well in school under your care. Not that I expected otherwise."

My nostrils flared and I forced my breathing to slow. "Lilly is my daughter. Your daughter abandoned her here. Of course she's having an adjustment period, but that's none of your concern."

"Face it, Wesley. You couldn't take care of yourself and you can't take care of Lillian. She's better off here with Gerald and me. We can provide for her, and she'll want for nothing. I'll put her in the best private schools money can buy."

"Because you did such a bang up job raising Savannah," I said. "Throwing money around doesn't equal good parenting."

"Neither does working sixty hours a week and letting your ridiculous parents mind her either. Clearly, you've tried your best and you're lacking. You're not fit to be a parent. You have until the new year to do the right thing or I get my lawyers involved. Goodbye, Wesley."

Her words took root in my mind, spiraling around with my own negative thoughts. Maybe she was right. I'd been telling myself that I couldn't do this. That I wasn't fit to be a single parent. Look at the damage I did with Lilly already in a few months. The new year was only a couple weeks away. Could I change that much in such a short period of time? Did I want to?

Chapter 11

Olivia

EVERY TIME I WATCHED Alex struggle to get in and out of the car my heart broke. I knew soon enough he'd be done with physical therapy and back to his old rambunctious self again. But seeing my kid in pain, even temporarily, was the worst kind of hell a parent could go through.

A chilly ocean breeze bit at my skin. The closer we got to the holidays the more I felt the slight change in season. My body wanted to hibernate, even though it was still sunny and warm during the day.

We both went through our nighttime routine. For me it was packing Alex's lunch for school, tidying up the kitchen and getting into comfy PJ's with thick socks. While Alex showered and got ready for bed I thought about how to approach the failing school conversation. I knew I couldn't come across as mad or disappointed or he'd shut down. Did I threaten to take his video games away until he got his grades up? Or was that too harsh?

I groaned. This parenting gig was so hard. Everything was easier when Alex was little and my only worry was taking him to the park and helping him learn his alphabet.

He padded out into the kitchen with his damp curls combed straight down. "Can I have a snack before bed?"

"Sure. Grab whatever you want and come sit on the couch with me."

"Whatever I want? Even the stash of candy you put on top of the fridge?"

"How'd you know? You know what, nevermind. Go ahead, but let me take it down first." I grabbed the bowl and snagged a Reese's for myself before heading to the couch. When Alex sat beside me, unwrapping a Kit Kat, I figured it was now or never. "I talked with Mrs. Nolan tonight. Looks like you're not doing so well in school. Want to talk about it?"

He crunched into the chocolate, chewing slowly. "Not really."

"Are you having a hard time with the lessons? Maybe we can find you a tutor. I'm sure Aunt Mia could help with math."

"I don't need help." He balled up the wrapper, sticking it on the coffee table and got to work opening a bite-sized bag of Skittles. Out of instinct, I reached for the garbage but remembered this was my home, not my parent's. I could leave a wrapper on a table for ten minutes.

"Okay," I said thoughtfully. "If it's not that, then what's going on? I know it's been hard since your accident. Did you fall behind from missing school?"

"Nothing's going on. School is dumb, okay?" His voice was laced with agitation. "Can I go to bed now?"

I sat back, confused and overwhelmed. Alex has had his moments like any kid, but he's never disliked school or gotten irritated over it.

"Alex, I only want to help you. If you don't get your grades up there's a chance they won't let you move on to sixth grade. Maybe we can make a plan tomorrow? Try and catch up over the holiday break? We could ask Lilly to join us?"

"Whatever. I don't care." He got up and started to walk away. I clenched my teeth as anger flared through me.

"It's rude to talk to me that way. You're grounded. Bring me your gaming remotes."

"Fine." He stomped off with his head hanging low and returned with two controllers. I looked away to hide the moisture collecting in the corner of my eye. This was new ground for us. He was my little buddy. My sidekick. He'd never shut me out this way before.

I wiped my eyes and turned to say goodnight but he'd already gone back into his room and closed the door.

"How'd it go?" I found Wes sitting at his desk the next morning when I went to stash my purse away. It looked like he had about as rough a night as I did telling from the shadows under his eyes and his extra day of stubble on the normally shaven parts of his face. I fiddled with a messy pile of paperwork on his desk to break my focus from how good he looked with a soft, sleepy expression.

He scrubbed a palm down his face. "Not great. She was quiet. One word answers."

"Alex, too. Well actually, he got irritated with me for caring." Guilt gnawed at my gut. "I kinda let my anger get away from me. Grounded him." I sunk into the extra chair facing him. "Did you tell your parents?"

"No." He blew out a breath. "Not yet. I'll have to tell my mom about her grades though. They've been letting Lilly do whatever she wants from what I've seen. I wonder if she's even having Lilly do homework at all."

"At least their break is coming. It'll give us a chance to figure this out, catch them up." At the mention of the holidays, I caught him grinding his teeth. "I wanted to ask if I could pick up more hours here too. Since Alex will be home with a sitter, I won't have to rush out to get him from school." And I needed the extra money, but I didn't tell him that. Hospital bills were coming in the mail every other day and the physical therapy costs alone ate up my entire savings.

He blinked, focusing his tired eyes on me. "Don't you need to be home with Alex? What about his physical therapy?"

"Don't worry about it. I'll figure it out." He held my gaze for what felt like minutes before I looked away. I was afraid if he stared too closely he'd see how much I was fumbling through every aspect of my life. I hadn't even been to Krav class in the past few weeks since Kendahl moved to LA. All this pent up frustration and fear swirled through me but I tugged a smile in place everyday. I had no choice anymore but to figure my shit out.

The door creaked and Thea peeked her head in. "Getting busy out there, Boss."

"Be right out," he said. She nodded and turned the corner toward the kitchen.

"I should get out there too."

He stood and grabbed his chef coat from the back of his chair. I had to leave but I caught myself watching the way his black undershirt fit against his chest as he slipped his arms into his jacket. I needed some sort of Wes flooding program. Where I'd get shown peeks of him in his street clothes everyday so when I was in front of him this way I could function normally. He cleared his throat.

"We can talk about the schedule later. Can't go overworking yourself."

My first instinct was to thank him but then I let his words sink in. "I can decide what's too much for myself." I stuck my chin out for emphasis.

He studied my face with a raised brow and that only annoyed me more. "Alright Tiger. Just looking out for you."

A crash from the kitchen caught our attention and we hustled out the door to help.

Toward the end of my shift I spent a few minutes tidying the prep area in the kitchen. Empty mixing bowls filled with onion and potato skins cluttered the counter, so I made myself busy cleaning them up before moving on to the trail of crumbs scattered around the toasters.

"Isn't your shift over?" Wes turned from the stove and pressed his back against the counter.

"Almost. Figured I'd help clean before I go."

"You don't have to." He sounded exhausted.

I tossed the handful of crumbs I scraped into the trash and faced him. "You almost done for the day?"

"I don't know. Depends on how busy we get." He blew out a breath and rubbed his shoulder, clearly hurting.

"Do you ever close up early?" I asked. Sunshine was always open. Breakfast, lunch, and dinner. I figured they needed the money to keep the place going. Restaurants like this one probably didn't bring in loads of income. But at what expense?

"Couple times a year." He winced, digging his thumb into his shoulder. I couldn't take watching him hurt anymore.

"Turn around." Tossing the rag I'd been holding onto the counter, I stepped up to him, making a twirling gesture with my finger.

He narrowed his brows. "What?"

"You heard me. Take off your coat, too."

He chuckled. "Damn, Tiger. At least buy me dinner first."

"Shut up and do as I say." I smacked his arm playfully and was reminded how solid it was. Not only his arms. All of him. His body was built like a tank.

He slipped off his coat and turned, leaning his palms on the counter. Even with him slouching I felt like I was facing a brick wall. I stood on my tiptoes, ignoring the way my pulse began to speed up and placed my palms on his shoulders.

When I squeezed gently he hitched a breath, the muscles of his back expanded in front of my eyes. "This okay?"

"Yeah, Tiger. It's—uh—more than okay." He turned his head to glance at me and I could see that some of the tightness left his face. That handsome freaking face. I dug in a bit, kneading what felt like rocks under the tight layers of muscle. "Mmm."

"Sorry! Did I hurt you?" Holy crap why did that sound send heat straight through me. I pulled my hands off him, although that did *not* sound like a pained groan. It was for sure a pleasure groan. A hot pleasure groan.

Clearing his throat, he stood straighter. "You didn't hurt me."

"Okay. Because you groaned and everything and I wasn't sure... so I stopped and—"

Wes's body started to vibrate before a laugh burst out of him. "You're adorable, Tiger."

I smacked his brick wall of a back. "Jerk." He stretched his neck from side to side and laughed again. "Also no more groaning. It's weird and I thought I hurt you and—Wait. Why are you still facing the counter?"

"I think you know why." His laughter died down and that gravelly voice was back. That voice that made heat rush into my cheeks.

"I don't." *Oh.* Wow, I was dense. "Ah." I patted his back. "I'll just give you a minute to—um—*calm down*."

"Might take more than a minute. But yeah, good plan."

"Old ladies, rainbows, poodles... um—shopping?" I listed off whatever nonsense came into my mind. Wes chuckled and shook his head.

"Are you trying to list unsexy things?"

"Is it working?"

"Yeah, Tiger, it's great." His voice was filled with humor.

I grabbed my cleaning rag again and turned the corner. It was right about time for me to get ready to pick up Alex. The longer I waited in the tension-filled space with Wes, the more I thought about how good it felt to have my hands on him.

Chapter 12

Wes

IT TOOK ME ANOTHER few minutes before I felt my dick go down enough to face my employees. Olivia only made it worse the more she talked. Every time that woman opened her mouth, I found myself more and more enamored by her. And that was before she put her hands on my body. Hell, I wasn't prepared for that.

Caleb came into the kitchen from his break and looked at me with a raised brow. "You good, Boss?"

"Never better, my man." He tilted his chin at me and went to wash up.

After a peek at the dining area, which was blissfully empty except for two tables finishing up, I followed Olivia into my office. Do I talk about my... reaction? Shit. I didn't want to make things awkward.

As I got closer I overheard her talking to someone. Her voice trembled and then I heard an unmistakable sharp intake of breath. I pushed the door fully open and found her stock-still, holding her phone up to her ear.

"Tiger?" I kept my voice low so I didn't interrupt. But something was wrong.

She spoke into the phone. "Okay. Yes. I'll be right there." As she hit end, her wide eyes met mine. "It's Alex," she whispered, like she was there with me but somewhere else at the same time.

"What happened?" Adrenaline pulsed through my veins, tightening every muscle in my body.

"He's on his way to the hospital again."

I felt like I was living in a time warp. Only this time, thank God, Alex didn't need surgery again but he looked like hell. I helped Alex into the front seat of Olivia's car, moving the seat back as far as it could go to accommodate his new cast. They gave Alex a wheelchair this time around, to minimize any more chances of a secondary fracture.

Olivia stood outside the car, her back against the driver's side window. She held her hand against her face to block the rays of the setting sun from her eyes or to keep me from seeing the anxiety written all over her. I didn't need to look her in the eyes to know how she was feeling. I'd lived with the same feelings so many times they were a part of me now.

"Hey." I tipped her chin up. She'd been frozen since she got the call. Going through the motions robotically. I was almost glad to see her reacting. "It's going to be okay."

She wiped her eyes and let out a dry laugh. "I wish I could tell you that you were right. But, no, Wesley. It will not be okay."

I searched her eyes. My life situation was fucked beyond belief but I'd be damned if I couldn't help hers in any way. "What can I do?"

"Nothing. There's nothing anyone can do. Come on, let's get him home." She went to open the driver's seat but I blocked her way, cupping her jaw. She blinked up at me, wetness coating her dark lashes.

"There's always something someone can do. I need you to believe in that." I swallowed a lump in my throat. "Because if someone like you can't believe that, then a jaded motherfucker like me is doomed." Dazed, she nodded slowly. I hoped she realized how serious I was. "I'll drive."

I helped them inside Olivia's place, where she settled an exhausted Alex in bed. He could barely keep his eyes open from the pain meds.

While she was getting him settled, I called my mom to check in on Lilly and ask her to come pick me up in a bit. I'd left my car at Sunshine earlier.

When Olivia came out into the kitchen, it ached to look at her. It was as if a physical weight laid on her back. From the slump in her shoulders, to the grimace lining her lips, every part of her screamed, "I'm hurting."

"I'm sorry," she said. "You keep getting mixed up in all my issues." She opened the fridge and shuffled a few things out of the way before pulling out a beer. She held it out to me. "I only have one. You take it."

"Let's share it. You need it more than me." I wrapped my hand around hers and pulled her and the beer closer. What would she do if I wrapped her in my arms? Would she stiffen up? Back away? She pulled out the chair beside me and slumped into it. I missed my chance where it would happen naturally.

"I need to know what happened."

"Did he say anything?" I asked even though I'd been with them all evening and I knew he didn't.

"No. Not a word. I didn't press though, not while he was in so much pain." She closed her eyes and brought the beer to her lips. "I know something isn't right."

"You mean, besides your kid breaking his leg twice in only a few months time?" My joke didn't land. Olivia brought her hand to her forehead and rested it there. "Bad timing for a joke," I muttered.

"No, it's fine. I'm just exhausted. I can't even process a joke right now." She passed me the beer. "There's no way he got those bruises from falling."

"We can talk to Lilly? Maybe she knows what's going on?" I offered.

Her eyes snapped open. "I bet she does."

"I'll call my mom, have her bring Lilly over."

Luckily, I caught my mom right before she left the house. Lilly was in her room drawing. Apparently, she'd been there all afternoon. We passed the beer back and forth, taking swigs until there wasn't a drop left in the bottle. Olivia had gone quiet and I respected that. She needed to retreat into herself and that was okay. As long as she knew she wasn't alone out here.

They knocked lightly but Olivia was already there waiting beside the door for them. "Oh, Olivia. I'm so sorry." My mother cooed over her and brought her into a hug. "I'm going to set you up with the church. Pastor John will mention Alex in his sermon so he'll have speedy healing and the ladies will all get together so you won't have to worry about meals for weeks."

I unwrapped my moms arms from Olivia. "Thanks Mom, but can this wait?" I asked, conveying a look that said, *you're being a bit much.*

She let out a small laugh and backed away. "Sorry dear. I'll wait in the car so you can talk with Lilly."

"Thanks so much, Mrs. Reed," Olivia said with a weak smile.

"Honey, please, just call me Val." My mother squeezed Olivia again before heading outside. Lilly hasn't said a word, which was out of character.

"Let's go sit on the couch," Olivia said. "Lilly, can we talk?"

Lilly brought her gaze to mine and I nodded. "Okay." Even her voice sounded off. Like it took effort to say one word.

I settled on the loveseat, fighting a groan from how good it felt to sit on something comfortable. I needed to get my prosthesis off for the day and relax but that would have to wait. Oliva sat next to Lilly, facing her. As the silence grew, I wished then and there that I could read minds.

"Lil, we need to talk to you about Alex," I said. "I promise you won't be in trouble. Whatever you say can stay between us."

She played with a loose seam in her shirt, keeping her eyes trained on the floor.

"We think something is going on at school. Is that why Alex keeps getting hurt?" Olivia asked. Silence stretched between us and I huffed out a breath, ready to push a little harder but then Lilly nodded. "So that's a yes? Something is going on at school?" I could hear the barely restrained panic in her voice.

"Yes, but I can't talk about it."

I sat forward. "You can talk to us, Lil. We need you to tell us."

"Is Alex okay?" she asked in such a hushed tone I could hardly hear her.

"Not really," Olivia said. "His leg is hurt again and he'll have to be in a cast for a while."

"Forever?" Lilly asked, finally looking up at Olivia with wide eyes.

Olivia took her hand. "No, not forever. But I'm worried if we don't figure out what's going on, he'll keep getting hurt. Can you please tell us what happened today?"

"Okay." She clutched her knees to her chest, resting her forehead against them. "It was Brady and his friends. They pushed Alex and he fell off the playground."

She had to be kidding. I clenched my jaw and zeroed in on what she was saying.

"Today?" Olivia asked.

"Not today. That was the first time." Lilly hesitated and looked at me. I nodded for her to keep going. It was like her letting that one piece of information slip cracked the whole dam open. She told us that Alex had come to her aid when these kids were pushing her around and they shoved him. His flip-flop got caught and he fell from the playground in a way that had him landing on his leg. This group of bullies had been targeting Lilly, and then Alex, all year long. Finally, she told us that today Alex said he was going to end it once and for all and he challenged Brady to a fight by the parking lot. He didn't want Lilly to be there but she hid and watched anyway. Brady brought three other kids and they pushed Alex. They knocked him to the ground and one of them kicked his leg.

"That's when I ran to get help," she said, tears welling in the corner of her eyes. "But by the time I came back, the kids were gone and Alex couldn't feel his leg. I'm scared."

"Come here, sweetheart. It's going to be okay." I opened my arms and Lilly collapsed against my chest. "Thank you for telling us. I'm so proud of you." She nodded against me. I looked up, realizing Olivia left the couch.

"Last time they said if we told they'd kill us."

"Like hell they will." I rubbed circles against her back. "I won't let anything happen to you. I promise."

"Or Alex?" she asked.

"Or Alex."

Or his mom.

I found Olivia outside, leaning against the wall and staring at the inky water. She hugged Lilly, thanking her, without taking her eyes off the distant waves. I sent Lilly to the car where my mom was still waiting. I wanted to stay here and comfort Olivia while our minds were reeling, but my mom had waited for a while already.

"Listen, Tiger. We will get this figured out. These little shits will be held accountable, okay?" I spoke with a sureness I didn't possess but it was what she needed.

"I let this happen to my boy. I grounded him when he was hurting." She looked at the sky. "I've been taking self defense classes when I should have been putting Alex in them. And oh God, I'm sorry."

"Why are you apologizing again?"

"Lilly. She's a part of this, too." Anger simmered low in my gut. If those asshole kids were here right now I didn't think I could keep my cool.

"Don't worry about it tonight. We'll take care of this. You should get some rest." I should take my own advice. Slim chance of that happening.

I got into the passenger seat and my mom instantly started asking questions. "Is Olivia okay? What happened? Lilly said there's bullies."

"Mom, I love you but can I please have a minute to clear my head?" Translation: if I continued to talk about this any more tonight I'd lose it.

"Sorry," Lilly said from the back seat. I pulled myself together enough to turn my head and offer her a weak smile.

"I meant what I said. I'm proud of you. How about you play hooky for the rest of the week? Christmas break is around the corner so I doubt you'll be doing anything important."

She leaned forward, I could glimpse a glint in her eye from the passing streetlights. "Yes!"

With the addition of a group of bullies thrown onto the steaming heap of shit I was in, I needed the time to figure things out. I only hoped Sav's parents wouldn't get wind of this newest information. They'd find a way to blame me for school bullies. Fuck that and fuck them. I was done sitting around. It was time we all fought back.

Chapter 13

Olivia

I TRIED TO TAKE Wes's advice and get some rest. I even watched a few episodes of reality TV, which always put me to sleep. Something about petty drama helped me relax. Maybe it was my messed up way of seeing that there were people out there with crazier lives than me. It gave me comfort to see that my parents weren't the only hyper-materialistic phonies. Either way, it wasn't working.

I checked in on Alex a few times, finding him sleeping peacefully. By eleven, I'd drafted a strongly worded email to Alex's principal, and when that wasn't enough to calm me down, I dusted my bookshelf, cleaned my bathroom sink, and organized my sock drawer. When I sat perched on the edge of my bed, bouncing my knee at full speed and staring at a spot of chipped paint on the wall, I finally gave in and picked up my phone. It was late but I knew she'd answer me.

"Liv? What's wrong?" Mia's panicked voice came through the phone. I breathed deeply, pushing the surge of emotion down so I wouldn't cry again.

"I'm sorry to call you so late."

"What's going on?" I heard the squeak of her bedframe and knew she'd gotten up.

"Alex got hurt again today. He's fine, thank goodness. But he's in a cast again." I gave her the short version of what happened and what Lilly told us.

"I don't even know what to say. I'll kick their asses. So what if they're ten? No one messes with my nephew."

"I believe you. You're fierce when someone messes with the people you love." And she threw a mean punch. "I hate to ask, but would you be able to come over and stay with Alex for a bit? I need to clear my head." I peeked in on him again and he had Quackers slouched over his eyes like a mask. "He's fast asleep but I don't want to leave him alone."

"Of course, sis. I'll be there soon."

When she showed up fifteen minutes later the trembling in my limbs had started again and my chest was clenched tightly. I kept replaying my own version of Alex getting pushed from the playground over and over again with more and more disturbing outcomes. Ruminating wasn't helping, but I couldn't turn it off.

Back home there was only one thing that helped me when I'd spiral and I knew exactly where to go to do it.

I hadn't been to Sunshine at night since I volunteered to help before we moved. Darkness blanketed the building giving it a deserted feel that sent my alarm bells ringing. A lone streetlamp cast a circular glow near the entrance to the parking lot, so I parked my car as close to it as I could.

It was rare that I left the house at night. Like a reverse vampire, I planned my schedule so the majority of my errands had me home by dinner time. The sad thing was I loved nighttime. The moon and stars. The quiet stillness. But sometimes the dark of night brought out the darkness within others. Pulled it from them like a mother beckoning her child. Not boogeymen or ghosts like we're told to fear. It's the ones hidden behind perfect smiles and designer clothes. The ones who call you pretty and try to get to know you. Those were the monsters I feared.

I pulled my emergency key to Sunshine out of my purse and fit it between my index and middle finger. With a sobering breath, I sprinted out of the car, keeping myself as alert as I could in the dim light.

Once inside, I locked the door behind me and waited there while my pulse returned to normal. The place perpetually smelled of breakfast foods. Maple syrup, buttery pancakes, sizzling bacon. I breathed in the comforting scent and for the first time that night, my shoulders relaxed.

I left the main lights off and headed toward the kitchen, flipping on only the lights that I needed. One of Wes's chef coats hung on a hook outside his office door and I grabbed it, putting it on over my camisole. I'd only just realized that I'd left the house in pajamas. Not the kind that could pass for actual clothes but loose bottoms covered in gray and white hearts and a gray cami. At least I had sneakers on. With my current mental state I was shocked I didn't leave barefoot.

"Okay, time to bake." This was what I needed to clear my head. Focusing on one step at a time, precisely measuring and pouring. Even the physical aspect of mixing the ingredients would help wear me out. I pulled out my favorite cake recipe, threw on a pop music playlist and got to work.

I'd cleared my head by the time all the measuring and mixing was done. Finally the fifty pound dumbbell weighing on my chest felt more like a five pounder and my thoughts focused on cake and only cake. The massive commercial oven beeped that it reached the right temperature so I bent over to slide the pan in while bobbing my head and singing along to Taylor Swift.

"Nice jacket."

"Shit!" I jumped, clutching my chest. I knew who the gravelly voice belonged to, but I spun on my heels anyway. Wes, wearing a thin white undershirt and black sweats, leaned against the swinging door frame grinning. "You scared me! What if I was holding the cake pan?"

"You weren't. I watched you put it in." He took a few steps toward me, touching the whisk and bowl I still had laid out on the counter.

"How long have you been here? Oh God, were you here the whole time?" I grabbed my rag and started to wipe the surfaces down. Mainly to avoid the intense eye contact Wes was giving me. Please, let him not have seen me singing "Shake It Off."

"Long enough." His grin told me he'd absolutely seen my one woman musical production. Lovely. Where was the nearest hole to hide in? "Do you always break into restaurants all hours of the night to bake cakes like some sort of musical elf?"

I cocked my head. "Musical elf?"

"You know that fairy tale... *The Elves and The Shoemaker*. The elves come at night and make shoes."

"Ah... I do know that one. Not an elf and *not* a burglar. You gave me a key, remember?" Why did I find him knowing obscure fairy tales kind of hot?

He ran his finger along the side of the mixing bowl and tasted some of the remaining batter. The way I watched his finger slip between his parted lips, his tongue darting out just a touch, connecting with the tip before he sucked was nothing short of erotic. Those five pound weights were settling somewhere else... much lower.

What was wrong with me? I needed to focus but something about being in close proximity with Wes Reed always got me feeling things I didn't need to be feeling.

"Delicious. Is that a hint of rum I'm tasting?" He went in for another swipe and God help me, I watched him repeat the whole finger sucking thing.

"Rum?" My brain took a moment to catch up. "Oh, yeah. It's a recipe I found a while ago. Vanilla butter cake. Rum's the secret ingredient."

"You're full of surprises, Tiger." He smiled and scratched his jaw. "Back to my original question... Why are you baking a vanilla butter cake, in my restaurant, at midnight?"

"I'm sorry. I should have called and asked." I stacked the dirty utensils into the bowl and carried them to the sinks.

"I'm not upset. You can come here anytime." His expression was open and honest.

"I appreciate that." He walked beside me, so close that I could smell the body wash he'd recently used. "Sorry about your coat."

"Don't be." He turned the faucet on and reached in to grab the whisk. "It looks good on you." Between the sound of the water and his low voice I almost didn't hear that last comment. I held it close, smiling slightly.

"Why are you here so late?" I asked. He handed me the clean whisk and I started towel drying it.

"Same reason you are, I'm guessing. Couldn't sleep." He worked on a measuring cup, lathering it with precision and rinsing the suds away. Watching him was almost meditative.

"Yeah. And believe me, I tried everything to relax." He studied me with a raised brow. It took me a second to catch on to what he was implying, but when I did I used the damp towel to smack his burly arm. "I know what you're thinking and I was hardly in the right mood for *that*."

"What?" he asked innocently. "I have no idea what you're talking about."

"Right... no idea at all," I drew out my words. "Anyway... I couldn't sleep either. I kept thinking about Alex getting hurt over and over again until I was almost in tears. Mia came by and we talked a bit but I knew I needed to get out of the house."

"So you came here to bake?"

"Yeah. Back home, baking was always the one thing that helped when I'd..." I hesitated, unsure of how much of myself I wanted to give to this man. His eyes met mine and they were full of understanding. Wes had shown me nothing but kindness all these months but still I couldn't finish the sentence. I couldn't tell him how bad my mental health was—could still be. "It's a hobby. Something I enjoy. We didn't have any ingredients and Alex was asleep so I figured I'd come here."

"My mom's a night owl too, so I had her bring me to my car. I saw yours here and wanted to make sure you were okay," he said, continuing to rinse the already clean measuring cup.

"I think this one's clean." I took it from him gently.

"Yeah, sorry," he muttered. Turning the faucet off, he faced me, taking his time to speak. "I needed to get out, too. Everything's fucked, isn't it?"

I thought about all the things going on in my life. Alex's injuries, the hospital bills, the bullies, the support system that I'd relied on for the past ten years falling apart. "Yeah. I can say with total certainty, everything is fucked."

"You got a recipe and a song to help this mess, Tiger?"

I heaved a breath. "Wish I did." Spotting the bottle of rum still out, I grabbed it. "But I do have rum."

"Do I look like a pirate?" He glanced down then back at me with a grin. "Don't answer that."

I shook my head. "I would never!"

"Screw the rum. I have something better," he said, wiping his damp hands on his pant leg. Normally, I'd be against drinking hard alcohol after midnight while alone with a guy. But with the day we've both had—the month, more like—I threw caution to the wind.

He came out of his office with a bottle of golden liquor. I grabbed two glasses from the clean dish rack and set them down. "What's that?"

"Sipping tequila." He poured us each a few ounces and slid one toward me.

"Tequila? What am I a teenager on spring break?" I picked it up and gave it a sniff. Didn't quite burn off my nostril hairs. That was a plus.

"This isn't your average cheap shit." He sipped with a sigh. "Go ahead, try it."

Narrowing my eyes at him, I said, "Fine, but if it's gross, I'm pouring it into your glass." I closed my eyes, for no reason other than maybe it would somehow make it go down easier, and sipped. It went down smoothly with only the slightest of burns.

I opened my eyes an inch to find Wes watching me with his head resting in his palm. "Good, right?"

"I wouldn't call it good, but I don't think it'll burn off layers of my esophagus going down." He laughed and downed the rest of his glass in one gulp. I peeked again at the contents of my glass and thought, *why not?* "Cheers to our shit show lives."

"Cheers to that." He shook his head and watched me fill my mouth and swallow down every last drop.

Chapter 14

Wes

I KNEW TWO THINGS. It was two in the morning, the bottle of reposado sitting on the table between us was almost empty, and Olivia was even feistier drunk than she was sober. Okay, so maybe I knew more than two things.

"What would happen if I beat up a ten year old?" She waved a hunk of cake in her hand as she spoke in between bites.

"I don't know... jail? But I know a guy... We don't have to do the dirty work." I laughed, picturing one of my gym buddies showing up at an elementary school.

"What kinda friends do you have anyway?" She chomped a bite of cake, getting crumbs all over herself and the table in the most un-Olivia like way I'd ever seen. I was still relatively sober, thankfully there was one of us who was.

"You know I was kidding right?" I laughed. "We can't hire a hit man for a ten year old bully, Tiger."

"But what if we're doing the world a favor? Maybe this kid will be the next... I don't know. The next... dictator guy."

"Well, then I guess we'll have to kick ourselves in our old wrinkly asses thirty years from now."

"Pffft. I thought you were cool, but you won't even help me commit a crime." She flopped her head back onto the vinyl booth, dropping her cake into her lap. "Oh no, cake down." Her whine turned to chaotic laughter in the span of two seconds.

"You are a mess, aren't you?"

"If I'm a mess, so are you," she said before picking up a hunk of cake and tossing it at me. I'm pretty sure she was aiming for my face but it landed on the seat next to me.

"Who are you and what have you done with Olivia?" There was no use in bothering to clean the crumbs. They were bound to multiply and spread before the night ended.

She blew a raspberry, flicking more crumbs my way. Man, I wish I had a camera rolling. The footage would be pure gold.

"Who am I? I'll tell you who." She grabbed the cake from her lap and nibbled. "A mentally unstable, broke as hell twenty-seven year old with no health insurance, a mountain of hospital bills, and an unhealthy obsession with this cake." I listened quietly while I pushed my water glass toward her. She took a long sip and smacked her lips. "Oh and I forgot to mention unloveable. Yeah... I'm that, too. Wait, this isn't tequila? You tricked me!"

She gripped the edge of the table for support and fumbled her way out of the booth faster than I would have thought she could move. "Where are you going?"

"To the tequila," she singsonged in a way that reminded me of one of those preschool cartoons Lilly used to watch.

Oh, no. That was the last thing she needed. I could tell when a person was dangerously close to crashing and Olivia was one shot away from blacking out. I followed her, letting her drunken declaration mull around in my mind. Did she really think all those things about herself? She couldn't be more wrong. And the health insurance thing... that must have been weighing on her.

"Hey Gretel, you're leaving a trail," I called to her retreating frame. "You trying to reenact two fairy tales tonight?"

Stopping at the door to the kitchen, she turned and matter-of-factly said, "Only if it involves a fairy godmother or a magic genie. Anyone in the wish granting department would work."

"What would be your first wish?"

Her gaze wandered as she thought, bouncing from a blank space on the wall to the floor, then finally locking on my face with a far away expression.

"Besides unlimited wishes... I guess it would be for an answer to my problems." After a pause, she shrugged and let out a dry laugh. "For tonight though, my fairy godmother has a name and it's tequila."

As she pushed into the kitchen, I sat back against the vinyl booth. I was positive I'd put my head onto a smear of cake but I had other issues to think about. A headache was beginning to take root at the base of my neck but something else was brewing, too. An inkling of an idea. It was absolutely ridiculous to even consider. But maybe not.

Two things were certain. One, I needed to get Olivia home and to bed before she reunited with her friend tequila. And two, for this plan to work I'd have to let Olivia into my life—fully in. Which meant pulling her into the custody shit with Sav's parents.

I glanced out the window at the dark sky. "Dylan, am I crazy for thinking what I'm thinking?"

I'd already answered my own question. Yes. I was talking to my deceased best friend out loud.

Either way, I'd sleep on it. Every idea looked better by the light of day.

Did I say every idea looked better by the light of day? Because it was just after seven and I was still certain the idea was bonkers.

"Here's your coffee, sleepyhead." Mia, looking fresh as a daisy, held a steaming mug out to me. I blinked and rubbed a crusty out of my eye. I'd forgotten how I ended up crashing on Olivia's couch last night. My back would be reminding me of the sleeping arrangement all day though.

I glanced at my prosthesis and sock next to the couch. I must have been exhausted enough to get that comfortable.

"Thanks. I need this." The steam hit my face, rousing me further. "Olivia still asleep?"

"Oh yeah, she crashed hard when you guys got back last night. She woke me up mumbling about cake and tequila but within five minutes she was out like a light. I've never seen her like that before." She plopped next to me on the couch, holding her own mug.

"Yeah, I can't picture her hitting the bottle hard like that on the regular." I chuckled remembering the way she manhandled that cake. "She'll be hurting today."

"Oh, yeah, she will. Us Murphy women don't hold our liquor well. You should see our mother the morning after a gala. It is not pretty or fun."

I sipped my coffee again and stretched my other arm, realizing too late that I probably didn't smell great. Putting my coffee on the side table, I reached for my sock and leg.

"Just going to take care of this so I can use the bathroom," I said, hoping Mia would be kind enough to give me some privacy.

"Go ahead. I have to head out. I'm meeting a client for breakfast soon. Tell my sister I'll call her later." She took one last sip out of her mug and stood to bring it to the sink.

"Sure. If she wakes up before I leave." Mia shrugged and grabbed her purse.

"Oh, and Wes?" She stopped at the doorway. "Thanks for taking care of her last night. She'll kill me for saying this, but she needs someone to take care of her sometimes, even though she won't admit it."

"Anytime." Fuck if I didn't feel similarly. A sinking feeling settled in my chest at the memory of Olivia's wish last night. I may have asked her the question as a cute joke, but I knew deep down that I wanted to know what she needed. Maybe I even wanted to be the guy to give it to her.

Mia left and I found the small bathroom in the hall. After taking care of business, I stepped out and heard Alex calling for his mom.

Olivia stirred, not that I was exactly peeking at her in bed. Her bedroom just happened to be adjacent to the bathroom and Mia had left her door halfway open.

I made my way toward the other bedroom and knocked gently on Alex's door. "Hey, your mom's still asleep. I can wake her if you need me to?"

He tilted his head, studying me. "What are you doing here? Is Lilly here, too?"

"I had to fix a leaky faucet in the kitchen for your mom this morning." The lie slipped out easily. I didn't need to be telling a ten year old that his mommy got drunk last night and needed to be carried inside.

"Oh, okay." He yawned and stretched his arms above his head. I looked over his small bedroom and it reminded me so much of my own childhood room. Video game posters hung on the wall, a few Lego sets were displayed neatly on a bookshelf, and stacks of well loved comic books were on his nightstand. It would have been so much easier to connect to Lilly if she were a boy. I didn't know what to say to her anymore. She was growing so fast and her interests changed all the time. By the time I picked up on a game or hobby, she'd dropped it like yesterday's news.

"How are you feeling? Does your leg hurt?"

"A little." He stared off toward his blank TV screen. There was so much I could say to him. I could bring up the bullies and how I was grateful he stood up for Lilly. I could spout off for hours about injuries and the healing process. Out of all the things, I felt confident in my knowledge when it came to that stuff. He was tired though, hurting too, and I was sure he wouldn't want to talk with me. I was an adult who he barely knew.

"Why don't I go get your mom?" I said, turning back into the hallway.

I opened her door a few inches wider, careful not to make any abrupt sounds. Olivia was flopped across the bed, arms cradling her head and her ass up, with a thin white blanket covering her lower legs and feet. I forced myself to avert my gaze from her ass and took in her room.

Her bedroom was only a bit bigger than Alex's, with a queen-sized bed taking up most of the space. The walls were empty of photos and the only other furniture to be seen was a basic floor lamp in the corner and a white wooden nightstand.

Olivia was still wearing what she wore out last night—those cute heart pajama pants smeared with cake. But as I got closer I noticed the strap to her tank top had slid down her shoulder.

Wes, don't be a creep.

Too late. I was a sucker for side boob and Olivia's tits were too perfect not to peek. *One peek. Then I'd wake her.*

Except at that very moment she flipped onto her side and her tit came popping out to say hello.

"Oh, fuck." I backed away, smacking my elbow into the lamp which, of course, knocked it over. And because it was my lucky day, she heard the commotion and bolted upright, tit still out.

"Wes? What's wrong? Wait... did you knock over my lamp?" Her voice was heavy with sleep.

I did what any respectable person would do... clenched my eyes shut. "Uh," I cleared my throat. "I did, sorry. But um..."

"Why are your eyes closed? Is Alex okay?" Panic laced her tone.

"He's fine. It's just..." I let the words tumble out in one breath. *"Yourtitisout."*

"What?"

"Your tit is out," I repeated slowly.

"Oh my God!" she shrieked. "Were you creeping on me?"

"Is it put away? Can I open my eyes now?"

"Yes... it's put away. Seriously? I never thought you'd be the type." I opened my eyes as she was checking over the rest of her body and straightening out her hair.

"Wait? You think I was looking at you on purpose?" I crossed my arms and tried to manage a casual stance. While I didn't come in here to ogle her, I didn't *not* check her out. But that information would live and die in my brain. If my cock could get the message and simmer down, that would help too.

"Why else would you be in here?" She climbed out of bed, but then thought better of it and perched on the edge, rubbing her temples.

"How about because your son woke up asking for you? I don't need to creep on sleeping women, Tiger, so put your claws away."

She scoffed. "Oh, because you're beating the ladies away with a stick?"

"I didn't say that." I huffed a breath. She was staring up at me with flared nostrils and narrowed eyes. "I meant that I don't need to be a creep to see a pair of tits, okay? Plus, you're *you*... I don't look at you that way."

Fuck. I was a grade A, lying dick.

Her face fell, but only for a heartbeat, before her scowl returned. "You should go."

"I'm sorry. I don't know what just happened, but I promise I wasn't looking at your tit."

"It's fine. I need to check on Alex."

"Yeah. Okay."

I remembered my idea and the conversation I'd hoped to have with her this morning. It would *so* not go over well now, but I had to try.

"Thanks for getting me home last night," she said quietly. "I can come by Sunshine later and clean the mess."

"Wait. Can we please talk for a minute? After you check on Alex?" I pulled on the back of my neck while she contemplated. "Something you said last night had me thinking and I wanted to talk... That's all."

"Fine," she resigned. "Give me a little while to get cleaned up."

I lifted my hands in surrender. "Take all the time you need. I'll be out front."

If my dad were here he'd have smacked me upside the head a dozen times in the past ten minutes. There was no way Olivia would go for my plan. Only an idiot would start their morning the way I did and then follow up with a marriage proposal. But I never claimed to be the smartest guy in the room.

Chapter 15

Olivia

WHAT A JERK. No, jerk wasn't strong enough. What a douche. *You're you.* What the hell was that supposed to mean? Not that I cared what Wesley Reed thought of me. But rejection still stung.

After checking on Alex and getting him settled on the couch with some breakfast, his meds, and a show, I took a steaming hot shower. Memories of the previous night flashed through my mind like a fuzzy 1980's home video. I'd dreamed of the vanilla cake and almost thought it never happened, but the chunks of it in my hair were evidence enough.

I wasn't sure what hurt more, my head or my ego. To top it all, a wave of nausea hit me in the shower. Decision made. I was never drinking again.

Finally clean and semi-refreshed, I steeled myself for whatever conversation Wes wanted to have. It seemed important, otherwise I was sure he'd have left with his head hung in shame after the boob incident. Another reason to keep my guard up, even with people I thought I could trust.

"Hey Alex, I'm going to be outside for a few minutes." He was so deep into an episode of some Netflix show that I doubted he heard me.

I grabbed a hoodie off the back of a kitchen chair to help ward away the morning ocean breeze and dug my sunglasses out of my purse. Wes stood near his car, on the phone. He juggled a brown paper bag and cup of coffee in his other hand.

"So close up if you need to," I heard him say. "Caleb can. He's just being lazy." I realized he must have been talking with someone at work. It was well past opening time and he was here with me. In the months I've worked there he rarely missed a day of work. To the point where he *always* looked exhausted. When he noticed I was outside, I raised a corner of my lip in the smallest smile of acknowledgement. "I don't know, Thea, but I've gotta go. Yeah, talk soon."

He shut his ridiculous flip phone and shoved it into the pocket of his sweats.

"What's in the bag?" I asked, lifting my chin. He pulled out a lump wrapped in foil and tossed it at me.

"Breakfast."

I yelped and stumbled forward to catch it before it landed on a wet patch of grass. "You realize my reflexes aren't great this morning, right?"

"Nah, you had it in you. I could tell." He chuckled while I glared at him. "Let's sit and eat. These are the best hangover cures I've ever had."

"I'm afraid to ask what they are."

"Don't worry, I wouldn't poison you. Then I'd be short staffed." He smirked and lowered himself into one of my out-door chairs.

"Ha, ha. You're a real comedian." I sat beside him and un-wrapped what turned out to be an egg sandwich.

"I thought it was a good one." He took a monstrous bite and chewed with a moan. "Hits the spot every time. Try it."

I bit into it, tasting bacon, cheese, and fried egg with a kick of spice. He watched as I chewed so I made it a point to keep my expression neutral. "It's okay, I guess."

"Just okay?"

"Yeah, just okay. At least I can rule out poison," I said.

He held out a cup of coffee. "Here. Wash it down with this."

Reluctantly, I thanked him and took his peace offering. "So what did you want to talk about? I'm sure you have to get to Sunshine soon so I won't keep you."

"It's fine, Thea and Caleb can manage for one day. And if not, I'll deal with it later." He took another bite and chewed slowly, staring out at the waves. A few minutes passed in silence while we ate, until finally he turned to me. "I've been thinking about what you said last night."

"Oh God," I groaned. "I said a lot of things if my memory serves. What do you mean?"

"How you said you're in debt with the hospital and you have no insurance... and all of that." He closed his mouth but looked like he had more to say.

"I can't believe I told you about that."

"I'm glad you did. All jokes aside, it's not healthy to keep that all in." He laughed dryly. "I'm one to talk."

Now I was curious. "What do *you* mean?"

He pulled on the back of his neck, giving me a peek at the underside of his thick bicep. "I haven't told anyone about this, so please keep it between us."

My pulse picked up. I didn't like the emptiness in his tone, the desperation. "Of course."

"My ex-wife's parents are trying to come after me for custody of Lilly." He stared absently at the horizon while I let his words sink in.

"Can they do that? I'm no expert in that sort of thing but don't the biological parents have rights first?"

"I don't know. Shit. I've been so all over the place since Sav dropped her off, every day has felt like survival mode. They have eyes and ears everywhere though. They know Lilly's failing school, they know I'm working all the time, they even know she wanders when my parents are supposed to be watching her." A muscle in his jaw ticked as he continued, "Maybe they're right. Maybe she would be better off with them."

"Do you really mean that? I know Lilly's having a hard time adjusting but she loves you." My knee shook on its own accord.

He blew out a long breath. "No, I don't mean it. Regina and Gerald are some of the worst people I've ever met. I can't let them have Lilly, but I don't know what to do. They said they'd come after me with their team of lawyers if I didn't make a decision by the new year. If that happens it might be out of my hands."

"I'm sorry. I don't know what to say. What can I do to help?" His gaze met mine, a question in them.

"I think I have a solution. Something that could help us both." He wrung his T-shirt between his fist.

"Okay..." I drew out the word. "Now I'm curious."

"You're going to think I'm crazy but hear me out."

"Just tell me. I'm already anxious and the hangover isn't helping."

"Let's get married."

I searched his expression for any hint of jest, finding none. He sat straight as a rod, hands fiddling with his shirt, jaw clenching as he ground his teeth.

"You're serious?"

"Dead serious," he responded. I stood and started to pace the space in front of me, my head spinning. "Talk to me, Tiger."

"Why—How? What would us getting married accomplish?"

"Health insurance for you and Alex, plus I'm happy to help pay his hospital bills. I'd offer that anyway, since he got hurt helping Lilly. And for me, it would show Regina that I was settling down—a family man. Lilly would have a stepmother and stepbrother. From what I researched, having two parents in the house is ideal in custody situations, if it came to that."

Everything he said made sense in a pragmatic way but my brain couldn't wrap around the notion of marriage. Husband and wife, till death do us part, marriage. My feet left divots in the seagrass, moist with morning dew, as I paced the space in front of my door.

"Say something, Tiger," he pleaded.

"Something."

"You know that's not what I meant."

I stopped in front of him. "I don't know what to say. I want to help you and Lilly, truly, I do. And although I hate that I admitted my baggage to you last night, I'm glad I talked about it… but marriage as a solution? I'm sorry, but that's absurd."

The way his shoulders sagged had guilt clawing at my gut. I knew there was no reason to feel bad. This plan was bonkers and I wouldn't hold myself responsible for a man's bruised ego. But still… maybe I'd been too harsh.

"Wes, I'm sorry. I appreciate the sentiment and if there's anything I can do to help I will, but I can't marry you." I huffed, picturing the shit show of us as a married couple. "We bicker all the time and you just said you don't like me that way. And what about our families? Would we lie to them? It would be a mess."

He pulled his hair out of the barely kempt ponytail and ran his palms over the strands, staring off in the distance. A breeze blew through the loose waves and I couldn't break my eyes away from the fluidity of their movement. Wes really was beautiful. He finally pulled his gaze from the ocean back to me, hurt clear on his face.

"I understand. It was an idea. Now that you talk about it… you're right. I guess I'm just out of ideas but I'll keep trying to figure this out. Talk to a few lawyers and see what they say. For all I know, Regina could be bluffing."

I nodded. "That's a good idea."

"What about you? I wish we offered affordable health insurance, but last I checked, the cheapest one is still a lot. Can you ask anyone for help? " My mother's last tirade about my parent's divorce and their frozen assets ran through my head. No way would I ask them for a penny. Besides the fact that they were in their own crisis, asking my parents for anything always came with a price, and I was done being their stand-in for everything they were missing in their own lives.

"Don't worry about me."

My phone started to vibrate in my pocket and I pulled it out. The hospital number flashed across the screen. *Great timing.* They could leave a message. Wes studied me with a curious expression.

"Do you need to get that?"

"No, it's fine," I said quietly.

I finished off my now lukewarm coffee, willing it to counteract my hangover from hell.

"I guess I'll get going." He stood, balling up the paper bag that was on the ground next to him. "I'm sorry again about earlier. And what I said."

"It's fine." Fine seemed to be my word of the week. Wes saw right through me though. I could tell.

"To put it out there, if we did this thing, I know it wouldn't be real, but I'd make sure you and Alex were taken care of. And yes we bicker, but we make a good team." He shrugged. "I can understand you holding out for love, though."

"Love? That's not it. I mean, yes, that's the dream for everyone, right? But it's not on the radar for me. It hasn't been for a long time."

"Why is that?" He stepped so close I could smell his comforting scent, before cupping my chin and tilting my face toward his. His calloused fingers scratched against my sensitive skin. It felt good—too good—every time Wes touched me like this. I could picture those strong fingers tracing their way lower. Skimming my collar bone, the swell of my breasts. My breathing quickened and Wes stepped closer still. Close enough that a strand of his hair brushed my cheek. I couldn't think straight like this.

"I—I don't know. It's just not. I'm not the love type, I guess." My voice trembled as the words spilled from my lips. "No one's loved me before."

Wes blinked and stepped away, leaving me breathless and frustrated. "You're telling yourself lies, Tiger."

I caught my breath and mentally smacked myself for letting his close proximity rattle me. "Oh, yeah? What do you know?"

"More than you think," he answered, like he was stating something glaringly obvious. My damn phone started to buzz again. I cursed under my breath and pulled it out. The hospital again. "You should probably get that."

"Yeah, yeah," I grumbled, answering the hospital number. Wes watched me, arms crossed over his broad chest.

"Mrs. Murphy?"

"Yes," I answered, ignoring the Mrs. part.

"This is Dr. Farrow, I'm the orthopedic surgeon who did your son's surgery a few months ago. I was forwarded his X-rays and records from his emergency room visit last night. I'm so sorry to say this, but it looks like he'll need to be seen for a follow-up in the office sooner than later."

My ears rang—a high pitched, grating sound that pierced straight through my skull. It was starting, the tightening of my chest muscles, the lump forming in my throat. I held onto the front door as my legs turned to jelly.

"Mrs. Murphy? Are you there?"

"Yes—sorry." I cleared my throat and felt a tap on my shoulder. Wes was beside me reaching for my phone. I passed it to him with a shaky hand.

"Hello, this is Alex's father." He'd spoken those words before but this time, with the proposal on the table, they conjured a different feeling. Comfort, maybe? Safety? I didn't know but, I was grateful he was here for me again.

"Okay, I'll check our calendar and call the office first thing to make an appointment. Thanks." He hit end and passed me the phone.

I peered through the front window where Alex was relaxing, leg elevated on a pillow, laughing at his show. It wasn't fair that he had to go through all this crap. I'd do anything to take it on myself.

"I told her we'd call to set up an appointment," Wes said in a muted voice.

"Thank you." I needed to get inside and calm myself down. These reactions I had to stress were compounding and I was afraid I'd reach a point where I was unable to care for myself or Alex. I couldn't even do a telephone call with Dr. Bannen since his rate was at least $200 an hour and it's been almost a year since I'd seen him for counseling.

Wes wrapped his arm around my shoulder and guided me inside. "Sit with Alex. I'm going to go grab Lilly from my parents and come back, okay?"

I shook my head. "You don't have to. We're fine."

"You're not fine," he whispered. "Please... I'll be back in fifteen minutes."

A tear fell down my cheek as I whispered, "Okay."

Chapter 16

Wes

THE DAY WENT BY in a contented blur. I didn't know how I could feel simultaneously torn up and at peace here with Olivia, Alex, and Lilly. The kids played video games, while I walked Olivia's exhausted, hungover ass straight into her bedroom and forced her to nap. She fought me tooth and nail, but eventually gave in. I knew she needed the rest... The panic attack plus the hangover had zapped the remainder of her energy.

I made the kids some PB&J's and checked in with Thea, who seemed to be handling the kitchen like I knew she could. By the time Oliva came out of her room a few hours later, I'd almost forgotten that we didn't live like this every day.

Her features looked softer. Like sleep siphoned the heaviness of the morning from her body. I knew better when it came to Olivia. That stress and anxiety was bubbling at the surface waiting for the next pin prick to let it free.

"Hey." She crossed the kitchen to find the fresh pot of coffee I'd brewed a few minutes ago, checking out the kids zoned into their games and the absence of disaster or mess. "Thank you for keeping an eye on him."

"It's no problem. They ate lunch and have been hanging out. Truth be told, Alex was pretty vocal about letting you rest. I think he can sense your stress level."

She sighed and rubbed her eyes. "You're probably right. He's a perceptive little guy."

We sat in comfortable silence while she checked her phone and I drank my coffee. It wasn't lost on me that this is what it would be like if we were a family. An average day spent lazing around, kids playing, Olivia and I getting a few minutes of peace and quiet. Only, in my fantasy version, I'd be carrying her into the bedroom and we'd be doing things that were neither peaceful nor quiet.

She caught me checking her out and raised a brow. "It's unnerving that you can sit there in silence like that."

"What do you mean?" I chuckled.

"You're not scrolling a phone or reading a book. You're just sitting there."

"It's not that weird. Lots of people don't like to have a screen in their face all the time."

She plopped her phone on the table and rested her head in her hands. "You're an odd one, you know that?"

"Says the person who ate an entire cake with her bare hands."

"Touché." She spotted a few crumbs on the table and used the edge of her palm to scrape them into her hand. "This day has been freaking weird, huh?"

"Apart from the phone call, it's been nice." I was telling the full truth. I liked being here with her.

"Oddly domestic," she said.

"Almost like a happy little family."

She played with a strand of hair. "Say we went through with this marriage thing—"

"Yeah?" I asked.

"How would it work? Do we tell our families the truth, that we're doing it to help each other? What about the kids? I don't want to mess them up even more when they're already going through so much. And what about living arrangements? I'm sure your in-laws would need to see that it's real."

"We'd need to figure that all out." I blew out a breath. "But I'm a shit liar, at least to anyone close to me. I guess I'd want to tell people that we were getting married. Make it as believable as possible."

"But behind closed doors?" She searched my face for an answer.

"It'll be business as usual, right?"

"Right. Friends who work together, help each other, and happen to be married." With each word she spoke she nodded her head like she was listing off a grocery order. Marriage held the same weight as a gallon of milk.

"Exactly. And we don't have to figure it all out at once. Most important thing is getting Alex fixed up and telling Regina where she can shove her lawyers."

Olivia watched the kids bickering over something in their game. Lilly wrapped her arms around her chest, refusing to unpause, while Alex bugged her to in a chorus of pleases.

"I can't believe her name is pronounced like that?" Olivia said, holding in a laugh. She repeated Regina's name. It just so happens to rhyme with vagina. "That should have been your first warning not to marry into that family." The laugh burst free and even though it was at my expense, I joined her because hell, I was glad to see her smile.

"You're not wrong," I said. "So, does this mean you're considering?"

"God, I feel like I'm in one of those Regency romance novels where the duke needs a bride to inherit his manor house or something absurd like that." She blew out a breath and wrung her hands together. "But yes, I am considering your bonkers plan."

My lips tipped up. "Aw, I feel so special."

"I have one requirement if we're going to do this."

Curious, I tilted my head. "Okay?"

"You ditch that stupid flip phone into the nearest body of water and get an iPhone. I can't be married to someone who doesn't text."

"That's your one requirement? Not, I don't know, money or needing to know if I close the seat after I pee?" I pulled out my trusty phone and spun it around on the table. "You hate this thing that much?"

"I do. But now that you mention it, I also like money and a person who puts the seat down after they pee."

"Sorry, you already laid out your conditions." I put my hands up in surrender. "Too late to add in anything else."

"You're the worst," she said as she shook her head and grinned.

"And we haven't even tied the knot yet."

"I think I've changed my mind. You're too insufferable."

"I have an idea." I grabbed a deck of cards that I spotted in one of her kitchen drawers earlier. She eyed me with curiosity as I opened the box and started to shuffle. "You ever play Spades?"

"No, the only card game I've ever played was a Pixar Cars version of Go Fish."

"It's easy, I can give you a rundown of the rules and we can play a few practice rounds." I did one of my fancy shuffles to break in the stiff deck of cards. "If you don't play cards, where'd the deck come from?"

"Oh, I think Alex got it at the dentist in one of those prize bins."

"Gotcha." I nodded. After a quick lesson on the rules of two-player Spades we started to draft our hands. "Spades was our go-to when I was a dumb teenager. Me and my best friend would bet shit like sticks of gum or whatever cash we had on hand, which was usually none."

"I guess I should be worried then since you're such an expert. What are we betting anyway?" We finished drafting, each of us held our hands of thirteen cards.

"If I win, I get to keep my beloved phone."

She scoffed. "You love that thing that much?"

"Yup. Me and her go way back and she's never done me wrong. I dropped her out a moving car window once and she survived."

Olivia laughed, the sound squeezing the organ beneath my ribs. "And if I win? I'm assuming you retire her and get yourself a shiny new iPhone?"

"Exactly. So you better keep your wits about you because I intend to win."

"Game on."

"You totally took me for a ride. There's no way that was your first time playing Spades," I said, double checking the final score.

"I'd never lie. I guess I'm a quick learner." She had the most smug grin on her face as she collected the pile of cards and fit them back into the package.

"Hey, Alex," I called. "Has your mom ever played card games?"

"What? You really don't believe me?" Oliva asked.

"Card games? Like Go Fish?" Alex asked, turning his head in our direction.

"Yeah, like Go Fish."

"I don't think so. Not with me, and Mom doesn't really have any friends to play with but I don't know." He went back to playing *Mario Kart* with Lilly.

"See?" Olivia said. "I'm too pathetically friendless to play card games according to my ten year old."

"Not anymore. Prepare to be texted nonstop. It'll be your punishment for winning the bet."

"Better than getting seven consecutive voicemails asking where you put your wallet."

"True." I flipped the phone open and closed a few times in my palm. "I'll miss you, Old Betty."

"Now it has a name? You've got to be kidding me."

"I just gave her a name. She deserves one. It'll go on her headstone."

"And I thought our ten year olds were dramatic." She laughed. "That thing belongs in a museum."

"Don't listen to her, Betty. She's jealous of our love."

"There has to be a reason why you're so against a smartphone. Come on, Wesley, give it up."

"Wesley? You're hitting me with the full name?" She narrowed her eyes until I relented. "I don't want to become one of those zombies who stare at their tiny screen nonstop. Life is too short, you know. Plus, me and phones... We have beef. But that's a story for the next time you kick my ass in Spades."

"Fair enough." She stretched her arms over her head with a groan that sounded more than a bit suggestive. "How about we give Betty one last assignment before she retires in her old age?"

"I'm listening."

"Order a few pizzas. All that winning made me hungry." She smiled and her dark eyes gleamed.

"As you wish, Queen of Spades."

"Oh, and don't forget the pineapple."

As if I could forget anything about her.

Chapter 17

Olivia

"Thank you again for offering to cook." I dropped the homemade apple pie I'd brought onto Shawn's kitchen island and took in his spacious great room. We were celebrating Christmas early since they'd be out of town.

"No problem. I enjoy cooking and it's nice to have more people to cook for. I thought I was going to have to eat an entire turkey on my own."

"He really did," Mia said. "We were looking at teeny frozen turkeys the other day at Publix, which weirded me out because they looked like babies. But then I was like, wait, Livvy and Alex live here now! I can't believe it, sissy. Our first holiday together in forever."

"It's been too long." I thought about Christmas last year and how the entire meal was cooked by caterers while we all stayed in our separate areas of the house until it was time to eat. I tried to make it fun for Alex by putting together a craft project in his playroom, but he declared he wasn't a baby anymore and didn't like finger painting. I ended up scrapping it, and cleaning the rest of the playroom while I was at it.

"Appetizers are set up in the living room," Shawn said. "Just keep an eye on Remy. He likes to table surf."

On cue, Shawn's adorable golden retriever sniffed my leg, tail wagging. "I think Alex already snuck him some cheese."

"Tell Alex to prepare to have a new best friend. Remy loves cheese almost as much as Mia."

Mia poured us a few glasses of wine and announced that she'd be back to help once Shawn was done making love to the turkey. I laughed, but she wasn't too far off, the man was massaging that thing with herbed butter like he was in love.

"Hey, it's called dressing the turkey. We can't have it all dry and flavorless."

Mia shot back a sassy, "Sure," before leading me out back to Shawn's deck. Being twenty minutes inland, Shawn's yard was far greener than my own. I breathed in the smell of pine coming from a tall tree at the back of his property mixed with the damp air.

"It's nice out here, right? Almost reminds me of New York," Mia said. She plopped in an Adirondack chair and motioned for me to join her.

"Yeah, I can see that." I sipped my chilled wine, feeling my body relax. I hadn't had time to catch up much with Mia the past week, with Alex recovering and me trying to get a few hours of work in. I knew I didn't want to say anything about Wes and our plan. If that was even happening. We talked about it that day and neither of us had brought it up since. Maybe he changed his mind.

"So sissy, when are you coming back to Krav? I know Kendahl left, but there's other nice people you can work with. Or if you want, I can be your partner for a few classes?"

"I don't know. I'm honestly exhausted between Alex and work and realistically I can't afford the membership." I knew how important Krav was to Mia and I understood where she was coming from. I should continue. Learning self-defense after everything that happened to me when I was seventeen was not only therapeutic but necessary. Mia pretty much begged me to join when I moved and I knew it helped her anxiety to see me there and learning. I guess I needed a big shove back in the right direction.

"I can pay for you. It's important to me that you go, even if it's just for level one. And I know you love it as much as I do." Mia gave me the biggest puppy dog-eyed look.

"That look is so not cool."

"What?" She feigned innocence and widened her eyes even more.

"I won't let you pay for me. You're my little sister. I can't accept money from you. But I'll recommit after the new year."

"Promise?" she asked.

"I promise. I think I want to get Alex in the kids classes, too. Once he's healed and gets the green light, of course."

"That would be great for him. Especially with the whole bully situation. Have you figured out what you're going to do about that? I bet you have grounds to get a lawyer involved. What does Wes think?"

"He hasn't talked about it much. I guess I'll call the school first before jumping to legal action. From what Lilly told us, and the bits that I've been able to get out of Alex, the first fall seemed like an accident. His flip-flop was as much the problem as the kids up there teasing them. I think he got shoved though, even if it was unintentionally off the edge. The second time, I'm not sure. Alex started the fight, but it was self-defense and one of him versus a couple of them." I gulped a sip of wine. "I should have him switch schools after the holiday break. I'm afraid these kids will keep at it."

"Maybe. I don't know though, I feel like these little shits need to be held accountable," Mia said. "I hate bullies. It makes my blood boil to think about Alex and Lilly having to deal with all this. And for what? Because they're new?"

"I can't imagine any other reason why. Not that kids like that need a reason."

Mia twirled a loose curl while she stared out at the yard. "If I can do anything to help, you know I'm there. What happened at the doctor's?"

I finished off the rest of the wine in my glass. "She said there's a strong chance Alex may need another surgery. I opted to wait and see how he heals with the cast and recheck after the new year."

"Damn. I'm sorry. Fingers crossed it'll heal up and won't need any more interventions."

"Fingers, toes, and everything else," I added. Mia's phone chirped from the pocket of her hoodie. She took it out, smiling when she looked at the screen. "That can't be Mom." I laughed.

"God, no! It's Ken. She's sending her love and says she has some big news. I'll Facetime with her later, this is sister time."

"Are you sure? I don't mind if we call her. I'm sure she's missing us." And I was missing her, too.

"If you're sure?" Mia asked.

I grabbed her phone and hit Facetime while Mia laughed beside me. Kendahl answered on the first ring.

"Mi, I miss you! Oh, hey Liv!"

"Hey Ken," I smiled and passed the phone to my sister but not before noticing that Kendahl was sitting in a car.

"Where are you?" Mia asked. "Please tell me you're not driving."

Ken flipped the camera to show Coby in the driver's seat. A blurry landscape of a tree lined highway flashed by from his driver's side window. "Guess what?" she singsonged.

Mia perched forward in her chair and pressed her face closer to the phone screen. "You're killing me, spit it out lady!"

"We're on our way back to Palm Cove!" Kendahl's voice burst through the phone at an octave that would wake hibernating animals.

"For the holidays?" Mia asked.

"For the holidays and all the days after," Kendahl said, while snuggling against Coby's shoulder.

Mia jumped from her chair and screeched. I knew how much she missed her best friend. I missed her too, it wasn't the same here without Kendahl and her bubbly personality. While they chatted about details, I excused myself to check on Alex and get a refill.

Alex was sitting in the kitchen with Shawn, talking about video games like old buddies. I joined them, helping peel potatoes and dice veggies, until Mia came in and relieved me of my duties.

Her and Shawn were so obviously in love. The way they looked at each other and their subtle flirtatious banter and gestures made it clear as day. I couldn't help but feel a pang of jealousy watching them together. Even if love was off the table for me, I guess I still craved that connection. I'd never felt something like that before. Never had a person who looked at me the way Shawn looked at Mia.

Back home I was used to getting wide-eyed looks of pity from everyone I knew. I was the pathetic single mother, knocked up as a teen. The daughter my parents paraded around to their friends to show how caring and charitable they were. The damaged one.

I could move 2,000 miles away and start fresh, where no one knew me, but I knew myself. I was still that girl on the inside.

Still unloveable. Still helpless. Still capable of breaking at the drop of a hat. Who could love a girl like that?

"Should we play a couple rounds of Uno while we wait for the turkey?" Mia asked as she wiped down scraps of potato skins from the counter.

I blinked and cleared my throat. "Yeah, sounds fun."

Mia came across the counter to where I sat perched on a stool and slung her arm around my shoulder. "You okay, sis?"

I forced my lips into a grin. "Yup, all good. I think the wine's getting to my head. I'm going to grab some cheese and crackers."

"Good idea. I'll start shuffling," she said.

As I loaded a plate with cheese and crackers in the living room, I spotted my phone sitting there next to the platter where I'd left it earlier. The screen lit up with a message, so I grabbed it, seeing Wes's name on the banner.

Wes: *Hey, Tiger. Yes, your eyes are working, this is me, Wes, texting you from the abomination that is my new iPhone.*

I laughed at the drama that poured from this man while I typed out a response.

Me: *Welcome to the cool kids club, old man. How's Betty feeling about being replaced?*

Alex giggled in the kitchen and I felt my mood lift. Wes may have had something to do with it, too.

Wes: *I'm in mourning and halfway afraid Betty might become sentient and exact her revenge. Can this phone Google what to do if your old tech becomes deadly?*

Me: *It can. But you might want to start by Googling, "What to do if I have an unhealthy obsession with a flip phone?"*

Wes: *It's showing me a list of therapists in the area... saving for later*

Was I actually laughing and twirling my hair while texting with my boss? I had to admit, he could be witty when he wasn't being an annoying man-child.

Me: *Good plan. Maybe find one who enjoys a challenge :)*

Wes: *Don't worry, I'll share their contact info with you too, sweetheart*

And there's the man-child again. Mia came into the room as I was shaking my head and huffing a laugh.

"What's got you blushing, sis? Or should I say, who?"

She tried to get a peek at my screen, but I swiped away quickly. "Nothing."

"I bet I know who," she hummed.

"It was Kelly from work," I lied.

"Liar! It was Wes, wasn't it? You like him... You like your boss." She chanted the tune like a five year old.

"I do not." I hid my screen as another text from him flashed. "He drives me crazy."

"I hate to break it to you sis, but the right guys usually do. Shawn drives me nuts everyday, but it's usually endearing. Except for when he tosses his dirty laundry next to the hamper. Like seriously... the hamper is *right there*. I don't get it."

"Glad I only have to deal with that from Alex. I think I've bugged him enough about it that he's trained now, though." I grabbed a piece of cheese, stacked it on a cracker and passed it to Mia before making one for myself.

"Thanks." She took a bite, chewing thoughtfully. "Well if you're not into Wes, at least let me set you up with someone. I saw this new guy at class talking to Mark and oh my God, Liv." She lowered her voice. "He's so hot. I shouldn't say this about someone since I'm taken and all but I had to wipe drool off my mouth when I saw him. His jaw could cut glass and he has dimples. You know I have a weakness for dimples."

I shook my head, even though I knew she'd keep pressing me. "Tempting but I don't think so. I'm too busy to date, especially now with Alex's leg."

"I'm happy to babysit. Promise me you'll think about it?"

"Fine, I'll think about it."

"Good! Now come on, I'm going to beat Alex's smack-talking butt in Uno." She pulled me up by the hand and I followed her into the kitchen, tucking my phone into the pocket of my jeans.

We had a great day at Mia and Shawn's place. Amazing food, laughs, and a fair amount of shit talking was exactly what I'd needed to get myself into a better mindset. Back home, Alex declared he was exhausted and put himself to bed, while I spent a few minutes straightening up the already tidy kitchen.

After the full day of conversation, my place felt extra quiet with only the two of us. Maybe we needed a dog like Remy. But I knew I'd constantly battle all the hair. While I scrolled our local animal shelter's list of available dogs, Wes texted me.

Wes: *Can you talk?*

Adrenaline immediately began to flow through me. It may have been my first official day of texting with Wes, but I knew he always at least said hello first.

Me: *Sure, I'm home*

I paced my kitchen, imagining the worst case scenarios. What if they'd taken Lilly? Or she got hurt? Were his parents okay?

Me: *Is everything okay?*

I waited for the little read notification underneath my message to pop up, but after five minutes it didn't. My kitchen felt too small, like it lacked enough air, so I grabbed my sweatshirt and walked outside. I knew the moment Wes stepped out of his car that something was wrong.

Chapter 18

Wes

OLIVIA'S FACE FELL WHEN she saw me. I couldn't blame her, I knew I looked like shit.

"What's going on?" Olivia asked as she approached my car.

"Regina surprised me with a text." I pulled out my phone and opened the message, handing it to Olivia.

Her eyes widened as she read. "She could be bluffing?"

"She's not. She sent me the file in my email. It's notarized from wherever Savannah is." I pulled up the image of the letter from Sav and showed it to Olivia. "She's starting the process. Giving up her parental rights to them. What am I gonna do?"

Her eyes focused on the ground while she paced back and forth. "My father is a lawyer in New York. Let's call him in the morning."

I nodded as she continued. "What were your custody arrangements before?"

"Savannah has sole custody. It was a cut and dry divorce. I didn't contest anything." I thought back to my mental state when I'd gotten served with divorce papers. Our relationship was toxic as hell and I'd just caught her cheating on me. I signed the paperwork without even reading through it, like the pathetic asshole I was. That's how I ended up giving Sav most of my monthly income and rarely seeing my own kid. Then we got back together, but that only lasted until the accident. I couldn't imagine her giving up her rights to Lilly, but especially not to her parents.

"That's good. I know my father will be able to help. He has colleagues everywhere, maybe he can put you in touch with someone?" I heard her voice but not her words. My head was all over the place. "Wes?"

"I don't know anymore. Maybe I shouldn't be a father? Maybe they're right? I'm not a good person, Tiger. People I love end up hurt." I pulled on the back of my neck, looking up instead of in her eyes so I couldn't see the questions in them. The silent judgment.

"Wes, I say this with all the care in the world. Pull your head out of your ass." She stepped closer, so her body was inches from mine. It didn't matter that her head barely reached my collarbone, she wrapped her hands around my neck and forced me to meet her gaze. "You're a good person who loves his daughter. We're not going to let those assholes win."

She looked at me with undeserved reverence. I wanted to believe her with everything in me. Her hands gripped me with strength I wished I had. Even my quickening pulse betrayed me. Why should I let myself react to Olivia's touch when it didn't mean anything? "I'm not strong enough to fight them."

She glided her fingers from my neck, catching a loose strand of hair and tucking it behind my ear. The small gesture caused me to shiver. "Then we fight them together."

"What are you saying?"

"Marry me."

"You're serious?" Her eyes blazed into mine as she nodded. A rebuttal almost slipped from my lips before I caught myself. Hell, I didn't deserve her for all the reasons I didn't deserve Lilly but I was selfish enough to take her offer. I knew I needed her much more than she needed me.

"You said it yourself, it'll be mutually beneficial. You'll help with health insurance and I'll help you with the custody stuff."

I had said that. "Right. But are you sure? I thought—"

"I'm sure. Like we said, nothing else will change. We're two friends helping each other who happen to be married."

She stepped back, leaving a chill in her wake. "Okay, then. When do we do this?"

She inhaled deeply and blew out a breath. "As soon as possible. I have this feeling in my gut that we shouldn't wait."

Who was I to argue her? I focused on her face with a renewed sense of purpose. "Alright, let's do this then."

Olivia searched on her phone, while I made a list of things we'd need and people to call. By the time I left an hour later, I'd almost forgotten about Regina's message.

I checked in on Lilly, sleeping soundly in my bed, before heading to the couch to pass out.

All night I tossed and turned, ruminating on everything that could go wrong. I was so damn scared. Scared of hurting Lilly and fucking up her life. Scared of dragging Olivia and Alex into my shit. Scared I'd hurt them all.

I kept picturing Dylan's face in those last moments. The way he held on for me. I let him down. He was gone because of me. Why did I think I deserved Olivia's kindness?

Chapter 19

Olivia

OH MY GOD, THIS was happening. I was about to marry Wes. All morning I'd been pacing my bedroom, talking to myself like a lunatic. Now that it's come down to the day of, I wish I'd told Mia. Even if I did, she was a few hours away for the holiday and I didn't want to ruin that for her.

Not like this was real anyway. She'd fuss over me and make sure we did all the customary traditions regardless—bridal shower, bachelorette party, dress shopping. She wouldn't take no for an answer. It was better this way, quick and simple.

I peeked at the to-do list I made when we decided this was happening. Honestly, my one regret was waiting until the week of Christmas. Like we weren't already busy enough. Only one thing left on the list: meet Wes at the courthouse.

I took one more look in the mirror, adjusting the loose curls I'd attempted. Maybe I didn't look like a traditional bride, but I felt good about myself in the white sundress I found on clearance. That was all that mattered, right?

With a bewildered Alex in tow, we made our way to the Palm Cove courthouse, my nerves eating away at my gut the entire ride.

Twinkle lights decorated the lobby and instrumental holiday music drifted through hidden speakers. We turned the corner and there he was, wearing dress pants that fit snugly over his thighs, a loose button up shirt and an unbuttoned jacket. His hair was pulled back, and his beard was neatly trimmed. I stopped in my tracks, taking him in before he saw us. I thought he was beautiful when I first laid eyes on him and that only intensified, which scared the hell out of me. I should not be finding my future husband mouthwatering hot. Not in our situation.

"Lilly!" Alex called to his soon-to-be sibling. They all turned their heads in our direction. Wes, Lilly, his parents, even the few random people scattered around waiting for their own appointments. He hobbled their way as fast as his crutches would allow.

Wes and I locked eyes from across the room. Each step I took toward him, toward this new crazy future, made unanswered questions spring into my mind. Oh, God. My mouth was a desert and my legs trembled. Maybe it was the heels... but probably not.

I spotted an open door and scrambled through it, not giving a damn if the room was off limits. *Shit, shit, shit.* Should I leave? Slip out through some back door. I'd figure out the health insurance somehow, and the money... No biggie.

Except it was a biggie. And I couldn't go. I finally looked around, realizing I'd infiltrated someone's personal office. They must have been out, but still, I shouldn't have been in there. A knock sounded on the door and I jumped, grabbing a stapler from the desk in front of me.

"It's me." Wes pushed the door open, immediately filling the space with his frame. He had this way about him that was more than his size. It was his presence. When he was near, you felt him. I hugged my arms against my chest as he froze in place a few feet from me.

"Sorry." I couldn't look at him. I felt like a scared child, hiding away in here when we'd already made this decision.

"Don't." His voice was clear and calm, the opposite of how I felt. He stepped closer and I didn't look up until his fingertips brushed my chin. "Don't apologize."

I nodded and made a noise of agreement.

"What can I do?" It took everything in me not to wrap my hand around his and bury myself in his chest. I craved that comfort and he could sense that.

"When I was standing there looking at you, I realized we never set an end date for this." He dropped his hand and took a step back. "I didn't mean it in a bad way," I corrected.

"No, you're right. We never did discuss an end date. I'll leave that up to you." He shrugged, which irritated me. This was important. We needed rules—boundaries—or someone was bound to get hurt.

"You don't care then? What if I said five years? You're really willing to shackle yourself to me and my kid for that long?" I crossed my arms and stared him down.

He shrugged again. "Like I said, up to you."

"Okay, then. Prepare to live the rest of your good penis years in a sexless, fake marriage."

"Good penis years?" Ha... I knew that would catch his attention.

"Yup. The years before ED kicks in. I've heard it can start as early as the thirties for some men," I said in a serious tone.

"I don't think I'll have to worry about that, Tiger." Ugh, I wanted to wipe that smug expression off his face. Was I now seriously wishing for this man to experience erectile dysfunction out of spite? He chuckled and my ears flamed. Yes. Yes, I was.

"Fine," I huffed. "How about six months? That should be enough time for the custody situation and for me to get my life in order."

"Six months," he repeated. "Like I said, whatever you think."

"Why are you being so agreeable? It's annoying the crap out of me."

"Would you rather I argue with you?"

"Maybe! I don't know!" I paced in front of the desk, which according to the nameplate belonged to someone named Larry.

Too bad Larry didn't have a stash of chocolate next to his keyboard, that would have really taken the edge off for me. Wes's chuckle brought my gaze back to him. "What's so funny?"

"Nothing, Tiger. Come on, we should get back out there before the kids get antsy." I hated that he was right. "Anything else you want to bang out now before we make this official?"

"Nice choice of words," I grumbled.

"I'm quite proud of them, thanks."

I heaved a sigh that I was sure could be heard in the lobby, even over the instrumental version of "We Wish You A Merry Christmas."

"Wait," I said. He stopped in the doorway and I almost piled into his brick wall of a back. "Did we ever figure out the living arrangements?" He stared at me with deer in headlight eyes before blinking slowly. "We didn't, did we?"

"No," he laughed. "Of all the things, we never decided on that."

"I think as soon as I get that insurance card I'm scheduling a brain scan for myself. How? Of all the things, how did we forget to discuss that?"

We paused, both clearly trying to figure out the answer to that particular issue. Neither of our homes would work. Not in the long term at least.

"We'll figure it out, okay? Let's just get your beautiful ass out there and do this damn thing before the judge makes us reschedule."

He thought I was beautiful? I couldn't dwell on his comment. He was right, I'd stalled long enough. Plus, plenty of guys have called me beautiful. That didn't mean they meant it, or that I could trust them. I needed to remember that, even when it came to Wes. Especially when it came to Wes. Out of all the times I've been broken, he had the capability to shatter me beyond repair. If I could keep that in mind and keep my walls intact, these six months would be cake.

"Welcome to the family, Mrs. Reed!" Walter enveloped me in a hug that lingered long enough for Wes to pull him away with a groan. Val focused on hugging the kids, who the judge had sweetly included in the quick ceremony. I still wasn't sure they realized what had happened. Maybe Lilly had, but Alex still looked dazed.

I couldn't blame him. I was dazed too, but for a different reason. Wes kissed me... right there in front of his parents, our kids, and the judge. He kissed me and it felt real. The moment replayed on a loop in my head for the next hour. It went something like this:

Val asking if we should go to lunch—*me replaying the feeling of Wes's palm on my cheek as he pulled me in.*

Us arriving at Pebble Grill on the beach—*me thinking about Wes's lips brushing against mine. Gently, like the tip of a lit match touching a wick.*

Me ordering a chicken sandwich—*his lips parting mine, the tiniest touch of our tongues. Flames burning through me, setting my blood on fire.*

Slowly and methodically eating, while nodding and answering basic questions—*him breaking the kiss, pressing his forehead against mine. The scratch of his beard against my face. The warmth of his lips, moist from our kiss, against my nose.*

Wes tapping my shoulder—*me thinking about how I wanted him to kiss me again.*

"Tiger?" he spoke low next to my ear and the skin on my arm pebbled. "You okay over there?"

"Hmm?" I blinked, pulling myself into the present. "Sorry, I'm tired. If you see the waiter, remind me to order a coffee."

"Sure," he said. "Alex was just asking if Lilly is his sister now."

I smiled at my son. "Stepsister, but yes. How do you guys feel about that?"

They gave each other goofy looks and Lilly answered, "I always wanted a sibling. Specifically a sister, but I'll take him."

"As long as she doesn't mess with my stuff," Alex said. "My Lego display is off limits."

"Like I don't already know that. You've told me a hundred times." They went back and forth with each other and Wes leaned in again.

"Looks like we'll have to find a bigger place soon. Them sharing a room might end up in World War III." He was right, those two bickered more than me and Wes.

"Alright kids," Val said. "Settle down. Santa's watching, you know."

"Santa... right." Both kids laughed conspiratorially and Val gave me a thumbs up.

Walter cleared his throat. "I want to say how happy I am for you both. Olivia, when you first came into our lives, I knew you were special. You were our angel that night, stepping in to help at Sunshine, and you've been there ever since, keeping this guy in line." He gestured toward Wes with his water glass. "Wesley has been through so much grief. After the accident and losing his leg..." He glanced at the kids and paused for a moment. "After what Savannah put him through. I never thought he'd find love. But the way he looks at you, I know he's found it. So welcome to the family. We're so blessed to have you and Alex."

My eyes watered as Walter came around the table to give me a side hug. I whispered, "Thank you," not knowing what else to say. Had Wes told them this wasn't real? If he did, then what was that speech?

"Walter, you're making the poor thing tear up," Val said. "Sorry, love. He gets emotional sometimes. What he said is true though. We are excited to have you in the family, right Wesley?"

Wes cleared his throat and met my gaze. My eyes drifted lower, settling on his lips. "Right. Couldn't be happier."

"I was going to wait to tell you but it seems like the right moment. We know you can't have a real honeymoon like your father and I did, but we booked you a room for tonight. A honeymoon special. We'll stay with the kids, so don't worry about them." Val beamed as she ruffled Alex's hair. I waited for Wes to say something. Clearly, he hadn't told his parents this whole thing was a ruse. He massaged his temple and I reached for my water to clear the sand in my throat. As I sipped, Val lowered her voice and added, "We know you could use the privacy."

My water slid down the wrong tube and came spewing out onto the table as I heaved a choking cough. I coughed again, gasping for breath.

"Shit, are you okay?" Wes asked as he thwacked my back a few times. I nodded and made an unintelligible sound of agreement through another bout of coughs.

"Be right back." I stood and gestured toward the restroom across the floor. If I was dazed before, now I was wide awake. We had to get out of this, but I had a feeling Val wouldn't take no for an answer.

"Oh, I'll join you," Val said, getting up to follow me.

"Great," I muttered. There'd be no five minute break to collect myself. I guess I should get used to having attentive and overly friendly in-laws. I didn't think my mother had accompanied me to the restroom since I was out of diapers. She was usually too busy schmoozing someone at the club, drink in hand.

I glanced back at Wes and he flashed me a look that was a cross between a wince and a grin. He'd be hearing a piece of my mind later. Val caught up to me and squeezed my hand. I flinched out of habit before taking a breath and squeezing back.

"Sorry, I'm a bit extra affectionate today. I'm just so happy, I could burst. You two make such a sweet couple. Walter and I knew for months that something was going on."

She radiated joy. Lord help me, I didn't want to burst her bubble. "That's so sweet of you," I responded. "You and Walter are the best."

We pushed through the restroom door as she went on. "Let's sit down for coffee this week and I can go over some of his care needs. It's been years now, so he's more or less healed and with all the therapies he's come leaps and bounds, but still, I'd like you to be aware of some things to look out for. You know since he won't be living with us anymore."

I hadn't thought about any of that. Not that I wasn't aware of his limb loss, but sometimes, it slipped my mind that he needed accommodations or special care. "Oh, okay... sure."

"Don't worry, love, he's a grown man fully capable of taking care of himself." She paused in front of an open stall. "It's just, we all need someone to watch out for us too, you know?"

My heart swelled at the pure kindness of this woman. I did know, because it's how I felt about Alex. It's what I'd needed from my parents but never received. "I know what you mean." I smiled. "He'll be in good hands."

"And so will you," she said, smiling back at me before heading into the stall.

I didn't even need to pee, but I sat there anyway, thinking over our conversation. There was so much I didn't know about Wes. So much he didn't know about me. I'd be lying if that didn't scare the crap out of me. I pulled my phone out of my sundress pocket and swiped to his name.

Me: *Sooo... your parents don't know?*

My phone chimed, and I scrambled to put it on silent. Val was still hovering out there, humming to herself while she washed her hands.

Wes: *Not exactly*

Me: *You didn't think to clue me in? I almost died out there.*

Maybe that was a bit dramatic, but warranted.

Wes: *I'm sorry. They went apeshit when I told them, I felt too bad bringing them down. I can tell them now if you want?*

"Great," I mumbled under my breath.

"You okay in there?" Val asked. She must have been waiting for me.

"Yes, almost done. You don't have to wait for me, I'm okay."

"It's no bother. I'm going to fix my lipstick so I can get the waiter to take a group photo for us."

"Wonderful," I said, sounding overly sweet.

Me: *No, it's fine. Now's clearly not the time... just next time I need you to communicate please. You have a real phone now, even a quick text would do.*

Wes: *Understood... sorry again*

Wes: *My father is out here singing your praises by the way... he's not wrong*

I snorted but covered my mouth in time.

Me: *Flattery isn't going to help, big guy. But nice try :)*

Wes: *I guess I'll have to figure out a way to make it up to you later*

Was I reading into that too much or was that innuendo?

"Do you want to use my lipstick? This pink would look great against your skin tone," Val said. Luckily she interrupted my train of thought since I was two seconds away from asking Wes how he planned to make it up to me.

Shoving my phone away, I walked out of the stall to see Val layering on the brightest shade of pink lipstick I'd ever seen. "Wow, that color is... vibrant."

"Isn't it? Here." She passed it to me. "For the picture."

I couldn't say no to this woman. She had some sort of kindness superpower that made it impossible to refuse her. I painted on the hideous lipstick while she chatted about the church. Maybe it was a good idea to make myself look worse... if anything, it would keep Wes from calling me beautiful again. We didn't need complications like that.

Chapter 20

Wes

OLIVIA CAME OUT OF the bathroom wearing flamingo pink lipstick and all I could think about was how that color would look smeared around my cock. I'd been on edge since I woke up that morning, a mix of normal wedding jitters and fear that she wouldn't show. I mean, fuck, the last time I got married I was a dumb kid who'd knocked up a pretty girl and was trying to do the right thing.

Today was different.

Olivia was different.

I saw her walking through the lobby and literally lost my breath. She'd curled her dark hair into loose waves that touched her bare shoulders. Her dress was simple—white cotton, fitted at the bust before flowing loosely around her hips. Each step she took in my direction seemed fluid. I zeroed in on her face, glowing with a hint of makeup, light enough that her freckles still peeked through.

My breathing quickened and I swore I could feel a bead of sweat forming on my brow. She was too good for me. I knew it, but fuck, I wanted her. Selfish or not, I couldn't take my eyes off of her... and she was almost mine.

I barely heard the ceremony. Just went through the motions, afraid that any sudden movements would trigger Olivia and she'd bail. That was until the judge said those last words—kiss your bride.

Her eyes met mine and the air around us buzzed. I didn't think. Hell, maybe I should have. No, I acted on instinct.

Now I was addicted.

Her soft skin under my palm as I drew her close.

The hushed exhale that escaped her lips the moment my tongue met hers.

Her taste, her smell, her sounds.

That kiss was like a single domino, toppling and causing a chain reaction.

And now she was sitting next to me—in that lipstick—pulling on my growing infatuation with her lips.

"I already took care of the check," my father said. "If everyone's done, we can take these two back to the house so you can get your alone time." He finished with a not so subtle brow waggle.

I groaned. "Seriously, Dad?"

"What? I didn't say anything." He shrugged and gathered his box of leftovers. I turned my attention to Olivia, who'd gone quiet next to me.

"You okay?" I asked in a low enough voice that only she'd hear.

"Mhm." She nodded, her movements stiff.

"I'll meet you at your place," I said once we got to the cars. Maybe the drive back would give her a chance to clear her head. My gaze lingered on her lips again until she lowered safely into the driver's side of her car. I bent to secure her buckle, noticing her quick intake of breath as my palm grazed the top of her thigh.

"I can buckle myself, you know?"

"I know you can." *But I like to make sure you're safe.*

"Okay then." She started the engine, and I stepped back, anxiety swirling in my gut from seeing her drive away.

Because she's yours now, the little voice in my head noted.

I stopped at home to grab an overnight bag, unsure if we were actually going to check in to the hotel. If we didn't, I still couldn't stay at home. My parents would shoo me out the door like a housefly and they'd know something was up.

On my way back, I decided I'd let Olivia choose. If she didn't want to go, I could crash on her couch. With the kids gone, we wouldn't have to play pretend for anyone. Telling myself the lie that I didn't care either way worked until I reached her doorstep and took one look at her in that dress again. Fuck, she was beautiful. I'd be a moron not to want a night away with her one on one.

"Hey." I knocked on the door as I let myself in. She was sitting at the table with a steaming mug in front of her. "Coffee?"

"Yeah, I'll probably regret it when I can't sleep later, but I needed one more cup."

"Got anymore?" I asked.

"Go ahead and help yourself. There's more pods in the drawer." I fiddled with her half Keurig, half coffee pot contraption and started the brew. While I waited, I peeked over Olivia's shoulder to see an email open on her phone screen. She scrolled to the bottom and blew out a breath.

"Everything okay?" God, I felt like a broken record with that question today. My vocabulary was usually better than that... It was the Olivia effect. Being in her presence siphoned my ability to think with the head on top of my body.

"Eh, could be better. Another email from the hospital billing department. Yay, happy wedding day," she replied, her tone dripping with sarcasm.

I grabbed the milk from the fridge and poured a splash into my mug. "Don't worry about that. We'll get it taken care of."

"Wes," she said softly, closing out of the email. "I don't expect money from you. That wasn't part of the deal."

"Yeah, well, my money, my choice." I smirked at the glare she threw my way. There was my Tiger. I loved to egg her on. Did that make me a bastard? Probably. But I wouldn't be stopping any time soon. She crossed her arms, ready to give it to me, when the door sprang open.

"What are you two still doing here?" my mother asked, waltzing inside like she owned the place. The kids and my father followed behind.

"Mom!" Alex said, moving slowly toward Olivia on his crutches. "Grandma Val and Grandpa Walt are going to let us decorate gingerbread houses with extra candy and then tomorrow there's a Christmas party with presents!"

I eyed my parents, whose faces were lit with wide smiles. *Grandma Val and Grandpa Walt.* Now that was fucking adorable.

"Wow," Olivia said as she pulled Alex in for a quick hug. "That sounds so fun. Maybe I can come, too."

"Are you nuts?" Walt bellowed. "You two better get out of here. I paid good money for that room." He crossed the space and physically pulled Oliva up from her chair. "You packed, young lady?"

"Umm, not exactly," she said while hiding her laughter behind her palm.

"What? Get to it, then. My father narrowed his brows, about to give her a fatherly talking to until she stopped him. "Okay, okay. I'll go pack."

"What are you guys doing here anyway?" I asked.

"Alex wanted to grab his things," my mom answered. "I remembered I have that emergency key Olivia gave me a while back, so we stopped over before heading home. Alex, go grab what you need for the night, okay love?"

He listened, heading toward his room with Lilly in tow. The two of them were already so close. I loved it but it also scared the hell out of me. If anything were to happen between Olivia and me, anything... unpleasant, they'd be devastated.

My dad gave my shoulder a firm squeeze. "You lock it down tonight, son. Show her a good time."

I groaned. "Dad, I really hope you're not implying what I think you're implying."

"Well, I know it's been a long time since you—you know—"

"Walter, dear Lord," my mother scolded. "I think our son knows what he's doing. He doesn't need your pep talk."

"How do you know, Val? Maybe he does." They bickered back and forth for a minute until I interrupted.

"You realize I'm sitting right here and I'd very much like to avoid a conversation about my sex life, with my parents, while my new wife is right in the other room." I grumbled again and finished the last sip of my coffee as Olivia reentered with a small suitcase.

I stood, offering to take it from her, but she insisted she was *fine*. That damn word again.

"Have fun, you two," my mother crooned. "Don't worry about a thing! The kids are in good hands." Olivia met my gaze with a grimace. She knew their track record, but as the kids came out laughing, Lilly carrying Alex's bag in one hand and stuffed animals in the other, she shrugged.

We hugged them, thanked my parents, who said they'd already texted Olivia the hotel address, since they knew I "sucked" at phones.

Once they practically shoved us out the door, we both stood awkwardly, waiting for the other to speak. When we did, our questions spilled out at the same time.

"Should we—"

"Want to—"

I laughed. "You go."

"I was going to ask if we should take your car?" Her ears were tinged with pink. Was she embarrassed?

"Sure, I can drive. Want to plug in the address on the GPS? You're better at that than me."

"You're not wrong there. I bet you haven't even used the GPS yet."

"Haven't had a reason to. I have a sophisticated navigation system right up here," I said, pointing to my head.

"Right..." She hopped in the passenger seat and typed in the address as I stowed the bags. With one last peek toward the door, where I caught both my parents spying on us, I pulled out and onto the main road.

"This place is something," Olivia said as she checked out our room. With a pinched expression on her face, she picked up a bottle of sparkling wine that was already chilling in a plastic ice bucket and peeked at the label. "Where did your parents find this place?"

"No clue. Knowing them, they had a discount from AARP." Goddamn, I should have thought to ask about the hotel. I'd bet this was my father's doing. He was always looking to save a buck. My mother would never book a place like this.

Situated right next to a truck stop off the interstate, The Cozy Inn and Suites looked more like Bates Motel if it were abandoned for fifteen years. The lobby "concierge" spotted us wheeling our luggage onto the chipped tile floor and spent twenty minutes trying to sell us a time-share in Albuquerque. Once he admitted defeat, he handed us our key card along with a complimentary honeymoon gift bag. I peeked inside—it was mostly full of lube and sketchy twenty-four hour energy tablets.

"This place is a disaster." I sniffed the air and covered my face with my palm. "And what in God's name is that smell?"

"Yeah, it's pretty bad." Her eyes widened. "Wait, hand me that bag."

"You mean the bag full of scented lube? Wait, don't tell me you're going to spread that around as an air freshener." I thought about it. "Actually that's not a bad idea. Here, pass me some."

"Seriously?" She shook her head and sifted through the bag, pulling out a small metal jar candle. "I thought I saw this when we peeked inside." She dug around some more. "And they even thought of matches."

"What's the scent?" I asked. She checked, snorted and tossed it at me. I caught it and read the sticky label. "'Cream pie scented massage oil candle.' Wow... subtle." I took a whiff. "Thankfully, it smells like the baked good... not the other kind."

"Wes!" She grabbed a packet of lube and tossed it at me, laughing. God, I fucking loved her laugh. I'd make sure she laughed every single day.

"So what do you think, Tiger? Should we tempt fate and stay? I'd bet there's a fifty-fifty chance we'll contract a deadly disease and die... but hey, at least we'd have each other. Solidarity and all."

"I'm not sure I'm ready to die... especially not from a deadly disease. But it's getting late and I really don't feel like getting back in the car." I followed her gaze to the queen-sized bed in the center of the room. "I just realized there's only one bed. That should be..." She paused. "Interesting."

"You don't hog the blankets, do you?" I sat on the edge of the bed and smirked.

"No! I bet you do though." I laughed as she huffed, coming around to feel the flat pillows. "I guess we should start getting used to sleeping together. Might as well start tonight."

"Sleeping together? Getting straight to the point, aren't you? I figured I'd at least wine and dine you first. Was it the cream pie candle that got you all hot and bothered?"

Lucky for me, the closest object in her vicinity was only a pillow. She tossed it at my head and said, "On second thought, the floor is looking pretty comfortable for you. Just ignore that questionable sticky spot over there."

"Aw, Tiger, you wouldn't make me sleep on the cold, hard floor on our wedding night. I promise, I'll be good."

She crossed her arms. "You better or I'll find a creative way to utilize that candle wax."

I smirked again. "Don't threaten me with a good time." She huffed a breath and grabbed her phone, typing on the screen. "What are you looking up?"

"The nearest place to get alcohol... That bottle over there won't be enough."

I looked over the bed again, knowing my body would take up more than half of the thing. Yup, alcohol was a great plan. Too bad there was no way I'd lower my inhibitions. Not this time.

Chapter 21

Olivia

Lucky for us there was a bar on the other side of the truck stop. Head held high, I hauled ass across the crumbling gravel.

"Slow down, Tiger. You're going to get run over by a semi. The bar isn't going anywhere."

It may not be going anywhere but the longer I was alone with Wes, thinking about that kiss, the more I itched to touch him. Which was entirely inappropriate considering he was my boss. My boss, my friend, and this was all fake. So very fake. *Keep telling yourself that.*

I paused when I reached my target, but it looked different from the Google listing. Wes caught up and stopped at my side.

"Is this The Cozy Inn and Suites' shameful cousin? Because judging from the outside, I'm pretty sure anything we consume in there will give us hepatitis." He looked at the entrance. "There's no sign. Maybe the listing is old?"

"There's a neon beer sign over there." I pointed toward the only sign glowing in the window.

"You mean, EER?" he asked. "What if they mean ear—" He tugged my ear lobe. "—and are terrible at spelling. We could be walking straight into a house of horrors."

"I'm going to pretend you didn't just bring up cannibalism on our wedding night." I hesitated, searching for the right words to describe the dilapidated structure in front of us. "Just because the place is in need of a facelift, doesn't mean we won't have fun. Don't be a snob. I bet it's fine."

I took another glance at the neon sign and walked inside. Wes huffed behind me and grabbed the door to hold it open. I wouldn't admit this to him, but I'd only ever been to a handful of bars in my lifetime. Drinking was a newly acquired... What should I call it? Hobby? One that I didn't intend to pursue much further unless the situation called for my brain to go on autopilot.

Although I had few examples for comparison, this place seemed like your average dive bar. Scuffed dark floors that looked like they hadn't seen the wet end of a mop in a decade. Dim lighting from a few dusty overhead fixtures. Behind the bar, a boxy TV played a NASCAR race with the volume turned all the way up. Which would have been fine, if the revving of engines wasn't competing with a twangy country song coming from overhead speakers. Ten or so people, mostly men, sat at the bar with drinks and plates of food in front of them, while another group was midway through a game of pool. They looked harmless enough but the muscles in my chest decided to tense anyway.

Wes placed a palm on my lower back, clearly sensing my sudden unease. His lips grazed against my ear. "We can always grab a few beers from the gas station and hang out in the room?"

The heat of his warm palm burned through the thin material of my dress. His touch put me at ease and the way he drew slow circles with his fingertips had me taking in a strangled breath. "I'm fine."

We took two empty stools at the corner of the bar, somewhat away from the other patrons. I'd been so busy internalizing my feelings that I hadn't noticed how frazzled Wes seemed until we sat down with sticky plastic-covered menus in front of us.

"What's up? You look like someone kicked your dog."

He set his attention back on me and clenched his jaw. "I don't know. We've been joking around and that's great but I feel like shit that this night is a disaster. Look at this dump. You shouldn't have to eat here."

I fiddled with the edge of the menu and thought of what to say. He was right about how we've been joking around and teasing, but that was us. Or at least that's how we've always been. As much as I was starting to trust him, there were layers to me that I haven't shown. Hiding behind jokes made it easier to feel normal.

"This isn't your fault and honestly even if you did book this on your own, I'd still be grateful," I said.

"Grateful? That guy over there just farted louder than the TV. Tiger, this place... That hotel... You deserve so much better. I can give you better." He glanced over his shoulder toward the door. "If we leave now, we can find a decent restaurant on the way home."

Maybe I was nuts, but I was tired of fancy restaurants and luxury hotels. I wanted real. Wes may have seen this place as a dump, and yeah it was run down, but I saw the beauty in all its flaws.

"How about a game?" I asked. He raised his brow and scrubbed a hand over his scruff.

"You're avoiding my suggestion," he said as he cocked his head. I shrugged and offered a half smile that had him huffing. "What kind of game? And don't say Spades. I'm not falling for your so-called beginners luck again."

"Do you see me busting out a deck of cards?" He narrowed his eyes, like I could be hiding cards in my nonexistent bra. "Not cards. It's a game I used to play with my sister when we were bored at our parent's parties. Do you know the kids game, Guess Who?"

"Guess Who? Yeah, the one where you ask yes or no questions?"

"Exactly. So we each pick a person, but be sneaky about it! Don't let me see you staring." He chuckled and shook his head.

"I'm serious, it'll be fun. Pick a person and I'll ask yes or no questions to see if I can guess who it is."

"This place is like ninety percent old dudes," he said. He stared off for a moment before asking, "What do I get if I win?"

"The pleasure of my company."

"Tempting, but I think you can do better." He stretched his arms and rested one on the back of my stool.

"Okay." I paused to think. "How about whoever loses has to answer questions about themselves?"

The bartender, probably the only other woman in the room from what I could tell, finally greeted us. She looked rough around the edges, like she'd seen her fair share of shit in her forty or so years and it made her stronger. "What can I get you two?"

"Two beers, whatever you recommend," I said. Wes covered his hand with mine on top of the bar and cut in.

"One beer actually. I'll take a Coke."

"Sounds good," she said and turned to get our drinks.

"You're not drinking?" I asked.

"Nah, I'm not in the mood."

Interesting.

"You're a mysterious guy sometimes, Wesley Reed." I glanced down at his hand resting on top of mine and smiled. "So, our game? Do you accept the conditions?"

"I accept. No cheating this time."

"You'll never let me live that game of Spades down will you? I swear I didn't cheat."

The bartender brought our drinks and we ordered a plate of wings and fries, figuring deep fried food had less of a chance at being undercooked. Wes's theory, not mine. Once she walked toward the kitchen, Wes leaned in close and brushed my hair off my shoulder. The graze of his calloused fingertips against my bare shoulder lit a heated path along my skin.

For the second time that evening, he brought his lips to my ear, his voice a throaty whisper that had me inching closer. I angled my body until our knees touched. "You ready, Tiger? Because I have so many questions."

All I managed to say in reply was a breathy, "Yeah?"

"Oh, yeah. I'm ready to win. Go ahead, ask me a question." I swallowed and reached for my beer, putting a few inches of space between us again. I hadn't picked my target yet, but as I glanced around I noticed a man sitting alone. His shirt said something about grandkids, but I couldn't read it without staring. I knew better than to pick someone with features that stood out. This man was perfect.

I sipped my beer and asked the standard first question, although I was pretty sure I knew the answer. "Is your person a man?"

"Playing the long game, good call," he said. "Yes, he's a man." I nodded and he snuck a look around the room. "Is your person old?"

"How am I supposed to answer that? Old is relative. You're old compared to me."

"I'm older than you, but I'm not old, Tiger. You know what I mean but I'll rephrase—"

"No, no. No rephrasing. You already used your question."

"Such a stickler for rules." He laughed and sipped his Coke. "Go ahead and answer the question then."

"No." I smirked and raised a brow. That would throw him off. Yeah, he was old compared to us, but compared to say... the president, my pick was a spring chicken.

"You're up to no good again," he said. "I swear you made the same face during Spades."

I shrugged, sipping my beer. "Okay, my turn." I glanced around the room and zeroed in on a guy in a camo trucker style hat. From what I could see there were only two other guys in hats, so that would narrow it down. "Is your person wearing a hat?"

"There's no way you're not cheating." He leaned back in his stool, stretching his legs.

"How could I be cheating? I'm not a mind reader." I followed his gaze toward one of the younger guys at the pool table. He wore a baseball cap and Miami Dolphins shirt. *Bingo.* "So is that a yes?"

"Yeah, he has a hat." He grumbled while the waitress dropped off the plates. All of a sudden my stomach rumbled. Food poisoning be damned, I was going for those wings. Wes turned the plate so most of the food was on my side. "Eat up, Tiger."

We took a few minutes to polish off some food. For a dive bar, the wings weren't bad. I finished my first beer and ordered another, feeling that comfortable warmth spread throughout my limbs.

"I think it was my turn," Wes said. "Let's see..." He looked around, paying extra attention to the group of guys at the pool table. I couldn't blame him, since they were getting rowdy. He nodded his head toward a guy with black hair and tattoos. "How about that guy?"

"That's not a yes or no question. Who's cheating now?"

"You got me there," he said.

"He's not my guy, to answer your question. And I think I know yours."

"Oh, really? Let's see then."

I made a show of tapping my nose and looking around the room, until I inched closer and said, "Baseball cap and Dolphins shirt."

"Witchcraft." He chuckled. "That's the only explanation."

"Or how about the fact that you were staring the guy down. Your poker face sucks, Reed."

"Reed? So now we're calling each other last names? I could call you Reed too, you know. *Mrs. Reed.*" Blood rushed to the tips of my ears. "You're blushing, *Mrs. Reed.*"

"Okay, point taken," I said, looking away from his heated gaze. "Let me think of a good question."

He picked up a fry and dipped it in ketchup. "Go ahead. You and your cheating earned it."

There were so many things I wanted to ask him. His past was a mystery to me and I knew he kept certain parts of himself guarded. I could relate. I took another sip of my liquid courage, licking a drop from my bottom lip. Wes's stormy eyes followed the movement of my tongue and lingered on my lips until I felt myself squirm from the attention.

"Tell me about your first girlfriend."

He told me about his secret fling with his best friend's older cousin during the summer between junior and senior year of high school. How he followed her around like a puppy for a month until his friend found out and kicked his ass.

"Dylan was pissed. Not at her of course, just me. So anyway, I started my senior year friendless and single. Wasn't the highest point of my teen years. Thankfully Dylan realized he was being a dick and apologized. We made a pact that family members were off-limits, and if I fucked up again he'd hit on my mom." He shook his head and let out a dry laugh.

"You know what they say..." He quirked a brow. "Bros be-fore—actually, I kind of hate that phrase." I expected him to laugh but he stared absently at a spot on the wall. "So are you and Dylan still friends? I'd love to meet him."

"I—uh..." Wes pushed up from the stool and gave the bar top a tap. "I'm going to use the bathroom and check on Sunshine real quick. You going to be okay?" He tilted his chin toward a hall in the back, which I only assumed led to the bathrooms.

"Oh, yeah. Of course. I'll be here." He got up and walked over without another word.

Weird.

While I waited, I flagged the waitress and ordered another beer. Might as well keep drinking while I figured out how I could have offended him.

As the waitress dropped off my drink, I glanced to my left where Dolphins shirt guy and his tattooed friend were leaning against the bar ordering whiskeys. Dolphin guy spotted me looking at them and his lips spread into a crooked grin. As quick as I could, I turned my head in the opposite direction, clutching my beer close to my chest.

Alarm bells reverberated through my head, mixing with the sounds of their raucous laughter. I pulled my phone from my purse and opened Instagram to give myself something to look at.

"Can we buy you a drink, gorgeous?" His voice slid over my skin like a thick oil. Against my better judgment, I looked up from my phone and saw that it was Dolphins shirt talking to me. They'd come closer, close enough that I could see their glazed eyes and foreheads beaded with moisture.

"No thanks, I'm good." I pursed my lips into a tight smile and lifted my half-full beer to make my point before going back to scrolling Instagram.

"What's the matter? Don't like what you see up close?" he added. "I know you've been watching me all night. Me and my friend."

I huffed, not giving them the satisfaction of looking up. My skin crawled as the tattooed one stepped closer.

"That's right. And we like to take turns, don't we, Brian?"

I took a deep breath and faced him. "What's your problem?"

Dolphins shirt, aka Brian, took a step closer. "My problem is that you've been eye fucking me all night and now you're acting like a little cocktease in that dress."

My limbs trembled as adrenaline flooded my system. *Get the hell out of there.* I grabbed the strap of my purse and pushed out of my stool. Where the hell was Wes?

"Don't worry, our friend is taking care of your cripple boyfriend," tattoo guy said as he moved closer. "Come with us. We promise you'll have a good time." He reached out and groped my shoulder, pulling on the thin strap of my dress.

"No, I'm good." I shrugged away and searched the room. If they meant what they said, Wes could be in trouble. "Leave me alone."

"Fine, we'll go." Brian raised his hands in defeat and I finally felt air reach my chest. I took a step away from them so I could get Wes and get the hell out of there, but Brian grabbed my arm and yanked me toward him. "We'll go... after you suck our cocks in the parking lot." I pulled away, flinching from the bite of his fingertips into my skin. "And if you even try to scream right now, Mike will make sure your boyfriend watches."

"Hel—" Mike slapped his salty palm over my mouth and the full gravity of my situation washed over me. This was happening. *Again.*

The deafening buzz in my ears replaced their snickering voices as they pulled me toward the door. My limbs were nothing but phantom parts. Why couldn't I do something? Fight them off? Once they had me outside, it was over.

"Get your fucking hands off my wife."

Chapter 22

Wes

"YOU HEARD ME. STEP away from my wife." I clenched my fists, ready to strike if those motherfuckers didn't back off. The tattooed one slipped his hand off Olivia's mouth and she whimpered my name.

That was all I needed to hear.

Red hot rage pulsed through me and all thoughts left my mind except for one.

Pain.

I stepped closer, grabbing the nearest bar stool, and they shoved Olivia aside.

"Hey man, it's all good." The tattooed one backed away with his hands raised. Smart guy had a shred of self-preservation. "Brian, let's go. Lenny just started another round."

"Nah. I'm not in the mood for pool." The scumbag in the hat glanced at Olivia and smirked. "This one promised us something. Isn't that right?"

"Fuck you," Olivia spat.

He laughed and reached for an empty tumbler. "Come closer, cripple. I'd love to see how many hits it takes to break this glass on your face."

"I don't think you want to do that."

He laughed again. Such a cocky bastard. "And why not? What? You going to beat me up with your fake leg?" He turned toward Olivia again. "You must love to fuck that stump, don't you? Kinky bit—"

Before he could finish speaking, I swung the barstool against his knees and he lurched forward. I took advantage of his compromised position and brought the stool up again, this time smashing it against his back. When I stepped away, he crawled to his knees.

"Fuck yeah, cripple!" He let out a maniacal laugh that seemed to beckon his friends. "Let's do this."

That was when all hell broke loose. Shouts bounced through the room while a group of men surrounded me. Olivia screamed. The same man who alerted me in the bathroom came to my side. Between the pounding of my pulse and my rage clouded vision, it was as if all the movement happened at half speed. I stood to my full height, readying the stool to strike, when the sound of a gun cocking broke through my haze.

"Not in my bar, motherfuckers!" The bartender held her shotgun, pointing it toward us. "Brian, Mike, Lenny... You all get the hell out of here. Brian, your uncle will hear about this!"

"Simmer down, Shelly. We have it taken care of. No need to tell him." Brian grabbed a stool and pushed himself up, wiping fluids off his mouth. "We're leaving."

The place grew silent except for the blaring TV and the scraping of stools. I finally blinked and looked around, noticing that every single person in the place was standing at attention, clutching something in their hands. My gaze reached Olivia's and a breath whooshed out of me.

"You both pay and get outta here, too. I don't want any more trouble." The bartender looked at Olivia directly. "You should know better than to go to bars dressed like that."

Olivia's mouth gaped open and she hung her head. I wanted to yell on her behalf, to hit someone else. But I pulled her against my chest and wrapped my arms around her. *Thank God.* As I breathed her in, relief flooded my system.

"Did you call the cops?" I managed to whisper although my throat was clogged with emotion.

"Not yet. My phone's over there." She gestured toward the bar with her chin.

I nodded. "Grab your stuff. I'll pay, and as soon as they step outside, we'll call."

We waited the few minutes until the group of offenders walked through the door, urged on by the shotgun still clutched in Shelly's grip. My body prickled with awareness, clocking every move around us. Olivia called the cops, while I kept a protective arm around her waist.

"You two okay?" I turned to face the voice, coming face to face with the older man who got my attention in the bathroom. He looked to be in his early sixties. He wore a shirt that listed all the names of his grandkids.

"I think so," I said. "Thank you for having my back. I don't even want to think about what would have happened if you didn't get me."

He smiled at Olivia, who was still on the phone. "I would have stepped in myself, but I had hip surgery not too long ago. Too many years behind the wheel. Glad I could help, though. I've seen those fools in here a few times. Their uncle owns the bar. He oughta be behind bars, if you ask me."

"Yeah, my wife is on the phone with the police."

"Good. Well, if you need me to leave a statement, I'll be over there for another hour or so." He pointed to a booth across the room.

We shook hands and he walked off as Olivia finished her call. "Well, that was frustrating."

"Are they coming?" I asked.

"They said they'd get a patrol car out here but since it's not an emergency, it may take a while."

"That's bullshit," I said. My jaw ached from clenching it and a headache made its way from my shoulders up the base of my neck. "What should we do? I'll wait for them all night if you want."

I followed her wide-eyed gaze to Shelly's shotgun leaning against the bottle-lined shelf. "Let's just go. By the time the cops get here those guys will be long gone."

Cupping her chin, I angled her face toward mine. Staring at the gun wouldn't help either of us. Neither would sitting here replaying the past twenty minutes in our minds. Guilt was already clawing its way through my gut. "I'm sorry. Fuck. I'm so sorry that I let them touch you."

I was too busy being sad in the bathroom while the woman I'd sworn to protect above all else was in danger. There were too many close calls. What if that guy hadn't warned me when he did? What if I couldn't have taken down the asshat they sent to the bathroom?

I forced myself to breathe Olivia in while I brushed my fingertips over her soft skin. A tear spilled from the corner of her eye, trailing down the apple of her cheek and onto the pad of my finger. I swiped the moisture away but it kept coming.

I wanted to kiss her tears away. Taste the salt she shed while I whispered promises of safety. Hold her until she knew in her bones that I'd never let anything happen to her.

But I stepped away and wrapped her trembling hand in mine. "I've got you. Come on, let's go to bed."

Chapter 23

Wes

I DIDN'T TAKE ANY chances while we walked the short way back to the hotel. Olivia shined her flashlight ahead of us and I clenched an empty beer bottle, ready to use it as a weapon if I needed to. Thankfully, we made it back to the room in one piece and locked every lock on the door.

"This room feels like a palace compared to that bar," I said, trying to break the tension. I sat on the edge of the bed and patted the spot beside me. "Come sit. You're shaking."

"Just the adrenaline," she said, sitting beside me. "It'll wear off."

I yanked the comforter out from under her and wrapped it around her shoulders. "Do you want to talk about what happened?" I asked.

She shook her head. "I'm fine."

"You're not and neither am I." I groaned and reached down to take off my shoes. She followed the movement with her eyes.

"I'm sorry about what they said. You know, about your leg."

Tossing my shoes aside, I leaned back on my elbows. "Don't worry about that, Tiger. I've heard much worse."

"That's horrible. Why are people so awful?" She wrapped a strand of hair around her finger and chewed her lip.

"Not all. Unfortunately, assholes make up the loudest of the bunch." I pushed up and grabbed the now warm bottle of sparkling wine from the bucket of melted ice. "Drink?"

"Why not?" she said. "My nerves could use it." I twisted the cap and brought the bottle over. We took turns sipping in silence.

"Earlier, when you went to the bathroom," she started. I knew where the question was headed. "Did I say something that bothered you?"

I took another swig and passed it to her. No time like our wedding night for a load of trauma dumping. "No, Tiger. You didn't upset me."

She swallowed a sip. "What was it then? I could see the change in your expression. Your whole body sagged."

"It's a long story, but Dylan—my best friend—he died about eight years ago. It's been a while since I've talked about him." Even saying his name out loud again brought too many feelings to the front of my mind.

"I'm sorry," she murmured. "You must miss him so much." I cleared my throat and she passed me the almost empty bottle.

"I do. He was more like a brother to me than a friend. He loved the shit out of Lilly too, even if he only got to be her uncle for a short time." I thought about how Dylan always gave her piggy back rides and brought her toys even when we told him she had too many. He was one of the only people who didn't give me shit for marrying Sav when I was nineteen. He'd do the same in my situation.

"I bet she loved him." Olivia smiled softly and reached out her hand. I went to hand her back the bottle, but she reached past it, settling her palm on my forearm. I stared at the plain gold band, an heirloom from my mother, and my chest swelled.

"Yeah. Everyone who knew him loved him." I played with the ring, running my fingertip over the band. "You need a better ring than this."

"Changing the subject?" she asked.

"No, not really. Just saying."

"I like this ring. It's simple and it was your mom's, but if you want to buy me something else I won't object. Seems silly though." She reached for the bottle and took a long sip.

"Silly?"

"Yeah, no reason to buy a big diamond when this isn't even real, right?" She shrugged and put the empty bottle on the floor. "Anytime you want to talk about Dylan, I'm here. We're friends. And about earlier, I'm fine. Or at least I will be. I've handled worse and lived through it." My stomach bottomed out and I grimaced, not knowing how to respond. She climbed up on wobbly feet and stretched. "I'm going to take a shower. Hopefully it's at least clean-ish in there. Be right back."

She grabbed a few items from her bag, walked into the bathroom and closed the door behind her.

I sat there stewing in my thoughts. One part of me wanted to barge into the bathroom, yank the shower curtain open, and show her how not fake this was for me while the other part wanted to curl up in a ball and forget this day ever existed. What I felt for her got more and more real everyday, but clearly she didn't feel the same way. The last thing she needed tonight was another man mauling her like a fucking horny bastard anyway. *Fine* may be her favorite word, but one look and I knew she was anything but.

I pulled out my phone charger and checked my phone for messages before plugging it in. As I lifted my eyes from the screen, Olivia came into the room in another of those tiny tank tops and shorts. Her hair dripped water onto the front of the fabric, making a wet spot spread right above her tits. Because of course that would happen. When she caught me staring, she cleared her throat.

"Shower's not too bad, it you need one." I did, but I didn't want to grab my seat from the car. Probably should have thought of that when we carried the bags inside. I remembered my crutches though.

"I'll just wash up. I can shower in the morning."

"Okay." She bent down to grab her charger from her bag, and the curve of her ass peeked from the bottom of her shorts. Fuck.

Why did she have to have such an amazing body? "Have you heard from your parents?"

"Yeah, my mom texted. All is well." I ran a hand through my hair, releasing it from the hair tie. "I'll go use the bathroom now."

Leaning on the edge of the vanity, I gave myself a pep talk. *Do not look at her body. It's sleep time. That's all.* I splashed water on my face and ran a brush through my hair before retying it up. As I brushed my teeth, I thought about her lips and how fucking good she tasted. How she moaned when my tongue touched hers. Shit, now my cock was hard as a rock. I couldn't go out there like that.

But after five minutes of willing my brain to think of other things, it was no use. This night was the definition of whiplash, and apparently even my dick was confused.

I opened the door, and thank God, she'd turned off the lights except for a small table lamp on the nightstand. "How's the bed?"

"Scratchy and lumpy, but could be worse." She pulled the comforter up to her chest and sighed.

I plopped on the bed and laid on top of the blankets. "You forgot to mention the musty smell."

"I was trying to think of the positives." She rolled to face me, but I knew if I looked at her gorgeous face in the dim light I'd lose any hope of calming my dick down. Instead, I tried to find shapes in the popcorn ceiling. "You didn't change?"

"I usually sleep in my boxers," I said. "I figured that would make you uncomfortable." I focused extra hard on the ceiling and finally found a menacing looking face in the bumps.

"Oh." She fidgeted beside me, moving her legs under the blanket. "You should get comfortable. Seriously, however you normally sleep is fine with me." I huffed a laugh. "What? I'm serious! And get under the covers, you're being a weirdo."

"Fine, but turn off the light."

She reached over and clicked the light off, blanketing the room in darkness, except for the occasional flashes of headlights from the interstate peeking through the curtains.

"Better?" she asked.

"Yup." I pulled my shirt off and tossed it on the floor first, then hesitated.

"Do you normally sleep with your prosthesis on?"

"Depends," I said. It had been years since anyone other than my family and doctors had seen me without my prosthesis. Not since right after the accident, but even then, I rarely left the house. It took years for me to gain a small fraction of my confidence back.

"Wes," she said softly, settling her palm on my bicep. "I want you to be comfortable. Please."

Fuck. She sounded so damn sweet and her hand on my arm was too distracting. "I normally take it off."

"I thought so," she said. "Do you need any help?"

Not with my leg. I smirked and shook my head. "I've got it." I tried not to let those fuckwads words get into my head as I sat up and pulled it off. Olivia tried to pretend she wasn't watching me, but I could see her glance over every few seconds.

"Does it ever hurt?" Her soft voice broke through my thoughts.

"Sometimes. My hips and back hurt a lot after long hours at work but as far as my residual limb goes, I don't have as much pain there anymore. It took a bunch of adjustments to my prosthesis to get the right fit." I slipped my liner off and ran my hand over my scars, massaging the area gently. Sometimes I needed that reconnection after wearing my prosthesis for a long time. Finally, I slid my shorts down and added them to the pile on the floor.

"Better?"

"Much," I said with a sigh.

"Wes? You said Dylan passed eight years ago?"

"I did," I answered, wondering where she was going with the question.

She rolled onto her side and propped her arm under her pillow. "Wasn't your accident eight years ago?"

"It was." My throat dried up. After the night we'd had I didn't think I could talk about the accident. Not fully. It was as if I could hear her thoughts. Sense the questions forming on the tip of her tongue. "Goodnight, Tiger."

"Oh," she said. "I'm keeping you up. Sorry." Bright lights from trucks passing by the window flashed by. I closed my tired eyes against the glare and felt myself drifting. "Goodnight, Wes. Thank you."

Chapter 24

Olivia

Wes's back muscles rose and fell in a steady rhythm, which made the tattoo stretching from his shoulder to the middle of his back seem to move. Fitting that the ink swirled in a wave-like pattern. With each peaceful breath he took, I itched to trace my fingers along the lines.

No matter how tight I shut my eyes or how many times I rolled from side to side, sleep evaded me. It wasn't abnormal for me to have problems sleeping. It was a lingering effect of PTSD, or so my doctors said. My body was heavy with exhaustion, so why couldn't my mind get the memo?

Wes murmured in his sleep and I sat up to peer over at him. It was truly unfair how attractive he was. And sleep only softened his features. I flopped back down and faced the other direction with a huff. "Freaking bed," I muttered.

"Why are you flopping around like a fish?" I startled from the break in the silence. The bed creaked as he rolled toward me.

"Shit, I'm sorry I woke you."

"Come here."

"What?"

"Nevermind," he said, his voice extra gravelly from sleep. He scooted closer and wrapped his massive arm around me, pulling me against his chest.

"What are you—"

"I'm cuddling you, Tiger." He slid his other hand under my pillow and tucked his chin above my head. Instead of relaxing into him, my body decided to become a wooden board.

"I don't cuddle," I said. Which wasn't the whole truth. I'd cuddled Alex before, but that was obviously different.

"Then what do you call what we're doing right now?"

"A human straightjacket?" He chuckled and his chest shook. "Is your plan to gorilla hug me to sleep?" I asked.

"If that's what it takes." I wiggled and adjusted my pillow, letting myself get used to the feel of his arm draped over my waist like a weighted blanket. His warmth sank into my skin, and after a few minutes I realized that my shoulders weren't touching my ears. "You done squirming yet?"

"I think so." Was I? Maybe. But being in Wes's arms made me feel equal parts relaxed and hyperaware at the same time. I didn't know what to do with my hands, so I laid them against my side.

"Good. Get some sleep." He cleared his throat and whispered, "And maybe try not to grind your ass into me like that."

"What? Oh God, sorry!" I started to scoot away but he held me steady. Another of his sleepy chuckles rumbled against my ear and he inched closer until my back was pinned flat against his torso. He stroked my arm with his long fingers, up and down, sending electric tingles in their path.

"Shh, relax, Tiger. I'm just playing with you." I'd relax if my nipples weren't aching pebbles. I closed my eyes and focused on the drag of his calloused fingertips along my sensitive skin. How it felt incredible when he touched me like that. I hadn't been touched in so long. Behind my closed lids, I pictured him trailing lower, tracing the curve of my hip with his strong hands, dipping down to where I throbbed. Pressing into my wet heat. Could he feel my heart hammering against his chest? "Better now?"

"Mhm," I lied. I'd never fall asleep this wound up.

"Goodnight, wife," he whispered and tucked his hand under my arm. *Wife.* I didn't think I'd ever get used to that.

I tripped over an action figure left on the living room floor and cursed under my breath. The worst part was that I couldn't even scold Alex, since his cast made it difficult to clean up fallen Christmas toys.

"Where do you want these stockings?" Mia asked, holding our empty Christmas stockings.

"There's a bin. Let me grab it." I hustled into my bedroom closet and grabbed the red plastic bin I'd bought to store our new Christmas decor. "Why does it feel like there was so much less when I was putting it up?"

"No clue, but don't worry, we'll get it all down before Shawn and Wes get back with the truck." Mia still sounded mopey. I'm pretty sure she was experiencing the stages of grief since I gave her the news that she'd missed my wedding. If only I could tell her that the whole thing was fake, but I couldn't risk her telling my parents.

"I appreciate your help, sis." I dropped a few plastic ornaments into the bin. "Between the Christmas exhaustion and taking care of Alex, I haven't had a chance to get things ready for move in day."

"I'm always here to help. When you let me," she added under her breath. I sighed and went back to taking down the rest of our three foot mini-tree. I'd already apologized and given her gifts, there wasn't much else I could do other than let time heal that wound.

"Are you sure Shawn didn't mind helping today? He's been a lifesaver, building the bunk bed and loading his truck. I'm so grateful."

"It's fine," she said, avoiding my gaze.

"Okay, well, in case I don't say it enough today, thank him again." I grabbed the last ornament from the tree and picked it up along with the full bin. "I'm going to go put these in the storage shed on the side of the house. Be right back."

"I can do it," Mia said, taking everything from me. "Go ahead and finish in your room."

She was right, I still needed to make room in my closet for Wes's clothes. Luckily I didn't have much furniture in there as it was, so it shouldn't feel too cluttered once he added whatever he was bringing.

I couldn't believe Wes and Lilly were moving into my small place. We'd be working together, eating together, sleeping together... Not in *that* way, although all week I'd stared at the left side of my bed imagining him there. But was I prepared for tornado Wes twenty-four hours a day?

My chest tightened and I paced my room, ruminating about all the changes.

Single parent to having a partner.

One kid to two.

Doing things how and when I wanted, to having to make decisions together.

Oh, God. I think I made a mistake.

"Mom," Alex peeked in, resting his crutch against my door frame. "When is my sister getting here?"

Just like that, the spiral stopped. Alex wanted this. He was happy, even if he wouldn't admit it. I could tell. Call it motherly instinct.

"You like calling her that, huh?" I said with a smile.

"I'm getting used to it. It's not a big deal, Mom."

"Alright, Mr. Eye Roll. She'll be here soon. Did you do as I asked and make room in the closet?"

"Yup. But Mom, how are we going to fit her desk in there and all her stuff?"

Fair question. "Once Shawn and Wes get back, we'll get it all set up. Don't worry. Why don't you go hang out on the couch with Aunt Mia while I finish in here."

I watched him make his way down the hallway, asking myself the same question. This would make for an interesting day.

"Six boxes of cookbooks?" I double-checked my counting and scrunched my nose at Wes. "Does anyone need that many cookbooks?"

"It's not about need," he said. "I collect them."

"You realize that you can pull up any recipe in the world on your handy-dandy iPhone now?" He met my gaze with a glare. "Okay, well what about this box?" I pointed to an open box filled to the brim with license plates. "I'm honestly questioning if you're a criminal now."

"They're vanity plates that I've *bought*. I didn't steal them off peoples cars." He crossed his arms. "What? You're telling me you don't collect anything?"

I picked up a rusty Florida plate and shrugged. "Not since I was a kid. I don't like clutter."

"But it's not clutter if it makes you happy." I watched with a raised brow as he lovingly stroked the outside of a box.

"Would you like some time alone with your boxes?"

He picked his hand up and smirked. "Funny."

"Okay, how about this? For now, we put all of this," I fanned my hand at the dozen or so boxes filled with Wes's collectibles, "in the storage shed."

He rubbed his chin and finally huffed in agreement. "But first thing tomorrow we need to buy a dehumidifier and air purifier to go in there."

"Deal," I said while mentally thanking whatever higher power being saved me from having to stare at a wall of hideous license plates.

He stretched his arms above his head with a groan. "I'll go check in on the kids and see if they're ready for bed before I shower. You need anything from the kitchen?"

"I'm fine." I pushed a box against the wall and yawned. My muscles were screaming at me to relax, but there was so much left to do to get this place organized. I stood up from my stooped position to find Wes watching me with his arms crossed. "What?"

"We've been at it since seven this morning. Let's call it a night. We have work tomorrow and then Alex's appointment."

"But it's a mess," I groaned.

"And it's not going anywhere. Come on, you go shower first. You'll feel better." He pressed his palm against my lower back and gave me a small push toward our en suite bathroom, where yet another unpacked box waited for me.

"I forgot about this box. Where are we going to fit anymore stuff in here? What time does Target close? Maybe I can go pick up some more shelves." I poked around the bathroom, taking mental measurements.

"My suggestion is still on the table," Wes said. "You know you want to."

"Absolutely not. We're not moving into a bigger house." He's brought up his *suggestion* everyday since we got married. And yeah, it would be nice to have more space, but why would I uproot Alex and get him used to that, just for us to have to move again in six months?

"We could find a place with double sinks in the bathroom," he teased. "And extra closets."

That did sound amazing but I'd stay strong. "As much as I'd love that, no. I can barely afford the rent on this place and I already told you I didn't want to have to move Alex again."

"Money isn't an issue. If we need more space, I'll take care of it."

"Wes," I narrowed my eyes at his stupidly handsome, smirking face but decided I was too tired to argue. Instead, I sighed and pushed the box aside so I could shower.

"No argument? You're getting soft on me, Tiger." He chuckled and added, "I'll start looking for bigger places."

I pulled my hair tie out and started the water, ignoring his comment. If he wanted to I wouldn't stop him, but there was no way I'd move.

"Oh and I forgot to tell you, Shawn said he'd help me go through my storage room and load the truck up."

Wait, was I hearing him correctly? "You're telling me you have more stuff?"

"Yeah. Did you think this was everything?"

Oh, hell no.

"Let's talk about this later." Steam fogged up the glass shower door and I couldn't wait for the hot water to hit my tired muscles. Wes cleared his throat and walked out, hopefully to go check on the kids.

I closed the bathroom door, pulled off my sweaty clothes, pushed Wes's teakwood shower bench back, and stepped into the blissfully hot water. Damn I was tightly wound. This entire day had been more than a reality check. I'd call it a reality smack to the face.

Wes's bench caught my eye again, along with his body wash. Without thinking, I opened it and took a whiff. My whole bedroom would smell like this now... Like him.

My face flushed as I pictured him soaping up his tight abs, grazing his hand lower until he teased the base of his cock. I squeezed a small amount of it into my hand and lathered it into my skin, copying the path I'd imagine him taking. Hot water pulsed against my sensitive nipples and I opened my eyes with a frustrated huff.

I needed a release and there was no way I'd ask Wes to help me out with my predicament. Not like he'd want to, anyway. Grabbing the shower head, I eyed his bench. It felt wrong to sit on it to get myself off, but God, I was exhausted.

I sat and twisted the setting until it reached the perfect amount of pulsing pressure. With my legs spread, I slowly lowered it until the spray hit my clit just right. It felt so good, I knew I could get there fast. I let my head fall back against the cool tile and closed my eyes, focusing on the building tension wrapping itself around my muscles. The water pounded against my sensitive clit as I climbed higher and higher. I rocked my hips, grinding the head against me and moving it in a circular motion. *Yes.* Wes would work me like this. I knew it. He'd talk me through it, calling me his Tiger while his dark eyes devoured me.

I was so close. *Right there*. My legs shook, my pussy spasmed, and the mounting tension snapped as a wave of euphoria washed over me.

"Wes... Oh, God!" *Shit.* My breaths rolled out in heaving pants and I bit my bottom lip hard to keep quiet.

There were no words. I'd never made myself come that hard. Maybe I should have been concerned that I came with Wes's name on my lips, but I felt too damn good to care. I stood on shaky legs to put the showerhead back in place, laughing at the absurdity of my life. How in the world was I supposed to sleep next to this man after what I'd just done?

Chapter 25

Wes

HOLY FUCK. I CLOSED my eyes and forced my breathing to slow. Maybe she wasn't getting herself off? Maybe I'd overheard her talking to herself?

No, the way she sounded, she was definitely coming. My cock thickened almost painfully imagining what she was doing in there. Was she sliding her fingers through her slick pussy right now?

Fuck.

It was literally day one of living together and my cock was already about to fall off. Then again, I've wanted Olivia for months, picturing scenarios just like this one when I've fisted myself in the shower.

I needed to make a move.

But shit, what if she didn't want me? She freaked out when I'd accidentally seen her tit. I could picture how it would go—me coming on to her and her shooting me down. Then what? We'd have to live together and it would be awkward as hell. Or worse—she'd end our arrangement and kick me out of her life.

I couldn't lose her. She was too important to me.

My cock would have to deal. There were fates worse than an extended case of blue balls.

She turned the shower off while I was standing near the door with an erection that could double as a steel rod. I scrambled backwards just as she stepped out of the bathroom.

"Oh, I didn't think you'd be in here." She looked so damn beautiful with her face flushed pink. One towel was wrapped in her hair and the other fit snugly around her chest. I clenched my fists to keep from reaching for her.

"Sorry, kids are going to sleep... I should have waited to come in. Won't do it again." If some blood flow could return to my brain that would be nice.

"It's fine," she said, narrowing her eyes. "You're being weird."

"What? Am I?" I coughed and shrugged. "So, I guess I'll go shower since you've finished yourself... I mean since you're done."

This is what celibacy for eight years looked like. I was a complete bumbling fool.

"Okay…" she said, drawing out the word. "I, uh, left your bench in there for you, all set up."

"Good, great. Thanks." I passed her as I walked toward the bathroom door and got a whiff of my body wash. She hurried past me and into the walk-in closet, closing the door behind her. She used my body wash while she got herself off? I was truly and seriously fucked.

I undressed quickly while the bathroom filled with steam, careful to soak up any remaining water on the bath mat before I removed my leg. Fuck, it felt amazing to get some air on my residual limb after a long day on my feet. Removing my sweaty liners gave my brain something else to focus on, other than Olivia in the shower.

I situated myself on my bench and leaned into the stream of hot water. It pulsed hard and fast against my tired shoulders. A little *too* hard and fast. Looking up at the showerhead, realization hit me like a vibrator to the face. She used the *showerhead*. So much for calming my dick down.

While the stream pounded my back, I soaped myself up. The bottle had already been uncapped. *I knew it.* Now my own body wash was turning me on. I took hold of my uncomfortably hard cock and slid my soapy palm along the length. It felt so good, so wet and slippery. *Not as good as she'd feel.*

I let my mind run wild—Olivia's soft palm stroking me. *"You're so hard for me, Wes."* Fuck yes, I am. You feel incredible. *"Mmm, this hard cock is all mine."* All yours. No one else's. I fisted myself harder as I pictured sinking into Olivia's tight pussy. Her moaning my name with each thrust. Squeezing my cock as she fell apart. She loved every second. God, I was seconds away from blowing my load. My muscles contracted and I pumped myself faster. Bright spots burst behind my closed lids as my cock pulsed. *"Come for me Wes. Fill me up."*

"Fuck!"

My cum shot out, mixing with the hot water pulsating around me. I flopped my head back against the tile, breathing hard while I floated back into my body.

"Holy shit." I hoped she didn't hear me. Or did I? Maybe this would be our new life. Us overhearing each other getting ourselves off while we pretended we didn't. I could work with that... for a while. I'd take any part of her.

I finished showering, taking extra time to regain strength in my trembling thighs. That had to be the hardest I'd ever come from my own hand. My heart still hammered against my ribs.

I turned off the shower and faced the bathroom to grab my towels. I'd always needed at least two to make sure everything was dry before putting my leg back on.

"Shit." I could smack myself. In my stumbling stupor, I'd forgotten to grab any towels at all. My clean liners were also sitting discarded on my side of the bed. Looking around, I realized my only options were either the thoroughly soaked bath mat, or the hand towel. My hair dripped water along my chest, not helping my situation in the slightest.

"Olivia?" I called. If she answered, I'd ask her to pass my stuff through the door. If she didn't, I'd take my chances and try to make it to the bed without face planting. "You in here?"

No answer.

I dried myself as much as I could with the small hand towel, grabbed my leg, and held onto the door for balance. In the eight years since my surgeries, I was more than used to the "hop across short spaces" game, but it was never fun. I'd take hopping over crawling though.

The coast was clear, so I held the wall for balance and made my way slowly toward the bed. If I could grab a clean towel then I'd be able to dry off and get my prosthesis back on right away. But where did she keep clean towels?

"You decent?" Oliva opened the closet door as I stood buck naked steps away from the bathroom.

"No!"

"Oh, fuck!"

We yelled at the same time and I was so damn frazzled I let go of the wall and fell right on my ass. She covered her eyes with one hand and removed an AirPod from her ear with the other.

"Shit, are you okay? I'm so sorry, I thought you'd be done. I should have waited longer. I was listening to music and unpacking and—"

"I'm fine. I need a towel though."

"Right. One second." I chuckled as she attempted to walk across the space with her eyes firmly covered by her hand, bumping into boxes and almost knocking over her lamp.

"That lamp so needs to go," I said, remembering how I'd knocked it over before. Still on my ass, I figured I may as well at least try to get closer to where I needed to be. Not like Olivia was looking, thankfully. Because crawling across a floor, ass in the air, wasn't a good look for a guy like me.

"The lamp?" she asked. "Oh yeah, I forgot you almost broke it." I was halfway there, close enough that I could almost pull the blanket off the bed to cover my junk. Just a few more steps. "Hold on, I think I put the clean towels over here to make room for—"

And... she tripped and fell on top of me.

Turned on the spot and walked right into me, flopping forward against my ass.

"Oh God... shit," she yelped, scrambling to get up but having trouble gaining purchase on my wet body. "I'm on your ass."

"Yup," I said.

"My eyes are still closed, I swear."

"Tiger, open your eyes. I don't care if you see my ass at this point. I just need a towel." I pushed up from the floor as she climbed off of me and opened her eyes. Maybe it was my imagination but as her eyes fell on me, she took me in. All of me.

Kneeling, I ran a hand through my wet hair and chuckled. "Like what you see?"

She blinked and turned her head, groaning. "Oh God. I just fell on top of your wet, naked ass."

"I can't believe you thought you had to close your eyes."

"Well, what was I supposed to do? Stare at your giant dick?" She rested a hand on her hip and crossed the room.

"You think it's giant?"

Her face flushed crimson, so fucking pretty. "Well... I'm not going to lie. That thing is a monster." I chuckled as she groaned again and headed back into the closet. "Seriously, have you broken someone in half?"

Never had any complaints. I laughed and kept that comment to myself.

She came out holding a stack of folded towels and tossed them my way. I started to towel off and gestured to where I left my prosthesis. "Can you grab my leg?"

"Yeah, sure." She grabbed it then perched on the edge of the bed, watching me.

"You gonna watch me get dressed?" I smirked.

"I might as well. I've seen it all now anyway and I'm curious about how you put your leg on."

I shook my head and laughed. "Okay then. Way to make a guy feel like a science experiment."

"Stop... You know what I mean," she said. "If we're going to be living together I need to know."

" I know, I know," I teased. "Lemme at least put my boxers on. Me and my monster dick are feeling kind of vulnerable with you staring."

She handed me a pair from the pile on the bed. I caught her biting her bottom lip out of the corner of my eye. I needed to get dressed, before I got hard... again.

"I have to ask," she said once my boxers were on.

"Yeah?"

She brought her palm up to cover her face, muffling her voice. *"Howbigisit?"*

"What? I couldn't hear you with your hand over your face."

"Nevermind," she groaned through her palm.

Oh, I heard her. I just wanted to see her face as the question left her lips. Reaching up, I wrapped my hand around her wrist and tugged her palm away. Her cheeks were still flushed pink all the way to the tips of her ears. "Ask me again, Tiger."

She held my gaze and shook her head. "No. Nevermind."

"Okay." I dropped my hand, deciding not to press her. Instead I walked her through the steps I took to get into my prosthesis and then once we brushed our teeth and got into bed, I showed her how I took it off.

"Is this awkward or is it me?" she asked beside me. With the room blanketed in darkness other than a small nightlight, I could make out the silhouette of her curves shadowed against the wall.

I flipped onto my back. "Not for me," I lied.

"Right," she said with a huff. She fluffed her pillow and rolled onto her back. "Can we play the question game again?"

"Which game is that?"

"Where we ask each other questions. Please," she begged. "I'm worried about Alex's appointment and stressed about this mess and my mind keeps replaying that whole... incident."

"You keep thinking about me naked?" I teased. She yanked her pillow out from under her head and smacked me with it. "Okay, okay. You've already tackled me, I don't need to be beaten with a pillow, too."

"I think you do," she said. My mind traveled to the gutter, because of course it did whenever Olivia was concerned. *You can spank me with whatever you want.* "How about one question each?"

I grabbed her pillow and stuffed it under my head. It smelled like her shampoo—mint, lavender, and something I couldn't name, but it was all her. "One question each... and I'm stealing your pillow."

"Hey, you have your own pillows." She grabbed it and pulled.

"But yours is softer," I said, chuckling and giving in.

"It's called a high thread count. You should try it."

"Yeah, yeah," I said. "One day. But for now my Walmart pillowcase is doing just fine."

"Oh Wes, I'll bring you to my side eventually." She plopped the pillow on my head and laughed. Her voice had a raspy quality to it this late at night that was so damn sexy.

"I believe you. So, the question game? Ask away."

"Hmm, let me think." She played with a loose strand of her hair. "Tell me about your last relationship."

I figured this conversation would come up eventually. "Not really a question," I responded.

"You know what I mean."

"I do. I can't help but give you shit," I said with a laugh. "Last relationship, huh?" I pretended to mull it over, although it was a simple question. There'd been no one since Savannah. "It's embarrassing but I want to be honest with you."

"Embarrassing? Is it like *a lot* of women?" she asked.

I chuckled. "Uh, no. How about the opposite of a lot. My last relationship was with Savannah."

"And when did that end again?"

"Officially, eight years ago, but we were on and off. I found out she'd been cheating on me while I was in the hospital with my first surgery." I realized as I let those words into the open air, that I didn't feel the tightness in my chest that I used to. I barely felt anything at all.

"I'm so sorry. That's deplorable."

"Yeah, well, that's Savannah. She's never been the empathetic type." I turned to face her, taking in her warm expression in the dim light. "Anyway, to answer your question, I haven't been in a relationship since my marriage ended. Haven't wanted to be in one, if I'm being honest."

"Why is that?" Her voice was a soft whisper.

"I thought we said one question each. Someone is cheating again," I teased. She didn't tease me back. Instead, her question hung heavy in the air between us.

I took a breath, and as my chest expanded I knew Olivia was breaking down another brick in the wall I'd built around my heart. That loose piece of hair fell into her eyes as she shifted. As I released my breath, I reached out and took it between my index finger and thumb, gently brushing the back of my hand along her cheek as I swiped the hair behind her ear. I didn't miss her sharp intake of breath or how she released it in a ragged rhythm with my name on her lips.

"I haven't wanted to be in a relationship, Tiger, because I've been hurt so deeply I didn't think I was capable of caring for another person again. The old me who was whole and unbroken could have bounced back after Savannah betrayed me. But after losing Dylan and my leg... it didn't matter anymore. Not much did."

I let my gaze stay locked onto hers for a second longer before I rolled onto my other side. I couldn't bear to see the pity in her eyes. "Wes." Her voice trembled.

"It's okay," I said with resolve. "Let's get some sleep. It's been a long day."

"Yeah, okay." I hated the sadness in her tone but was too exhausted to put up a fight. My body was so in tune with hers that I could feel her inch closer until her small frame nearly pressed against my back. My skin prickled with need to turn over and pull her into me. To press my lips to hers and kiss the sadness away. But I wouldn't. I'd hate for our moment to be laced with pity and tears.

As I forced my eyes closed and felt myself drifting into sleep, I could have sworn I heard her whisper, "You're not the only one who's broken."

Chapter 26

Olivia

BEING BACK AT WORK again was equal parts miserable and joyous. I'd only been out for a little over a week, but it felt like a year with everything that had happened in that short time. My feet ached and mind whirled, but by the middle of my shift, I'd gotten back in the groove. Or at least, I'd gotten out of Kelly's way.

I grabbed my plates from the back, careful to avoid too much eye contact with Wes, and made my way to the booth in the corner, where my sister and Kendahl sat waiting.

"One grilled cheese and fries for Mia," I said, placing the plate down in front of her, "And one deluxe burger with onion rings for Ken."

"This looks amazing. Thanks, sis," Mia said. "Are you sure you can't sit with us for a few and catch up?"

"Yeah, use some of that wife privilege and take a load off," Kendahl added.

I winced. "Shh, we haven't told anyone here yet." I gestured for Mia to scoot over and slid in. "I only have a minute."

"Wait? Why haven't you told anyone?" Kendahl asked, always one to get straight to the point.

"I don't know. It hasn't come up, I guess. It's only my first day back anyway." I snagged a fry from Mia's plate and took a bite.

"It'll only make things weirder if you wait. I can see it now—you and Wes making out by the walk-in freezer and Kelly dropping a plate in shock," Ken said.

"That would never happen," I said, narrowing my eyes.

Mia laughed and held another fry out to me. "Come on, you can't tell me you guys haven't at least made out here. You're newlyweds and crazy in love."

Shit. They don't know. For some reason, I kept forgetting that it's only me and Wes in on our plan.

"Please tell me you disinfected the counters after you—" Kendahl started.

"New subject please. I refuse to talk about my sex life at work."

Mia's lips turned up. "Does that mean we can discuss it at the Krav party tomorrow when you've had a few drinks?"

"No. It means I'm not discussing it," I said.

Kendahl pouted. "I hope when I'm married I don't turn into a grump, too."

"She's not a grump, she's just private," Mia said. She leaned her head against my shoulder. "Sorry for bugging you. No more sex talk."

"Thank you," I huffed.

"How was Alex's appointment? You didn't get a chance to fill me in the other day," Kendahl asked.

I cracked a smile. "So far he's healing well, but he still has a few more weeks in his cast. The doctor gave us options and we decided to go the less invasive route for now."

"So the wait and see option?"

"Exactly. With all the changes going on, we thought it would be best to let him settle in."

"When you say we, this means you and Wes?" Mia teased.

I grabbed another fry. "Yes, it means me and Wes. He came with me to see the doctors."

"Aw, you guys are such a cute family," Mia said. She took a bite of her sandwich and added, "I'm so happy for you, sis. I know I was crabby about you doing this behind my back and everything but I think I'm starting to get over it."

"I had to talk to her," Kendahl added. I shot her a grateful smile.

"Ooh, speak of the giant, sexy devil. Hi, Wes," Mia said, waving.

I turned to find Wes walking across the floor toward us. His chef's coat was unbuttoned and gaping open, showing off his fitted white undershirt. I swore his abs rippled as he walked like some anomaly of nature.

"Ladies," he said, grinning at them. "Enjoying your food?"

"So much," Kendahl said, her eyes lingering on his chest. "It's yummy." I kicked her under the table and she yelped.

"Excited for the party tomorrow?" Mia asked Wes. He met my gaze and I raised a brow. I had no input there. We were roped into this New Year's Eve party and there was no backing out.

"Yeah, sure. I haven't been to a party in a long time. It'll be fun." He sounded as excited as someone who opened a pack of socks for Christmas.

"And you'll get to meet my fiancé finally," Kendahl said with a bright smile. "His name is Coby. I love to say fiancé. It makes it feel real."

I could relate. Every time Wes said *my wife,* it was a dose of reality.

"Looking forward to it," Wes said. He ran a hand through his hair and adjusted his bun. Mia nudged me with her shoulder and waggled her brows. I was definitely checking him out. "I've gotta take care of some paperwork in the office. See you tomorrow ladies."

"I should go, too," I said. "I have to clean up and check on my other tables. You guys need anything else?"

"You sure you're not following Wes into the office for a little afternoon quickie?" Kendahl teased.

I groaned. "You two are the worst. I'm giving you to Kelly."

"No! She never gives us free cake like you do," Mia said.

"That's what you get for being annoying." I smiled and turned on my heel, but with my gaze still focused on them, I smacked face first into someone. Why did I never pay attention when I walked? I looked up into the face of dimple guy. *Great.* "Sorry!"

"Olivia, you okay?" He held my shoulders to steady me and I nodded. "Glad you weren't carrying anything."

I blinked, noticing someone familiar at his side. "Sifu?"

"How's it going, Olivia? Haven't seen you in a while." What was my Krav instructor doing here with dimple guy? Mia and Kendahl spotted them and hopped up to say hi. "Looks like the whole gang's here."

"Hey, Mark," Kendahl said. "Happy holidays."

"Nice to see you," Mark said. "I heard about the engagement. Congrats."

"Thanks. Coby took me by surprise." They chatted for a minute about Kendahl and Coby's plans until Kendahl turned to dimples and asked, "Mark, who's your friend?"

"Sorry, that was rude of me. This is my old friend, Damon. He's opening a gym in a few months, so I'm teaching him the ropes."

"A Krav gym?" I asked, intrigued by this new development.

Damon smiled, and even though I hated myself for it, my stomach flipped. He was way too hot to be smiling at me like that. "Not a Krav gym, although I'd love to offer self defense classes. It's a general fitness club... Personal training, classes, equipment. Back in New York, where I'm from. I'm grateful to Mark for all his help."

"That's awesome," Mia said. "We'll have to check in with Mark once you're up and running to see how it turns out."

"I can do a walk through on Facetime." He looked right at me and grinned. "Olivia don't forget to text me your number. You still have mine, right?"

Mia and Kendahl shared a look of shock before they regained their composure. "Yeah, I think I do."

"You can chat more tomorrow night. Damon and his partners will be at the party," Mark said. Damon's face lit up. "This worked out well. Now you'll already know a few people." Mark smiled and gestured to an empty booth. "We okay to sit here, Olivia?"

"Yup." I gulped. "I'll be right with you."

"See you gorgeous ladies tomorrow," Damon said.

Mia and Kendahl about swooned right there. I turned on my heel to get some air but Mia stopped me. "Liv, I think Ken and I need to order some tea."

"Yes. Tea. We need two tall glasses of it," Kendahl said in a much louder tone than normal.

They're the actual worst. Why did I want to move here again? Oh right, because I thought living near my sister would offer support. Instead all I got was meddling. I groaned internally and met them at their booth.

"You have his number? That's the guy I was telling you about the other day. Dimples! I met him at the gym briefly." Mia spoke in a whispered shout. "You're married, young lady!" Kendahl leaned her elbows on the table to listen in.

"It was before me and Wes," I whispered. "He put it in my phone one day when I was serving him. And keep your voice down."

"Spill the tea," Kendahl added.

"I have to work." I gestured around to the multiple full tables. "These people aren't going to serve themselves."

"Fine," Mia said. "But we are so finding out more later. Good Lord, that man is hot."

I crossed my arms but huffed. "I know he is. But I don't know, he gave me weird vibes when I met him. Not my type. Plus, you heard him. He doesn't live here. Anyway, I'll talk to you two nosy meddlers later."

"We'll text you," Kendahl called as I retreated to the serving station. *Didn't I know it.*

I hustled to check on my tables and quickly took Mark and Damon's order without any more small talk. Once I had a second to breathe, I poured myself a glass of ice water and leaned against the serving station, looking over my receipts.

"You okay?" I almost spilled water down my shirt as Wes sidled up next to me.

"I didn't see you coming," I said, putting my glass down. His arm brushed my cheek as he reached beside me to grab a glass. I took a steadying breath.

"Busy day. Did you get a break yet?" he asked. I stepped aside so he could fill his glass with water.

"I'm fine. It feels good to be up and about again, even though my feet would beg to differ." I took another sip of water.

"I can massage them when we get home." He lowered his voice and added, "I'm great with my hands." The water went down wrong and I coughed, spewing water onto his white shirt. He chuckled and patted my back. "If you wanted a wet T-shirt contest, all you had to do was ask."

"You're all trying to kill me today," I said when I finally stopped coughing.

"What did Mia and Kendahl do?" he asked.

I wiped my wet mouth with the back of my hand noticing Wes's eyes intent on my lips. Heat bloomed against my cheeks and up to the tips of my ears and I drew a steady breath. "They're just teasing me. Nothing serious."

He reached out and swiped a bead of water from the corner of my lip with his rough, calloused thumb. If I wasn't bright red before, I was now.

"They're probably happy for you. You landed such a great guy." He smirked and wiped his hand against his thigh.

"Lucky me," I deadpanned. "Speaking of that, when are we going to tell everyone here? Kelly keeps eyeing me. I swear she knows."

He peeked around the corner into the kitchen. "Let's tell them now. I have nothing to hide."

"Not now! Shouldn't we, you know... break the ice a little? Maybe you can offer them raises or nice fat bonuses first."

"Why would I do that, Tiger? Do you think they're going to strike? Rebel? They'll be thrilled for us."

"I don't know," I cried. "I'm still the newbie and I want them to like me. I feel like they'll think I'm getting special treatment."

He leaned in. "You are getting special treatment. I can promise I've never once offered to rub Kelly's feet."

I crossed my arms. "You're impossible." He chuckled with his whole body and in Wes-like fashion knocked over his glass of water. I sighed and bent to pick it up, even as he put a hand on my shoulder to stop me. "I've got it, no worries. It's just water this time, thankfully."

While I was on the floor scooping up ice cubes, I looked up to find Damon hovering nearby. Our eyes locked and he took that as his cue to come over.

"Sorry, your food should be out any second," I said, dumping the ice cubes into the sink.

"Oh, thanks," he said. His gaze slid over to Wes and he offered a friendly grin. "I was heading to the restroom. But since I ran into you again I wanted to say that it was nice to see you. I was worried about you when you weren't here last time I came in and you hadn't called."

Wes stiffened beside me. I wiped my damp hands on my pants and let out an awkward laugh. "That's nice of you. I'm doing fine. Just took a few days off for the holiday."

"I'm glad. Well, I'll see you tomorrow then." He flashed another bright, panty melting grin and waved to Wes, who didn't return the sentiment. His hands were busy gripping his glass so hard it was a wonder the thing didn't shatter.

I turned to Wes and winced. "I should go check my tables."

"Tiger," he uttered through gritted teeth. "What was he talking about?"

"Wes, I'm not getting into this with you right now. We're at work." I pried the glass from his grip and he flexed his fist. I lowered my voice and explained. "Calm yourself, big guy. He's just a customer who has a thing for me. Nothing's happened. He's friends with Mark and he'll be at the party tomorrow. Unclench your jaw and take a deep breath. There's no need for a *my wife* moment."

His eyes met mine and he massaged his jaw. "Sorry. I didn't mean to make you uncomfortable."

"It's fine. I'm fine. Everyone's fine. I'm going to get some actual work done now." I didn't wait for him to respond before I marched away, leaving him staring after me. This shift couldn't end soon enough.

Chapter 27

Olivia

"ARE YOU SURE YOUR parents are okay watching the kids? Maybe I should call them again to check in." I adjusted my skirt and climbed out of the passenger side of Wes's car.

"They're fine. But if you want to leave, I'm okay with that," he said. He stepped out of the car and stretched his arms over his head, exposing a sliver of abs. I knew he was as uncomfortable in a party setting as I was. Although, I hadn't shared my reasoning with him yet. My parent's boring galas were one thing. Parties like Mark and Dina's made me about as uncomfortable as a person could be. No matter the setting, certain sounds and smells set me on edge.

At least fifteen cars lined the road and their driveway was packed. From what Mia told me these parties could be wild.

Think of Mia. We've missed out on years of holidays together and I wasn't about to miss another.

"Let's go before Mia starts calling me." Wes came around to my side of the car and took my hand in his. "Good idea. We need to keep up appearances."

I felt him stiffen, then relax as we walked down the driveway. "Yeah, exactly."

Mark and his wife Dina greeted us at the door, each already holding drinks. Music pumped through speakers throughout the main floor of the house as they walked us through to the backyard.

"Nice place," Wes said loud enough that only I heard him. "I'd give anything for a pool."

I looked over their paradise of a yard—pool and spa, cozy patio furniture set up around a fire pit, tiki bar. It reminded me of a resort. For a moment, I got a small pang of homesickness. My parents have the nicest backyard. Or at least they did, who knows when they'll sell the place, now that their divorce is in the works.

"There's Mia and Shawn," I said, spotting them with a large group around the bar. I forced a smile and pulled Wes over.

"Sissy!" Mia squealed, pulling me into a hug. She smelled like a bottle of wine. "I'm so glad you're here!"

"Me too, sis." I laughed at the way her bun bobbed as she tilted her head. Shawn patted Wes's shoulder and introduced us around the circle. I'd recognized some of the people from the gym, but most of them were higher level.

"Nice to finally meet you." A tall woman with cropped pink hair offered her hand to shake. "I'm Avery and this is my girlfriend, Bethany." The girl beside her smiled awkwardly and waved. "Don't mind her, she's not a fan of parties."

"Me either," I said. "Don't worry, you're not alone."

"One time my roommate had her stomach pumped after a party. What a night." She looked off past me and I nodded.

"Sounds awful," I said.

"I liked riding in the ambulance. Got me out of the party."

Avery chuckled. "Social anxiety, huh? It's a bitch."

"Right..." I said.

"Can I get you guys a drink?" Shawn asked. "Anyone else need a refill?"

"I do," Mia sang. Shawn shook his head and took her glass.

"I'll just have some water," I said.

Wes met my gaze. "You don't want a drink? Don't worry about driving, I'll stay sober."

"I'm good. Not really in the mood," I said.

Shawn led Wes over to the bar and I overheard him saying, "Glad I brought an extra set of clothes for Mia. Looks like she'll be worshiping the porcelain god tonight."

Kendahl and Coby showed up a few minutes later, looking more than a bit disheveled. Kendahl pulled me aside and told me they needed a quickie in the car before they came in. I glanced at Coby, who was beaming from ear to ear and chatting with a few of the guests. Seeing them so blissfully happy was great. But why did a teeny piece of my chest ache for what they had?

I sipped my water and listened in on conversations about class and inside jokes a few of them started at the wedding they went to in the fall. I laughed when everyone else did and smiled around the room, but inside a restless energy thrummed through me. I wanted to leave but it wasn't even close to midnight. I hated that I couldn't relax like everyone else. If anyone needed to de-stress it was me. The new year meant school starting back up for the kids and all the custody issues coming to a head. Our very own countdown of doom.

Wes was off chatting with Shawn while everyone else seemed to be in on a joke I knew nothing about. I turned to find the restroom and saw Damon coming outside with Mark and two other insanely tall and handsome guys. Those must be his partners.

Damon spotted me right away and waved. He tapped his friend's shoulder and said something before turning back in my direction. *Shit.* He was heading toward me.

"Bathroom?" I blurted, louder than I meant to.

"You need the bathroom?" Mia asked. I nodded. "I'll bring you. Be right back. Don't finish the story until I get back," she said to Kendahl.

She started to go toward the door, right where they were standing, and I pulled her arm. "Did I say bathroom? I meant pool."

"What?" Mia asked, clearly confused.

"Show me the pool. It's so nice," I said. I glanced over my shoulder. Damon was still heading my way.

"It's right there, sissy." She felt my forehead. "Are you feeling alright?"

"Yup, I'm fine." I gripped her arm so she wouldn't leave me.

"Olivia! Hey," Damon said, reaching our side.

Mia's eyes met mine and widened. "Oh," she said as I gave her arm a pull.

"Hi. This is my sister, Mia. You met the other day," I said. "Mia, didn't you want to talk to Damon all about his gym?"

Mia shifted on her feet as someone from the group called her name. Distracted, that little traitor pulled herself from my grip and bounced away. "Be right back, sis!"

I let out an awkward laugh.

"I'm trying to be smooth here, but it's hard around a woman like you." He rubbed the back of his neck. "Olivia, you look gorgeous tonight."

My face flushed and I looked at my feet. "Thank you."

"I don't want to come across as too forward, but I'd like to get to know you better. Can I get you a drink? Let's go somewhere to talk."

Let's go somewhere to talk. My chest tightened as his words echoed in my mind. I sucked in a ragged breath and bolted toward the door.

I didn't stop until I reached the bathroom, shutting the door and locking it behind me. I sat on the toilet seat, holding my head in my hands.

The smell of pine trees and damp earth floated through my nose. But how? I closed my eyes and counted down from five, but the words kept repeating on a loop. *I really like you, Olivia. Here, you can have my beer. Let's go somewhere to talk.*

My bare legs pebbled. *It was so cold in the dark woods.* I rubbed some warmth into them but my palms shook.

No, no, no. I opened my lips to say it but the words were no more than a whisper suffocated by the thick blanket of laughter surrounding me.

Tears streamed down my face as I struggled to suck in a breath. "I'm fine." I repeated the phrase, in between focused breathing, until my tears dried up and my throat ached. I had no idea how long I'd been in the bathroom, but as soon as I splashed water on my face and made myself presentable again, I opened the door to see Damon waiting for me.

"Olivia, there you are," he said. "Are you okay?"

I cleared my throat. "Yeah, I'm not feeling well. I'm going to find my sister and let her know."

His smile didn't reach his eyes. " I understand. I hope you feel better. Maybe we can get together another time?"

I gave his forearm a sympathetic squeeze. "I'm actually recently married." I flashed my left hand, showing him the simple band on my ring finger. "Sorry I didn't tell you sooner."

"Oh, wow." He let out a dry laugh and scrubbed a hand over his face. "I feel like an ass."

"You're not! I'm the one who should have spoken up earlier." I hugged my arms to my chest. "Anyway, happy New Year, Damon. I'll see you around."

"Happy New Year," he said. "And congratulations."

I plastered on a fake smile and turned the corner to find Wes leaning against the wall, arms crossed with a deep frown on his face. "Shit, Wes. Where have you been?"

"I could ask you the same question," he said. I knew instantly something was off by the tone of his voice.

"You could, but you didn't." I huffed. "Can we go? I'm not feeling well."

"I was just leaving." He ran a hand through his hair and turned toward the front door.

"What the hell, Wes?" I called after him. He didn't stop or even slow down. "You're going to leave me here?"

That got him to stop. His hands clenched at his sides and he faced me. "You have plenty of company already, don't you think?"

"What are you talking about?" My pulse picked up as I stepped up to his chest.

"You and that guy go missing at the same time." He paced the front hallway, not meeting my gaze. "I couldn't find you for half an hour, Olivia. Then I see you with your hands all over him. Tell me that's just a coincidence." A laugh bubbled up from my throat. As much as I tried to hold it in, I couldn't. He glared at me. "I'm glad you think this is funny."

"Wes, are you serious right now? Nothing happened with me and Damon." I shook my head at the absurdity of it.

"Then where were you?" His tone dropped the edge it carried and he finally met my gaze.

"Do you really want to know?" I let out an exasperated breath as tears welled in my eyes. *Let's go somewhere to talk.* My hands trembled again and I knew I needed to get the hell out of there. "I don't need this," I said, pushing through the front door.

This night was a total shit show. Why not throw the end of my fake marriage on top of the heap? If he couldn't trust me, then what did we even have?

I had no idea where I was going, only that I needed space from him and everyone at that party. The front yard was quiet and empty. The only light came from a single fixture hanging above the front door. I rounded the corner until my chest heaved in a shallow breath. Pulling my phone from my pocket, I swiped until I found my Uber app, and clicked to re-download it. I knew my chances were slim of finding an Uber at eleven at night on New Year's Eve in a residential area like this, but I had to try.

"Olivia, I'm sorry. I'm a fucking idiot. Please, don't shut me out." Wes turned the corner but I didn't glance in his direction. I couldn't let him see the hurt in my eyes. I'd break if I saw that he was hurting, too. Even through my anger and panic, I cared for him. I cared for him too much. "Tiger, please."

His voice cracked. I ignored the blaring alarms in my head and glanced at him. He looked small with his shoulders caved in and head held low. A cry caught in my dry throat and I fought the urge to go to him. Anger blocked my path.

"I wouldn't hurt you like that, Wes. I know this isn't real, but we have an agreement. No one else." I held up my left hand for emphasis. "I was in the damn bathroom having a panic attack, okay? That's the truth. I don't know what else to say to you right now."

"You were? Are you okay?"

I let out a dry laugh and checked the progress of my download.

He spoke again and as much as I didn't want to look at him, I met his gaze. "I'm sorry I wasn't there to help you through it. I'm so fucking broken, Olivia. I know you won't hurt me." He spread his palm on his chest and pounded once. "But inside, in here, I can't help but wait for it to come. Look at you, and then look at me."

I swiped my tears away with the back of my hand. "Stop. Don't put yourself down. You have to trust me when I tell you I won't fuck you over like that. We made a deal. A promise. I don't break promises."

"Is that all this is for you?" My pulse raced as he stepped closer. God, he looked destroyed. Like one push and he'd shatter into a hundred pieces.

"What are you asking me?" He reached me and cupped my chin in his hand. I wanted to close my eyes. To protect my heart. His fingertip drew a line down my quivering bottom lip, and my legs trembled. I forced my eyes open to find his blazing into mine, so dark they mirrored the night sky.

"Us. Me and you. Is this just a deal for you?"

"How could I answer that when I don't even understand what you're asking me," I said.

He boxed me against him, resting one hand above my head on the rough exterior wall. His warmth and smell surrounded me and for the first time that night my chest loosened. All I wanted to do was curl into him. He bent his head until we were so close his breath mingled with mine. An ache grew—hot and heavy in my throat, in my chest, between my legs. Pure need coursed through me and I tested him by grazing my cheek against his. The rough stubble scratched my sensitive skin. "Wes," I cried.

He captured his name from my lips with a light teasing kiss. It was too much and not enough. My knees buckled but he wrapped his arms around me, lifting me against the wall.

"I've got you, Tiger. I always have and I always will." I crashed my lips against his in a frenzy of need. I'd wanted this for so long, there was no denying it anymore. I melted against him as he pressed his tongue along the seam of my lips. I opened, tasting him as he licked into me. Scrambling to get closer, deeper, I dragged my fingernails into his thick shoulder muscles and he groaned, sucking my bottom lip between his teeth. "Fuck, I need you."

"You have me," I said through a panting breath and he trailed the column of my neck with kisses. I pulled his bun loose and fisted my hands into his hair. God, it was so soft and full. I gave it a light tug, eliciting another groan from his lips. "I love that sound."

He groaned again and I hummed an easy laugh.

"Your laugh is so hot," he said, sucking on my lip again. He gripped my ass, grinding me against him with each stroke of our tongues. My skirt rolled up to my stomach but I didn't care. I needed more.

Noise from the party pulled me in, and I angled my head to listen. "Do you hear that?"

"No, I only hear you." I kissed him lightly and brought my forehead against his.

"I think it's almost midnight," I said once I could make out what the voices were saying. "Kiss me, Wes."

"Always," he said, brushing his lips against my cheek and down to my mouth.

"Kiss me and then take me home."

Chapter 28

Wes

THANK FUCK THE KIDS were sleeping at my parents house. I unlocked our front door and gathered Olivia into my arms in one quick motion. Fifteen minutes of her hands on my thigh, teasing me while I drove had me about ready to throw her over my shoulder and toss her on our bed. One taste and I was completely feral.

"You know I'm going to make you pay for your teasing in the car," I said. She gasped and made the most delicious humming sound as I sucked her earlobe into my mouth.

"I don't know what you're talking about," she said sweetly. *Right.* Her hands slipped under my shirt, exploring the ridges of my abs. "God, I love these. Lose the shirt."

"Damn, Tiger... You don't waste time." I pulled my T-shirt up and over my head, basking in her praise. I worked my ass off to keep my body fit, and to have her appreciating it made me so fucking grateful.

Wrapping her arms around my neck, she kissed me softly and whispered, "I'm done wasting time, and yes, I like being in control. Let's go to bed."

"You mean *bed*, right?" I asked to be sure I was actually hearing her correctly and this wasn't my imagination running rampant. I'd pictured this so many times and in so many ways.

She stepped back and pulled her shirt off, tossing it next to mine on the floor. Standing in front of me in only her short skirt and bra, she cocked her head to the side. "Does this answer your question?"

My heart was about to burst through my chest. She was so fucking gorgeous. I'd never felt this fierce need for anyone or anything. I barely recognized the deep timbre of my voice as I said, "I think so, but I want to be sure."

The corner of her lips tipped up in a smirk and I knew she caught on to my game. Games were our thing. Our icebreaker. I loved to see her play.

She slid her skirt down her legs and stepped out of it, letting her palms trail up her thighs and across the thin straps of her panties. My cock grew uncomfortably hard against my boxer briefs.

"You next," she said, pinning me with her dark eyes.

I fumbled with the button of my jeans, too distracted by the outline of her curves in the dark room. Holding onto the wall for balance I pulled the jeans off and kicked them aside. Need mixed with insecurity as I stood in front of her with nothing to hide. I'd grown to accept my body, for the most part. Having a metal leg was pretty badass generally. But she was perfection. What if she didn't like what I had to give?

I cleared my throat and scrubbed my hand down my face. This was easier in my clothes. Easier still, if she was the sole focus. "I, uh, understand if you've changed your mind." My tone dropped so low, my voice cracked. "Seeing me—"

"Wes," she said, stopping me. "You're beautiful. All of you." Stepping forward she buried her face against my chest and I held her tight. Her lips traced a path of kisses up my chest and neck until she reached the shell of my ear. "Take me to bed and fuck me."

With her cheeks in my hands, I angled her face so I could look into her eyes. "You're going to make me come in my pants if you say shit like that."

"Not allowed. You have to come in me."

"Fuck." My mouth covered hers and I kissed her with renewed hunger. Our hands were everywhere. Grasping skin, tugging hair, palming curves. My body buzzed with need to sink into her and claim what's mine.

We made our way to the edge of our bed, never breaking contact. She moaned against my lips as I unclipped her bra and slid my hands down her back to cup her ass and lift her onto me. She straddled me, legs wide, her beautiful tits right where I wanted them.

Sliding her bra down her arm, I sat back and took her in. "Perfection."

"Give me your mouth," she said, tugging me forward and arching to feed me her tit. I had no idea she'd be so dominant, but I was fucking loving every second. I pressed her into me so there wasn't an inch between us and sucked one tight nipple, then the other, living for the way her body responded. Her hips rolled against my cock with every pull. "Mmm," she moaned. "Feels so good."

"You like having your tits sucked?" I wrapped my lips around one and sucked then nibbled until she writhed against me.

"Yes... Oh, God." Her nails scraped my neck as she held me in place. I licked and sucked while she rocked against my length until I felt myself losing control.

I flipped her onto her back and watched her tits fall to the side, pretty pink nipples wet and tight. Her face was flushed the same color and her hair was wild from my hands raking through it. I knew her pussy would be soaked and so fucking perfect. My mouth watered.

"Slide up the bed for me."

"Like this?" she asked when her head reached the headboard.

"Right there." I brushed my knuckles over her soft stomach, down to the dip above her pelvis and stopped. I was almost feverish with need—to taste her, to fuck her, but I wanted her to feel in control.

Slowly, I dipped one finger into the band of her panties while I watched her eyes glaze and her chest heave. I added another and slid the thin fabric down, exposing the top of her neatly trimmed pussy. She lifted her hips for me to finish sliding her panties all the way down, but I took my time, grazing the tops of her thighs, brushing the outside of her pussy lips.

"You're playing with me," she groaned. "Touch me, Wes." She reached down and placed her hand over mine, guiding me to her wet heat. "Yes... right there."

"Show me how you like it, Tiger. Tease that pussy for me."

"Mmm," she moaned again and moved my fingertips between her slick pussy, getting them nice and wet. "Your fingers feel so good. So much better than mine."

"You love to touch yourself, don't you?" She guided us to her clit and dragged my fingers in slow circles.

"Yes, I love it." I palmed my aching cock through my boxers as I watched her use my fingers. She circled them faster, tensing her legs and clenching her eyes shut. "Oh God, I'm so close."

Her clit swelled, and I added more pressure, circling in rhythm with Olivia's hand. Our pants and moans mingled with the rocking and creaking of the bed. I was so close to blowing my load from watching her, but I didn't fucking care. I could watch her like this everyday—face twisted in pleasure, cheeks flushed, plump lip between her teeth.

"Come for me. Soak my hand."

"God, Wes." Her legs trembled and hips arched as she called out. I stilled, letting her ride out her release on my fingers until her clit throbbed. With a tug on my hair, she pulled me up to her lips. "Too sensitive... please... come here."

"You're so pretty when you come." I sucked my fingers, savoring her taste. "I'm dying to eat your pussy. Taste yourself." She caught my index finger between her lips and sucked hard until I groaned against her.

"Not tonight." She gave my chest a push until I was flat on my back. "I've been waiting for this for too long."

I was transfixed watching her take charge. She straddled me and shimmied down my body to my thighs, pulling the waistband of my boxers until my cock jutted out, hard and aching. Wrapping her hand around me, she stroked me from my leaking head to my base. Rasped sounds left my lips as I pumped my hips into her hand. "Too good... I'm gonna come if you do that."

"I have an IUD," she said. "And I've been tested. I haven't been with anyone in an embarrassingly long time." She slowed her strokes and lightly teased my lower abdomen.

I hissed when her nails scraped against my side, sensations overwhelming me. "Same. I've had more blood work in the last eight years than the majority of the population does in a lifetime."

"Thank God," she said. I pulled her to me so I could kiss her. Those lips—I couldn't get enough. I planted kisses down her neck and chest and licked her sensitive nipples. "Mm, I'm ready. But Wes?" Her quiet voice had me stopping to look into her eyes. "Let's go slow, okay? It's been awhile."

"Of course. You take the lead," I said. She looked down at me with a soft smile and angled herself over my cock. The anticipation of being inside her was killing me, but watching her take what she needed was so worth the wait. She dragged her body up and down my length, grinding into me, and taking her pleasure. "You're so wet. God, you feel so good."

Hold on. Don't fucking come.

"Mm, yes. Wet for you." Gripping her soft hips, I helped steady her as she slowly positioned herself over me. As much as I wanted to drive my hips up, sinking my cock into her, I waited, letting her relax as my tip slipped into her tight heat.

Fuck. She felt too good. I wouldn't last.

She lowered herself until most of my cock filled her and cried out, "You're not even fully in and I feel like I'm breaking in two. I don't know if I can."

"You can. Take all the time you need, Tiger. You're perfect. You're doing so well." She bit down on her lower lip and squeezed my chest as she sunk all the way down, throaty moans slipping from her lips. "You're made for me. Feels so fucking good inside you."

"Wes," she hissed, rocking her hips, her eyes glazed over.

"Look how perfect we fit together." I stared at the spot where our bodies connected—skin to skin—and thanked the universe for this woman. For months I've imagined this moment and now she was mine.

"Yes," she gasped, rocking her hips harder. I kept one hand on her hip, guiding her motion, and reached for her clit with the other. With a matching rhythm, I pressed into her clit as she rode my cock, harder and faster. "Feels so good... Just like that. Don't stop."

"Never." I was so far gone, squeezed by her tight pussy, it would take an army to pull me out. "Come on me. Use my cock to get off."

"I'm so close... so good." Incoherent cries left her lips as I kept a steady pace on her clit.

Our bed creaked, sounding like it was about to fall apart but fuck if I cared. I lifted my hips, thrusting into her. Again and again. While her walls tightened like a fist around me.

"Fuck... I'm coming," she said as she threw her head back and dug her nails into my chest. I fucking loved the feeling of her letting go. "Wes... come in me."

Christ. Her filthy mouth was so sexy.

I flipped her onto her back and pounded into her while her pussy spasmed around my cock. "Fuck," I grunted. "Fuck... Olivia." My muscles tightened and my balls grew heavy... I was so close.

"Wes!" My name spilled from her lips again and that was all I needed. With one last thrust into her my cock swelled and pulsed, shooting cum deep inside her. She wrung me dry, grinding against me a few more times until we collapsed in a heap side by side, breathing hard and fast.

My body was boneless, every inch of me strung out from pleasure. I stroked her hair away from her face. "You're so beautiful, always. But especially right now."

She laughed with a breathy, raspy sound. *My favorite sound.* "You're not too hard to look at yourself."

I gathered her into my arms and she buried her face in the crook of my neck. With our bodies flush against each other, I breathed her in. I couldn't ask for a more perfect woman.

"So... happy New Year," she said, laughing again. "When can we do that again?"

Chapter 29

Olivia

MY PHONE BUZZED AGAINST the end table, waking me up. Low light filtered in from the window and rain pattered against the house. I rolled to reach my phone, but I was trapped underneath Wes's huge arm. He was still asleep beside me.

"Hey," I whispered. "I need you to move your arm." He shifted and pulled my back against his chest... in the complete opposite direction of my phone. *Someone* was waking up, if the hard length poking my ass told me anything. But crap, what if it was the kids calling? I had to at least check.

With careful maneuvering, I slid my body under the blanket toward the end of the bed so I could untangle myself from his hold. Except now, I was staring at his erection head-on. My mouth watered at the sight. In terms of penises, his was pretty damn perfect.

"Tiger, if you wanted to suck me off, all you had to do was ask." Wes shifted and rolled to his back so that his cock was tenting the blanket.

I yanked the blanket down and gave him my best *you're an idiot* grin. "You had me trapped by your giant man-arm. I was making an emergency escape to check my phone."

"If that's the story you're going with," he said, his voice gravelly. I crawled up the bed and leaned on his chest, already turned on from our naked bodies sandwiched together. He looked at me reverently with his half-lidded, sleepy eyes and soft face, peaceful from a good night's sleep. I'd capture this moment if I could. Hold onto it in my mind's eye and come back here whenever I needed a reminder of joy.

"Yup, that's my story. It's riveting, isn't it?"

He scooped me onto his warm chest and held me close. "All your stories are."

Sorry, phone. You'll have to wait.

I opened my legs so my knees fell on either side of his body and leaned forward to brush a soft kiss against his lips. He palmed my ass, ran his hands up my back, and sunk them into my hair to deepen the kiss. I couldn't get enough of his calloused hands on me. I wanted them everywhere, memorizing my body inside and out.

He sucked my bottom lip and I whimpered. "I love when you do that."

"These lips should be sucked every single day," he said, repeating the motion and sending heat right to my clit. Needing to move—to feel any amount of friction—I rocked against his pelvis. "Fuck, you're so hot. Sit on my cock. Squeeze me with that tight pussy."

I was sore from last night, but I needed him inside me. Yanking the blankets away, I scooted lower, grabbed his giant cock and rocked myself against him, hitting my clit with the perfect amount of pressure. "Mm, I love your cock. I don't think I told you that last night."

"My cock loves you," he said with a groan. "Get me nice and wet. God, you feel so good already, baby."

He'd never called me baby before. Something about it coming from Wes's lips had me grinding harder and crying out. That familiar feeling started in my belly and moved down my legs. Tightening and throbbing. Soft whimpers mixed with his groans. "So close, Wes."

He lifted me up and into position. I cried out from the lack of pressure. "Not yet. You're coming on my cock."

"Oh, God—I—" He thrust me down in a quick movement, slamming me onto his cock. I gasped. "Fuck... So big."

"You're soaked for me, Tiger. God, I dreamed of fucking you again all night." He pistoned his hips up into me, hitting places I didn't know existed. I adjusted my hips until I was fully seated on him and circled them, grinding my sensitive clit against his pubic bone. This Wes was different from last night. Rougher. Dirtier. I loved it.

He pinched my hard nipples, sending a jolt of heat into my core. "Yes, do it again."

I rocked harder and faster while he pinched and played with my nipples. Every muscle in my body tightened in delicious anticipation and when I started to tremble and moan, he grabbed my hips, guiding me faster.

"Fuck. *Oh, my God.*" I didn't recognize my own voice as incoherent sounds poured from my lips. My orgasm peaked, shooting through me. Wes groaned, and with one last jerk he filled me up.

"Baby... Fuck. *Fuck.*"

I fell forward, panting hard. He slung his arm around me, pressing our damp skin together. His pounding heartbeat against my cheek as we worked to calm our breathing. An overwhelming feeling of euphoria washed over me and I felt tears leaking from my eyes onto his chest.

I pushed up, sliding his cock out of me as my chest heaved. *Shit.* What was wrong with me? Tears streamed down my cheeks and I went to move but Wes sat up.

"Did I hurt you?" He sounded like I'd shot him in the chest.

"No... no, I'm fine." I closed my eyes and wiped my tears with the back of my hand.

"What's wrong?" He reached for me and I let him pull me back into his arms. A sob escaped my lips. "I've got you," he murmured against my ear. "You're safe with me."

That was just it. I knew I was safe with him. He was unlike anyone I'd ever been with and all these unknown feelings flooded me. It was too much to handle. I'd never felt so raw before, even with everything we'd already been through.

He held me for a long time, rubbing my back and whispering sweet words until my tears dried. I pried my face from his chest and kissed him softly, letting out a choked whisper. "Thank you."

"Do you want to talk about it?"

I shook my head. "I'm fine." There was no reason to worry him and I didn't even know how to put words to my emotions. "Sorry I ruined our morning."

"Tiger," he growled. "You didn't ruin shit. You're incredible." He planted a kiss on my forehead and I leaned into him. "Remember you told me not to hold in my emotions? I believe you said 'that shit would be a ticking time bomb.'"

"Was that me?" I said. "Sounds like someone else."

"That was, in fact, you. And I'm glad I took your advice." He smoothed circles over my back.

"Glad I could help." I forced a small smile. "I don't think I'm able to talk right now, but maybe soon." That was all I could give him. I still wasn't ready to open up about the toughest parts of my life and why our closeness meant so much to me.

"You know I'm here whenever you need me."

"I know." I kissed his cheek and climbed out of bed, finally checking my missed call. It was Mia, likely checking in since we left the party in such a hurry the night before. "I'm going to get cleaned up. Want to call your parents and see when they're bringing the kids home?"

I'd spoken too soon. The unmistakable sound of the front door unlocking was like a siren in our ears. Wes scrambled to the edge of the bed, finding his boxers and slipping them on while I ran into the bathroom to shower.

Before I started the water I could make out the kid's excited voices and Walter grumbling something to Wes. I was sure those two wore him out, especially on a night they were allowed to stay up late.

While waiting for the shower to heat up, I stared at the stream pounding against Wes's seat and thought about how for the first time in forever I didn't have to rush my shower because I felt guilty leaving Alex alone for too long. I didn't have to worry about him bothering my parents or touching their stuff if I wasn't watching him. I wasn't afraid he'd get into something dangerous while my eyes were away from him for ten minutes. I could trust Wes to take care of things. As a single parent for his entire life, I'd never had that luxury. My brain was hardwired to always be on, only taking a reprieve for the few hours I slept each night.

I stepped into the hot water, sighing at how amazing it felt against my sore body. I used muscles that had been inactive for many, many years last night and oh my God, I couldn't believe this is what I'd been missing for so long.

I squirted some shampoo into my hand and took my time lathering and rinsing, thinking of all the ways I wanted to explore with Wes. I loved how he let me take charge. After what happened to me when I was seventeen, that was the only way I was able to be intimate. Not that I'd had much experience. There were a few hookups with this single dad I'd met at Alex's preschool, but that ended as soon as his ex took him back. I liked him enough, but I never felt truly comfortable with him. I knew I needed to have sex again and get it out of the way, and he was there and willing.

I soaped up my body, taking extra care to wash my sensitive areas. Maybe I could open up to Wes tonight. Tell him that I'd been assaulted by Alex's father and I had no clue who he was. God, I wanted to share that so badly, but something held me back. Even though he said he was a broken man last night, I didn't know how he'd react hearing how truly broken I was. Damaged. Barely holding on some days.

My mood turned dark as I stared at the wall, watching as the drops of water collecting on the tile turned to misshapen blobs before slowly sliding down to the drain.

I closed my eyes when they turned red.

Why are my legs like ice? It's cold... too cold. Robins are singing their familiar morning call. I guess I left my window open last night. I pry my eyes open and instantly shut them against the assault of sunlight streaming through an opening in the trees. Trees? Where am I? My temples are throbbing, but I force a breath and open my eyes again, this time shielding them with the back of my hand.

I'm lying next to a huge evergreen in a dense forest. Dew covered patches of grass create a pillow under my head and the smell of damp earth overwhelms my senses. Pushing forward onto my forearms, I scan the area for people... anyone who could tell me what's going on, but my head starts to spin so I quickly roll to my side, retching and emptying the contents of my stomach into the grass.

I curl myself into a ball, hugging my arms to my chest and rubbing them to get warm. Think, Olivia. What's the last thing I can remember? Closing my eyes, flashes of memories drift into my head. Sasha and me showing up at The Hill... the party. There were so many people, not just from our school, but people I'd never seen before. Sasha went off with Craig and I tried to find familiar faces in the groups. It was so dark already... I used the light on my phone to watch my step.

Shit, where is my phone? I feel the dirt around me but my phone and purse aren't there.

I try to remember what happened next, but it's like watching a movie through static. There were these guys and they started talking to me. Their faces are unclear. A red cup... warm beer. And one of them saying, "Let's go somewhere to talk."

I push to a sitting position and wait for my head to stop spinning. When I feel like I could stand, I take stock of my body, realizing my core aches almost as badly as my head. My legs are covered in dirt and my shoes are missing, too. I grab hold of the tree and stand on weak legs, taking my time as a wave of nausea hits.

That's when I see the dried blood on my thighs. Fresh drops dripping down my leg, landing in the dirt like crimson teardrops. Adrenaline spikes through my veins and my pulse shoots up so fast that I slide against the tree so I don't fall.

Why am I bleeding?

What happened to me?

Knock, knock, knock. "Mom, you almost done? I want to show you the cool drawing Lilly made on my cast."

I blinked and brought myself back to the present. Alex. Wes. Lilly. I was home and I was safe. "Almost done," I called.

"Okay!"

I finished up, taking a few more minutes to center myself. Once the holidays were officially over, the first thing I needed to do with my new health insurance was find a therapist in Palm Cove. My life was going too well to jeopardize it by letting my mental health issues take the wheel again. No. I wouldn't allow that to happen.

Wes and I both worked the morning shift the next day. I'll admit that it was difficult to focus. We kept staring at each other through the window and making excuses to touch when we were close. At one point, he tried to get me into his office. I would have gone if I didn't have three tables.

He met me by the server station. "Hey, I got a voicemail a few minutes ago from my tattoo artist reminding me that I have an appointment this evening. I totally forgot about it. I think I made the appointment over the summer."

I paused refilling the glass in my hand. "Oh, cool. What are you getting done?" I let my eyes rake over the ink peeking out from his rolled up sleeves and wondered if there was room anywhere for another piece.

"I have an idea or two. I'll have to see what he thinks." The green in his eyes looked extra bright as he smiled. "Would you want to come with me?"

"Aw, do you need me to hold your hand?"

He chuckled and crossed his arms. "As a matter of fact, I do. I'm a big baby. You should know that by now."

I laughed and squeezed his arm. "Of course, I'll come. I'll see if your parents wouldn't mind hanging out with the kids a little longer."

"Don't worry about that. I'll ask them," he said, taking out his phone. I watched him slowly type out a text message, biting back the urge to tease him. His phone dinged and he smiled. "She said no problem. That us 'two lovebirds' should take our time."

"She's the best." Without caring if anyone could see us, I stood on my tiptoes and kissed his cheek. "Let me get back to work."

The rest of the day dragged, mostly because I couldn't wait to have more alone time with Wes. We grabbed lunch at a taco shop nearby and made it to his appointment right on time.

The moment I stepped inside, the shop intrigued me. I'd never been in one before and always wondered what they'd be like. Maybe somewhere in my brain I pictured black walls and people screaming in pain while getting poked by intimidating biker dudes. But this place was nothing like that. Artwork hung in frames around the large room and the smell of marijuana lingered in the air. Everything was brightly lit along the burgundy painted walls. There were three stations set up with massage tables and equipment, but only one was occupied when we came in by a woman getting her arm worked on.

Wes introduced me to his artist, Mac, who was anything but intimidating. He looked like your average guy—short-ish hair, dad bod, dressed in cargo shorts and a Fleetwood Mac T-Shirt. He wasn't completely covered in ink, but had about as many as Wes that I could see. When he shook my hand, I noticed right away that he was gentle and soft spoken.

"Mac, meet my wife Olivia." Wes rested a palm on my lower back and beamed as he introduced me. I couldn't help but grin, too.

"Nice to meet you," I responded. "I don't want to get in the way, so please feel free to make me move."

Mac chuckled. "You're completely fine where you are." He faced Wes. "So man, what are we working on today?"

Wes pulled out his phone and sneakily showed Mac a photo he'd saved. "Something like this, but obviously however you want to draw it. I was thinking right on my left pec area, black and gray."

"Hell yeah, let's do it," he said. "I'll draw something up. Shouldn't take long."

Mac went down a hallway toward where I'm assuming his desk was and I turned to Wes, teasing him. "That phone's coming in handy, isn't it?"

"I plead the Fifth." He pulled me in and wrapped his arms around me.

"So, are you going to let me see what you're getting?" I was curious and also a bit suspicious since he was being so secretive about it.

He kissed my cheek. "You'll have to wait and see."

I scowled, which only made him chuckle. Mac came back out ten minutes later so I let them chat and took a peek at some of the portfolio binders they had set out on a coffee table. Flipping through each one, I noticed right away how different the artist's styles were. One focused more on colorful, cartoonish pieces, while the other two did mostly black and gray. I stared at one of the pages when I noticed Wes's wave design on his back. It looked amazing when it was first done.

Once they got started, I peeked and saw that he was getting a gorgeous tiger's head on his chest. "For my Tiger," he said.

I had no words to describe how touched I was. Maybe I should have been put off by this grand gesture, but somehow I only felt cherished. He'd look at his heart and think of me.

While they worked, the other artist across from Mac introduced herself and invited me to check out the piece she was finishing up. The woman she was tattooing got a gorgeous, detailed Medusa on her bicep. I couldn't take my eyes off it.

"I absolutely love your work," I said to them both.

"Thanks," the client said. "This one was a long time coming." Her eyes were damp but she had a proud smile on her face.

"I hope it helps you heal," the artist said, giving her forearm a squeeze. I watched enraptured as she squirted liquid onto a paper towel and wiped her arm down. It made the tattoo pop and Medusa's eyes looked vibrant enough to be real.

Once the client stood to look in the mirror, Mac and Wes took a break to come check out her work, telling her how awesome it came out.

An hour later, I sat by Wes's side, watching Mac tattoo smooth lines across Wes's skin and making chit chat. "I loved that Medusa."

"Yeah," Mac said. "Sarah did an awesome job. It's always a difficult tattoo to do and I know her client was emotional about what it represents."

I had no idea what he was talking about, so I nodded and quietly pulled out my phone. A quick Google search told me that Medusa is a symbol of survival, often from sexual abuse or rape.

I schooled my features into a neutral expression but inside my heart pounded and my mouth went dry. I'd met another survivor and didn't even know it.

"Hey, Sarah," I called. She looked up from cleaning her station. "Can I book an appointment with you?"

"Of course! Let me check my schedule."

I knew I couldn't afford it, and maybe I was acting on a whim, but none of that mattered. Not when I'd be taking another step toward healing.

Chapter 30

Wes

I LEFT WORK EARLY so Oliva and I could take the kids on a picnic at the park. Was this my real life? There was no way I deserved this woman, but fuck if I was going to let her slip away.

I hadn't heard back from Regina since I sent her an email, telling her my happy marriage news. Knowing her, she was probably moving her chess pieces around, figuring out a new angle to ruin our lives. She could try, but I'd never let her win.

I spotted them setting up at a table under a big oak tree. Alex sat with his cast leg out in front of him, tossing a ball up and catching it, while Lilly helped Olivia pull containers of food from a paper bag. Olivia beamed while she spoke to Lilly. She was so fucking gorgeous it hurt to look at her. And seeing her interact with Lilly had all these feelings bubbling inside my chest. I looked up at the blue sky, like I always did when I wished

Dylan was here. "How'd I get so lucky, man? I don't deserve her."

A car drove by in the parking lot behind me, blaring country music through their open windows and Olivia turned her head toward the noise. Our eyes locked and her smile broadened. Those feelings in my chest danced around like carbonation from a can of soda. I quickened my pace, needing to wrap her in my arms, even though it had only been a few hours since I last saw her.

"Slow down. We're not going anywhere." Her teasing voice had me smirking like a fool. I pulled her into me, breathing her in.

"Maybe I couldn't wait to do this," I murmured into her ear. "And lots of other things later tonight." She swatted my ass, which thankfully was facing away from the kids. I growled into her ear. "Tiger, save it for later."

"You're the worst," she said, laughing.

"Eww, guys," Lilly said. "No PDA."

"How do you know what that is?" I asked.

"Duh, I'm in fifth grade. I know a lot, Dad." Olivia and I gave each other mortified looks and she shrugged.

"Okay, fifth grader," I said. "You too old to give your dad a hug, too?"

She laughed. I hugged her and ruffled Alex's head of curls, which had him rolling his eyes.

Olivia finished passing out the sandwiches her and the kids picked up at the deli while I opened containers of potato salad and sliced fruit. We chatted about our day in between bites and the kids showed each other memes on their phones, laughing.

A heavy weight rested on our shoulders since it was the last day before school picked back up. I didn't know how I felt about sending them back to the place that failed to protect Alex twice. He still had two more weeks in his cast, and we could only hope that his X-ray results would be positive at his next appointment. The kids had finally started being themselves again, and we were about to reset any progress we'd made during their break.

"So guys, how are you feeling about tomorrow?" I asked.

They looked up from Alex's phone screen and I'd never seen faces morph so quickly from happy to morose.

"Awful," Lilly said.

"Same," Alex echoed.

Olivia sighed. I knew she'd been trying to figure out a work around for weeks but the private schools in the area were full, and homeschooling wasn't an option since we both worked. Between them failing subjects and getting bullied, we had to find a solution. Even a temporary one. Regina and her spying on Lilly's grades was an added issue.

"We'll figure something out," Olivia said. "But I want you both to tell a teacher if anyone messes with you. Don't try to take matters into your own hands, okay?"

They nodded. "Not like I could fight them, even if I wanted to," Alex said.

"No fighting!" Olivia chided.

"I feel like such a loser in this cast. Stupid crutches and not being able to run around. I just want it to be over." Alex physically sagged as he grabbed his bottle of lemonade and chugged.

"I know how you feel, buddy. It's hard not being able to do all the things we want to do." I rubbed my palms together and rested them on the table. "Crutches suck but hey, at least they let people get around easier, right?"

He nodded and I noticed his eyes ping downward toward my legs.

"Trust me, when I had my accident and the doctors told me that they couldn't save my leg, I thought it was the end of the world. And in a way it was... It was the end of the way I'd lived for twenty years. But it got easier and before long, I was grateful for crutches and wheelchairs." I stretched my leg out and tapped my prosthesis. "And my badass metal leg."

The kids giggled and I apologized for saying "ass." Olivia shot me a grateful smile as their conversation switched to video games. She shimmied closer to me on the bench and whispered, "Thank you."

"Of course. I understand how hard it is for him. He's a kid with a shit ton of energy. Being in a cast for as long as he has is hard. No one likes feeling limited, but especially a kid his age."

I felt the comforting warmth of her palm on my thigh under the table as she leaned her head on my shoulder. "Will you tell me more about your accident?"

"I want to," I said, taking a moment to think. "But—"

"It's fine," she interrupted. "Maybe one day?"

I could agree to that. "One day."

After the kids finished eating, they decided we were being too gross with our hand holding and went over by the swing set. Alex perched precariously on a swing, swaying it back and forth, while Lilly sat on the other drawing in her sketchbook.

We basked in the peaceful moment, side by side, watching our kids enjoy being young. The weather was a perfect seventy degrees but started to get chilly in the shade of the oak, so I pulled Oliva to my side and wrapped my palms around her shoulders.

"You're getting goosebumps," I said. "Want to go home?"

She shook her head. "Not yet. I want to let them stay and have fun a bit longer." She took a sip of her water bottle and sighed. "What are we going to do about the school thing?"

"I don't know what there is to do," I said honestly. "Maybe we can schedule a meeting with the principal and the teachers to start?"

"For sure. I'll follow-up first thing tomorrow. When I emailed the principal before the holiday break, I requested a meeting." She crossed her legs and started to vibrate them with nervous energy. "I've been thinking we can put them in the kids classes at the gym, too. Well, Lilly first and then Alex when he's healed. You think she'd like to give it a try?"

"Your guess is as good as mine," I said. "I barely know what she's into these days."

Olivia raised a brow. "Time to start asking questions then. Make an effort with her. And while we're on the topic, I'm taking the poor girl clothes shopping... with your money, of course."

"Oh, really?" I chuckled. "What's wrong with the clothes she has?"

She planted a soft kiss on my cheek and squeezed my thigh. "I've seen some of the clothes you put in the closet, Wes. You know when things get holes you're allowed to replace them, right?"

She found me out. "Snoop."

"Yup," she said. "I won't deny it."

I fished my wallet out and grabbed my Amex. "Here, keep this one on you. Use it for anything you need."

"I'm not going to rack up your credit card," she said. "But I will treat your daughter to a girls' day."

"Thank you. She'll love that." I rubbed circles on her thigh and grinned.

"Don't be surprised if you come home and half your wardrobe is replaced, too," she teased.

"Better not... My old T-shirts are sacred. You can't find that level of softness anywhere."

"Because they've been washed a thousand times. But okay, I'll leave the T-shirts alone... For now." She started to clean up the picnic, balling up sandwich paper and stuffing it into the bag.

"I'll talk to Lilly about joining Krav. I think she'd love it, and then at least she'll learn some self-defense."

"I like that plan. Are you going back to class this week, too?" I picked up the bag of trash so I could toss it.

"I'm planning on it. I miss moving my body and getting stronger. And I'm pretty sure Mia will bug me if I don't. She'll be so happy to see the kids in classes, too." She directed her gaze back toward the kids. "It wouldn't hurt to call more private schools, I guess. I'd hate to ask them, but maybe my parents would help out with tuition."

"I can look into it tonight, try and find one that has openings for mid-year. And as for tuition, I'll take care of it." I thought about Regina using private school as a part of her case against me. "I know one thing, if Lilly went to private school that would be another thing off Regina's 'Wes is a terrible father' list."

I watched Lilly finish her drawing and show it to Alex, who said something animatedly in response. Would I be willing to grovel to private school snobs for my daughter's benefit? I hoped it didn't come to that.

Later that night while Oliva packed school lunches for the next morning, I grabbed my phone and looked up more private school options nearby. I wouldn't admit it, but the damn iPhone was growing on me. It was convenient and I looked forward to my daily texts with Olivia.

Like I thought, the few options we had were at least thirty minutes away and cost about thirty thousand per year. Thankfully my savings would cover it for the first year or two.

As I was about to put my phone away for the night, it buzzed as an email notification popped up. *Regina.* Did I summon her by speaking her name earlier? She was the Wicked Witch, after all.

I clicked the message, but before I read it, I decided I wanted Olivia to read it with me. We were in this together now, and I wanted us to behave like a couple. Passing the kid's room, I listened to them chattering away. The dread of reading Regina's email lifted for a moment, until I reached the kitchen. I knew I couldn't put it off.

"You got a sec?" I asked Olivia. She was listening to a podcast on her phone while slicing apples.

"What's up?" She touched her screen and the room went quiet. I stopped behind her, wrapping my arms around her shoulders and holding her tight. She dropped the knife and rested her palms on my forearms. The small amount of comfort from holding her bolstered me.

"I got a reply from Regina, and was hoping we could read it together."

She twisted to face me and her eyes widened. "Of course. Let me get this stuff in the fridge and we can read it in the bedroom."

She finished up and we said goodnight to the kids before shutting ourselves in our room. "Alright, ready?" I asked.

I clicked and we read through. Olivia turned to me after we took a moment to swallow the unfriendly response. "I don't know this woman, but I think she and my mother would get along well."

I grimaced. "Maybe Regina has an opening in her evil witch coven? Your mother could apply."

"I'll have her write up a resume." I let out a dry laugh. "In all seriousness, it wasn't as bad as I expected. I don't mind letting her do a background check on me. I have nothing to hide. Honestly, if Alex was going to be living with a stranger, I'd want to meet them and check up on them, too."

"I still think it's a bunch of bullshit. I'm Lilly's father. She doesn't need to sniff after me like a watchdog. Our life is our business." I tossed the phone onto the bed behind me.

"If all she's asking for is that and a poke around the house, then I say we give her what she wants. When should we set it up?"

Never.

I rubbed my hands against my thighs and groaned. "That depends."

"On?" she asked, crossing her arms. Maybe it was my tone, but she was already reading between the lines.

"Us getting a bigger place." She crossed her legs and started to vibrate them. "You're shaking the bed, Tiger."

"Sorry... anxious habit. I don't know, I'm worried about something happening and not having a place to go and—"

My first instinct was to clam up. So much had changed in a short amount of time since we'd made our original *deal* and we hadn't talked about what it all meant for us. I was scared to admit I had feelings for her. And fuck, moving into a place that was ours seemed like such a big step for me, too. But looking into her eyes, I knew I was all in. Six months with her could never, ever be enough. I needed six lifetimes.

An idea popped into my head. She'd hate it, but maybe it would help her feel better about moving. "What about this? We said six months right?"

"Yeah?" Her face pinched in and I hurried to finish my thought.

"How about I pay the rent here until the six month mark is over?" She opened her mouth to argue but I put a hand on her thigh and said, "Hold on, hear me out. I pay the rent here and then we split a bigger place. That way you'll have this house as a back up plan. And before you argue about money, it will be fine. I have a decent amount of savings from living with my parents for a while and some money I got after the accident."

I watched the wheels in her head spin while I rubbed circles on her thigh. In reality, I wouldn't take a dime from her, but I knew she'd object to that. Me getting a place has been a long time coming. I'd been at my parents since the accident and Sav leaving. In the beginning, I needed the help while I recovered and was too fucked up in every way to handle living alone, but then it became the norm. Yeah they bugged me, and sleeping on the couch when Lilly was over wasn't ideal, but having their help with her was a bonus. Being with Olivia was the push that I needed to get my shit together on so many levels, not only for her and the kids, but for myself, too.

"You're right about the kids needing their own rooms," she finally said. I smiled and planted a light kiss on her lips.

"And I know how much you love closets," I teased.

"I hate to waste the money on keeping this place and I'm sorry if that hurts you. But I have to look out for Alex. I can't go back to my parents for help again... Not in the way I used to."

"I wouldn't have offered to do it if I didn't want to. I know this," I gestured between us, "is new to both of us. And I want to protect the kids most of all. That's the main reason I think we should do this. I could live in a cardboard box with you and be happy." She narrowed her eyes. "You know what I'm saying. I don't care about fancy houses or having a bunch of closets. This is about what's best for the family."

She gazed downwards, her knee still gyrating the bed. Fuck. I must have said something wrong. Turning to face her, I tipped her chin upward with my palm. Emotion clouded her eyes and her lip quivered.

My chest caved in as a single tear streamed down her cheek.

Chapter 31

Olivia

"I'm fine," I said. "It's nothing."

Just the sweetest thing a person has ever said to me.

He pulled me onto his lap and cradled me against his broad chest. We stayed like that for what felt like hours, quietly holding each other. Why did I keep losing myself like this? He probably thought I had serious issues. Why else would I keep breaking into tears randomly? He kept saying all the right things and making these grand gestures and I didn't know how to react. No one had ever cared for us this way and it was... a lot.

If my mother could see me now, she'd give me hell. Real ladies held it together and cried in private if we had to. She was a real "stuff it all down deep and make a cocktail" kind of woman. Funny how that turned out for her.

"I'm sorry. I feel like such a mess lately." I got up to grab a tissue and dab at my damp eyes. "I promise I'm fine."

I swore I saw his jaw clench before he covered it up by rubbing his palm over his chin. "What can I do to help?"

I straightened my posture and stepped between his knees. "Let's do it."

Wrapping his arms around my waist, he pulled me onto his lap again. "Do *it?*" He waggled his brows in the dumbest, cutest way.

"Not sex—although—hold that thought. I meant let's move. You've convinced me. Reply to the Wicked Witch's email and tell her we need a few weeks."

He beamed and my stomach actually fluttered. So cliche, but it was true. I felt safer with him than I'd ever felt before. It scared the shit out of me but also gave me the feeling of butterflies racing through my gut. "I'll take care of everything. It'll be great."

Our eyes connected and I studied the tiny speck of green in his iris. My skin prickled with electric energy, soaking in the warmth of his hands against my waist. I moved closer and kissed his smiling lips, keeping my touch like a soft caress. Barely lifting my lips from his, I whispered, "Why don't you go check on the kids and I'll get ready for you." Then I slowly kissed along his jawline and toward his earlobe until I heard him hitch a breath.

"Give me less than thirty seconds," he said, as he squeezed my ass and lifted me off his lap, depositing me next to him. I laughed watching him launch off the bed and out the door.

While he was out of the room, I shut the lights off and lit a few candles. Both of us were still getting used to being naked in front of each other and the dim lighting helped settle my nerves.

I rushed to my closet and pulled out the one silk nightgown that I'd owned. It caught my eye at Victoria's Secret a few years ago and I bought it on a whim, more for myself than anything. I deserved sexy things, even if they were only for my own pleasure. It was thigh length and a deep red color with lace trim around the bust. I quickly undressed and slid it on, opting to take off my underwear too. My body flushed with heat all the way to the tips of my ears and my nipples already pebbled through the soft fabric.

Wes was sitting on the edge of the bed in nothing but his boxers when I came out of the walk-in closet. His legs were parted and hands were loose at his sides. When he spotted me, his mouth opened and his eyes traveled over my body.

"Christ... You're sexy as fuck." His tongue darted out to moisten his lips and that tiny movement had me aching for him.

"So are you," I said, stepping closer. "Kids asleep?"

"Yup," he grinned. "I turned up the sound machine, too."

"Good."

"Come over here, baby." He leaned back on his forearms while he watched me with hunger in his eyes. "I need my hands on you."

I settled myself between his legs and he reached out, running his hands down my waist, over my hips and lower to graze the spot where the lace edges of my nightie fell. "Wes..." My voice was a rasped whisper. Having his hands on me was all it took to turn me on. "I want to make you feel good."

"You always make me feel good." He kissed my abdomen and dipped his head lower until he reached right below my belly button. His fingers trailed under my nightie, reaching behind to palm my ass. "Fuck... You're bare under here. I knew it."

All my attention shifted to my throbbing core while his hands explored me. He traced the dip of my hip bones and the curve of my ass until he slowly trailed his hands to my inner thighs, so close to where I ached. His eyes darkened in the flickering light. He looked ready to devour me whole.

His finger dragged up my thigh and between my slit, softly teasing around my clit until I was desperate for pressure.

"You're soaked for me, Tiger." Pulling my nightie up with his free hand, he kissed and licked my belly, craning his head lower until he hovered right above my center. His fingers teased, dipping into me just enough that my hips arched toward him. "I'm going to eat this pussy until you're shaking."

"Oh, God." He plunged a finger into me and cupped the rest of his palm against my clit, finally giving me the pressure I craved. I dug my fingers into his shoulders, biting back a moan. "Wait... You first."

That had been my plan for tonight. I'd never given a blowjob before and I was nervous, but I wanted Wes everywhere. My mouth watered for his cock. But mostly, I wanted to show him how much I appreciated him.

"You think I'm letting go of this pussy before you've come at least once?" he said, sounding desperate. He increased the pressure on my clit, grinding his palm until my knees shook. "Lay down for me."

"Wes, but—" Without letting me finish, he lifted me and deposited me on the bed. Seeing him losing his mind with need was so damn hot. *To hell with it.* Wes wanted this and I wouldn't deny him. I slid down the bed until my head hit the pillows. He kneeled between my legs, running his hands up my thighs. "Before we do this," I started. My cheeks flamed in embarrassment. "I've never had anyone go down on me before."

There, I said it.

His palms froze in place. "Really?"

"It's the truth. I'm obviously not a virgin and have done stuff with guys. Yeah. Um. I've explored and everything but never that." I closed my eyes and kept rambling. "And while I'm telling you this, you should know I've never given a blowjob either."

I wrenched my eyelids open to see his reaction. His chest heaved and he looked up at the ceiling for a second before meeting my gaze with a grin.

"I'm the luckiest man in the world to be the first one to taste you. Fuck... You're so perfect." He kissed up my leg. "Everything about you."

"I'm embarrassed," I admitted. His mouth and the stubble from his beard felt so amazing against my skin. I gripped onto his hair while he paid extra attention to the crease of my thigh.

"Don't be. Pull my hair. Guide me like you did with your hand." I relaxed into my pillow and let my knees fall open for him. "Tell me what feels good." He parted me with his fingers and delved in, sliding his tongue up my slit. He did it again, but flattened his tongue against my clit, pressing in. "So good," he groaned, only lifting his mouth for a moment before sealing his lips against my clit.

"Oh, fuck," I cried out, gripping his hair and bucking my hips. "There... right there."

He flicked his tongue, circling and teasing while sucking. I'd never felt so much pleasure before. Not by my hand or anyone else's. He slipped a finger inside me, curving it and massaging.

I was on another plane... That had to be it. The edges of my mind went blank. There was only feeling.

My legs shook as he upped his pace and I grabbed onto his hair, grinding against him. "Don't stop."

He added another finger, stretching me. Oh, God—the sounds he made while he sucked and slurped, groaning and humming. I grabbed a pillow and threw it over my head to keep myself quiet but between both of us, it was no use.

My legs trembled and my muscles went taut... I was chasing, climbing higher and higher, until my walls clenched as the most intense orgasm I'd ever had slammed into me.

He lapped me up, his tongue massaging my pulsing clit. I squeezed my legs against his face and gripped his hair, holding him in place while I rode out my release. "Oh my God... Oh. Fuck. Wes... please."

When my legs turned to jelly, I dropped them open and he finally slipped out of me, kissing my pussy and my thighs until he reached my lips. "I can't move," I said, panting. "That was too good."

"Taste yourself. See why I'll never get enough of you." I lifted my head to cover his lips, tasting myself on him. Salty and sweet. I deepened our kiss, tangling my tongue with his and sucking it into my mouth.

I reached down to grip his cock through his boxers. "You're so hard and wet." I sucked his lower lip, teasing it with my tongue. Ready to taste all of him.

On shaky legs, I pushed up and slid out from under him. He still had his prosthesis on and I knew he felt more comfortable wearing it, but I wanted to let him know I wanted him either way.

I sat back on my knees while he scooted toward the headboard. Running my palms from his chest, down his body until I reached his thighs. "Are you comfortable?"

"Yes. Why?" he answered.

"I'm just asking." I ran my nails over his skin and he shivered. "If you're more comfortable without your prosthesis, that's okay with me," I said, gently. "Whatever you want."

"Thank you, baby. You're too fucking sweet." He pulled my hand up to kiss my palm, sucking a finger between his lips. "Come up here and ride my cock. I need to be inside you."

I grinned and tugged his boxers down, gripping his massive cock in my palm. I had no idea what I was doing, other than what I'd seen the few times I'd watched porn, but I was relaxed. Wes made me feel comfortable to explore and learn. I brought my head down and wrapped my lips around his tip, giving him a quick suck. Beads of precum hit my tongue, tasting saltier than I'd expected.

"Your mouth... Christ, I'm not going to last." He tried to pull me up. "You don't have to."

"I want to. Please... You taste so good." I slid my palm up his thick cock, squeezing the tip and he hissed a breath. "Let me take care of you."

Getting my mouth nice and wet with my spit, I took him in as deep as he could fit while I wrapped my palm around his base. He groaned, clenching his thighs and bucking his hips. "Shit, sorry. I don't want to choke you."

He wasn't. I loved him losing control. I stroked his base, using my saliva as lube and swirled my tongue around his cock, alternating between sucking and licking. He groaned and wrapped his hands in my hair.

"Is this okay?" he asked, tugging, guiding me up and down on his length. I answered by hollowing my cheeks and sucking harder. "Fuck... Baby, you feel so good."

Moaning from his praise, I slurped him down, taking him as deep as I could without gagging and quickening my strokes with my palm. I loved his groans and curses. I felt so good. So powerful.

"I'm so close." He gripped my hair, jerking his hips. "Can I come in your mouth, baby?"

I moaned around his cock, nodding my head and sucking harder. His body tensed and his cock twitched as he groaned his release, shooting cum into my throat.

"Holy... shit," he panted, winding his fist in my hair. His cock kept twitching, filling me up until it dribbled out my lips. I swallowed down as much as I could before I pulled him out of my mouth. The rest spilled onto my chin and chest. "Did you just swallow, Tiger?"

"Yes." I wiped my mouth with the edge of my nightie and crawled up his torso, resting my head on his chest. His heart beat like a drum against my ear.

His voice rumbled and chest shook as he spoke. "You're so incredible, you know that?"

I didn't feel that way, but maybe I could learn to believe it. He kissed my head and stroked my back, sliding his fingers beneath the fabric. I stayed quiet, listening to our mingled breathing and the sound of waves crashing in the distance beyond our walls.

"I wish we could stay like this," I said. "Not have to worry about jobs and lawyers and school bullies and life."

"That would be fucking perfect," he said. "But we got this. Together."

I melted into him and fell asleep to the sound of his heartbeat.

Chapter 32

Olivia

NERVES TORE UP MY gut as I waited outside the school to pick up the kids at the end of the week. Even though Wes and I sat for a meeting with their principal, and he assured us he'd keep an extra eye on things, I was still a nervous wreck. Alex's shoulders were scrunched up to his ears every afternoon. Like he'd been wound tightly all day and needed to let loose. Lilly wasn't much different, but she still chatted with me like usual.

I decided to forgo our usual route home and drove into town to Cone Cove, a little ice cream shop that Mia told me about. The owners had recently hired her on as their accountant and Mia hadn't stopped raving about their homemade ice cream.

After too many samples, each of us ordered and Alex grabbed a table in the corner while I waited for his shake and my cone.

The place was cute and bright. Beach themed, like most places in Palm Cove, decorated in sea blue colors and whimsical artwork.

"Thanks for taking us here," Lilly said, digging into her massive hot fudge sundae. "This is sooo good."

"I'm glad you like it." She walked over to join Alex at the table as the employee handed me the rest of our order.

"So guys, catch me up. How was your first week back?" I smiled and passed Alex his cotton candy shake.

"Well, nobody messed with us. So there's that," Lilly said. "But we're starting something hard in math. Problems with numbers and letters. I'm completely lost."

"I can help you," Alex said. "It's easy."

"Easy for you," I said. "Math doesn't come naturally to everyone." I tasted my cookies and cream cone and almost moaned, it was so good.

"I'll do your math if you do my dumb project for me," Alex said. He rolled his straw wrapper between his fingers.

"What project?" I asked.

Lilly winced and stuck her spoon into her cup. "A family tree. It's going to count as a big portion of our grade. She wants us to interview family members and stuff."

"I don't want to interview my grandparents. They're so boring," Alex said. "Like, what would I even ask them?"

"Ask them about the olden days," Lilly said and laughed. "Where were you when dinosaurs roamed the earth?"

Alex snort laughed mid-sip and I couldn't help but join them. My parents were kind of the worst.

"What if Mrs. Nolan asks about my father?" Alex asked.

I froze and almost dropped my cone. I hadn't even thought about that when they mentioned the project. Shit. How was I supposed to answer that question? In all these years he hadn't asked much and what he had asked I was able to give my standard response. *He hasn't been in our life.* A part of me knew this day would come. I hoped it would have been when he was older.

"Um, well," I hesitated. "Like I've said, I don't know much about him. He hasn't been a part of our life."

"So you never met your dad?" Lilly asked with an air of nonchalance.

"Nope," Alex said as he shrugged.

"That's tough," she said. "But I guess it's better than knowing him and having him not want you."

Well, fuck me sideways. How was a sweet ice cream hangout turning into talk of their childhood trauma?

"We'll figure out the project guys," I said, ruffling Alex's curls. "Don't worry."

Within a few seconds, they were on to talking about something else. Thank God. But I still felt terrible. I pulled out my phone and texted Mia.

Me: *Found out Alex has to do a freaking family tree project for school. He just asked about his father. WTF am I supposed to do?*

My chest loosened a bit from typing out the words.

Mia: *Wow... who assigns a project like that these days?! Okay... I know you're probably freaking out.*

Me: *Of course I am. I don't want him to show up with half a tree. It's hard enough that he knows he doesn't have a father... but to say that out loud in class, where he's already getting bullied. Maybe I should email his teacher...*

Mia: *You could, but I can't see her axing a whole project because of one student. And it's fifth grade sis, no one wants to be the odd one out. If she lets Alex do something else, that would be equally bad.*

Me: *True.*

Mia: *Why don't you ask Wes?*

I licked my dripping cone and responded.

Me: *Ask Wes what? He'll have to help Lilly with her project.*

Mia: *Ask him to be on Alex's family tree :)*

Mia: *You are married... it wouldn't be that weird.*

I could do that. But would Wes be uncomfortable? I'd never want to put him on the spot. Finishing my cone, I finally answered back.

Me: *I'll talk to him. But... I don't think that'll keep Alex from asking questions. And I haven't told Wes everything yet either. I don't know if I'm ready to open up like that. Not yet.*

Mia: *I understand. Crap, I gotta go. Sorry, am walking into a meeting. See you in class later?*

Me: *Yeah I'll be there.*

I snapped a pic of the kids with their ice cream and hit send.

Me: *BTW Cone Cove is amazing... you weren't kidding.*

A few minutes went by before she replied.

Mia: *OMG JEALOUS!*

"Ready to go kiddos?" I asked once I slipped my phone back into my purse.

"Can we go to the beach?" Lilly asked.

"No, not the beach. The arcade. Please, Mom. I'll do extra chores."

"How are you going to do chores in your cast?" Lilly asked, hand on her hip. "Wait, nevermind, I want the arcade, too. Pretty please, Olivia. I'll do his chores and extra."

I laughed at how they totally outnumbered me, but in the best way. "Okay, arcade for an hour. Once I'm out of cash, that's it." I looked at Alex. "No begging for more credits."

They whooped and got up to toss their trash while a wave of gratitude washed over me.

Wes had taken a rare Saturday off to go look at houses and Alex was going with him. In his words, he needed a house picking wingman. I would have gone too, but I had plans with Lilly for our girls' day.

I watched from the bathroom vanity as Wes ran a brush through his hair and grabbed a baseball cap, putting it on backwards. That was new and I didn't hate it. Not at all.

"Has Lilly talked to you about the big project they have at school?" I asked, putting on some mascara.

He wrapped his arms around my waist from behind and kissed my neck. "No, I don't think so. Why?"

"It's kind of a big deal. Worth a chunk of their grade. It's a family tree project." And the pit I thought had left was back in my stomach.

"Sounds cool," he said. "Except that her unfortunate mother's side will have to be included." He grabbed his deodorant from the counter and swiped some on under his shirt. I loved the smell... Cedar and sandalwood.

"Yeah, about that. I wanted to talk to you about something." He capped his deodorant and turned to me, studying my face with his deep eyes.

"Anything," he said.

"You know how I told you Alex's father has never been in the picture?" He nodded and I went on, that stupid pit feeling like it weighed a ton. "Well, that's not the full story."

I focused my gaze on my tube of lipgloss, turning it around in my palm. "I'm listening, Tiger."

Sighing, I finally met his gaze. "The truth is, I don't know who he is."

His eyes widened, but only for a moment before he blinked and nodded. "Shit... So, what does that mean?"

The whole story sat on the tip of my tongue waiting to spill out. The way he looked at me with such care had my chest cracking in two. I wrapped my arms around my chest and breathed deeply.

"It's a long story, but let's just say it wasn't consensual." His brows turned in. "My main reason for bringing this up is Alex's project. It might come up and I don't want you to be out of the loop. Alex doesn't know anything. Thankfully he hasn't asked much and... Yeah. It's a mess."

"Tiger, are you saying what I think you're saying?" He rubbed a hand over his mouth and down his chin. "Did someone hurt you?"

Stay strong. Do not cry.

Inhaling deeply, I met his gaze. I'd only ever talked about that night to my therapist, other than bits and pieces when Mia asked years ago. I wasn't ready to tell him everything. Not while we had such a good day planned, but I couldn't leave him in the dark.

"Yes, but it was a long time ago, and I promise I'm doing okay. I won't lie, it's hard sometimes. Smells and sounds... Certain things will trigger a memory or even a subtle feeling. I get these lumps in my throat that won't go away. But I promise I'm fine. I have Alex and he's everything to me... no matter how I got him. But yeah... I don't know who his biological father is. I don't remember anything from that night and I'm grateful for that. If I knew his face it would be harder to pretend that I'm the only one who made Alex. That there's no trace of that monster inside him."

Wes opened his arms and I fell into them. "I'm so sorry, baby." I buried my head in his chest, breathing him in and letting his comfort settle my racing heart. "If I could find him, I'd fucking kill him for touching you."

A strangled laugh escaped my lips because I could actually picture that after seeing him go crazy at the bar. "I promise I'm fine. I guess I'm mostly worried about Alex. All these years, I'd never planned what I would tell him when that time came."

He held me at arm's length, searching my face. "Don't tell him anything yet. As far as I'm concerned, I'm his father now and that's all any school project needs to know."

My throat clogged with emotion as I stared into his eyes. "Are you sure?"

"Of course." I brushed my lips against his, asking myself how I got so lucky.

"Thank you. You don't know how much that means to me."

"You mean the world to me," he said. "You and Alex."

I love you.

It sat on the tip of my tongue, dying to break free. I'd been thinking it for a while, if I were being honest with myself. But I wasn't ready to say it. What if he didn't feel the same? What if I was setting myself up for heartbreak?

After a few minutes, Lilly came bursting into the room, full of energy. "Olivia, are you almost ready to go?"

"Yup. Give me five more minutes."

Wes squeezed me again and whispered in my ear, "I can do a lot with five minutes."

"Keep it in your pants, buddy," I whispered back, giving him a little smack on the arm.

"Who said anything about my pants? I was talking about yours." He turned to grab his shoes with a devious smirk on his face.

"Not nice," I said. Now I had to take his daughter shopping with the image of him in my pants rolling through the back of my mind.

"What?" he feigned innocence. "I'm always nice."

"Right," I said, squeezing his ass as I walked by. "Have fun with Alex. Take lots of pics of the houses for me."

"We will. And hey, are you free tonight?"

I stopped at our door frame and smiled. "I don't know. Let me check with all my other male suitors."

He scrunched his brows and growled in the most feral way. I loved it.

"Consider all those male suitors erased from the earth, Tiger." I shook my head, laughing. "Let me take you out tonight. I'll get my mom to stay with the kids."

Butterflies fluttered in my ribcage, but I pretended to think about a response, tapping my chin. He grabbed me and nuzzled into my neck, nibbling until I yelped. "Okay, okay... it's a date. Where are you going to take me?"

"You'll see. Now get that sexy ass out of here before I shut the door and take those five minutes and then some."

Lilly sprinted to our door again, giving me an impatient look, so I kissed his cheek and headed out.

Hours later, after more than a few hundred dollars were spent, Lilly and I sat at a tiny table in the mall's food court sipping boba tea. She'd asked to try it and I'd been curious about it for a while. Turns out, it's freaking yummy.

"Are you excited about your new outfits?" I asked. We talked about the style she liked and I helped her find at least five new outfits in varying shades of primary colors. She said she was going for that aesthetic and talked all about what she meant by that while I listened and absorbed. She even snagged some new yellow Converse and some accessories.

"Obsessed is an understatement," she said, her voice full of joy. "Thanks so much for today."

"It's been fun. I love hanging out with you." My cheeks lifted in a grin as I realized I'd genuinely meant that. Lilly was an amazing kid.

"My mom and I never did stuff like this. She was always busy with Jeff or her boyfriends before him." Her tone grew somber. "Are you and my dad going to stay together forever?"

I gulped down the sip of tea that had been in my mouth before I choked. "Umm, well," I said, while she stared at me with her big eyes, identical to her father's. "Forever is a long time. But I can promise you this. I like your dad a lot and we care about each other. And you're so special to me." I held her hand and she grinned. "I'm here for you, always."

"I love you, Olivia." She sipped her tea and looked around at people passing by like she didn't just touch my freaking soul. "Can I get my ears pierced?"

I choked down the swell of emotion in my throat and squeezed her hand. "I love you too, sweetie. And sure, but let's text your dad first. I doubt he'll mind."

"Yes!" she said.

After Wes gave us the thumbs up, we finished our shopping spree with ear piercing and a trip to Sephora for some face wash for Lilly and a new lip shade for me. My heart overflowed already and I still had a date night with Wes ahead of me.

Chapter 33

Wes

WE PULLED UP TO Sunshine and Olivia turned to me with a raised brow. "Do you need to get something from your office?"

"Not exactly. Come on, you'll see." I got out of the car and walked around to open her door. She looked fucking stunning in a formfitting dress that hit mid-thigh, heels, and her hair tied back in a low ponytail.

I was more than a little nervous that she wouldn't like what Alex and I set up this afternoon. But I wanted her all to myself tonight and this made the most sense to me.

I unlocked the door and stood in front of her. "Okay, close your eyes." A shaky laugh left her lips. "I've got your hands."

"What's going on?" she asked as she closed her eyes and followed my lead.

"Just a little something Alex and I came up with," I said, walking her toward my office.

"Alex helped? That's so sweet."

"He did. You've raised quite the gentleman. I could take a few lessons from him." She smiled wide and I took a mental picture of this moment. "Almost there. Okay, stop here and don't open your eyes yet."

She rolled her red bottom lip between her teeth and let out a nervous laugh again while I lit the candles I arranged earlier throughout the restaurant. Caleb and Thea helped me set up a private dining space in my office, moving my desk into the corner and lugging a spare table and chairs in here. I had Caleb coming to cook for us any minute now. I paid him a few hundred bucks to make it amazing and to leave as soon as he finished cleaning up. Hopefully, he wouldn't flake out on me. The last thing I did was turn on the playlist I made on my phone, which it pained me to admit I'd been using daily.

"Okay, you can open."

She took in the space and grinned. "Oh my God, I didn't even realize this was your office at first. It looks great in here."

"Thank you. I had some help." I pulled out her chair. "Come have a seat. We have the place to ourselves. Well, except Caleb, who's coming to cook any minute now."

"I love this. It's perfect. There's not a pile of paperwork in sight."

I heard a sound from the back door, which had to be Caleb. "One second, I'll go grab drinks. What are you in the mood for?"

"Whatever you're having," she said.

I went into the kitchen to pull out the wine I had chilled at the same time that Caleb came in. "Hey, Boss. Your lady liking the surprise?" He grabbed a chef coat from a hook on the wall and slipped it on.

"So far," I said, uncorking the bottle. "You know what you're making?"

"Yup, all set. Go be all romantic and shit." He smiled a goofy grin and smacked my arm lightly.

"Don't burn the place down. I'd hate to ruin my date," I joked.

I came back into the office, poured our wine, and sat across from Olivia, quietly taking in how gorgeous she looked in the candlelight. After what she told me earlier, I was even more set on taking care of her. I'd never felt so angry and possessive at the same time. And I meant what I said. I'd make sure that asshole never took another breath if I ever found him. I didn't need to hear details, what I heard was enough to make me out for blood.

I watched her slender neck bob as a sip of wine slid down her throat. If Caleb wasn't here, Olivia would be my appetizer.

"Did you guys like any of the houses?" she asked, dabbing her lips with a napkin.

I pulled out my phone to show her the pictures I took. "We looked at three and I loved one of them. Here, take a look. Let's see if we have the same favorite."

She scrolled through the pics with a thoughtful gaze, pinching the screen on a few to zoom in. She flipped my phone to show me the exterior shot of the beach house I loved. "This one has to be it."

"I knew you'd love it."

I told her all about the features as she beamed back at me, asking questions in an excited tone. I could see us living there long-term. The place was perfect.

"Want to go check it out tomorrow?" I asked. "We can bring Lilly, too. Although, Alex already called dibs on the better bedroom, and who am I to argue the rules of dibs?" I shrugged, laughing.

"Of course... I can't wait. I was secretly upset that we may have had to find something inland but this is perfect. Are you sure it's in our budget?"

I knew she'd ask that question and while it was pricey, it wouldn't be a problem for me. I slung my arm around the back of my chair and pushed my tongue against my cheek. "It won't be a problem."

"Wes..." She narrowed her eyes. "I don't want us to take on a lease that's too expensive. I don't need beachside. We can find cheaper."

I leaned forward and took her hand in mine. "If you want beachside, you're getting beachside." I brought her hand to my lips and kissed the top of her palm. "You're going to have everything you want, no matter what."

She closed her eyes and inhaled. "I appreciate that. Really, I do. I guess it's tough for me since I've always relied on my parents for everything and I'm finally on my own and then bam—you're here to support me. I don't want to feel like I'm not pulling my weight."

"I understand. Should I find someplace else?"

She nibbled her bottom lip and sighed. "No, I do like this one. I'll make sure to contribute half to everything."

I clenched my jaw and nodded. "Of course, whatever makes you happy."

Caleb knocked and carried in two fresh green salads sprinkled with shaved parmesan and cracked black pepper. Oliva gave him a hug and thanked him for helping us before he turned to leave.

"He's come so far since I met him," she said. "I'm proud of him."

She wasn't wrong. I hadn't even had to gripe at him about being on his phone in a few months.

"Did you talk to Lilly about starting those self-defense classes?" I asked, hoping Lilly agreed.

"Yes, and she said she'd try it. She was especially keen on learning how to punch properly. I love that kid."

A warm glow flooded my chest. *Love.* She loved my kid. "I'm glad she agreed to try. I feel like she's really turning a corner." I sipped my wine and swallowed. "Or maybe I've gotten to know her better the last few months and feel closer to her."

"Keep on doing your best. Ask questions, spend time with her, and your relationship will continue to grow."

"You're right. I probably over complicated everything because I was scared. Even my mom mentioned the other day how much happier Lilly seems." I took a bite of my salad, chewing slowly.

"Once Alex gets his cast off, he'll be right there with her. Fingers crossed we get good news next week. He'd be devastated if he has to wear it longer or, God forbid, have another surgery."

I could understand that. "Let's hope for the best," I said. "Let's talk about you, though, my sexy wife." Her cheeks flushed, so I said it again. "My wife."

"It's so weird when you say that. So possessive."

"I am possessive. And I love to say it. Every time I do, I'm reminded of how fucking lucky I am to have you."

She touched her face, hiding the smile I could see peeking through her palm. "I don't know what to say."

"You don't have to say anything."

She took deep, heavy breaths. "No one's ever treated me this way. It's hard to accept compliments, you know?"

"I understand. Come over here, let me hold you." I pulled my chair out a few inches and gestured for her to sit. She pushed up and I drew her against me, settling her on my lap and cradling her in my arms so I could look into her eyes.

"You make me so happy, Wes, and that scares the shit out of me. I don't know what to do when you say all these nice things. A part of me is waiting for the other shoe to drop."

I held her face in my palm and brought my mouth to hers, kissing her softly. "This is new to me too. I've had so much bad shit happen to me that I feel like if I don't acknowledge the good, it'll slip away."

I kissed her again, sliding my tongue against the seam of her red lips. My cock thickened against her ass as she deepened the kiss.

Knock, knock. Of fucking course.

"Should I fire him?" I asked against Olivia's panting lips. She laughed and stood, adjusting her dress. "Because I'd really like to right about now."

"Come in," she called. Caleb came in holding the first plate. A chicken and pasta dish that smelled delicious.

"Okay, we can keep him," I said, and he looked at me with a raised brow. "You can bring in the rest and then head out."

"Dessert, too?" he asked.

"Yeah, that would be great."

"Thanks again, Caleb. This looks amazing," Olivia said, digging in. Caleb left for the kitchen and came back in holding a cake stand. Olivia eyed it curiously. "Wait... is that rum cake?"

A grin stretched across my face. "It is. That's one of my surprises. Alex helped me bake it this afternoon. Your recipe, of course."

"Oh my God, I'm going to cry. That is so sweet." She turned to Caleb, who was lingering in the doorframe. "Beat it, buddy. I'm about to thoroughly thank my husband."

After the initial shock on Caleb's face died down, he spun on his heel and left.

"Fuck, Tiger. I've never been more turned on than I am right now. Say it again."

She stood up, walking back to me slowly. "My husband."

Her words soaked into my skin, filling me with a fiery glow. "Game time, Tiger. Are you up for it?"

She nodded, biting her lip. "Eat your meal and then hide. If I find you, I fuck you so hard you won't be able to walk out of here."

My cock tightened, bursting against the seam of my zipper. I wasn't hungry anymore. Not for food. Only Olivia could satisfy my appetite.

"What if I'm not hungry?" she asked in a breathy whisper.

"Then I'll give you ten seconds to hide. Make it good. I know this place inside and out." I closed my eyes as she let out a rasped expletive and scrambled out the door.

I let her voice replay in my mind. *My husband*. It felt like her finally claiming me and fuck... I needed to sink so deep inside her that I etched myself into her bones.

She'd be wet and panting for me when I found her, and that only made me harder. I counted down from ten, loud enough that she could hear me over the music. I loved our games, but this had to be the sexiest by far.

"Ready or not, here I come." I stood up, pushing in my chair and turned toward the kitchen. There were a few nooks and crannies where she could fit her small frame. "You know I'll find you, Tiger. Get that pretty pussy ready for me."

I peeked around corners and listened for her panting breaths, not finding her anywhere in the kitchen. The more I looked, the more I ached to be inside her.

"Clever," I called. "Where can she be?" Making my way into the dark dining area, I noticed a tiny movement out of the corner of my eye and narrowed my gaze. She scrunched her body under the table in the far corner of the room.

"Found you," I said, moving toward her. She let out a squeal and made a run for it back toward my office. "Cheater! That's going to get you fucked even harder."

I let her have a head start while I removed my clothes as I walked, dropping each item on the floor. I wanted nothing between us when I caught her. My heavy cock bobbed in the cool air, already dripping at the tip.

When I stopped at the doorframe, I found her perched on my desk with her eyes blazing. "I guess I'm caught," she said, huskily.

"Pull up your dress, Tiger. I need to be inside you." I made my way over to her as she lifted her ass and hiked up her dress.

"I have a game for you," she said as I stepped between her open legs. "Find where I hid my panties."

I looked down, moistening my lips, and found her bare and glistening. "Fuck, say it again. I need to hear it from your lips as I fuck you."

I lined myself up at her slick entrance, pressing my thumb against her sensitive nub until she cried out.

"You're my husband, Wes." *Fuck, yes.* Without a second's hesitation, I pushed into her, balls deep as she moaned my name. "My husband fucks so good."

I pulled out and thrust back in, harder. Her nails dug into my shoulders for purchase. "Fuck yes, I do. This cock is all yours, wife. Rub your clit for me."

She reached between our damp skin, circling her clit with her fingertip while I rocked in and out of her slick heat. Every time she moaned my name, I let it sink into me, filling me with pride.

"You feel so good." She bit down on my shoulder until I hissed.

"Who feels so good?" I said, gripping her ass in my hands and slamming home.

"My husband feels so good." The slap of our skin and our feral moans filled the air while I fucked her hard and fast. "My husband's cock is perfect. Oh, God... Shit, I'm so close." She sucked my bottom lip between her teeth, biting down until I tasted copper.

"Yeah, baby. How close?" I groaned as I pulled out and slammed back in.

"Shit... Don't stop. Please." I yanked her as close to the edge of the desk as I could and lifted her legs up so they were flush against my chest.

"Hold on to the desk, Tiger... and don't stop playing with your clit until you're squeezing every drop out of me."

The change in position had us both crying out. She felt so fucking good. So tight. I wouldn't last much longer. She held onto the desk with one hand and picked up the pace against her clit with the other until her pussy clamped down on my cock like a vise.

"Come in me, Wes. Fill me up," she moaned as she rode out her release.

I pumped into her one more time as my balls tightened and cock spasmed.

"Fucking hell," I roared, coming so hard blackness laced my field of vision. I wrapped her in my arms and held tight while she squeezed every drop out of me.

Soreness didn't hit until minutes later, when I finally pulled out. My hips and back were feeling the brunt of our activities, and I needed to sit. We kissed, and I smoothed her dress down before grabbing a napkin from the table and wiping her dry.

"I'm exhausted now," she said with a laugh. "Should we take the food and the cake home and snuggle?"

"I like that plan. After I find your panties, of course."

"Good luck. I hid them well." She stood up and planted a kiss on my lips.

"Finders keepers. When I find them, they're mine." I gave her a lascivious grin and squeezed her ass.

"Fair is fair... My husband, the panty snatcher."

I smacked her ass and she yelped before jogging into the kitchen.

"Round two, at home now," I called. "Nobody calls me a panty snatcher and gets away with it."

Chapter 34

Olivia

"I DON'T CARE HOW many desserts you ply me with. Don't expect me to unpack boxes for you again for a long time," Kendahl said, dropping a box at my feet.

"I'm sorry! Thank you again. You don't know how much I appreciate you guys." I opened the box she'd brought over to me and stacked books on my bookshelf.

"I want the good wine with our pizza tonight. No box crap," she said with a smirk.

"Anything for you, my loyal helper." I bent my head in a mock bow and she snort laughed.

In all seriousness, I don't know how I would have survived the past few weeks without our support system. Alex's appointment went well. They discharged him with a referral for physical therapy three times a week and a follow-up visit in six weeks. He was like a new kid without his cast—optimistic and energized. Although, the school situation was still iffy. He and Lilly stayed pretty quiet about it though, and my emails to the teacher haven't answered much. At least their grades have gone up, thanks to us rocking their family tree projects.

If the teacher thought anything of Wes's family being on both Alex and Lilly's project, she said nothing and for that, I was grateful.

After that good news, we found out they accepted our application for the beach house but wanted a fast move. Two weeks! It's been a whirlwind of work, pack, sleep, repeat.

But it would be worth it. The house was more than I could ever hope for. It fit our little blended family perfectly and we had room to fit a table big enough for family dinners. There was no way Regina could object to a home like this for Lilly.

Wes and Walter came into the living room, each carrying table lamps. "Where do you want these, Tiger?"

"Tiger?" Walter asked. "Is that some kind of sexual innuendo?"

Wes groaned. "Dad, seriously?"

Walter put the lamp down on the floor and walked toward the front door, shaking his head. "I don't need to know."

"Your father cracks me up," I said to Wes. "Such a character." Wes came up behind me and squeezed me around the middle.

"That he is. The place is looking great. What else can I do?"

I settled the last book from the box onto the shelf and stepped back against Wes's chest to survey my work. "It's missing something."

"Looks good to me. I can bring in some of my license plates if you want to jazz it up."

I twisted my neck to glare up at him. "Hard pass."

"Your loss." He shrugged with a smile. "Maybe you should quit listening to your dirty audiobooks and buy books instead. Fill these empty shelves."

"Oh yeah, because that's what Regina needs to see when she comes over. Half-naked man books lining the shelves. I'll stick to audio, thank you very much. Plus, I like their voices." I watched Kendahl and Coby walk inside, chatting to themselves and carrying a box of toys into the kid's room.

"If you want me to talk dirty more, you should have said so." He leaned his face against the crook of my neck and whispered in my ear. "Now what did that book I caught you listening to say? Hm, I remember." He lowered his tone to a deep timbre. "Shut the fuck up and take that dick like a good girl."

I'm ashamed to say that I melted right there. Yeah, Wes's dirty mouth did it for me.

"God, Wes... You can't just say stuff like that with our family around." I said through closed lips, although I couldn't help myself from smiling. "Save it for later."

"Roar, Tiger. Put your claws away, I'll be good," he crooned. "Now, where do you want those lamps?"

"Over there." I pointed to the corner of the room as Mia and Shawn walked inside.

"Sorry we're late!" Mia called. "Shawn had to deliver some furniture to a client. I brought snacks though." I grabbed the empty box to break it down for recycling and went to hug my sister.

"Where can I help?" Shawn asked, getting right to the point. Maybe I was imagining things, but he looked more frazzled than usual. I hoped he wasn't having a rough time with his mental health. Like me, he had flare-ups with his PTSD symptoms now and again.

"I think Wes is planning on assembling our bedframe. I'm sure he could use some help." I smiled and pointed toward the bedroom. He hugged Mia and whispered something in her ear before heading that way.

"Bring anything good?" I asked, peeking into the shopping bag Mia had put down on the kitchen counter.

"Always. Check it out. Take whatever you want but, uh, leave the crackers for me." She plopped down in one of our kitchen chairs and took a sip from her water bottle.

I pulled out a bag of sour cream and onion chips, a container of pre-cut fruit, two packages of cookies, and a box of saltines. Opting for the chips, I opened them and sat next to my sister.

"So how's it going? I haven't talked to you much the past few weeks." I pulled out a chip and took a crunchy bite.

Mia wrinkled her nose at me and I swear her skin took on a green tinge. "Do you mind eating those somewhere else? Sorry, I've just been a bit nauseated today."

Crinkling the bag shut, I brought it back to the counter and grabbed her the box of crackers. "Do you want something else? Some ginger ale maybe? I can have Wes run to the store."

"No, I'll be okay." She held up the box of crackers for emphasis. "Have you heard from Mom? She called me yesterday."

Joy. Talking about our parents was my favorite. Sarcasm intended.

"Not since I updated her on Alex's leg. She was busy, so we didn't stay on the phone long. Why, what's up?"

"Well... don't hate me, but I kind of let it slip that you married Wes. Before you freak out, she took the news as well as expected."

"You did what?" I asked. "I was purposely keeping her and Dad out of the loop. They'll meddle now. I know it."

"She promised me she wouldn't, but she mentioned taking a trip down here soon. They're in the final stages of the divorce, so once that's done she's free. Her words." Mia opened the box and took out a few crackers, stacking them in front of her.

"Let's hope something comes along to distract her before she plans a trip here," I said. I needed a longer break before dealing with my mother in person again. As amazing as Wes and his family were, I knew she'd find a way to pick apart their flaws. That was her superpower. Which was the absolute last thing we needed when our relationship was so fresh and in this weird limbo.

"She had a few things to say about not including her in your wedding plans. I told her it was a spontaneous thing, and I wasn't involved either, but she still took on that tone. You know the one she uses when she's hurt but pretending like she's not."

I winced. "I know the one. Have you talked to Dad too, or just Mom?"

"Just Mom. You know Dad and I don't talk unless he needs something from me." She nibbled the edge of a cracker. Our father was a real ass in general, but especially to Mia. That's how it's always been, and us growing up didn't change much. He may have viewed me as the damaged one but he still loved to parade me around. When it came to Mia, nothing she did was ever good enough.

"Talking about them is bumming me out. God, I'm so happy I moved." I stood up and stretched my tired arms over my head. Moving boxes and getting used to Krav classes again was kicking my ass. "Want to help me unpack the dishes? I'm good with doing most of the house little by little but leaving the kitchen in boxes will drive me bonkers."

"Yeah, I think I can handle that. As long as I don't have to bend or lift much." I raised a brow her way and she quickly added, "I think I pulled a muscle."

A few hours later, we all sat around on towels and camping chairs at the beach to watch the sunset. I tugged my wagon through the sand, stacked with boxes of pizza and drinks while Alex and Lilly ran beside me.

"Alex, please be careful! I don't think you should run yet." He rolled his eyes but they both slowed. It would take a long time before I got over the trauma of his injuries. If I was a nervous mom before, he was in for it now.

Once everyone settled into their spots with their plates of pizza, I leaned into Wes's chest, watching the people I loved chatting happily. "This is perfect. Thank you."

He kissed the top of my head. "For what?"

"Being a part of my life," I said with a genuine smile. If I took a snapshot of my life a year ago, it looked nothing like this. I was lonely, estranged from my sister and wrapped up in my parent's toxic lives. While I stayed busy enough taking care of Alex, I didn't have anything that filled my cup as a woman outside of being a mother. It took stepping into this new life to see how much I'd needed that.

"I should be thanking you. You don't know how much you've turned my life around." He took a bite of his pizza, chewing slowly. "We have one more big obstacle with Regina, and then I hope things will settle down and we can enjoy each other without so much stress."

We hadn't had a conversation about the silent changes to our original plan since New Year's Eve, but hearing him now, I had a feeling this was as real for him as it was for me. Those words felt like he was in it for the long haul.

My chest swelled with warmth, knowing I wasn't alone in those feelings.

While I was in the middle of waiting on a particularly difficult table, my phone buzzed in my pocket.

"I want my eggs cooked for exactly three minutes. No more and no less," the woman sitting at table five asked. She had her glasses perched at the tip of her nose while she scrutinized the menu. "And I'd like the whole wheat toast, dry. Lightly toasted. No burned bits or I'll send it back."

I forced a smile. "Of course. Can I get you both anything else?"

Her companion held out his empty mug to me without making eye contact and after getting distracted by my phone once again, I grabbed it from his outstretched hand. "Regular or decaf, sir?"

"Regular. Strong. Whole milk." He closed the menu and thrusted it at me without tearing his gaze from his phone.

"Coming right up," I said in the sweetest tone I could muster.

Kelly bumped into me on my way to place their order. "I've had that couple before. Good luck, Wifey."

She hadn't stopped teasing me since Caleb spread the word that we were married. We finally confirmed it to be true about a week ago and were met with nothing but love from everyone. Teasing, too.

Caleb was at the grill, so I made sure to give him their order verbatim. On my way back out, I popped into Wes's office to check my phone. Wes was sitting at his desk, getting together our weekly produce order.

"Hey, beautiful," he said, looking up from his paperwork.

"Hey, I got a call. Do you mind if I check in here?"

"Go ahead. Oh, and if you're interested, the woman who supplies our desserts took a leave for a few weeks. I was thinking maybe you could give it a try? I know you love to bake and what I've had has been incredible."

"Oh, wow." I thought for a moment. I'd always loved baking and people said I had a knack for it. But was I ready to bake for a restaurant? "Can I think about it?"

"Of course. And hey, even if we only serve rum cake for a few weeks, that'll be enough." He adjusted his hair and went back to his paper, not realizing how much he'd melted my heart.

I pulled out my phone and my stomach dropped. "Shit."

"What's wrong?" I met his gaze with a face that surely looked mortified.

"The school called. Hold on, they left a message." I scrolled to my voicemail and hit play, turning the speaker on so Wes could hear too. My stomach tied itself in knots waiting for the caller to start speaking.

"Ms. Murphy, this is Principal Adams over at Sunset Elementary. Unfortunately there's been an incident and Alex is here in my office. He's unharmed, but I do need a parent to pick him up. Call the office back at your earliest convenience."

I hit end and stuffed the phone back in my pocket, holding back tears. "What the hell? I can't do this anymore, Wes."

His eyebrows pinched in. "What does he mean by an incident? I swear if it's those asshole kids again, I'll lose it."

I stepped closer, planting a hand on his shoulder. "If it is, we'll deal with it. I might just have to push for them to start private school earlier than later if this school isn't going to do anything."

Wes sighed and rubbed his temples. "I'll be ready to go in a minute. See if Kelly can cover your tables."

"You don't have to come. You're busy," I argued.

He narrowed his eyes. "I'll be out in a minute."

We found Alex sitting outside the principal's office. At first glance, he looked fine, but his sagging shoulders told me that wasn't the case. The office administrator let us through while she knocked on the principal's door.

"Hey, what's going on?" I asked Alex quietly. From this angle, I could see another boy seated in a chair a few feet away from us.

"Another fight," he said. "I didn't start it, Mom. And the teacher broke it up right away."

Wes put a hand on his shoulder. "Alright, we'll get this figured out."

Chapter 35

Wes

"I CAN'T BELIEVE HE suspended him," Olivia said for the tenth time since we got home with Alex. "How is missing school going to help? And it's a load of crap that the other kid got the same punishment and nothing worse."

"It's dumb as fuck, but I get that the principal has to go by the book. Not that I agree. Let's call the private schools and set up some meetings. Maybe if we explain our situation they'll fit the kids in."

She sighed and curled her legs underneath her on the couch. "Okay. I guess we don't have other options. I should have done that sooner but I was being optimistic. It seemed like the issue was over after their break."

"Don't worry about it, we'll get it figured out."

Staring out the window at the waves crashing in the distance, I let my mind clear. It wouldn't help to stress about the situation any more than I needed to. I had to be calm for Olivia, she needed me. But damn, it felt like everything was coming to a head. And to top it off, the anniversary of the accident was next week, the day after Regina was showing up. Because of course, the universe would screw me like that.

"I think I'm going to throw on a cheesy show and relax. Want to join me?"

I turned to see her pulling a throw blanket over her lap. "Nah, I'm gonna go to the gym for a bit. Do you mind keeping an eye on Lilly?"

"Not at all. Have fun." I leaned in and kissed her forehead before grabbing what I needed for the gym and heading out.

I was halfway there when my phone buzzed.

Tiger: *Dumb question, but do you know why the Wi-Fi isn't working?*

Fuck. I knew I'd forgotten something during the chaos of moving. I guess I could live without that shit, so it didn't cross my mind. I grabbed the phone and started to text back, but a car honked. I must have swerved into their lane. Fucking phone.

I tossed the thing into the passenger seat and left it there the whole time I was at the gym.

By the time I got home, I had worked off some of my pissy attitude and felt like shit for ignoring Olivia's text. The house was quiet and she was in bed, scrolling on her phone. At my footsteps, she lifted her head to meet my gaze. I couldn't read her expression, but it wasn't a happy one.

"Hey," I said, pulling off my sweaty shirt and tossing it in the hamper.

"Hey." She went back to whatever she was looking at on her phone. "How was the gym?"

"Good. I'm gonna hop in the shower." Before I went into the bathroom, I grabbed everything I'd need, including my crutches. "Oh, and about the Wi-Fi. I never set it up. It slipped my mind."

She gave a curt nod. "I figured."

"I can take care of it in the morning." I pushed the bathroom door open and set my things down.

"Don't bother. I'll take care of it."

"What's with the tone?" I was in no mood to argue.

"Oh, I don't know... Maybe the fact that you couldn't text me back in the three hours you were gone." Her voice was clipped.

"Maybe I don't want to be attached to that fucking phone nonstop like every other zombie out there." I sounded colder than I meant to. But I was being truthful. I hated the things.

"No one says you need to be a 'phone zombie.'" She used air quotes when she repeated my phrase. "But a text back is common courtesy."

"Why would you text me when you knew I was driving? Where's the common courtesy there?"

She dropped her phone in her lap and sat up straight. "You didn't have to look at it right away. That wouldn't be safe."

"That's my point. It's not safe. You have no idea how unsafe they are." I rubbed on the back of my neck. "I'm gonna shower. We'll talk later."

Except, we didn't talk later. When I got out of the bathroom, the lights were off and Olivia was facing the other direction. I contemplated tapping her shoulder to continue our conversation, but I was too exhausted to bother.

She'd never get why I felt the way I did. It would always be a matter of contention between us. Hell, I'd only gotten the thing because of her. She's been lucky I've even carried it on me to begin with.

I watched the rise and fall of her ribcage, wishing I could be different for her. Maybe if I held her in my arms, this pissy attitude would melt away? But fuck, I doubted she wanted that, at least not without resolving our argument.

I tossed and turned for a while before finally falling asleep.

The following days were tense between us. I apologized for being a dick, but I didn't promise I'd change regarding the phone shit. How could I promise something that I had no intention of sticking to?

Olivia's babysitter had been home with Alex for his suspension while Lilly begged to stay home, too.

On the plus side, Olivia called a few of the private schools and set up meetings. The negative being that they still insisted they were full until the following school year. With an end in sight, maybe it would be easier for us all to breathe easier, but it wasn't ideal.

It was Lilly's first class at the gym, and Alex and I were on our way to cheer her on for the last half. Olivia would be supervising as a volunteer assistant. I'd been curious about these classes for a while, so I was excited to see what went on in there.

Alex led me through the glass doors like he owned the place. I was instantly hit with a familiar gym smell—metal tinged with body odor, covered up by air fresheners. The place looked decent enough, nothing fancy. Red walls, concrete floors covered with rubber mats, bright overhead lighting. Electronica music pumped through speakers. But my eyes zeroed in on Olivia, standing next to Lilly, showing her how to punch a big vinyl pad.

There were about a dozen other kids in the class, looking anywhere from five years old to Lilly's age. Some didn't need help doing whatever their drill was. They were punching and circling their partner like synchronized dancers.

I caught Lilly's eye and her lips perked up in a lopsided smile. Pride swelled in my chest at my two girls working together, being fierce as fuck.

The instructor, a petite woman with long dark hair tied back, stood at the front of the room. She called for Olivia to join her.

"Before class is over we're going to practice a tough drill, but it's so important. What do we always want to do first, before anything else?" She pointed at a young boy who raised his hand. "Yeah, Tyler?"

"Be aware of our surroundings?" he answered.

"Very good," the instructor said. "Oliva and I are going to go through some drills to show you how being aware of my surroundings helps me stay safe."

I watched them role play a few different scenarios while the kids watched with rapt attention. Then they finished the class with a fun obstacle course game. Alex was chomping at the bit by my side, more than ready to jump in, too. Oliva had told him at his six week check up she'd talk to his doctor. We were both eager for him to start classes almost as much as he was.

We took two cars over to Sal's pizza for dinner before heading home. Like the past few nights, Olivia showered first and retreated to her side of the bed, phone in hand while I contemplated our situation.

"Want to play Spades?" I asked. Games always broke us out of any awkward tension.

"No, thanks. I think I'm going to finish my audiobook and go to bed." She reached for her earbuds on the side table.

"Okay, I guess I'll leave you to it then." I went to double-check the kids were all good and ended up sitting outside on the porch with a beer, listening to the waves.

Whenever I felt shitty, I turned to Dylan. He couldn't answer me. But it helped to pretend.

"I'm fucking up man. God, I wish you were here to kick my ass and make me a better man." I swallowed a swig of beer. "It'll be eight years soon. Can you believe that shit? How the hell I've made it this long is beyond me. There were more than a few times I was sure I'd be joining you up there. I guess that wasn't in the plans for me, though. And I know you'd be pissed if I left Lilly like that. It's just, shit... So many nights I lie awake thinking how it should have been me that night. I was the one fucking around. I was the drunk one."

I finished my beer in two more swallows. "Don't worry, I'll have a bowl of Cheerios and beer for you, you weird bastard. And brother, if it's possible, can you help me out with Olivia? I'm trying, but fuck... It's difficult to let her in."

I heaved in a breath, feeling it lodge in my windpipe. The air never quite reached my stomach when I thought about that night. With one more look at the charcoal sky, I headed into the house, feeling lower than I'd felt in a long time.

Chapter 36

Olivia

Wes woke up even more distant than usual. He'd barely uttered a word to me the entire morning and I didn't know how to feel. In truth, I hadn't been a peach either lately. Stress was getting to me. Every morning for the past week I'd woken up at three in the morning in a sweat with my heart racing. It seemed like we were clashing on so many small things, too. Obviously, the phone situation was a biggie and it was looking like that wasn't going to change. He'd actually stopped carrying it with him all together. He's been leaving a mess in the house, going out without letting me know when he'd be back, and has even been distant toward Lilly.

Something was going on with him. That much was a given. I'd bet it was the stress of Regina coming by today. I wasn't worried though. Clearly, Lilly is happy and well cared for. What could she hold against us?

Wes worked for a few hours that morning while the kids and I cleaned, making sure the house was spotless. When he came home, I initiated the conversation.

"How was work?"

I followed him into the bedroom to change. "Fine. Same old." He glanced around the bedroom. "Looks great in here. Thanks."

"The kids helped," I said.

I wanted him to come to me, wrap me in his arms, call me Tiger, and kiss me like he's missed me all morning.

But he went into the closet to get dressed without another word. I took the cue to give him space. I checked in with the kids, who were both feeling the tension in the house.

"Be yourselves guys," I said. "It'll be okay."

"My grandmother isn't very nice," Lilly said. "I've only seen her a few times, but I remember that she always yelled at me for touching her stuff."

"My grandma used to do that, too," Alex said. "I wasn't gonna break anything."

"No one's yelling today, I promise. Come on, let's fix your hair, Lil. We should clean your ears too."

The doorbell rang right on time. Wes took a deep inhale beside me and opened the door.

"Hello, Wesley," Regina said with an air of superiority. Everything about her screamed *I'm better than you*, from the way she sounded to the thousands of dollars of designer clothes. Little did she know, I grew up with people like her. Not only my parents, but everyone they surrounded themselves with.

"Regina," Wes said curtly. "Come on in."

She lifted her chin and stepped inside. I know I only saw Savannah for a few minutes the day she dropped Lilly off, but I couldn't help but wonder how someone like her came from a woman like this.

"Hi, I'm Olivia. Nice to meet you." I stuck my hand out to shake hers, but she ignored it and walked past me to the kitchen.

"Where's my granddaughter?" she asked, poking into one of the kitchen cabinets. She sniffed and turned back toward us. I noticed her eyes lingering on Wes's prosthetic leg for more than a few seconds.

"I'll get her. I'd like you to meet my son, Alex, as well. He and Lilly have become close friends. Wes, why don't you offer Regina a drink?" I widened my eyes at him trying to silently imply to get a move on since he hadn't left the front doorway.

"No, I don't think I will," he said. "She won't be here long, right, Regina?"

My face grew hot while Regina gave him a look of utter hatred. "Wes, that's no way to treat our guest," I said. "I'll go get the kids and then make you something. Tea, coffee, sparkling water?"

"Thank you. At least someone has manners. A sparkling water sounds lovely, Amelia." She went back to poking around our kitchen.

"It's Olivia," I said. "But sure, no problem. Wes, join me." I asked in an overly sweet tone. Once we were out of earshot, I turned to him and whispered through gritted teeth, "What is wrong with you today?"

He crossed his arms. "What? Because I'm not kissing the devil's ass?"

"You don't have to kiss her ass, but maybe try to be civil. Your future is riding on today." I leaned against the wall and racked a hand through my hair. This stress was more than I could take.

"I refuse to kiss her ass today or any day. She can do what she came to do and get out." He took on a harsh tone I'd never heard from him before. I wrapped my arms around my chest and turned away from him.

"Fine, if you want to make a bad impression, that's on you. I guess I'm the only one of us who cares about Lilly." I held back tears and stormed away from him and into the guest bathroom.

Patting my face with cold water, I took some deep breaths and tried to stop my brain from spiraling. This wasn't the Wes I knew. I had no idea who that man was. Yes, we've had a lot of stress but we've always been able to lean on each other and work toward our common goals. I had to pull myself together for Lilly. I loved that girl enough for both of us.

When I came out of the bathroom, Wes was nowhere to be seen, but I heard the kids talking with Regina in the living room.

I peeked in the bedroom but he wasn't there either. I was going to kill that man.

"Sorry about the wait," I said as I entered the living room. "Let me get you that drink."

"It's fine. The children are telling me all about what they do every day. Krav Maga classes for children? Is that safe?"

I put her drink on one of my wooden coasters in front of her, and sat across from her on the couch. "It's extremely safe. They teach confidence and how to stay safe in all kinds of situations. There's very little physical contact."

"I saw your son was recently injured. Was that from these classes?" She sipped from her glass and focused her gaze on me.

"No, that was from an accident at school," I said, keeping my tone clipped.

"Bullies," Alex added.

Was it a good time to smack myself in the face? I made eyes at Alex and he cleared his throat and fixed his gaze out the window.

"Bullies? That sounds serious. Lilly, have they bothered you?" She craned her neck toward her granddaughter and gave her the same intense stare down.

"Um—not so much." Lilly sounded so small, it broke my heart.

"I see," Regina said. "I'll be speaking to the principal about this."

Shit, shit, shit. "No need to bother yourself with that. They'll be changing schools soon. We toured this amazing private school and they've been accepted for next school year."

My cheeks heated as the exaggeration slipped past my lips. It wasn't a total lie, but somewhat truthful.

"Well, that's good to hear. Is it Bright Minds Academy? I have a few friends on the board."

I couldn't remember the name of the schools I looked at. Not while she was giving me such intense eye contact with those clear blue eyes that looked almost translucent. "I think so. I'd have to find the email and double check."

"If you don't mind, I'd like that information, so I can follow up with them," she said.

"Sure, I'll send it over." I chewed on my bottom lip wondering where in the world Wes went.

"Oh, and have you chosen the date for your psychological testing?" Regina pulled out her phone and tapped her screen. "Best to get it done and out of the way, don't you agree?"

"Psychological testing?" This was the first time I heard about anything like that. Background testing, yes, but not psychological.

"Yes, and I'd need to have backgrounds done on anyone else that will be in Lilly's life. What are the arrangements with your son's father?"

I choked on the lump in my throat. This wasn't a topic I was comfortable talking about with a complete stranger, especially in front of the children. Thankfully, Wes picked that moment to walk back inside. We turned our heads in his direction.

"It's time for you to go, Regina. If you didn't finish touring the house, that's on you."

She stood up and brushed her hands down her immaculate pants. "It's clear you're still ill mannered and classless. I hope you have a stellar lawyer ready."

"Get out," his voice boomed, making me flinch.

"Goodbye, Lilly. Grandmother will see you soon," she said as she grabbed her purse and walked with her chin raised past Wes and out the door.

The four of us sat in silence for a few moments, processing what had just happened. Alex finally spoke up. "Can I go play video games?"

"Yeah, go ahead." My voice cracked as I added, "Lilly, why don't you go, too?"

Once they were out of the room, I steeled myself for the difficult conversation I knew I needed to have.

"I know what you're going to say," Wes said. He sat across from me on the couch, knees wide and head in his hands.

"And what is that?"

"That I fucked up. That you're pissed at me for walking outside?" His voice broke as he sank lower onto the couch.

"If you already know that, then why? I'm so confused lately, Wes. Things were going so well, not just with me but with the kids, too. I know you were putting in the work to be better for Lilly. So why be like this? I need to know."

I tried to keep my voice even. To bite my tongue at the annoyance and frustration wanting to escape through cold words. It wasn't easy, especially since he was giving me so little.

He finally lifted his head but cast his gaze down at the floor. "I'm no good at this. Being a father... a husband... a friend. I can't take care of anyone when I'm such a fucking mess. Why bother with Regina? I refuse to kiss her ass when I know it won't get me anywhere."

I stood up and paced the living room. "I understand you don't like her but do you really want her to fight us for Lilly? It doesn't take much to use common courtesies. And then you left her with me... How could you? She asked me about Alex's father." My voice drifted off as I tried to hold back tears.

Something in Wes finally snapped back into place and he came to me, pulling me against his chest and wrapping his arms around me. He stroked my hair and kissed the top of my head. I was so frustrated. Not only with him, but with everything. Why couldn't things be easy? Back home when it was just Alex and me, no one else mattered. I didn't feel so raw all the time.

"I'm so fucking sorry, baby," he whispered into my hair. "I've been a dick and I know it. I don't deserve you."

I looked up at the devastation in his features and hated what we'd become. "I'm trying to help, Wes. It's harder than you realize for me to open myself up but I am because I care. I want to help you but you have to let me, and most of all you have to help yourself."

He blinked and nodded, letting my words sink in. "You're right. I'm going to try harder."

He tipped my chin up and brushed a gentle kiss against my lips. I wrapped my arms around him and buried my face in his chest, breathing deeply. I didn't know how much I needed this connection until that moment. There was still so much up in the air but at least I was getting through to him.

"Did you know about her setting up psychological testing for us?" I asked once we were sitting back on the couch.

"You mean background tests?"

"No—well, she's doing those, too. I mean getting cleared by a psychologist. She mentioned us scheduling our sessions. Can she force that?" I didn't need her looking up my psychological records. That was my business.

Wes ran his hands through his hair for the hundredth time. I loved when it looked all disheveled though. It gave him character. "I have no clue, but I found a good lawyer and set up an appointment for this week. I had a feeling today wouldn't be enough for her to back down."

I huffed but bit my tongue. It could have been enough, if he cooperated. "That was a good idea. Should I call my father, too? Ask him for advice?"

"I don't know. It seems wrong to involve them in my issues," he said.

"You mean our issues? This isn't only on you." After the day we've had, him not including me stung even more.

"Yeah, sorry." He stretched his arms over his head. "It's been a long day. Let's worry about Regina another day, okay?"

"Okay." I didn't have it in me to argue so I got up and went into the other room. Wes stayed at the opposite end of the house for the rest of the day, tinkering around in the kitchen and then cooking dinner. We ate in relative silence, each of us avoiding the Regina conversation.

After dinner, we went about our bedtime routines—showering, brushing teeth, getting comfortable. I missed Wes's hands on me, missed our physical connection.

"How are you feeling?" I asked, trying to make conversation.

"Honestly, not great. I've got some phantom pain in my leg, my hips hurt, all this stress is killing me, and on top of that I know I'm failing you." He adjusted the blanket and palmed his residual limb with a light massage.

"What does phantom pain feel like?" I'd been wondering about that, but always felt too nervous to ask.

He sighed and continued massaging. "It's hard to describe but it changes. It can feel like pins and needles some days or get so bad that it feels like being stabbed with a hot knife. It's gotten better over the years. Either that or I've gotten better at dealing with it."

I reached out and rested my palm on his thigh. "I'm sorry, I can't even imagine that kind of pain."

"I wouldn't want you to. I'd never wish this pain on anyone." He hissed a breath as he rubbed.

"Can I?" I trailed my palm lower, wanting to help in any way that I could.

His dark eyes met mine and softened. "You don't have to."

"I want to." With sure strokes, I worked my palms lower, paying extra attention to his scar tissue. "Is this pressure okay?"

He closed his eyes and leaned his head against the headboard. "Yeah, it feels good."

I continued massaging, working his thighs and hips above his boxers before going back down and repeating. His breathing slowed and face softened, filling me with a warmth that I hadn't felt in days.

We may be in a weird place, but this was a huge step for us. He'd rarely given me a chance to even see him without his prosthesis on, let alone touch him without it. It felt like he was giving me a piece of himself.

"Thank you, Tiger," he whispered. His eyes still closed.

I kept massaging until a light snore fell from his lips and his head flopped to the side.

With this small connection after such a difficult day, I fell asleep feeling like maybe we'd be okay.

Chapter 37

Olivia

I GOT IN MY car after Krav class the following evening feeling more than emotional. We worked on choke defenses and something about the drill had my mind spiraling. It wasn't a flashback or memory, more like a feeling. I shoved it down for as long as I could to finish the drill with Kendahl, but as soon as we took a break, I excused myself early.

I reached for my phone to text Wes but thought better of it. I'd rarely seen him carrying his phone lately. He was super quiet that morning and all afternoon at work, keeping to himself and barely saying two words to me.

I tried to bring up Regina but he brushed me off. He hadn't even gotten all grumpy and growly when Damon and his business partner came in for lunch and flirted with me.

I hurt too much to go right home, not without calming down first.

Halfway home, I turned around and drove toward Sunshine. Thea or Derek may have still been there cleaning up, but they wouldn't mind me coming in. Maybe an hour of baking in peace and quiet would help me refocus and get rid of the pit in my stomach.

As I pulled into the parking lot, I noticed Wes's car parked in his usual space. If he was here, who was with the kids? Once parked, I texted Alex.

Me: *Hey... Who's with you guys?*

I collected my purse and fixed my hair in the rearview while Alex replied.

Alex: *Grandma Val is here. We're watching a movie and having popcorn.*

Well, now I was both relieved and irritated. How could he leave without letting me know?

Me: *Ok, I'll be home soon*

Wes was about to be reminded of why he nicknamed me Tiger. Being here at the restaurant instead of home where the kids could eavesdrop was for the best. I could speak my mind and let out my frustrations.

I walked toward the front door and peeked in the window, surprised to see the dining area lit up. Then my gaze slowly fell on Wes sitting in a far booth with his back toward me. He wasn't alone. A gorgeous woman with chestnut brown hair hanging in waves at her shoulders sat across from him. Her hand covered his as they talked over mugs of what I guessed had to be coffee.

I quickly moved away from the window and into the shadows so I could collect my thoughts. Peeking around the corner again, I saw her shoot Wes a beaming grin. My heart sunk right to my toes. Whoever she was, I wasn't important enough in Wes's life for him to clue me in. To see him laughing and smiling with another woman when he'd been absolutely miserable with me was the cherry on top of my shit sundae.

"Screw this," I huffed. This was why I didn't let people in. I'd only set myself up to be hurt. Holding back tears, I got in my car and drove home.

I was done.

The lights were off and the kids and Val were watching a Marvel movie in the living room when I came through the door. Seeing them like that, happy and content, had an ache settle in my chest. I didn't know what to do. All I knew was I didn't want to see Wes. Not at all.

Val peeked her head up and smiled at me from the couch. I mustered a half smile in return before turning my back to put my bag away. I couldn't look at her, she was too sweet all the time and I knew myself. I'd break down in front of her at a single nice gesture.

She placed a palm on my back and I felt myself shudder. "How was your class?"

"Fine," I said. I made myself busy at the counter, anything to avoid looking at her.

"I thought Wesley would be home before you, but I guess he needed more time."

At that, I turned to face her. "More time for what?"

She studied my expression and her face fell. "He didn't tell you?" She shook her head and sighed. "I'm sorry, I know my son is hardheaded but I thought he'd opened up with you."

I couldn't take much more of this, not while my pulse already raced and I was two seconds away from crying. "Val, what's going on? Why did Wes leave?" *And who was that woman?*

She gave my arm a gentle squeeze. "This is a conversation for him to have with you. But today is the anniversary of his accident. It's a h-hard day for us all. You should talk to him when he gets back." Emotion clouded her eyes and she sniffed. "I need to get going, early morning at the church tomorrow." She gave me a quick hug and left without another word.

I stood there staring at the spot she'd just left. Everything made sense now. Wes retreating into himself, his moods. But who was that woman and why couldn't he tell me what was going on? As much as this wasn't about me, we're a team and being left out of important details in his life felt like crap.

With the kids still occupied by the movie, I went into the bedroom and paced, holding my phone. I was right in assuming he'd left his phone home. It was sitting on his end table turned off. But I could call the restaurant... Maybe he'd answer there? What would I say? *Oh hey, your mom told me it's the anniversary of the worst day of your life, want to talk about it? Oh yeah, who's the woman you're with?*

No. This was a face to face conversation. I'd opened up to him about my past, much more than I'd ever opened up to another person and it hurt that he didn't trust me enough to clue me in.

I took my time in the shower, letting the hot water beat against my tired muscles. He still wasn't home when I got out. At least I knew he was at Sunshine, or hoped that's where he still was.

I had the kids get ready for bed, telling them Wes was working late when they asked why he wasn't home yet. My stomach clenched from lying, but it was the best excuse I could come up with.

Laying in bed, I watched the time tick by on my phone, while trying to keep my mind busy scrolling social media. It was after eleven and he still hadn't come home. I'd bitten my lip so much that it bled while every negative possibility ran through my head. Abandoning my phone, I went out to the living room and turned on a cheesy reality show, curling up in a throw blanket. If he wasn't back by the time the episode ended, I'd call Mia to come stay with the kids. Hopefully, it wouldn't come down to that, but I couldn't just sit around while he was hurting, even with how upset I was.

As the credits rolled, I heard his keys turn the lock. I gave myself an internal talk to stay calm and let him explain. He walked inside and turned toward the sound of the television.

"You're still up?" He came to sit on the opposite couch as I nodded. I took in his slumped posture in the dim light. His eyes looked bloodshot and his hair was messy.

"Yeah, couldn't sleep." I waited a moment to see if he'd speak first, if he'd offer up any kind of information, but he didn't. He stared at the screen as the next episode started playing. "Wes," I said softly. "Talk to me. Where were you?"

I sat up straight, fighting the urge to go to him and offer comfort. "Sunshine. I had a lot on my mind. Sorry I didn't tell you I was leaving."

"What's on your mind? You can talk to me. I want to help."

He rested his head back against the pillows and scrubbed his palm over his face. "I'm not in a good headspace right now. I'm sorry. You deserve so much better than what I can give you."

He could say whatever he wanted but that didn't mean I'd stop caring. "Your mom told me what today is. I can't even imagine how you're feeling."

He met my gaze. "What did she tell you?" His tone lowered, taking me by surprise. I bit my lip again, silently cursing as I tasted blood.

"Not much, just that it's the anniversary of your accident. That it's a hard day. She said it was up to you to have the conversation with me."

"She should have kept her mouth shut," he said.

My throat tightened but I forced words out. "I don't understand you. I've shared so much of my past. You can trust me. Please. I promise I'm fine, you don't have to keep things from me."

"You're fine?" he said. "I don't know if you realize how often you say those words but you're anything but fine. I wish you'd admit that for once."

My cheeks heated like I'd been slapped but I ignored him. He was hurting and didn't mean it. And a part of me knew he was right, I did hide behind a wall of *"I'm fine."*

"Maybe it would help to write your feelings out. You can even text me or email if it's too hard to talk."

A dry laugh left his lips. My heart beat so fast I thought I'd pass out. "Fucking texting. You want to know something, Tiger? I'll tell you something. My fucking cellphone is the reason my best friend is dead. Why I lost my leg and my entire life crumbled to nothing. You keep pushing and pushing that fucking phone on me and you know what, I'm done."

He got up and stormed into the bedroom while I sat on the couch frozen. I'd never heard him use that tone with me or anyone else. He was like a different person, a stranger.

He came back into the room with his phone in hand. "Wes, please calm down."

"This is what I think about phones." He dropped it on the floor and smashed his foot against the screen until the glass shattered. He kept going, crunching the pieces into the hardwood floor.

His face was flushed and fists clenched at his side as he stomped. I couldn't watch anymore. Forcing myself up from the couch, I jogged into the bedroom and shut the door, locking it behind me. Tears streamed down my face, obscuring my vision.

This wasn't Wes. I knew he wouldn't hurt me, but seeing him lash out like that scared me. My hands shook as I pulled the duvet down and climbed into bed. It was clear that Wes didn't want my help. I could give and give, but it took two to foster a relationship. Communication was the most important thing other than trust and the way he acted today had me questioning everything.

If it weren't for Alex and Lilly, I'd have been packing my stuff and getting the hell out of there. I would have to wait until morning.

With the duvet pulled up to my neck, I listened for movement outside the door but heard nothing. After tossing and turning for at least an hour, I fell into a fitful sleep against my tear soaked pillow.

Wes was already gone when I woke up. No note, no message left with the kids. I figured he went into work early, but the way I was feeling, I didn't care. Falling asleep sobbing brought me back to my teenage years. Those were the darkest and most difficult times of my life and I'd worked so hard in therapy over the years to grow stronger. Maybe I was wrong in opening my heart. I needed to remember that being the best mom to Alex was most important and that meant caring for my mental health above all else.

I went about my morning, getting the kids off to school. As soon as I was alone again, I called Val. After a few rings, her voicemail picked up.

"Hey Val, I'm so sorry to call you like this but I'm going to need you to get Lilly after school. Alex and I are going to stay at my old place for a while." A lump in my throat made it difficult to get the rest of my words out but I pushed through. "Thank you for everything. I'm so lucky to have been a part of your family."

Shit. I hated this. Why couldn't Wes freaking talk to me? I'd be willing to work through our issues but I needed him to try.

I thought about calling Mia or even my mother, but I didn't want to bother them. *I was fine.* I'd go home and pack up our necessities while Alex was at school.

With a short-term plan in mind, I pushed back tears, turned up my stereo and drove along the coast towards the bungalow I called home.

Chapter 38

Wes

I FUCKED UP.

I didn't think I'd ever get the picture of Olivia's face as I lost it last night out of my mind. And maybe that's what I deserved. I sure as fuck didn't deserve her. Replaying her devastated expression would be my constant reminder of that.

I left the house before five, hitting the gym for an intense workout before going to Sunshine. It didn't help my spiraling mind in the way I'd hoped it would. Derek and Thea took one look at me when I came into the kitchen to prep and steered clear. I pulled an all-nighter when I already looked like shit, so I was sure I looked scary as fuck.

I threw myself into prepping our daily special and when customers trickled in, instead of going to my office and letting

Derek do his job, I stayed on the line to cook. Anything to keep my mind busy.

During a lull between the breakfast and lunch crowd, my old man came in and took his usual seat at the counter. He had his eyes trained on me, likely assessing my mental state. Funny how both he and my mother were absent yesterday other than my mother coming over to watch the kids.

"Wesley, can we talk in the office?" my father finally asked through the window when he caught me looking at him.

I ran my palms over my chef's jacket and groaned. I didn't need his guilt trip. I was already beating myself up enough. Derek stepped to my side and nodded.

"I got this, why don't you go take a break, Boss?" He took over sauteing onions and mushrooms for the burger I was making.

"Fine, I'll only be a minute."

My father was sitting in my chair when I walked into my office. It was his office for years, so it didn't shock me that he'd take up his old spot.

"You look like shit, son." His brows drew together and he leaned on the desk with his forearms.

"Thanks... Matches how I feel." I sat in the chair opposite him and brought my head into my hands.

"Pardon me for saying this but, what the fuck? Your mother called me a little while ago in a tizzy. Said Olivia is moving out. Care to fill me in?"

I looked up to see if he was bullshitting but his face was as hard as stone. "What did she say?"

"I just told you. She asked your mother to pick up Lilly and said she's moving out."

"Fuck," I groaned. "I don't know what you want me to say, Dad. I don't blame her. She deserves so much better than me. Lilly does, too."

"That's the biggest crock of shit I've ever heard. You've got to stop beating yourself up about what happened. It's been eight years. Dylan would kick your ass if he could. Yes, what happened was horrible and I know you'll never fully forgive yourself, but come on. You're a good man. A good father and from what I've seen, a good husband. You won't grow and get better unless you give yourself a chance." He pulled a hand through his hair, the same way I always did when I was stressed and stared me down.

"Dad, I hate to tell you this but my marriage with Olivia isn't real. We did it to help each other out. It doesn't matter anyway. Regina is coming after me with her lawyers and everything will end up fucked in the end."

"That's bullshit and you know it. Regina won't win, not if you fight. And Olivia—real or not you care about each other. Hell, I'd be willing to bet my life that you're in love with her. And I know that scares you but you can't throw that away. Take it from an old man, women like Olivia and your mother are once in a lifetime." He pushed to a stand, grunting from the effort. "I've gotta get home to console your distraught mother, but I hope you sit here and figure out a way to make things right."

He left without another word, while I stayed and went over everything he said. I couldn't believe she left. It made sense that she would, but still, I didn't expect her to up and leave so fast. My father was right about one thing. I was a fucking asshat. I needed to figure out how to make things right.

With my head hung low, I asked the only person I could ever really talk to for some guidance. "Dylan, if you're listening, help me out here. What the fuck should I do?"

I left work early, in time to pick up Lilly from school so my mom didn't have to. Maybe I'd catch Olivia and at least apologize for the way I acted with the cellphone. There was no reason for me to go off the way I did. No reason for anyone to act that way.

The sun beat down on my head from a cloudless sky as I walked across the parking lot toward the area where parents waited at the school gates. My tired eyes squinted against the brightness. I noticed a police car parked along the curb and a few people chatting near it. As I got closer, I saw Regina in the group, speaking quietly with an officer.

My fists clenched at my side but I pushed my anger deep down. Taking a breath, I greeted them in the most friendly way I could muster.

"Regina, what are you doing here?" I forced a smile through gritted teeth, nodding my head at the young male officer.

"I don't want any problems, Wesley." She handed me a document with a satisfied grin. I scanned the front page but before I could read it she said, "That's a temporary custody order. As you know, Savannah already signed over guardianship to Gerald and me. We're taking Lilly with us."

"Here at her school? I knew you were a piece of work but this is low." I glanced at the cop again, grinding my teeth. My entire body strained to let my pent-up anger loose. I let out a controlled breath and asked, "Why are you doing this? You have to know this is wrong."

She stepped closer to me, still wearing a smug grin. The fucking nerve of that woman. How could someone I once loved come from a mother like her?

"It's not me you need to blame. This is coming from Savannah. Maybe if you were a better father, this wouldn't be happening."

The end of day bell rang and within seconds, kids of all ages came flooding through the gate. I clenched my fists, wanting to turn and get the hell out of there, but I couldn't. Not without talking to Lilly.

I scanned the crowd for any sign of her, Olivia, or even Alex and finally I saw a head of dark hair I knew better than my own. Turning to Regina I shoved down my anger and pleaded, "My wife is over there. Please don't leave with Lilly until I can speak with her."

She narrowed her eyes at me but nodded. "Don't try anything. My friend here will make sure you won't get away with it."

What the hell did she think I'd do?

I walked over to Olivia as fast as I could. Out of breath and frantic, I tapped her shoulder. "Tiger, I'm so glad to see you."

A flurry of emotions played out across her face. Shock, disappointment, anger. She looked away from me, searching the crowd for Alex. "Not now, Wes. We can talk later. Alone."

"I know you're angry at me. Fuck." I lowered my voice as a mother scowled at me. "I deserve it. Please, Regina is here."

Her eyes widened and she twisted her body to look around. "Here? Like at school?"

"Over there." I pointed to where she stood waiting with the cop.

"What's—"

"There's no time for questions. She's here to take Lilly." I handed her the paperwork. "It's an order of temporary guardianship. I don't know the details but ... What should I do?"

Olivia scanned the front page, her eyes bounced from word to word and her face fell. "I don't think there's anything you can do. Not right now."

"No, that can't be. Read it again," I pleaded, grabbing her hand as I felt my limbs get heavy.

Tears collected in the corner of her eyes as she said, "I'm sorry."

Alex was the first to find us, jogging over with his heavy backpack. "Hey, you're both here. Are we doing something cool today?"

Olivia squatted low to speak to him. I couldn't hear what she said, but Alex scrunched his brows.

"Where's Lilly?" I asked Alex.

"She was talking to the teacher. They were taking too long, so I came out first." Alex looked back at the gate. "I can go get her."

"No, it's okay. I'm sure she'll be right out," Olivia said.

"Let's go over there." I didn't wait for their response as I walked to the gate. A few stragglers were still coming out, but the area was slowly clearing.

Finally, I saw her. She looked around with a hand shielding her eyes. Her teacher spotted me and halted momentarily, but Lilly kept walking faster toward us. She ran into my arms and her tears started.

"Mrs. Nolan said I have to go with Grandmother. Dad, what's going on?" Her words were muffled by sobs.

I glanced toward a crying Olivia, silently asked her for help. Every single word escaped me. My fucking heart was cracking in two.

"Baby, we're going to fix this, okay?" I held her tight as my voice wobbled. "It's only for a few days until I can get everything figured out."

"You don't want me? That's why I have to go?" She sniffed and pulled back. "Mom didn't want me and now you don't either."

"That's not true. I love you. You're my little girl always." Tears filled my eyes and thank God Olivia kneeled down to talk.

"Lil, we love you so much. Of course we want you. I'm so sorry sweetie. Like your dad said, we're going to fix this. Come here." She held her arms open and Lilly squeezed her. Olivia whispered into her ear and Lilly nodded.

"I'll take care of your stuff," Alex added. "You'll be back soon." I could see tears forming in his eyes, but he hung his head low.

Lilly nodded and took hold of Olivia's hand, as Mrs. Nolan cleared her throat. "I'm so sorry but I've been instructed to see that there's no issues. If you don't mind." She gestured toward Regina.

I cleared my throat. "Yeah, sorry to keep you." With a deep breath, I reached for Lilly's hand and walked her to Regina, who was still smiling like she loved the pain she was causing.

"Come Lilly, it's time to go home." She held the back door open and bounced her gaze between Lilly and me.

Lilly looked up into my eyes and squeezed my hand. Her voice was so small, it killed me. "I don't want to go."

"I know. I don't want you to either, but right now you have to. Come here." I pulled her in again for another quick hug and ushered her forward toward Regina before I lost it. "I love you. It's going to be okay."

Regina closed the car door as soon as Lilly slipped in. The officer moved to get back into his vehicle as I backed away a few steps. "You did the right thing," Regina said. "This is what's best for her and you know it."

"That's where you're wrong. You can hurt me all you want, but mess with my family and you're done." I took one more look at Lilly crying in the backseat and turned to go before I did something I'd regret. I may not have done my best to fight for Lilly before, but I knew then and there that I'd go to the ends of the earth to keep my family together.

Chapter 39

Wes

I WANTED TO SINK down into the dirt as I watched Regina drive away with a piece of my heart. I hadn't felt this out of control since the accident. No matter what I did, I couldn't change a damn thing. Not today at least. People I loved were suffering because of my actions, or lack of. My father was right. I needed to pull my head out of my ass and do something.

Olivia and Alex were still standing a few steps away, holding back tears. I could read their posture and expressions. They were as gutted as I was.

"I'm sorry," I said, coming toward them. "This is a mess. I don't even know where to begin."

Olivia wrapped her arm around Alex's shoulder. "I'm going to get him home. We can talk later."

"I'll meet you over there." As the words left my lips, I remembered what my father said earlier and met Olivia's gaze. She rolled her lip between her teeth and cast her eyes down, arm still slung around Alex.

"I meant my old place. Sorry, I just need time." I nodded and bit my tongue. This wasn't a conversation to have in front of Alex.

"Nothing to be sorry for. You've haven't done anything wrong."

"Let me get settled in for a bit. Call me later, okay?" I nodded and watched the other pieces of my heart walk away from me, knowing there was nothing I could do.

I must have stood there for ten more minutes staring off into the nearly empty parking lot, listening to birds chirping and cars driving by. I'd known rock bottom. I'd lost a brother and lived through hell. But this ache in my chest, so heavy it could drag me down into the dirt, was unlike any of those feelings.

When my leg and hip pain cranked up, I finally moved, getting into my car. The need to find the nearest bar and drink myself stupid was strong. I was tired of thinking and planning and getting nowhere.

Maybe Dylan was with me since it felt like I blinked and found myself back at home. The bastard knew I needed to stay in my right mind.

The house was empty and too quiet. Everywhere I looked reminded me of Olivia. Her smell even hung in the air. I pulled a bottle of water out of the fridge and collapsed on the couch to take off my prosthesis and take some pressure off my hips. What the fuck was I going to do?

I didn't even have a cellphone, thanks to my outburst. Olivia must have forgotten, since she'd asked me to call her. This had to be the worst possible time to be without a phone. I'd have to call my lawyer and see if she'd be able to move our appointment up, too.

After going through different plans in my head, I remembered my laptop, sitting dead in my closet and pulled it out to charge. It was my only form of communication. Driving to my lawyer's office unannounced seemed a bit too much and Olivia obviously didn't want me at her place.

I'd send Olivia a message first. Luckily, I had her email saved in my inbox from work related stuff. I clicked and sat back, head in my hands, trying to figure out what the hell to say. After staring at the blank screen for fifteen minutes, I typed a quick message.

Hey,

With everything that happened this afternoon I forgot I didn't have a phone. I'm sorry, Tiger. I miss you and I hope you're both OK. I'll let you know when I pick a phone up tomorrow. Can we sit down and talk then... about us and Lilly and everything? I don't even know if you're scheduled to work tomorrow, but maybe I'll see you there.

-Wes

As I shut the screen I realized this was the first time in months that I was truly alone. There's always been someone, either at work or my parents and more recently, Lilly, Alex, and Olivia.

I laid back on the couch for fifteen minutes but my body vibrated with restless energy. Unable to sit around and do nothing, I put my prosthesis back on and drove to my parents house.

My mom set a bowl of pretzels in front of me at the table. "I can't believe this is happening. What can we do?"

My parents were the quietest I'd ever seen them as they processed what had happened. My dad went for a walk to clear his head.

"I'm sure I'll need you with all the legal stuff but as of today, I don't know. I'll have to move up the appointment with my lawyer but for now, I can't sit at home, it's too quiet."

"I understand." She sighed and put a warm hand on my shoulder. "The timing couldn't have been worse, what with yesterday being..." She hesitated, but I didn't need her to finish, I knew what she meant.

"Yeah..."

She studied me with watery eyes. "What happened with Olivia? Did you tell her about Dylan?"

I knew this conversation was coming. "Not as much as I should. I pulled away like an idiot."

She tapped her nails on the table, thinking. "Maybe you should go to her. Did you apologize?"

"I have other things to worry about right now, Mom. Plus I think she needs time." I grabbed a pretzel and took a bite, chewing slowly. My parents didn't see how I'd acted. They didn't see the look in her eyes the night before when I absolutely lost my shit. Of course she needed time, anyone would.

"Or maybe she wants you to fight for her. She's been through enough in her life and I can tell you've been her rock. It's probably been hard to see you pull back this way. And I know she loves Lilly. I'm sure she's upset too and wants to help. We should all be together, we're a family."

My mother's words took root in my mind.

We're a family.

She's my wife.

What the fuck was I doing sitting here wallowing?

I stretched my arms over my head and pushed to stand. "You're right. I gotta stop being scared. My family needs me."

My mom beamed at me, nodding. "That's what I was waiting for you to say."

"One thing first. Can I use your phone? I think I have Savannah's number written down here somewhere."

"What happened to your phone?"

I rubbed my tight jaw and answered under my breath. "I kind of broke it."

She narrowed her eyes on me. "On purpose?"

I kept my mouth closed but she got her answer from my shame-filled expression. "Oh, Wesley. You need to accept that it wasn't your phone that caused the accident."

Yeah, I knew she'd respond that way. "I'm trying. Please just let me use your phone."

She scrambled up and grabbed it from the kitchen. "Go ahead. Why are you calling Savannah? You think you can reach her?"

"I hope so. I should have tried months ago before everything got this out of hand."

"Good luck," she said, as I walked down the hall to my old bedroom and dialed my ex's number.

I ended the call with Sav feeling more hopeful than I had in days. Before I gave my mom her phone back, I scrolled through her contacts and found Lilly's number.

Me: *Hey sweetheart, it's Dad. Listen, I don't know if your grandmother is looking at your messages so I'll keep it short. Everything is going to be okay... I promise. Hang in there, you'll be home soon.*

I grabbed my keys from the kitchen table. She looked up from the book she was reading with raised brows. "How'd it go?"

"Mom, I don't even know where to begin. I'll fill you in later, but everything's going to be okay."

"Come sit, tell me how the call went. I ordered take-out for dinner. It should be here soon." She patted the empty chair beside her.

"Sorry, I can't stay." I kissed her forehead and turned to leave. "I gotta go get my wife back."

"Wesley Gordon Reed, you stop right there," she boomed, stopping me in my tracks.

"Mom, I've gotta go. I promise I'll fill you in later." Anxious energy filled my veins each minute I was away from Olivia.

"It's not that," she said, gently. "You can't go to Olivia empty handed. Hasn't your boneheaded father taught you anything? You need a gesture. Something to win her back."

I leaned against the doorframe and pulled in a calming breath. "Mom, you're reading too many romance novels. We can talk this through like adults."

She picked up her novel, showing me the floral cover. "And you know who recommended this book?" I shrugged and she went on. "Your wife. Think about it, Wesley. If she's as important to you as you say, you need to show her."

Fuck. I hated when she was right. I walked back to the table and dropped my keys down before taking the seat next to her. "Any suggestions?"

"Oh honey, it needs to come from you. Dig deep and you'll figure it out." She kissed my cheek and got up with her book in hand. "Remember when your father filled the entire house with flowers when you were twelve? Well, you didn't know this but

I was two seconds away from leaving his ass for being an idiot. You've got this."

I remembered that, the house smelled like roses for a month. My father was so damn proud of himself too, strutting around like he was Casanova. I put my head in my hands and shut my eyes. *Think.* What could I do to show her she was everything to me? An inkling of an idea formed and the more I thought about it the more certain I became.

Tomorrow, I would get my family back.

Chapter 40

Olivia

I'D FINALLY GOTTEN ALEX to bed after hours of trying to cheer him up. Difficult to do while I was heartbroken on the inside. The hardest part of being a mother was keeping myself upright when all I wanted to do was collapse. I couldn't let him see me struggling, not when he was confused and upset.

We sent Lilly a few messages, letting her know we were thinking of her. She didn't respond, so it was likely Regina took her phone. I even called my dad to ask his advice, but got his voicemail.

After changing into pajamas, I flopped into bed, rolling to grab Wes's pillow. It still smelled like him, even though we hadn't slept here in over a month. Thankfully, we still had our beds here, and a few random belongings, but most of our stuff was at the other house—my kitchen utensils, all the living room furniture, even our bath towels.

I shouldn't have let my feelings for Wes sway my decisions. I knew deep down, it wouldn't work between us. Not when lines got blurry and we strayed from our original agreement. Neither of us were ready to fully let the other in.

I tried. I'd been as open and honest with him as I'd ever been with another person, but that was a mistake. And the worst part was letting Alex get attached. And Lilly, God, that poor girl. My heart hurt for her more than anything. Even if my relationship with Wes was over, I'd still do anything I could to help her. I meant it when I told her I loved her.

I rolled onto my back and grabbed my phone, swiping away a stray tear that had fallen onto my cheek. After months with Wes and Lilly, I needed background noise to fall asleep.

Tapping my screen, the first thing I saw was an email notification from Wes. I hated the flutter I felt in my stomach when I saw his name. But I couldn't help how I felt about him, even if he was a complete ass. Knowing he was hurting too was hard to bear.

With a sobering breath, I opened the email and read it slowly. He wanted to talk... That was a start. I appreciated his apology, but I needed more than that. I needed his actions to align with his words before I'd consider staying together. Living with emotionally unavailable parents my entire life was enough. I wouldn't have that kind of relationship with my partner.

When I hit reply, I stared at the empty space on my screen for a few minutes and tapped out the word, *Hey,* before deleting it and giving up. I turned off the phone, dropped it in Wes's spot and clutched his pillow to my chest. I was scheduled to work the following afternoon. If he was there, I'd talk with him. We both needed a night to think and clear our heads.

Mia didn't hide her shocked expression when she got to my house to pick up Alex for the day. I filled her in as briefly as I could but promised I'd talk more after work. It killed me to bother her, but I had no choice. I wasn't about to make Alex go to school when he was upset. I got lucky that she only had a meeting later that afternoon, but was able to reschedule it.

"I'm fine. I can get through this day. We'll figure things out." I repeated this mantra the entire car ride to Sunshine only stumbling my words when I pulled in and saw Wes's car in his usual spot.

The clarity I'd hoped for hadn't magically appeared when I woke up that morning. I doubted one conversation at work would clear things up but I was willing to talk to him. At the very least, maybe he could fill me in on the plans for getting Lilly back.

I braced myself for the conversation ahead and went inside.

It was business as usual. A few booths were occupied with families or couples eating lunch. Kelly and a new server named

Izzy were bustling around taking orders and running plates. Wes must have been in his office, since Derek and Caleb were side by side in the kitchen.

"Hey there, Wifey," Kelly said with a wide grin. "You look nice today. How are you doing?"

"Okay," I said, narrowing my eyes and drawing out the word. "How about you?"

She slipped by me, carrying a glass of water and said in a chipper tone, "Just peachy. Oh by the way, before you get settled in, can you clean table five? I haven't had a free moment."

"Sure, but Kelly?" I started to ask her if something was going on, but she'd already disappeared into the back like a wraith. *Super weird.*

I tossed my purse behind the counter and grabbed a rag. Table five looked clean. What was she talking about?

I gave the table a quick wipe-down anyway but stopped as I heard a phone notification. That wasn't my normal tone, but I pulled my phone out of my pocket anyway to double check. My screen was blank. It sounded again, so I kneeled and found the culprit discarded on the bench seat. A customer must have left their phone. When I picked it up the screen lit up and I saw a photo of me as the background.

What was going on? I glanced again and opened the message, too curious to let it go.

Unknown number: *The woman in my background picture is the most stunning woman I've ever seen. The first time I saw her on the beach against the setting sun, I stopped breathing. Her eyes* *remind me of the ocean at midnight and her smile could light up the darkest days. I've never known true beauty until I saw her.*

My heart sped up as I reread the message. It had to be Wes, but where was he and why did he leave this phone here?

I fumbled with the device while trying to slide it into my pocket, when another chime sounded from the next booth. This time, I saw the phone on the center of the table right away. I glanced around to see if anyone would claim it but after a moment, when no one came forward I picked it up and swiped it open. The background was a different photo of me.

Unknown number: *She is the strongest person I've ever known. Day after day she shows up for the ones she loves and never asks for anything in return. She makes me a stronger man. A better man. And I want to be the person she can lean on.*

I slid the phone into my back pocket as my eyes watered. The dining area was so quiet I could hear a pin drop when, across the room, another phone went off. This was absolutely ridiculous, but I felt a smile pull at my lips regardless.

Unknown number: *She makes the best desserts I've ever tasted.*

Another one went off on a table behind me.

Unknown Number: *No one sings Taylor Swift at midnight better than she does.*

A laugh escaped my lips as another chime sounded.

Unknown Number: *She kicks ass, quite literally, at Krav Maga. She's an inspiration to anyone she encounters.*

Behind me, two phones beeped, one right after the other. I was dizzy with adrenaline and from literally spinning around to find the sources of the sounds.

Unknown Number: *She always wins at games because she's superior to me in every way...(even though I think she cheats sometimes)*

Unknown Number: *She may not realize it, but she owns my heart. Every single beat, beats for her.*

I turned on my heel at the sound of another phone ringing, barely able to catch my breath. Kelly leaned against the counter, holding the phone out to me. "It's for you, Wifey."

I nodded while I wiped my cheek. Everyone in the restaurant was staring at me. I hadn't noticed it while I was busy reading the messages but I noticed now. I turned my back, walked to an empty booth and answered the phone with a shaky voice.

"Wes?"

"Hey, Tiger. God, I love the sound of your voice. It feels like longer than a day since I've heard it." He took a long breath while I waited for him to go on. "I have a few things to say, if that's alright with you?"

I sunk down into the booth, holding the phone close to my ear. "Okay, I'm listening."

"I know nothing I do or say can make up for the way I treated you this past week. You've opened up to me, treated me with love and care when I didn't deserve it, and I pulled away. Breaking my phone like that was uncalled for. You should never be treated that way. I'm so damn sorry. Will you give me a chance to make it up to you? I promise I won't ice you out anymore. I'll keep all these phones on me, if that's what it takes."

I was nodding before I'd said a word. It was too hard to speak with emotion clogging my throat but I managed a raspy, "Yes."

He released a shaky breath. "Thank you, baby. I'm the luckiest man alive. Will you turn around for me?"

I turned my head and Wes was right there behind me. His dark eyes were damp and his hair looked like he'd been pulling his hands through it all morning. As soon as our eyes locked, I couldn't hold my tears in, they spilled like an overturned drink.

He slid in beside me and pulled me against his chest. "Don't cry, please. It's all going to be okay." With gentle rubs along my back, and whispered praises, I finally looked into his eyes.

"I've missed you," I said.

"I know, Tiger. I'm sorry." He tipped my chin up and brushed a kiss along my lips. His eyes watered and voice cracked. "I love you. I love you so much, I can't breathe when we're apart."

I grabbed his cheeks and crushed my lips to his, tasting the salt of our mingled tears. His tongue slid against mine, exploring my mouth like he hadn't kissed me in years. Demanding and urgent, I buried my hands in his hair, raising myself onto my knees to get as close to him as I could.

When I heard someone catcall, I pulled back, remembering where we were. Wes chuckled and shook his head. "We should probably go home," he whispered and slid over to get up.

"Wait," I said, kneeling so we were eye level. My heart hammered in my chest but I knew how I felt and I couldn't wait another second to say it. "I love you, too."

"Come here." He held me close, kissing the top of my head, my cheeks, brushing soft kisses against my lips. God, I wished we were alone.

"Get a room!" someone from the kitchen hollered, garnering more than a few laughs from the surrounding people.

"I love my wife and my wife loves me," Wes yelled back.

Laughing, I wrapped my arms around his shoulders. "You're so loud. The entire street probably heard you."

"Good, I want everyone to know that I'm the luckiest bastard in the world." He kissed my neck and the shell of my ear. "Let's go home so I can show you how much I love you."

I shivered and felt tingles spread to my center. "What are we going to do with all these phones? Please tell me you didn't buy them all."

He stood up and pulled me with him. "Let's just say, you'll never have a problem getting a hold of me again."

"You're absolutely ridiculous," I said with a laugh. "We can't go home. I have to work."

"Nah, Kelly's going to cover for you. She already said she would earlier." He pushed a loose strand of hair behind my ear. "And Mia's watching Alex overnight."

My mouth hung open.

"You called Mia?"

He nodded and a smile spread across his lips. "I know we need to talk and she was more than willing to help. How do you think I got all those photos of you?"

I could see Mia squealing when Wes asked her to help. Everything made more sense now.

"Before you argue, she wanted to help. I see you biting your lips."

Damn, he caught me. "I hate bugging people. She has her own life and plans, I don't want to be a burden."

"You're never a burden. Come on, let's go home." He kissed me lightly and held my hand while we said bye to Kelly and everyone else, thanking them for their help.

My stomach churned as I left, knowing I was once again relying on others, even though Kelly genuinely smiled at us, a rare occasion for her. But like Wes said, we needed to talk and reconnect. Hash out our issues and figure out a plan to get Lilly home. This time I'd try to be grateful for the support we had instead of dwelling on my uncomfortable feelings.

"So, which phone number should I store?" I asked once we got in Wes's car.

He laughed. "Actually, I have no idea. Might need your help figuring that out."

"You're a hot mess, Wes. Ooh, that rhymed. Hot Mess Wes. I like it." I teased him until he looked at me with a smirk.

"Keep going... The more you tease me, the more I'll tease you." My cheeks heated as he dropped his palm onto the top of my thigh, curling his fingers against my inner thigh.

"You think your hand on my thigh affects me?" I cleared my throat and forced myself to stay still. "I'm dryer than the Sahara down there."

"Doubtful." He let out a gravelly laugh and inched his fingers higher up, brushing them side to side over my leggings.

Two could play this game.

"Still unaffected," I said in an overly sweet tone. It was a lie, but I needed to win this one. As he inched higher, I ran my nails over his arm, tracing a path up to his shoulder, neck and earlobe. He shivered but quickly stopped himself.

"I see what you're doing. You know I'm driving. We need to be safe." His voice shook the tiniest amount.

"What?" I feigned shock. "Do you think I'm trying to distract you? I'd never, not while you're driving."

He glanced at me with a smirk and shook his head. "Right, you'd never try to turn this into a game." I teased my fingers lower, over his tight chest, following the ridges of his abs and stopping right when I reached the waistband of his chef pants. "Tiger," he practically growled.

"Yes?" I answered, batting my lashes. I loved seeing him lose it over the smallest touches.

"I'm about to pull this car over."

He dragged his fingers against my core, holding them there lightly. It took all my willpower to not lift my hips and grind myself against him. I'd missed him, missed this. I slipped one finger into his pants, lightly brushing my nails against his skin until I reached his dripping tip, tucked up against his waist-band.

"I think I win," I crooned as I spread precum along his head. The car made a sharp turn so I looked out the window and saw that we were pulling into the beach parking lot. "Wes?"

"I warned you." He pulled into a shaded spot at the end of the nearly empty lot. Unbuckling his seatbelt, he reached into the backseat and grabbed the sunshade. "I'm about to come in my pants if you keep touching me like that." He spread the shade over the windshield for privacy. "But I'd much rather come inside you."

Our mouths collided in an electric frenzy—tongues clashing while we pulled at each other's clothes. Wes sucked my bottom lip and I moaned into his mouth. My skin was feverish. I couldn't get enough of his hands on me. I wanted him everywhere, to do anything and it shocked me that I was willing to give up that control.

"Lift up," he said before reclaiming my lips. I lifted my hips and he slid my pants and underwear down to my knees. "Off... All the way."

I slipped my sneakers off and pushed my pants all the way down, kicking them off completely, and followed up with my shirt, throwing that on the floor of the car.

I whimpered as he slipped his fingers into my slit with one hand and pulled my breasts free from my bra with the other. "So wet and ready for me, Tiger."

"Please," I begged, desperate for pressure.

"I should tease you," he rumbled against my ear, cupping my breast and kneading my tight nipple. I pulled at his hair and arched my chest into his hand. Slowly, he dragged his fingers through my folds, stopping right below my clit. "But I need to hear you come with my name on your lips."

He swallowed my moan as he finally gave me the pressure I needed. Circling my clit with an expert's touch, he brought me higher and higher.

"Feels so good... Don't stop." I felt my climax building with each urgent press of his fingers. He changed position, cupping my clit with his palm and slipping two fingers inside me. "Oh my God," I moaned, grinding myself against his hand.

He slowed, and I cursed under my breath. "Sit on my cock. Let's come together."

Panting, I wasted no time in pulling his pants to his knees and wrapping my hand around his cock. He messed with the lever under the seat and slid it all the way back. My heart thundered in my chest while I thought about where we were and what we were about to do, until Wes captured my lips again and wrapped his arms around my hips.

"I need you," I whimpered, not recognizing my own voice. I scrambled across the console and settled a knee on either side of his lap, lining him up to my entrance.

"You're so beautiful. So fucking perfect. I love you so much." His mouth found my nipple and he swirled his hot tongue over it, nibbling until I squirmed. "Ride me, baby."

Hissing at the size of him, I sunk down until we were skin on skin. He gave me a second to adjust, kissing my neck, squeezing my ass with his huge, calloused hands. I rocked my hips, riding him, while holding onto his shoulders. "Feels so good, Wes."

"Fuck," he groaned. "You're so tight, baby. You feel amazing." He drove his hips up and I ground myself harder, pressing my tits into his open mouth.

Each roll of my hips brought me higher and closer. My entire body tightened, and I cried out. Wes thrust up harder, taking hold of my hips and lifting me up and down on his cock. "Harder, please. Don't stop."

"Shit, I'm gonna fill you up." His thrusts became jerky as he buried his head into the crook of my neck, groaning.

"Wes." I threw my head back and rocked, feeling his cock pulse inside me. Waves of pleasure coursed through me as I followed him over the edge, crying out. "Oh my God! Holy shit."

I slumped against his chest and took a deep inhale. He smelled so freaking good. I planted a few soft kisses there, feeling the beat of his heart against my lips. "I love how you smell."

He chuckled and rubbed circles along my back, holding me closer. "You smell better, trust me."

"I slept with your pillow last night," I admitted. "It still smells like you."

He tipped my chin up to claim my lips. "I love you, Tiger. All of you, every day."

I kissed him again and smiled against his lips. "I love you too." Sighing, I reached up to smooth his hair. "We should probably get dressed. I can't believe we're in a parking lot."

We laughed, Wes's a deep chuckle. "I told you I'd pull over. I'm a man of my word."

"Maybe I should tease you more if it ends in this," I said, pushing up to climb back to my seat.

"I won't be so nice next time." Wes gave my butt a light spank and squeeze.

"We'll see," I said.

Chapter 41

Wes

MY CHEST LOOSENED AS we walked through the door of the house hand in hand. Olivia was my anchor, my person, and being in this house one day without her was too long. She went to get cleaned up and changed while I made us lunch. I knew we had to talk about everything and for once, that didn't scare me. I stared out the window at the cloudless sky and smiled.

"What do you think, brother? Am I doing right by her?" I grabbed a plate and arranged the sandwiches I made onto it. "I think I'm ready to tell her about the accident. Wish me luck."

Olivia came into the kitchen, pulling her hair into a ponytail. "Were you just talking to someone?"

"Yeah. Well, sort of." I set the plate on the table and grabbed the bowl of fruit salad that was in the fridge, two forks and a few napkins. "You'll think I'm nuts."

She huffed a laugh. "Doubtful."

"Sometimes I talk to Dylan. I know he can't hear me but I don't know," I hesitated. "It helps me clear my head."

She reached up and kissed me, wrapping her arms around my torso. "That's sweet." I gestured to the food and she sat down. "What were you telling him?"

I sunk into the chair next to her, biting back a groan. I'd been on my feet too much that morning and felt the consequences. "Nothing much, just telling him I'm ready to open up to you."

Her face softened. "Really?"

I nodded. "It's hard to talk about the accident and I'm scared you're going to view me differently. Hell, I don't think I'll ever forgive myself. Everything changed that night, but I want to try and move on. I have you and the kids and living in the past, beating myself up every single day, isn't healthy. You're all so important to me."

She folded her palm over mine and squeezed. "I don't want to pressure you."

"You're not, I promise." I pushed a deep breath into my chest and began. "I've told you a little about Dylan. How he was like a brother to me."

She nodded and rubbed circles on my hand. "He seemed like a great guy."

"He was. The night of the accident, I had been fighting with Savannah all day, so I left the house and went to Dylan's place. He had a small apartment not too far from here. He wasn't home yet, so I let myself in and drank myself stupid. Probably drank almost a bottle of whiskey by the time he got home from work. He was taking classes part-time and interning at this law office. He wanted to be a lawyer, to help people in need. Anyway, I was wasted when he came in. Sav had a babysitter come over to our place and was sending me pics of herself dressed up to go out, saying she was gonna find someone else. Egging me on. She did that kind of thing a lot. I begged Dylan to take me to find her and even though he was tired, he got changed and drove me to the bar nearby."

I shifted in my seat and took a sip of water. Images from that night flashed through my mind. Me stumbling out of the car. Dylan laughing at my drunk ass, taking pictures of me with his phone for some friendly blackmail. Us hitting a few different bars and still not finding Sav.

"We ended up going to a few different bars and Sav was nowhere to be found. She stopped texting me for a while so I gave up and we grabbed some drinks since we were out anyway. Dylan was always careful. He nursed a beer while I slammed down another few whiskeys. Then Savannah started texting me again."

"What did she say?" Olivia asked, her eyes wide.

"That she was out and she'd met someone. That she was dancing up on guys and they were buying her drinks. She told me all kinds of shit she knew would piss me off. It worked, too. I tried to get behind the wheel, but Dylan got me to relent and get in the passenger seat. He started to drive back to his house, but I didn't want that. I needed to find Sav. She kept texting me and I was shoving my phone at Dylan so he could see what she was saying. I wouldn't let it go. He tried to tell me to relax, that he'd read them at home, but I kept fucking pushing the phone into his face."

Olivia went as white as a sheet. She must have known what I was about to say.

"He didn't see the red light. There was a car coming fast. It slammed into the driver's side, killing Dylan almost instantly. The other driver suffered serious injuries too. My leg was crushed from the impact. The doctors tried to save it, but I would have had less than twenty percent mobility."

"Oh, Wes, I'm so sorry." She covered her mouth with her hand and leaned in closer.

"I'm sorry, too. I caused the accident and I'll never stop blaming myself. My brother should be alive today, kicking ass in a courtroom, maybe married with a couple kids. He had a girlfriend. It was casual... They met in law school. Every year on the anniversary of the accident she comes by Sunshine and we tell stories about him. I wouldn't see her the first year. I was too full of guilt, but eventually she wore me down."

Olivia's eyes widened and she sat up straight. "Dylan's girl-friend," she whispered.

"Yeah, her name is Emily. There's something else I need to get off my chest," I said. My hands shook but I took hold of Olivia's palm. "You've asked me about money and I haven't been very forthcoming but I want to tell you everything. Dylan's family was wealthy. I'd guess even wealthier than your family, but I don't know the exact numbers. When Dylan turned eighteen, his trust was made available to him and I didn't know this... but he'd listed me as his sole beneficiary on all of his assets. He was worth a lot, Tiger. I tried to deny it all. I was too guilt ridden to accept anything but thankfully my parents were smart enough to take care of the paperwork while I was in the hospital and the money's been sitting in various accounts all these years. Once a year I give Emily some money, even though I barely knew her... but I figure maybe she would have been Dylan's wife. Either way, it's helped my guilty conscience."

"I don't know what to say." Olivia stared out the window, eyes glassy and unfocused. "That was so kind of him. He didn't have family?"

"He had his parents but they weren't close. Honestly, they were cruel people, treated him like more of an asset than their own kid. He spent most of his time at my house. My parents thought of him as a second son."

Tears welled in Olivia's eyes. "I understand so much now. The phones... It makes sense."

I let out a dry laugh. "I'm a stubborn ass. It wasn't a phone that caused the accident, it was me and my drunken self. But it was easier to blame an inanimate object, you know?"

"I get it, trust me. If I could blame a random object for what happened to me, I would, too. It's easier than accepting that we don't have control over everything, that bad things happen to good people."

I blew out a long breath. "That's the fucking truth. Speaking of, I have so much to tell you about Regina, but first, do you have questions about that night? Or anything at all?"

She picked up her sandwich and brought it to her lips. "Not right now, but if I do I'll ask you. Tell me about Regina. What's going on? I've been a mess thinking about Lilly and how she must be feeling."

We dug into our lunch and I filled her in on my conversation with Savannah and the plans for the following day. As we talked my body relaxed, like a physical weight had been lifted from my shoulders. I was so fucking lucky to have this woman by my side and I intended to do whatever it took to be the best damn husband I could be.

The next morning Olivia and I made our way to Regina and Gerald's house. They lived in the next town over, Haven Harbor. We went over the plan again on the ride while she kept a gentle hold on my thigh. Having her with me helped settle my nerves.

"You're sure she'll be there?" Oliva asked.

"We rarely agree on much, but we agreed on this." She nodded and turned her head to stare out the window at all the mansions.

"You know, I was raised in a house like these and I have to say, they're overrated."

"I'm all for a smaller house, too. They're cozier. All these places seem cold and empty. That's how Dylan's home was. Did I tell you he's the one who introduced me to Savannah?"

"No," she said. "They were friends?"

I laughed. "I wouldn't call them friends, but their parents were acquaintances. They met at some dinner party and Savannah snuck Dylan out through the back door. We all got together at one of her friend's houses and that's when I met her."

"And it was love at first sight?" she teased.

"We were kids—eighteen with raging hormones and terrible impulse control. I thought she was hot, and we hit it off that night, so we started sneaking around. Her parents never liked me. They wanted her with someone like Dylan, rich and headed to law school."

Olivia huffed. "It's actually freaky how much these people sound like my parents."

"Can't wait to meet them," I said sarcastically.

"Oh, they're a barrel of fun. Go on, tell me about you and Savannah."

I drove through the lush neighborhood, passing bright tropical flowers and towering palms. It had been a long time since I'd been in this town.

"We started hanging out a lot the summer after graduation, going to parties, fooling around. Little did I know I wasn't the only guy she was seeing, but that's beside the point. Toward the end of the summer, she told me she was pregnant. Obviously, I was shocked and scared out of my mind. Her parents didn't react well. They tried to force her to give Lilly up for adoption, but Sav fought them. I have to give her kudos for that. She had no problem writing her parents out of her life, even when it meant losing their money, too. My parents helped us out and we had a small wedding, moved into an apartment near Sunshine. It didn't last long. By the time Lilly was born, we'd already broken up and gotten back together twice. It was a mess, toxic as hell. We even got divorced and then got back together for a small amount of time right before the accident."

"That's some history you two have," Olivia said, loosening a breath. "And what happened after the accident?"

I pulled onto Regina's street, slowing down as we approached the house. "She didn't come to see me in the hospital, not after the first night. I found out later that she was already seeing someone else before I was even released."

"That's vile," Olivia said. She turned to take in the enormous house in front of us. I spotted a black BMW parked along the road and guessed who it belonged to. She always loved German engineering.

"Ready?" I asked.

"Ready if you are," Olivia said. We slipped out of the car and walked over to the BMW where Savannah sat waiting for us.

The three of us walked side by side to the front door. I focused my gaze on Olivia for strength while Savannah rang the bell.

"I hope this is quick," Savannah said. "I can't stand this house."

You and I both.

After a few moments, a middle-aged woman opened the door. She seemed to recognize Savannah right away. "Ms. Robinson, so nice to see you." Her gaze bounced between the three of us and she stepped outside. "This isn't a good time. Might I suggest you call and get on Mr. and Mrs. Robinson's schedule?"

"No, Jean, we need to speak with them now. Why don't you step out and do your daily liquor store run for my father," Savannah said, sounding bored. "You won't want to be here for this."

Jean glanced behind her and then nodded. "I'll do that." She scurried inside and turned down a hallway.

Savannah walked inside like she owned the place, which I guess wasn't too far from the truth. She'd grown up in this museum of a home. "Mother, I'm home!" Her voice echoed throughout the expansive entrance. "Come down here, or I'll come find you."

Olivia and I stayed a step behind her, keeping our eyes open for movement. Savannah wandered over to a mirrored table and picked up an expensive looking glass object before slipping it into her purse. As she was about to climb the stairs, I heard footsteps from the hall.

"Mom? Dad? Olivia?" Lilly ran to us, crashing into her mother first. Sav kneeled and wrapped her in a hug. "You guys came for me?"

"Of course," Sav said. "Where's your grandmother? I need to speak with her."

"Right here," Regina said, coming out of the shadows of the hallway. She looked as prim and proper as ever, not like she'd been a caretaker to a child at all.

"Lilly, come over here," I said. Olivia and I each wrapped our arms around her shoulder. I craned my neck to whisper in her ear, "Why don't you go get your stuff? Grab anything you don't want to leave here."

She nodded and passed Savannah to run up the stairs.

"Mother, have you lost your mind? You tried to steal my daughter! How dare you forge my name on documents!" Pent up anger poured from my ex, while she continued her tirade against her mother. "There's a reason Lilly and I only come here once a year. You're a garbage person but I never pegged you as a criminal."

Regina finally stepped closer so she was eye to eye with her estranged daughter. "That's rich coming from you. Someone had to step in and raise the girl right. Clearly, I made mistakes with you." She glanced at me with hatred in her eyes. "You went and got knocked up at eighteen by this lowlife. He was letting Lilly wander the streets, fail school, get beat up by bullies. Is that how you want your daughter raised? And you, prancing off to

Europe like you're some jet-setter. Which loser are you chasing now?"

I clenched my jaw, listening to her spew her hateful thoughts. "I think I'm entitled to a break, Mother. I left Lilly with Wes because I know he's a good father. The audacity... I cannot believe you."

"A good father?" Regina laughed. "That man is a joke. He killed his friend! You think he can keep Lilly al—"

"That's enough!" Olivia shouted. Both Regina and Sav went silent.

"Who do you think you—" Regina began.

"I won't stand here and let you talk about my husband that way. You're an evil woman and I don't care if you're Lilly's blood, I'll make it my life's goal to keep you and your husband away from my family for the rest of our lives."

Regina's nostrils flared and she stepped back as if she were struck. Savannah laughed, but the sound was humorless. "I can agree to that. Like Olivia said, you're done. Try and be a part of our lives and I'll go to a lawyer with this little stunt you pulled."

I stood there with my mouth agape as my current wife and ex-wife worked together to take down Regina. Was I dreaming?

Lilly pounded down the stairs with a backpack slung on her shoulder and a stuffed animal in her arms. "Dad, I need my phone. She took it that day after school."

Savannah held her hand out. "Get my kid her phone and be sure to delete our numbers from yours."

Regina sneered and spun on her heel, coming back a few seconds later with Lilly's phone. "I only wanted what's best for her."

"Your intentions don't matter. You broke the law. You traumatized my daughter and made me leave the best opportunity of my life to come back here." Savannah's voice shook and she turned her back, heading out the door. "I'm done."

"Come here, Lilly," I said. "Do you want to say goodbye?"

Lilly stuck her hand out in front of her grandmother and waited for Regina to shake it. When she didn't, Lilly shrugged. "Have a nice life. Oh, and by the way, you smell like old rotten flowers and I hate this house."

With that she walked outside to her mother with her head held high. Olivia and I exchanged bewildered looks and followed, closing the door on a stunned Regina Robinson.

"Where's Alex?" Lilly asked as soon as we were by the cars.

"He's with Aunt Mia. We can pick him up on the way home," Olivia said. Lilly dropped her stuff in the backseat and hugged Olivia. "I missed you, kiddo."

"I missed you, too. I was worried I'd have to stay there forever."

"I'd never let that happen," I said, joining their hug.

Savannah walked over from her car and Olivia touched my shoulder. "I'll give you two some privacy. Lil, I saw some cool flowers over there. Should we go see?"

"Yeah, sure."

I smiled at Olivia, mouthing a *thank you*.

"She seems pretty great," Sav said, once they were out of earshot. "Too good for you."

I crossed my arms and leaned against the hood. "You're not wrong there. She's great. She and Lilly have really bonded these last few months."

"I'm glad. Lilly needs a mother figure in her life." Sav sniffed and turned her face away from me. "Thanks for calling me. I know it wasn't easy for you to reach out."

"I'm glad I did. I still can't believe she'd forge documents. What a piece of work. Do you think her lawyer was in on it?"

She pulled a cigarette out of her purse and lit it. "Knowing my parents, probably. They have connections everywhere. She's not dumb enough to cross me though. I know all their dirty secrets. Enough to ruin their lives." She took a slow drag and blew the smoke toward the sky. "She must have found out I left the country and decided to pounce. Wonder how long she's been keeping tabs on me?"

"Listen, I know we've had our differences, but I think it's time we set them aside and make a new custody arrangement. When are you heading back to Spain?"

"In a few days. I wasn't sure how bad it would be here." She gestured to the house and I understood what she meant. "What are you thinking for custody?"

"Joint custody and for us to work things out in writing. We need better communication, too." I pulled my new phone out of my pocket and Sav's eyes widened.

"Wesley Reed with an iPhone. I'm shocked."

I chuckled. "The things we do for love."

Savannah's face lit up. "I'm genuinely happy for you, Wes. Lilly looks happy too. I'm willing to sign a new agreement. Have your lawyer send it over to me."

"Sounds good, I'll try to get it to you before you leave. Did you want to spend a few days with Lilly?"

"I think she'd rather go with you, but if it's okay, I'd like to take her to dinner later." She dropped her cigarette and stepped on the butt. I cringed but then remembered we were on Regina's property and didn't feel so bad.

"That works," I said.

Savannah called for Lilly and they hugged, promising to see each other later.

I took one last look at Savannah's childhood home as I drove away, happy I'd never have to go back there again.

"Are we going home?" Lilly asked.

A contented glow spread through me as I smiled at my two girls. I took Olivia's hand and brought it to my lips, brushing a soft kiss along her skin. "Yes, we're going home."

Epilogue

Olivia

Three Months Later

"Is SAVANNAH MEETING US here?" I grabbed the water bottles while shoving granola bars into the kid's hands.

"Yeah, I gave her the address yesterday." Wes came to my side of the car and pulled me in for a hug. "What else do we need?"

"Nothing. I think I grabbed it all," I answered. "Alex, don't forget your gloves."

"Got them," he yelled as he started toward the gym doors.

"You mean I got them. You almost left them in the back seat," Lilly added, sounding too grown up. I laughed as they bickered back and forth like true siblings.

"Come on, no fighting. Save it for class," Wes teased.

"Dad, it's not an actual class. It's a test."

"I know, and you're going to kick butt. Both of you are." I smiled at Wes as we followed the kids into the gym.

The waiting area was packed with families. I loved how Mark and Dina invited parents to watch as their kids reached this incredible milestone. Seeing their loved ones there for them, cheering them on, was incredibly special.

Wes stepped outside to wait for Savannah. She was back from Europe for a few weeks now and getting used to our new custody arrangement. We weren't buddies with her or anything, but since everything happened with her mother we'd formed a sense of solidarity. It seemed to me like she wanted to be a good mom, even if her follow through wasn't always the best.

Mia popped out from the office, her baby bump leading the way. She hugged the kids first before pulling me in for a signature sister hug. "I'm so proud of them!"

"Me, too. They've come so far," I said. "How are you feeling? I swear you're showing more and more each time I see you."

She rubbed her bump. "Tired and hungry. This little one is like a tapeworm. I can't eat enough."

I laughed, remembering the feeling. "And Shawn? How's my favorite brother-in-law doing?"

She rolled her eyes but grinned. "Moody and overprotective to the max but you know me, I love that about him." Her cheeks tinged pink and she hugged her arms to her chest. "He's going to be the best dad."

"He really is. And Remy's going to be the best dog brother."

"I almost can't wait for the next few months to pass but I know I should live in the moment," she said. "My ovaries are actually going to explode when I see Shawn holding our baby girl."

"I think ovaries around the globe are going to explode." She giggled and turned her head as the man of the conversation stepped out of the gym and chatted with a group of parents. "Is he assisting?"

"Yeah, he was helping Coby set up in there." I watched her beam at her new husband and I couldn't help but feel an over-whelming surge of love for our family. "Oh, by the way, did mom tell you she was coming back next month?"

"Why so soon?" I asked. She was here last month for Mia and Shawn's intimate backyard wedding.

"Who knows? Maybe she's gone soft since the divorce? She has seemed much nicer than usual lately." Mia shrugged and chewed her lip. "I'm just glad Dad's staying away. She was telling me yesterday that there's rumors he's dating someone."

"I believe it," I said. "What about Mom? Has she reconnected with Senator Gillis?"

Mia laughed. "You think she'd tell me about her love life? She hasn't even admitted the affair to me out loud."

"True. She hasn't to me either. I'm okay with not knowing."

Wes came back inside with Savannah behind him. I waved them over as Mark hollered for us to come on into the gym.

Wes placed a hand on the small of my back and whispered, "You'll be in here testing next. I'm proud of you, Tiger."

I let his praise soak into my skin, absorbing it like a flower takes in the sun's rays. "Get your camera ready," I whispered. "We need pics of both of them."

"Already on it." He showed his iPhone at the ready.

"You've come a long way." I leaned in to kiss his cheek as Mark and Dina began giving their first instructions.

Our group filled the dining area at Sunshine. Everyone fawned over Alex and Lilly, giving them hugs and presents for passing their test. Thea and Caleb were in the kitchen putting the finishing touches on our lunch while Wes and I filled pitchers of soda and iced tea.

"I'm glad you thought of doing a little party," Wes said. He cupped my chin and planted a sweet kiss on my lips. "We're so fucking lucky, aren't we?"

I peeked around the corner and watched our Krav family mingle with Walter and Val and some of our Sunshine employees. A few of Alex and Lilly's friends from class joined us with their families as well and the kids all congregated around a single booth while Lilly showed them a hundred pictures of her new kitten. I couldn't hold back the grin that spread across my face.

"We truly are," I said.

We spent the afternoon laughing and eating too much food with the ones we love. Kendahl and Coby filled us in about their wedding planning. I already knew most of those details since my group chat was spammed daily with pictures and questions. I never minded though. I was happy to help.

I placed a hand on Wes's shoulder and he turned from his conversation with Coby. "Sorry to bother you, but can you come in the back and help me with the desserts?"

"Of course." He pushed to stand and told Coby he'd be right back. I led the way into the kitchen and started to assemble the desserts I'd worked hours baking the previous day.

"Okay, I know the platter I want to use is somewhere around here. You know the white one I'm thinking of?" I asked Wes. He stared off at the shelves behind me.

"I think so. White platter, can't be too hard to find."

"Thanks. I'm going to fix the icing on the cake while you look." I grabbed the piping bag and fixed a few of the smudged spots on the cake. A few dozen cookies sat waiting on baking sheets, ready to be brought out once he found the platter.

Wes searched for a few minutes before I heard a laugh burst out of him from around the corner. "What's so funny over there?"

He came out holding something black in his hands... black and lacy. "Look what I found."

Oh, my God.

I busted out laughing. "The panties! It's been months! How have you missed them?"

He tucked them into his pocket and stepped close. "I'm just glad I found them and not Caleb or Derek. I'd have to kill them for touching what's mine."

He boxed me against the counter and captured a kiss. "That's a little excessive, even for you."

I felt his hard length against my abdomen and bit back a whimper. It didn't take much for us to get feral for each other.

"No one touches my wife's panties but me, Tiger." His tone deepened and I immediately flushed. When he used his sexy voice, I was done for.

He lifted me onto the counter and I wrapped my legs around his hips while my hands went to his hair. "We can't. Our whole family is right there. They can literally see us through the window."

"We're not doing anything wrong," he said innocently. "I just want to kiss my wife."

I reached down and rubbed his erection through his shorts. "Seems like you're thinking other thoughts."

He pushed into my palm and I squeezed until a low growl left his lips. He buried his hands in my hair and pulled me closer. "You're bad, Mrs. Reed."

Without realizing what I was doing, I rocked against him, searching for friction. I could feel how soaked my panties were—I wanted my husband.

"You're the one who started this," I said, breathing against his ear and sucking his lobe into my mouth.

"Fuck, that's not nice." He tipped my face up and claimed my lips, sending a jolt of heat straight to my core. Our mouths moved together, sucking and nibbling, pulling hushed needy sounds from both of us. "You know I'd fuck you right here if I could. I'd bend you over this counter and spank you for leaving your panties on the shelf like that before pumping my cock into your perfect, wet pussy."

"Oh, God," I whimpered. His lips seared a path across my collarbone and up my throat.

"But that'll have to wait for later, Tiger." He backed away a step, leaving me panting and squeezing my thighs together. With a smug grin, he slid his finger along the frosting and sucked it suggestively. "Delicious. I can't wait to eat your cake."

A laugh bubbled up from my chest and I pulled him to me again, brushing a quick kiss against his lips. "You're going to be the death of me."

"Never," he teased. "You better let me go back out there before I forget my manners entirely and take you into the office."

I raised a brow and let the idea float through my mind but laughed it off. There was always time for a little kitchen play after the place closed for the night. Perks of owning a restaurant.

"Grab the cookies. We'll have to forget about the fancy platter," I said. It was only family and friends, no one would care. I still had to remind myself that my life wasn't for show anymore. I could be real and raw and not worry about perfection. There were no campaigns or charity galas in my life.

I could be me, ugly cookie sheets and all.

I glanced at my covered thigh, and grinned knowing right beneath the fabric was my badass new Medusa tattoo. I cried when I first saw the finished piece on my skin but it felt like a part of me had healed.

That no matter what happened in my past, I was strong. I'd survived.

I carried the cake out to the table with my head held high. If someone asked me how I was doing at that moment, I could have told them with full certainty that I was happy—truly and blissfully happy. And even if I was having a tough time with my mental health, I didn't have to keep it in anymore.

No more fake, "*I'm fines*," to show I was holding it together. Unconditional love was an incredible thing. With Wes by my side and the support of my family, blood related and not, I knew no matter what life hurled my way, we could fight through it together.

Acknowledgements

Thank you for reading Wes and Olivia's story. Writing this series has been such an incredible journey. There are tiny pieces of me left behind in each of these characters and it'll be tough to say goodbye to them.

I'm forever grateful for the amazing people that have been there with me each step of the way during the creation of this book.

Havoc, thank you times a million. I don't even know what this story would have been without you. You're stuck with me now.

Veronica, I'm so glad we met and bonded over books. You've become one of my favorite people and this book would not be where it is without you. Thank you for loving Wes and Olivia as much as I do.

Sean, thank you for sharing your experiences and answering all my questions. Your honesty and heart brought so much into creating Wes. I'm forever grateful.

Leah, I love and appreciate you and all you do! To my beta readers and everyone on my team, thank you for everything. A special thanks to M.J., Breanne, Enni, and Daleina.

My family, you've embraced this new life and all it's chaos and deadlines with nothing but love and support. I love you!

About Author

Lauren lives in Phoenix, Arizona with her full chaotic family. When she's not crafting her next happily ever after, you can find her playing taxi to her teenagers, being pulled by her two large dogs, and when she's lucky reading with a cup of coffee.

Also by Lauren

Palm Cove Series

Fight For It

Fight For Her

 instagram.com/laurengreenebooks

Made in the USA
Monee, IL
05 August 2024

63286939R00245